Dreams of the Thinker

A Novel

William Waldo

WestBow
PRESS
A DIVISION OF THOMAS NELSON

WestBow Press books may be ordered through booksellers or by contacting:

WestBow Press
A Division of Thomas Nelson
1663 Liberty Drive
Bloomington, IN 47403
www.westbowpress.com
1-(866) 928-1240

Because of the dynamic nature of the Internet, any web addresses or links contained in this book may have changed since publication and may no longer be valid. The views expressed in this work are solely those of the author and do not necessarily reflect the views of the publisher, and the publisher hereby disclaims any responsibility for them.

Any people depicted in stock imagery provided by Thinkstock are models, and such images are being used for illustrative purposes only.

Certain stock imagery © Thinkstock.

Throughout this book, the abbreviation AC, when used with dates, stands for "After Creation."

Some character dialog, particularly those of God/Jesus Christ, are direct quotes from the New American Standard Bible

Scripture quotations taken from the New American Standard Bible®, copyright © 1960, 1962, 1963, 1968, 1971, 1972, 1973, 1975, 1977, 1995 by the Lockman Foundation. Used by permission. (www.Lockman.org)

ISBN: 978-1-4497-8292-4 (sc)
ISBN: 978-1-4497-8294-8 (hc)
ISBN: 978-1-4497-8293-1 (e)

Library of Congress Control Number: 2013901585

Printed in the United States of America

WestBow Press rev. date: 3/20/2013

To Hannah Lee, my beloved niece

We are destroying speculations and every
lofty thing raised up against the
knowledge of God, and we are taking
every thought captive to the
obedience of Christ.

— 2 Corinthians 10:5

Acknowledgments

A special thank you to my family for their prayers and support—especially to my youngest sister Pam for helping me with proofreading and editing, and to my youngest niece Hannah for her input. Also a special thanks to Pastor Rod Skelton for his input and prayers.

Chapter 1
I Think, Therefore I Am

I've been called a great many things in my life, some not very flattering, but to my friends I'm known as the "Thinker". As you can imagine, I do a lot of thinking. I think about all sorts of things. Things that have no significance and accomplish nothing, and things more weighty that can change the course of a life for good or for bad—if anybody cares to take them seriously.

I particularly like to think about lies that masquerade as truth and to expose them for what they are. I used to think it was the Christians who were spewing lies that masqueraded as truth. After all, what is truth and who can know it? Who can honestly take the Bible seriously? Talking animals, the sun turning backward, dragons, the dead rising from their graves; I mean, these things don't happen in reality. Lest you think I'm being cynical, I admit that I have since learned differently.

The following is my story. It is a story I am compelled by God to share with you, for faith comes by hearing, and hearing by the Word of God. If people do not hear the Word of God, how will they believe? That is my mission. That is my purpose.

I was raised in a family of atheists and heard my father spew forth atheistic arguments against irrational Christian beliefs everyday. He was a strong atheist who believed all forms of religion, especially Christianity, were the worse form of evil on the planet. He believed all forms of religion should be abolished. That the world would be better off without religion. As a young man, I held these same beliefs and used the same arguments against Christians. I am now a professor of philosophy at a local community college. I have used these atheistic arguments to pin down Christians whom I felt were misguided, so I'm quite familiar with the logic atheists use—or at least, what *they* call logic.

Atheists like to assert that if God is love, then why does He permit suffering? If He is all-powerful, why doesn't He stop people from dying? Atheist claim that if anyone has the power to stop a catastrophe and doesn't do so, that person is evil. Therefore, since God has the power to stop catastrophes and doesn't, He is evil. They argue that if God created all things, yet evil abounds, He must have created evil also, and therefore He is evil. Since He is evil, He is not God. Therefore, He must not exist. I have never found a Christian who could give a sound answer to these questions.

Then, one day I was discussing these matters with a professor of religious history during our lunch break. He was a seasoned Christian gentleman who had no difficulty answering my objections. Few I have found who were able to adequately defend their faith but this gentleman was an exception. It was his first year teaching at the college, so I didn't know him all that well. I was surprised the school had hired him. Conservative thinkers generally aren't welcome on most college campuses these days— except for students, of course, as we can attempt to teach them how to think properly and along more acceptable lines.

In talking with him, he challenged me, saying that if I was

indeed serious about finding the truth, I needed to search out these matters as objectively as possible. That included looking at both sides of the issue, not just the side I agreed with. He told me that Jesus died on the cross to pay for my sins, that by faith in Him we may find salvation from eternal damnation and even from ourselves. Yes, we are very much our own worst enemy. Those who refuse to believe have been judged already and are destined to be gathered up like dry sticks and cast into the Lake of Fire.

I thought it rather bold of him to make these assertions. Naturally, I objected to this exclusiveness and intolerance for other people's beliefs. How did this promote peace in the world? How could a loving God cast people into hell? If Christianity sought to grow and prosper, it needed to be more accommodating and tolerant.

The gentleman said to me, "God is perfect and cannot allow sin in His presence. He has to be intolerant toward those who refuse to abide by His Word. God loves us more than we can possibly understand and desires for all to be with Him for eternity. He has provided the means for restoring fellowship with Him through the work of His Son. It is a free gift of God. All we have to do is believe in His Son. Those who refuse to believe must be cast out no matter how much they object. It is not God who actually sends people to hell but they themselves. In Jesus we find peace in the assurance of our salvation, which cannot be taken away from us. Only in Jesus can peace be found. As long as we abide in Him, He abides in us. Jesus specifically stated that He did not come into the world to unite the world, but to divide it. In the world there will never be real peace until Jesus Christ returns. If Christians do accommodate and tolerate other faiths it will be a spiritual disaster as we're already beginning to see in the apostate churches."

Starting at the Tower of Babel, Jesus has, indeed, divided the world and He keeps it divided. That —along with His demand to observe His law—is one of the reasons the world hates Him so much. He threatens the world's power-base and restricts our liberties. Christianity is the most hated religion on the planet for good reason. It certainly wasn't something I could get too excited about. I stated that I had no reason to believe in the existence of God. There was no scientific precedence to prove His existence. This was the biggest issue atheists had with Christianity. And since God didn't exist, I had no reason to believe, or to fear hell.

He pointed out sciences inability to observe—let alone *prove*—anything beyond the material universe. "The effects of God's presence are seen throughout the entire universe," he said. "All we have to do is be willing to open our eyes and look. I challenge you to prove God doesn't exist. To attribute those effects to evolution only seeks justification for your unbelief. It takes a mountain of faith to believe in evolution, but only a mustard seed of faith to believe in God. With evolution, which in realty has no scientific support despite the claims of evolutionists, you are staking your life on a known lie. Where is the logic of this?"

"It is the only logical alternative," I stated. "Belief in a nonexistent God is irrational and unthinkable. Where does it possibly get you? What if you're wrong?"

"What does it profit a man to gain the whole world yet loose or forfeit his soul?" he answered. "If I'm wrong, I have lost nothing. But if I'm right, you lose everything."

That certainly wasn't the answer I was expecting. I was expecting some unscientific creation nonsense. So I didn't have a ready answer. At first, of course, I wasn't able to accept his words. Why would anyone endure the hatred and persecution of others for no reason at all? This man was clearly misguided and needed to be set straight. However, his words kept ringing in my ears. What if I was wrong? It was an unthinkable concept for sure, but those two horrible words kept haunting me. What if? What if man was more than an animal? What if there was life after death? What if God existed after all? Then what? If such was the case, then I stood to burn forever. To be honest, spending eternity in hell certainly wasn't included in my retirement plans. Nor was it anywhere on my "places to see" or "things to do" list. So I set out to objectively find the truth.

I accepted the challenge and conducted an exhaustive study of the Bible and all things related to it. In my studies, I discovered I had been deliberately lied to. I won't go into the details of my search for truth, but suffice it to say that I saw the light. In my analysis, I realized that every one of the atheists' arguments against God and the Bible made the mistake of committing a straw-man logical fallacy. By this I mean that they misrepresented who God is, making Him like man and expecting Him to do what they expected men to do. They failed to understand that, unlike other gods created in man's image, man did not create God.

Instead, God created man in His image. His ways are above our ways, and His thoughts are above ours. Being the Creator, He has the right to make the rules and dictate absolute standards and values of conduct to mankind. And being the Creator, He is not bound by those standards and rules, and no man has a right to expect Him to. We are but jars of clay. How can the jar dictate to the potter what he must do?

I, therefore, reached the logical conclusion that God did indeed exist. Before the space-time continuum—the laws of physics that govern the universe's operation and the flow of time—God was, is, and always will be. God is all knowing, all powerful, and everywhere present. He is like a sphere that is all encompassing and has no beginning or end. God is self-existing and has existed for all eternity. He is timeless and exists outside of time. He is not bound by the restraints of time that bind the realm of the material universe.

God is also loving and just—two inseparable attributes that are two sides of the same coin. Without love, there is no justice. Without justice, there is no love. He is the Creator of all things seen and unseen. He is the all-consuming fire and the judge of all things. He is truth, the light of life, the giver of life, and the first cause and sustainer of all things. He is our Creator.

Considering all these things, I was now left with a choice. Like so many atheists before me who had tried to prove the Bible wrong, I likewise failed. Like them I had to decide whether to ignore what I'd just learned, or to put my faith in Jesus Christ. Being the logical person I am, there was only one logical choice. I chose to put my faith in Jesus Christ. To do otherwise would have been irrational.

Psalm 14:1-3 states, "The fool has said in his heart, 'There is no God.' They are corrupt, they have committed abominable deeds; There is no one who does good. The Lord has looked down from heaven upon the sons of men to see if there are any who understand, who seek after God. They have all turned aside; together they have become corrupt; there is no one who does good, not even one." Without exception we have all fallen short of God's standard. Nor are we able to meet His standard, for only God is perfect. This is why Jesus came to take our place on the cross. In so doing, He fulfilled the requirements of the law. Those who obey God's command to believe in His Son will not have to face His judgment. Jesus has promised to remove these believers from the earth, for God will not suffer the righteous to perish with the wicked.

After my conversion to Christianity, I was filled with an insatiable desire to learn all I could about God even beyond what I had already learned. I read everything I could get my hands on. I talked with other Christians about God and the Bible and was surprised at how little most of them actually knew. I found it troubling that so many so-called Christians were unwilling to engage in conversation about God and the Bible. Were they that ashamed of the gospel? I wondered about this and determined that it must be the institutionalized church's failure to properly disciple the children of God. They were too focused on feel good messages that left one feeling empty. They were too focused on providing an entertaining show to draw people in so as to fleece them of their free-will offerings. What would Jesus say to these churches?

In my search for more knowledge I prayed that God would increase my understanding that I might be a more effective witness for Him. During my afternoon naps in my recliner I had a series of dreams of how certain things unfolded. These were not direct revelations from God, so don't take them as such. God has revealed everything we need to know in His written Word. It is our responsibility to read, understand, and apply His revealed Word.

The first dream was about the creation. There are many who consider creation a divisive issue and ask, "Why are creation and the age of the earth important? Isn't the gospel of Jesus Christ the only thing that matters?" The idea that the earth is billions of years old and that life evolved from non-life, (1) destroys the Bible's teaching on death and suffering, (2) assaults the character of God by calling Him a liar, (3) contradicts what Jesus believed and taught, (4) undermines the gospel, and (5) nullifies the authority of Scripture. The first eleven chapters of Genesis are the foundation on which the rest of Scripture rests upon. Without this foundation, the authority of Scripture crumbles, including the gospel of Jesus Christ. Atheists understand this, which is why they actively assault the first eleven chapters of Genesis. Christians need to understand this also and be ready to give a logical defense for their faith.

My second and third dreams were of the corruption of mankind and catastrophic flooding of the earth as a result of that corruption. Dinosaurs were portrayed as coexisting with mankind. The evolutionists and old earth creationists will, without a doubt be crying foul. But the fact is, the Bible states the dinosaurs were created on day six—the same as all the other land animals. They were created on the same day as mankind, not sixty-five million years earlier. The earth was not created on top of dead things. It was created perfect with no death or suffering. Adam's disobedience to God and mankind's continued rebellion against God brought death and suffering into the world and corrupted God's perfect creation.

The fourth dream told of the scattering of mankind following the confusion of his language. It includes the birth of Israel and continues with the splitting up and exile of Israel for her continuous rebellion against God. It concludes with the prophecy given to Daniel in Babylon concerning the coming of the Messiah and the redemption of Israel—a prophecy concerning Israel's seventy weeks of years (490 years) to put an end to sin and iniquities, and to usher in the Messiah. These seventy weeks of years encapsulate Bible prophecy, for all Bible prophecy centers around Israel, which was why the birth of Israel was included in the dream. This is important to understand. Without the existence of Israel and Jesus Christ, the prophecies make no sense. The prophecies all point to the redemptive work of Jesus Christ—not just what He did on the cross but what He will do after His second coming.

My fifth dream told of the birth of Jesus Christ and the sixth dream portrayed the last week of Jesus' life and His redemptive work on the cross. It also illustrated fulfilled prophecy and the reason why Israel still has one more week of years (seven years) remaining.

The dreams I experienced were based on the Seven Cs of biblical history and salvation. They were developed by an Australian gentleman who founded the Answers in Genesis ministry in Kentucky near the Cincinnati area. The Seven Cs were inspired by the Bible. The first six Cs—Creation, Corruption, Catastrophe, Confusion, Christ and Cross,—lay the ground work leading up to the present age. The seventh C, Consummation, is the focus of prophecy yet to be fulfilled. It is the consummation of mankind and the hope of every true Christian. It is the restoration of mankind to his Creator.

The reason why God created us in the first place was for us to be with Him and to bring Him glory. At the consummation, the believers are made holy like God—though they will not be gods themselves—and will finally be with Him for eternity. Each of us having a perfect, immortal body, will have our fellowship with God restored and we'll never again be separated from Him. My dreams about the second coming of Jesus Christ and the Consummation occurred in three parts.

At the end of the book is a glossary for those who have trouble pronouncing the names of the dinosaurs or understanding the scientific and technical terminology. There is also an appendix showing the time line of earth's history from creation up to the time of Christ's crucifixion, from a biblical perspective. Don't take it as absolute truth, however. Some of the dates might be off a couple hundred years, but I believe they're close. Of course uniformitarian historians and evolutionists will naturally disagree with it. After all, anything that contradicts uniformitarian thinking is automatically rejected. Old-earth and progressive creationists who give science a higher authority than Scripture will also disagree with it, invoking the day-age theory, the gap theory and a few other strange things. I have rejected the gap theory because the plain sense reading of the Scriptures doesn't leave room for gaps. I have also rejected the day-age theory, because the plain sense reading of Genesis 1 clearly indicates that a day of creation was a twenty-four hour day, not an undefined period of time.

This book was written from the pre-tribulation point of view in which the rapture occurs before the start of the tribulation. The rapture can occur at any time prior to the tribulation, but it does not mark the beginning of the tribulation. The Bible does not teach a mid-tribulation or post-tribulation rapture. What would be the point of the rapture if it occurred half way through or at the end of the tribulation—not to mention that Jesus would be breaking His promise to remove the church before the tribulation? God will not suffer the righteous to be punished with the wicked. Who are the righteous? Those whom God has declared righteous in accordance with their faith in the Son of God—not according to anything we have done but according to what Jesus did on the cross.

One last thing before I share with you my dreams; there are many who think it is a waste of time to study Bible prophecy, that no good can come of it. They consider it, like creation, divisive. Prophecy was given to us to warn us of the consequences of unbelief. It also gives us hope and comfort that the wickedness of mankind and the suffering he wrought on others will be overthrown, and that death will be defeated. It is our light at the end of a long dark tunnel. It is our assurance of the return of Jesus Christ and our reunion with our Creator. The fulfillment of these prophecies proves that Jesus Christ is who He says He is.

He is the Alpha and the Omega; the beginning and the end, who was, and is, and is to come. He is God. Those who say they're Christians but don't believe this, I firmly believe, are not in right standing with God. What Jesus Christ has said He will do, will be done, and there is nothing Satan can do to stop Him. Satan can't even overpower an archangel. How does he think he can overpower His Creator? So, no matter how bad life's circumstances appear to be, take comfort in the words of Jesus Christ and the promise of His return. Don't let Satan and his minions steal your joy or your hope.

Chapter 2
Creation of the Earth

Year 1 (Circa 4106 BC)

In my first dream, I saw the creation of the universe and all that is in it. As stated earlier, this dream was not a direct revelation from God. It was just a dream. The same, of course, holds true with the other dreams. The first dream illustrates a number of scientific concepts that most people may not be familiar with. I refer you to the glossary at the end of the book for definitions and explanations of terminology.

The scenario presented in this dream is not to be regarded as factual. It is an unqualified hypothesis and the best fit interpretation—in my unqualified opinion—of the creation story in Genesis. It is based on observed scientific data and the study of creation science physics with regards to "white hole" cosmology and a literal interpretation of the biblical account of creation. White hole cosmology theory was conceived by a creationist nuclear physicist from the San Diego area. Note: being a creationist does not disqualify him from being a scientist as the evolutionists insist. He regards the theory as only an hypothesis that outlines a theory, so caution needs to be exercised. While we know that the creation story presented in the Scriptures is factual, the process God used to create the universe is highly subjective and unknowable in the present earthly realm.

In my dream, I was taken into the heavenly realm and saw One sitting on a magnificent throne outshining a thousand suns. He appeared to have no physical form. No one has ever seen the One who sits on the throne except the Son. All I could see was a shroud of brilliant light emanating from Him. This was God the Father who existed before all things; all powerful, all-knowing, everywhere present. His love radiated from Him like an unstoppable, unrelenting, immovable force.

My attention was drawn to something going on behind me. I turned and there appeared before me a great void. This void contained absolutely nothing. Not the tiniest speck of matter was found in it. A being descended into the void whom I understood to be the preincarnate Son of God.

I heard no spoken voice, but at the Father's command, there appeared—out of nowhere and from nothing—a huge sphere of pure water about twenty-two trillion kilometers (or about two light-years) in diameter. The vacuum of space it occupied and the laws of physics it obeyed were created in the same instant. It was wrapped in darkness and confined in space by a black hole with its event horizon about 450 million light-years farther out.

Somewhere near or at the center of the sphere resided the material matter that would become the earth, lacking any form of its own. At this instant in time, everything was in a state of stasis. The laws of physics were not a self starting process. As with matter, something had to act upon these laws to start the process. Once started, however, the laws of physics became self-governing as they were designed to do. The movement of the Holy Spirit started these processes.

At the very instant of creation, the Holy Spirit moved over

the surface of the waters. He didn't merely hover over the water, but immersed Himself in it to stir up and agitate it. In so doing, He set in motion the laws of physics that govern the operation of the universe. Electromagnetic and nuclear forces made the water molecules with their constituent atomic components fully functional. The laws of chemistry bound the water molecules together to form the sphere. Conservation of angular momentum set the sphere rotating about an axis. Gravitational forces within the black hole began to compress the water. The gravitational forces increased the pressure on the water, producing heat that kept the water from instantly freezing.

As I wondered why water had been chosen, a voice in my head gave an explanation. Water was chosen because it contains hydrogen and oxygen atoms. Between elements number five and eight on the periodic table are unstable elements that prevent the lighter elements from transmuting into heavier elements. The creation of water, which contains elements number one (hydrogen) and eight (oxygen), permits the possibility of transmutation of all the elements on both sides of the transmutation boundary. These two elements, which made up the sphere of water, contained all the matter from which the universe, both visible and invisible, would be created. The Holy Spirit's agitation of the water separated the water molecules and started the transmutation process.

I heard a thundering voice say, "Let there be light." God's first spoken command to the material universe brought forth light that illuminated the surface of the agitated water. The light appeared to have no source, but I assumed God Himself was the light source. The light pierced the darkness, which could not contain the light, and fled from it. The darkness was divided so that one side of the sphere of water was illuminated while the other side remained in darkness.

The movement of the Holy Spirit caused conservation of

angular momentum to increase the sphere's rate of rotation, so the center of the sphere made one complete rotation in a period of twenty-four hours EST (Earth Standard Time). An evening and a morning passed. This one rotation was defined as one complete day. It was not an undefined period of time, an age, or an epoch.

Then God said, "Let there be an expanse in the midst of the waters, and let it separate the waters from the waters." The crushing forces of the black hole's intense gravity overcame the water's incompressibility as the sphere of water began to collapse on itself. Before it could be crushed into a singularity, it rebounded out of the black hole as if bouncing off a spherical trampoline. This rebounding turned the black hole into a white hole. Shockwaves, produced by the rebounding, broke up the sphere of water into layers. As the layers separated, they broke up into globules of water that became subject to intense pressures, producing heat. The heat, in turn, caused the water molecules to transmute into hydrogen gas and plasma, and other heavier elements, starting in the center of each globule and progressing outward. As the transmutation progressed outward, fusion reaction processes began igniting each globule, turning them into stars.

The layers of matter and billions of newly formed stars progressed outward at specific intervals until they reached the event horizon. One would think that the newly created stars would take 450 million years to reach the event horizon at the speed of light—but relative to which clock? As the stars raced toward the event horizon, the rate of time increased relative to time at the center of the white hole. The event horizon was the mathematically defined point of no return. Outside the event horizon time flowed at a normal rate, while time inside the event horizon slowed significantly. At the center of the white hole time appeared to stop completely relative to time outside the event horizon. Assuming the rate of time increased in a linear fashion as it departs the while hole rather than algorithmically, some 450 million years would have passed outside the event horizon, while only one day passed on the as-yet-unformed earth.

Each successive layer, upon exiting the event horizon, caused an immense release of energy in a colossal flash of light. This made the white hole appear to explode. Over time, as seen from outside the event horizon, several flashes of light occurred as each layer exited the white hole until the last group of stars, including the earth, exited with a flash of light and the white hole ceased to exist.

The release of energy upon exiting the white hole pushed each layer farther outward and stretched the fabric of space. This stretching of space produced red-shifted infrared radiation. The infrared radiation added to the microwave radiation each star emitted. This produced the cosmic microwave background (CMB) radiation that filled the expanding universe. The CMB emanated from all directions as the stars spread farther away.

The event horizon began to collapse as each layer departed with the light from the newly created stars following right behind it. Some of those stars were so large, that they used up their hydrogen plasma fuel quickly and soon collapsed upon themselves. The resultant supernovas blasted matter outward, while the inner core continued to collapse into itself and produced massive black holes. These black holes formed a strong gravitational pull on nearby stars, which then orbited around the black holes. The resultant galaxies clustered together and began rotating around the white hole from which they had emerged forming a disk-shaped universe made up of concentric layers. These black holes didn't just draw stars around them; they also inhibited the formation of new stars.

While the galaxies formed outside the event horizon, the

few remaining globules in the vicinity of the waters below the expanse began their own transformation. Some of these globules were larger than the earth. They would later become the sun, planets, and moons. While God still directed the formation of the universe outside the event horizon with all its many splendors, like nebulae and unique planets circling distant stars, His primary focus remained on earth. Most of the stars that would form the Milky Way galaxy had already exited the white hole, reducing the event horizon to only a few light-years in diameter.

Within the white hole, which was only a few billion miles in diameter at this point, there was still significant gravitational pressure upon the sphere of water that would become the earth, producing enough heat to rip apart most of the atoms of the water molecules. Some of the disassociated subatomic particles transmuted into inert gases, carbon dioxide, and other greenhouse gases to form an atmosphere. Other disassociated subatomic particles transmuted into heavier atoms that solidified below the surface of the waters to become the minerals used to lay the "foundations of the earth". Below the surface water, the elements separated themselves according to weight in onion-like layers. Lighter basaltic elements rose to the top to form the crust and heavier elements sank toward the center. The upper strata of the crust sorted itself into sedimentary layers before cooling. As the crust cooled some the heavier elements that hadn't yet sank below the crust became trapped within it.

As the crust cooled, rapid radioactive decay occurred, producing heat to keep the continental cratons pliable. The heavier basaltic elements below the crust remained molten to form the mantle. Even heavier elements sank below the mantle to form the core. Within the core, the lighter iron and nickel elements formed the outer core while the heavier radioactive elements like uranium and thorium formed the inner core. The radiation from the inner core produced convection currents in the iron outer core, which produced the magnetic field surrounding the earth, protecting it from harmful radiation constantly bombarding it. The radioactivity of the inner core also kept it white hot, which kept the surface relatively warm.

God called the expanse *heaven.* Here, *heaven* refers to the visible arc of the sky where the clouds move and birds fly as well as the higher ether where the celestial bodies revolve. The heaven surrounding the earth is also known as the first heaven. There was another evening and another morning, the second day.

Then God said, "Let the waters below the heavens be gathered into one place, and let the dry land appear." The dry land God called *earth,* and the gathered waters He called *seas.* The rapid radioactive decay of the crust resulted in thermal expansion of the continental cratons, making them more buoyant relative to the rocks below them and lifting them up above the surface of the waters, which gathered the waters in the ocean basins. This upward movement thrust up low mountain ranges while the water runoff washed sediment into the sea and cut canyons and ravines in the land. The continental cratons formed a single supercontinent called *Rodinia.* Because life had not yet been created, and thus there was no death, it is logical that there were no fossils in the sedimentary layers of the newly formed crust. The original sedimentary layers that span ninety percent of the earth's assumed geologic history according to uniformitarian assumptions, are called the Precambrian ("before life") eon.

Then God said, "Let the earth sprout vegetation, plants yielding seed and fruit trees bearing fruit after their kind, with seed in them, on the earth." No sooner had the dry land appeared than vegetation began sprouting from seeds created from the dust of the earth. These plants grew rapidly to full maturity in a matter of hours. They were necessary at this time, not only for food for the animals that were created on days five and six, but also to clear the air of undesirable dense gases and to oxygenate the seas and atmosphere. Each plant sprouted according to its own kind and produced seed and fruit after its own kind. While many variations or species were produced from the original kinds, not a single kind sprouted from another kind. And God saw that it was very good. It was another evening, and another morning; the third day.

Then God said, "Let there be lights in the expanse of the heavens to separate the day from the night, and let them be for signs, and for seasons, and for days and years, and let them be for lights in the expanse of the heavens to give light on the earth". Several million years had passed outside the event horizon, while on the remaining spheres of water within the white hole only three days had passed. During day four, God gave the plants time to purify the air, while He concentrated on the sun, planets and moons of the solar system. The rocky planets and moons went through a process similar to what the earth went through on day two. There were originally five rocky planets and of them, only the earth had a moon.

The gas giants went through a different process, being made up of mostly gas. It is only reasonable to assume that they have a solid core to produce the gravitational forces that keep the gases contained. Because free-floating gas spreads out in a vacuum rather than coalescing into a gas ball, the water globules would have been converted into dense gases from the inside out, just like the stars. The gas giants were also accompanied by rocky moons, all different from one another. The sun went through the same process as all the other stars, with fusion reaction occurring within the hydrogen gases and plasma to ignite the sun. The planets with their accompanying moons were then set on their intended orbital paths about the sun, with conservation of angular momentum determining the speed of their orbits. The greater the distance from the sun, the slower the speed of the planets to keep them in their intended orbits. The earth was placed in a privileged position near the center of the universe at the precise distance from the sun that was perfect for the support of life. Despite the denials of secular scientists, the earth *is* special.

By the end of the fourth day the undesirable dense gases were cleared from the atmosphere. The beginning of the fifth day saw the disappearance of the event horizon. As the earth's solar system exited the white hole, the starlight was already present. First the outer planetesimals and comets exited the white hole. The gas giants followed and then the rocky planets. The white hole finally disappeared in the center of the sun in one last flash of glory.

The stars in all their splendor and the first full moon were seen for the first time on the surface of the earth. Dawn brought the rising of the sun. The sun, moon and stars were to give light on the earth for signs and seasons, and for days and years. Seeing the work of His creation, God declared it perfect. Another evening and another morning were the fourth day.

Then God said, "Let the waters teem with swarms of living creatures, and let birds fly above the earth in the open expanse of the heavens." Immediately the oceans around the earth along with the lakes, rivers and streams, were filled with swarms of living creatures—a great variety of kinds, each created according to its own kind. The sky above the earth was filled with flying creatures ranging in size from the smallest winged insect to the pteronodon. Though many varieties or species arose from each kind, each kind was created according to its own kind, not from another kind. Each of the species that later arose from these kinds were not able to evolve into another kind.

God blessed them saying, "Be fruitful and multiply, and fill the waters in the seas, and let birds multiply on the earth." And another evening and another morning were the fifth day.

Then God said, "Let the earth bring forth living creatures after their kind; cattle and creeping things and beasts of the earth after their kind." Out of the ground arose the beasts of the earth, including the dinosaurs—or *dragons* as Scripture and legends refers to them—and the cattle and creeping things. Each one was created according to its own kind, not from another kind.

Many varieties or species within a kind later arose, each one adapted to the environment in which it lived and to the food it ate, but no kind has ever become another kind. God clearly stated several times that He created each kind according to its own kind. Not a single kind arose from another kind by evolution or any other means.

Then God said, "Let Us make man in our image, according to our likeness; and let them rule over the fish of the sea and over the birds of the sky and over the cattle and over all the earth, and over every creeping thing that creeps on the earth." The Scriptures indicate that God created man in His own image; in the image of God He created them; both male and female He created them. Three times God made it specifically clear that He created mankind, and that He created them perfect. Mankind did not come from some ape-like creature, nor did the apes emerge from the same ape-like creature. Both may be primates but they are still separate kinds. (It is difficult to determine if mankind can be classified as cattle or beasts. I'm inclined to think he is neither.)

Twice, God made it perfectly clear that, unlike the animals which were created according to their own kind, mankind was created in God's image, according to God's likeness. That is, within man, God created a spirit. For while all living creatures that have the breath of life in them have souls, only mankind has a spirit—a spirit made in God's image. This is what separates man from the animals and why we don't fit the above mentioned classifications. It is also why we are the center of God's attention. God made man special and gave him dominion over all the earth.

And God blessed them and said to them, "Be fruitful and multiply, and fill the earth and subdue it (this does not mean to destroy it or rape it); and rule over the fish of the sea and over the birds of the sky, and over every living thing that moves on the earth (this does not mean to annihilate them)." Then God said, "Behold, I have given you every plant yielding seed that is on the surface of the earth, and every tree that has fruit yielding seed; it shall be food for you. And to every beast of the earth and to every bird of the sky and to everything that moves on the earth and has life, I have given every green plant for food." Every living thing, including tyrannosaurus rex, velociraptors, cats, dogs, eagles and vultures, were all originally herbivores—not meat eaters.

And God beheld all that He had made and declared it perfect. In six days God created the heavens and the earth and all that was in them. No imperfection was found in it—no mistakes in design, no death, no corruption, and no suffering. There was another evening and another morning, which were the sixth day.

On the seventh day, God rested from all His work. He blessed and sanctified the seventh day, because in it He rested from all the work He had created. He was the One who had created the heavens and the earth and everything in them. Nothing came about of its own accord.

There *must* be a first cause for everything that exists, without exception. God alone created all things and He created them perfect.

Chapter 3
Corruption of Mankind and the Earth

Circa 1 AC (After Creation)

In my second dream, I found myself in the garden of Eden. I was not by any means prepared for the beauty I saw there. There is beauty still in our corrupted world, but it could never compare to the beauty of the perfect world God created.

For about a year or so, Adam and Eve explored and tended to the garden of Eden. They were perfect in form and beauty being tall with bronzed skin, golden-brown hair and brown eyes. God gave them complete, autonomous free will to do whatever they wished. However, they had only one law to obey.

In the east in the land called Eden, God planted a garden in which He placed two unique trees. One was called the Tree of Life, which invigorated the bodies of the animals that ate of its leaves and fruit. This was the good tree, the tree of blessing. Adam and Eve had free access to this tree as long as they maintained a proper relationship with God. Toward the center of the garden grew the other unique tree called the Tree of the Knowledge of

Good and Evil. Adam and Eve were prohibited from eating of this tree, lest they die. This was the evil tree, the tree of the curse. God did not intend for mankind to know evil but the tree was put there as a test of obedience. Of all the wonders of the garden, it was this tree that proved most tantalizing for Eve.

Life in the garden was idyllic. There was nothing in the garden that sought to hurt them. The animals were exceptionally friendly and loved attention. The air was fresh and energizing, the temperature varying little from day to night or from season to season. The innumerable stars and the entire galaxy shone in the night sky like sparkling glitter on black velvet.

At that time, a mist rose out of the ground to water the earth. Eve often took delight in the colorful rainbows the morning mist produced in the rising sun. In childlike wonder she sometimes tried to capture a rainbow and find its beginning, but whenever she drew near to it, it disappeared. Adam had to laugh at her whenever she tried this, but he was just as captivated by the rainbows as she was. There are some who would have us believe that there were no rainbows before the world flood. But how can a mist not produce rainbows when viewed at the proper angle from the sun? The laws of physics at the time were no different than they are now.

Every day seemed to hold new wonders. The serpents were fascinating to watch climbing into fruit trees and knocking off the fruit. Back on the ground, if it was still there, the serpents coiled around the fruit to hold it in place as their unhinged jaws allowed them to swallow the fruit whole. Some serpents injected a dissolving fluid into the fruit to help digest it.

Spiders weaving their webs were a great fascination for Eve. Some spiders like the tarantula kind were quite ugly, but others were beautiful in form. Eve seemed to favor the black spiders that had large abdomens with two red spots on the bottom which looked something like a black widow. She sometimes picked up the spiders and studied them. They just walked around on her hand, very docile. No matter what she did, they wouldn't bite her. She occasionally noticed a bug fly into a spider's web and get caught. Before it could break free, the spider rushed to wrap it in a web. It injected a fluid into the bug to dissolve it to be consumed later.

Each day, God assumed the form of an angel of the Lord and walked in the garden with Adam and Eve. They greatly enjoyed this close fellowship with God and talked with Him of a great many things—the wonders of both the earth and heaven. In one of those talks, Adam asked how the rainbows were made. The Lord explained that light was made up of several different colors. Each color has its own wavelength that, when combined, made white light. When seen from a forty-two degree angle opposite the sun, the water droplets forming the mist acted like tiny prisms, separating the different wavelengths of the light to produce their individual bands of colors. These formed large circular bands of color. From the ground, only part of the circle was seen as an arch. From the sky above, the whole circle could be seen. This led Him to explain the nature of color, how the eyes worked to see color and how the brain processes the color images.

Somehow, no matter the subject—whether it was about rainbows or about how spiders wove their webs to be adorned by the morning mist like strung jewels, or about the stars in the sky, or what constitutes life—it always provided a spiritual parallel that the Lord used to help Adam and Eve mature in their walk with Him. The circular rainbows were used to illustrate that God is circular in nature, having no beginning or end and that He is all encompassing and everywhere present. The seven visible colors of the rainbow represented the seven facets of the Holy Spirit.

The rainbows and adorned spider webs weren't the only

by-products of the mist. The runoff from the mist produced numerous streams, which flowed into a single river, which in turn, flowed around the garden before dividing into four rivers. Adam named the first river Pishon, which flowed north around the land called Havilah. In Havilah were gold, bdellium and onyx stones. The second river was called Gihon, which flowed west around the land of Cush. The third was called Tigris, which flowed east around the land called Nod. And the fourth river was called Euphrates that flowed south from the land of Eden. These four rivers eventually wound their way to the ocean.

One large ocean surrounded a single continent, itself ringed by a floating forest. The roots of these trees extended below the mat that supported the trees and into the seawater below. Because the oceans were still freshwater oceans, the floating forests were able to sustain themselves from the seawater. Among the forest of roots lived a variety of animals, including the tiktaalik which used its limbs to "walk" from root branch to root branch.

The land scape was varied and held numerous unique wonders. Grasses and flowering plants covered the land along with flowering and nonflowering trees of various kinds, sizes and shapes. In the south grew a forest of glossopteris trees while in the west thrived the massive gopherwood trees that reached heights of hundreds of feet. Flowing among the forest and meadows were rivers and streams that tumbled over short cliffs, forming beautiful waterfalls. The waters collected in depressions to form lakes and swamplands in low-lying areas, which supported a diverse ecological system. There was beauty in the land that has never been seen since.

The garden proper was an exceptionally wondrous microcosm, more splendid that the rest of the world. Yet, of all the wonders of the garden, the Tree of the Knowledge of Good and Evil held the single greatest wonder for Eve. Often, while Adam was out tending the garden, Eve would sit and stare at the tree for hours on end. It was a beautiful tree, a one-of-a-kind tree. What was this knowledge she was forbidden to possess? What was so deadly about this fruit? For that matter, what did it mean to die? She had no concept of death other then that it was the absence of life. Even that mystified her. What did it mean to be absent of life? What happened when life was lost? It was not as straight forward an answer as one might imagine, for death is a great deal more than the mere absence of life. Did one just simply cease to exist? Was there nothing more afterward? The concept of nothingness and the hopelessness and purposelessness of it was completely beyond her ability to comprehend or imagine. Maybe the tree's fruit could provide answers. By the same token, if one had to die to learn the meaning of death, what would be the value of it? Still, she stared and wondered. Her hours of staring at the tree gave Adam cause for concern.

Immediately after Adam's creation, God put him in the garden of Eden and charged him with tending it. Tending the garden was his service to God but he needed a helper. God stated it wasn't good for man to be alone and He brought all the land animals living in the garden of Eden for him to name and to see if any of them was a suitable helper. Blessed with superior intelligence he named all the animals God brought to him in the course of a single day. Adam was given dominion over all the animals. By naming them he exercised his authority over them. As God intended, however, he soon saw that none of them was a suitable helpmate. Even the various species of primates, which resembled him in form and were closely akin genetically but were not of his kind, were not suitable helpers. They were too interested in doing what monkeys and apes do best; acting like monkeys and apes. Even the apes showed no interest in him apart from short-term curiosity.

So God put Adam into a deep sleep. He extracted a section of rib bone from the man and from it He created a woman. A rib bone was used because it was designed to regenerate itself. Eventually, Adam's rib regrew, so he didn't have to go through life with a gap in his rib cage. The very day God created Adam, He created a woman from Adam's rib. She was only a few hours younger than Adam. He called her woman because she was created from the man rather than from the dust of the earth as he had been. As with the animals, he exercised his authority over her by naming her, thus establishing his headship over his family. When God brought her to him, she was the most beautiful creature he had ever seen and he named her Eve. She was God's single, greatest blessing to him and he loved her mightily. In many ways he even desired her above God.

He feared of losing her if she ate of the fruit of the Tree of the Knowledge of Good and Evil. He grew frustrated when her chores didn't get done and he warned her about her infatuation with the tree. Her efforts to sooth his concern did little to comfort him. Yet, despite his concern, he wasn't overly worried. The idea of disobeying God was simply unthinkable to him. Unbeknownst to them, however, a war was waging in heaven that would change everything.

Lucifer was the most beautiful creature ever created. Full of wisdom and perfect in beauty, every precious stone was his covering. He was a created being, created along with all the other sons of God, sometime before or about the same time the earth was created. As a created being, he was not by any stretch of the imagination, equal to God. Nor was he a brother to the Son of God. He was no more equal to God than the precious stones he was adorned with. He was just an angel, who upon his creation, was placed on the holy mountain of God and walked among the stones of fire, the precious stones of heaven. He was anointed a cherub and covered with three pairs of grand wings. His purpose was to serve God in the temple and to minister and guide humans in their walk with God.

Lucifer was given power and authority over one third of the angels. Because of his beauty and power, he began to think of himself as something special. Pride welled up within him and he thought he should be the one being served. Instead of ministering to the humans, he wanted them to worship him. He chaffed at serving God and grew angry and rebellious. The thought of serving humans irritated him even more.

He was gifted with great wisdom and was highly persuasive in speech, which he used to persuade the angels he had charge of to join him in rebellion against God. Not that they needed much persuasion. Like their leader, they were filled with pride themselves and desired their own kingdom. Like Lucifer, these angels had been given the charge of ministering to the humans. Because of their pride, they thought themselves special and above the humans. The idea of serving and ministering to the humans annoyed them to no end. When they had enough of their humility, they rose up in rebellion against God. The fighting in heaven was fierce but they never stood a chance. The other cherubs and archangels, along with their angel charges, were too much for the rebels to overcome.

Lucifer and his angels were soundly defeated and cast out of the third heaven. Afterwards, all of the rebellious angels were stripped of their beauty. Some had the form of a human, while others had a mix of human and animal features. Some were so hideously deformed in their depravity, they were literally nauseating to look at. They were all condemned to an eternity in the fiery bottomless pits in the center of the earth. Until the time of judgment, however, they were confined to the second heaven.

The second heaven existed between the third heaven where God resides and the physical realm of the first heaven. It was located in the fourth dimension of space the three dimensional material universe occupied. Barriers between the dimensions prevented the three dimensional beings of earth from passing into the fourth dimension or even from being aware of or able to detect its existence. Fourth dimensional creatures like angels and demons, however, could pass through the barrier at will. The human spirit and accompanying soul could also pass through it, but only after being cut off from the body.

Upon being cast out the third heaven, the demon's were permitted to roam the earth, but were required to report their comings and goings before God on a regular basis. Lucifer, now called Satan and bearing the resemblance of a serpent, likewise still had access to the throne of God—but only at God's biding.

Seeing he was cast out of his place in heaven, Satan raised his fist in full defiance of God and said in his heart, "I will ascend into heaven, I will raise my throne above the stars (angels) of God, and I will sit on the mount of assembly in the recesses in the north. I will ascend above the heights of the clouds; and I will make myself like the Most High."

I've often wondered why God didn't just destroy Satan and his angels at that time. Why did He allow them to live and roam the earth? Why wasn't he permanently bound and separated? Why was he allowed to roam free? So much death and suffering could have been avoided. Knowing what would happen, does this make God evil? Of course not. His ways are above our ways and his thoughts are above our thoughts. Whatever His reasons for allowing Satan to remain free, they were for a righteous reason and for God's glory. Besides, the temptation to eat of the Tree of the Knowledge of God and Evil still tempted Adam and Eve.

It was only a matter of time before that temptation became too strong to resist, even without Satan's intervention.

Before Satan could raise his throne above the stars and ascend into heaven, he had to first capture the earth. But he could not forcefully take possession of the earth. In order to legally possess the earth, he had to deceive the rulers of the earth into handing dominion of the earth over to him. For the moment, the rulers of the earth consisted only of Adam and Eve. And he knew exactly with whom to start. At the Tree of the Knowledge of Good and Evil, he found Eve staring at it once again.

Having the form of a crafty serpent, he spoke to Eve, "Indeed, has God said, 'You shall not eat from any tree of the garden'?" He twisted God's words around and in essence, questioned whether the Word of God was indeed infallible and inerrant. From the very beginning, Satan has put into the hearts of mankind the desire to question the inerrancy of God's Word and to question whether or not it should be understood literally.

Eve marveled that the Serpent spoke to her. For of all the creatures on the planet, only she and Adam had the power of speech. In her wonder, she corrected his statement saying, "From the fruit of the trees of the garden we may eat; but of the fruit of the tree which is in the middle of the garden, God has said, 'But from the tree of the knowledge of good and evil you shall not eat, for in the day that you eat from it you shall surely die.'"

The Serpent replied, "You surely shall not die! For God knows that in the day you eat from it your eyes will be opened, and you will be like God, knowing good and evil." He seemed to imply, *He didn't mean it the way you understood it.*

She looked up at the tree wondering if she had indeed misunderstood. She thought about the Serpents words and liked the idea of being like God. In their morning talks with God, she longed to be as wise and knowledgeable as He, and to do the things

He could do. She wondered if maybe there was an alternative meaning to what He had said. What did "you shall surely die" really mean? Maybe He meant it allegorically or symbolically. How could she know? Seeing that the tree could make her wise like God and that the fruit was good to eat, she picked from it and ate, dispensing with any idea of the consequences it would bring. She didn't feel any sensation or experience a blinding flash of knowledge, yet she convinced herself that she was now like God. Especially since she didn't immediately drop dead as she'd thought God had meant.

On the surface it appeared that the serpent was right, but it was only a half-truth. This was a clever tactic of Satan to mix truth with untruth to get people to believe his lies. It's a tactic he continues to use to the present age, for it is highly effective toward those who don't know the whole truth. He still uses the same lie he deceived Eve with, and even with all mankind's advanced knowledge, he has not grown one iota wiser.

While Eve didn't experience an immediate physical death, she did experience an immediate spiritual death. At that moment, her body, which was originally intended to live forever, began the slow process of decaying towards a physical death. Thus she began to die before she eventually physically died, thus fulfilling God's Word, "you shall surely die." Not realizing this, she went to find Adam, who wasn't far away, and gave him the fruit to eat."

He took the fruit and looked at it. "What have you done, Eve?"

"See? I am not dead as you feared. But I am like God now. Don't you want to be like God? Eat. It is good."

Adam did indeed want to be like God but his desire was mostly for Eve. He wasn't deceived as Eve was, but he feared God would take her from him as punishment. So he foolishly chose the woman over God and ate of the fruit. Immediately their eyes were opened and they knew they had sinned against God. They knew they were naked and felt ashamed. Feeling exposed, they made for themselves loin coverings of fig leaves. Adam and Eve had only one law to obey. And they couldn't even keep that one law.

Come the cool of the day, the pre-incarnate Jesus Christ, Who was Himself God, walked within the garden for His daily chat with Adam and Eve. But when they heard Him coming, they hid themselves among the trees. When God couldn't find Adam, He called to him, "Where are you?"

They emerged from the trees, and Adam replied, "I heard the sound of Thee in the garden, and I was afraid because I was naked, so I hid myself."

"Who told you that you were naked? Have you eaten from the tree of which I commanded you not to eat?"

Adam felt ashamed, but his pride would not allow him to take responsibility for his actions. Instead he said, "The woman whom Thou gave to be with me, she gave me from the tree, and I ate." He didn't just merely blame the woman for his actions, but he essentially blamed God for giving him the woman in the first place.

God ignored Adam's innuendo of blaming Him and turned to Eve, "What is this you have done?"

It was the same question Adam had asked her, but in her pride she wasn't about to give God the same answer or take responsibility for what she did. Instead, she too shifted the blame to someone else. "The serpent deceived me, and I ate."

The Serpent wasn't allowed to quietly slip away. In God's presence, it too, was required to stand with Adam and Eve. The Serpent wasn't asked to give account of itself, for God knew what he was. Instead, God pronounced a sentence of punishment on the Serpent. "Because you have done this, cursed are you more than all cattle and more than every beast of the field. On your belly shall you go, and dust shall you eat all the days of your life." Then He prophesied of the promised Messiah. "And I will put enmity between you and the woman, and between your seed and her seed. He shall bruise you on the head, and you shall bruise Him on the heel."

When He turned to Eve, Adam feared the worse. He felt no fear for himself, for in his pride he still felt he had favor in God's eyes. To Eve God said, "I will greatly multiply your pain in childbirth, in pain you shall bring forth children. Yet your desire will be for your husband and he shall rule over you." Eve had yet to experience childbirth. She didn't know that childbirth was originally a relatively pain-free experience. Nor did she have any concept of what kind of pain she was condemned to suffer. But she was allowed to keep her life, and for that she felt her punishment was a light one. She found out differently when Cain was born. Aside from the pain, she also had a strong desire for her husband—not a sexual desire but a desire to control and usurp his authority over her. Oftentimes this issue of authority caused conflict that Adam had to learn to deal with. It is the woman's desire for control that men of every generation have had to deal with.

Eve's judgment was harsh, but God handed Adam a much harsher judgment. For Adam was responsible for much and from him much more was expected. More importantly, he was responsible for his wife's welfare, including her spiritual welfare. He had seen the warning signs that this would happen, but he had done next to nothing about it.

God turned to Adam and said, "Because you have listened to the voice of your wife and have eaten from the tree about which I commanded, saying 'You shall not eat of it,' cursed is the ground because of you. In toil you shall eat of it all the days of your life. Both thorns and thistles it shall grow for you, and you shall eat the plants of the field. By the sweat of your face you shall eat bread till you return to the ground, because from it you were taken. For you are dust, and to dust you shall return."

Adam was condemned, not just for his pride, but also because he chose the woman over God. He was relieved that Eve wasn't going to be taken from him, but he groaned when God handed him the death penalty. To make matters worse, it would be a slow death after a lifetime of hard labor and suffering.

Adam and Eve didn't die an immediate physical death, but they did die an immediate spiritual death. That is, they were separated from God and lost fellowship with Him. Because of their spiritual death, all of their descendants were likewise born spiritually dead. But God wasn't going to leave it at that. Instead, He provided a means of redemption, if only a temporary one. He looked upon their loin coverings of fig leaves they attempted to cover their shame with and determined that this would never do. Atonement for sin cannot be woven by the hands of mankind. He took an innocent animal suitable for sacrifice and slew it in the presence of the man and woman. As the earth drank up its blood, He took of the hide and made clothes for them to wear.

When Eve saw it, she was aghast. Never before had anything died on the earth. She thought about its death and about how it would never again experience life. For the first time she understood that death was not merely the absence of life. It was the terrible price of sin. As she watched the animal's life drain out onto the ground, she cried and kept willing it to get back up, but it wouldn't move. Only then did she realize how final death was. She knelt and cradled its limp, lifeless head in her lap and wailed, "What have I done?"

The Serpent laughed wickedly.

Adam looked on, just as shocked, as tears filled his eyes. It was his first experience with sorrow. It would be the first of many instances and was also part of the price of sin. The animal hadn't been slain merely to provide clothing for Adam and Eve. The shedding of its blood also served as a temporary covering for their sins. It was made known to them that this was something they would have to do every year for the rest of their lives.

Because Adam and Eve had eaten of the Tree of the Knowledge of Good and Evil, God said, "Behold, the man has become like one of Us, knowing good and evil. And now, lest he stretch out his hand and take also from the Tree of Life and eat and live forever—" So God drove the man and woman out of the garden of Eden and they were forced to scratch a living out of dirt. He stationed the cherubim with a flaming sword that turned every direction to prevent them from finding the way to the Tree of Life.

When Satan left the garden, he felt pleased with himself. He had his kingdom now. Adam had been given dominion over all the earth and had been made its governor. When Adam sinned, he handed the keys of the kingdom to Satan. But no land can permanently be taken from God's people. The loss of the land and the conditions for purchasing it back were written on a scroll that was sealed with seven seals. The conditions for purchasing back the land required a sinless person, a kinsman redeemer, to break the seals. That person would be our Lord and Savior, our Creator, Jesus Christ. But like an incurable disease, sin first had to run its course. The world would suffer mightily before Jesus would begin the process of transferring the administration of the earth from Satan back to man.

When Adam and Eve were driven out of the garden, they first found shelter in a cave. Adam learned how to make bricks of mud and straw and he built a house with a sod roof. The house was built beside a meadow surrounded with trees near the banks of the Euphrates River. He fashioned tools out of wood and stone, and continued his occupation as a gardener growing crops for food. He grew grains and vegetables from seeds he acquired from plants growing in the wild. These wild plants were quite different from todays wild plants that have devolved to the point where they can no longer be used to grow crops.

Around the house, Adam planted various flowers, including roses. Eve loved the scent of roses and wanted them around the house. He was surprised when they grew with thorns on the stems. This made tending them a prickly affair. Eve was supposed to take care of the rose garden, but because of the thorns, Adam ended up tending to them.

Not long after Adam and Eve were driven from the garden of Eden, the hydrologic cycle took effect and the mist stopped rising from the ground. Prickly things started growing that seemed to grow faster than anything else. The animals felt the corruption of the earth, and many became mean spirited. Many of the formerly benevolent insects became pests. It didn't take long for the earth to suffer the effects of sin's corrupting influence.

While plowing the ground to sow his crops, Adam noticed white fluffy things floating in the sky above him. He had never seen clouds before and wondered about them. The next day, dark and angry-looking clouds rolled in. There was a flash of light followed by a deep rumbling sound. A bolt of lightning flashed from the sky and struck a nearby tree. It split the tree in half and set it on fire. The light of the lightning briefly blinded him, and the thunder it produced was deafening. Frightened out of his wits, he raced to his house to get Eve inside. All the while wondering if he had done something to make God angry.

Adam watched the storm from his doorway with fear and wonder. A sudden gust of wind almost blew the house down and was followed by water falling from the sky. Adam knew about mist, but rain was something new. Chunks of ice fell from the sky and turned the ground white. This was also something completely new to him. He picked up one of the hailstones and watched in wonder as it turned from a solid into liquid. The coldness of the ice was a strange sensation. He had never known that water could become a solid and wondered how it was possible. He discovered a few months later how destructive hail was to crops, when another storm blew through. He learned that he not only had thorns and thistles to contend with, but the whims of nature—and wild animals and insects that wanted their share of the bounty of his crops. He had to plant a garden four to five times the size he needed, just to make up for his losses.

How Adam longed to discuss these things with God! But since he had sinned against Him, he learned that another consequence of sin was separation from God. He was cutoff from fellowship with God and was unable to talk with Him face-to-face. God still occasionally spoke with him through that still, small voice in the back of his head—a thought that appeared from nowhere, which he instantly recognized as the voice of God. But it wasn't the same as talking with Him in person. He greatly missed his daily walks with God. As much as he loved his wife and cherished her, he often felt lonely. Since his fellowship with God had been broken, a great void opened in his heart. One that his wife, children or anything else could never fill.

Other storms followed, and Adam and Eve learned not the fear them, though they still held a strong respect for the lightning and the power of water from the occasional flash flood. Apart from learning to farm the land, Adam also learned animal husbandry and raised various domesticated animals. He learned how to train them to do some of the work and sheared the sheep's wool.

Eve in turn learned how to spin this wool into thread and weave it to make clothing. From the mud she also learned to make clay pots and to weave plant fronds into baskets to carry and store things.

They also learned the joy of sex and wondered why they waited so long. Soon the time was near for Eve to give birth to their first child. Adam was working in the field when he heard a mighty scream coming from his house. Alarmed, he raced to the house and found his wife in childbirth. For hours she screamed and cursed in pain. "This is all your fault," she kept screaming and cried out for God to help. When the child emerged, and as the Lord gave instruction, Adam cut off the umbilical cord and tied the ends so his wife and baby wouldn't bleed to death. To force the baby to take a deep breath, he spanked the child to make him cry. He proceeded to clean the child and then wrapped him in a wool blanket. When he gave the baby to Eve to hold, she immediately forgot about her pain and rejoiced in her firstborn. As the child suckled, she stated joyously, "I have begotten a manchild with the help of the Lord," and she called him Cain.

This is the first recorded instance of Eve usurping Adam's authority and naming the child herself. In so doing she claimed authority over the child. She did this with all her other children as well. Instead of taking a hard stand, Adam permitted Eve to have her way and surrendered any say in raising the children.

In the following years, they had a second man-child whom Eve named Abel. Daughters were born to them in later years. As the two boys grew, Adam taught them everything he knew, including the knowledge of the Lord and why they needed to sacrifice a lamb every year. In time Cain became a farmer while Abel became a shepherd.

Eve often took her children out and taught them all that the Lord had told her about living things. She came across one of those black-widow-like spiders. Remembering how she had once held one, she plucked it off its web intending to teach her children a few things about it. Instead, it gave her a new lesson that none of them would soon forget. She screamed when she felt a sharp pain in her hand. She dropping the spider when she realized it had bit her. In her anger she stepped on it and killed it, but the pain in her hand increased. Her hand started swelling up and the pain spread up her arm. For several days, she was deathly sick. Adam feared he would lose her, but he had no idea how to help her. All he could think of was to pray that the Lord would help her. God showed him how to treat the wound, and she eventually recovered. From that moment on, they became fearful of spiders and never messed with them again. Spiders still held their fascination, but they learned to observe them from a respectable distance.

Come the spring of each year, they had to take a lamb without blemish and offer it up to the Lord as a sin offering for the temporary covering of their sins. At that time, they each had to make a sacrifice for their own sins. Abel offered up the firstlings of his flock and found favor with the Lord. Cain, however took great pride in his crops and was grieved that he had to buy a lamb from Abel to sacrifice for his sins. In his pride, he wanted to do things his own way and he grew angry when God would not accept them.

The Lord said to him, "Why are you angry? And why has your countenance fallen? If you do well, will not your countenance be lifted up? And if you do not do well, sin is crouching at the door; and its desire is for you, but you must master it." Sin's desire for mankind was the same desire Eve was cursed with. The desire for control.

Cain walked with Abel in the field and told him what the Lord had said. But he was unrepentant, and in his anger, he picked up a large rock and bludgeoned Abel with it. He found his brother's death fascinating and smiled wickedly, but he knew he had done wrong. He threw down the rock and calmly walked away as if nothing had happened.

The Lord, however, was not mocked. He asked, "Where is Abel, your brother?"

Cain answered, "I don't know. Am I my brother's keeper?"

The Lord replied, "What have you done? The voice of your brother's blood is crying out to Me from the ground. And now you are cursed from the ground that opened its mouth to receive your brother's blood from your hand. When you cultivate the ground, it will no longer yield its strength to you. You shall be a vagrant and a wanderer on the earth."

Cain cried out, "My punishment is too great to bear! I have been driven from the land and it will come about that whoever finds me will kill me." His attitude was the same as every criminal that followed him. Though he had killed his brother, he thought he had a right to get away with his crime.

The Lord had other plans for Cain, however, and branded him on the forehead, declaring whoever killed Cain, will experience vengeance sevenfold. Cain thought he had gotten off light, but his sons followed suit and became murderers themselves. Eventually Cain did receive his just due. After all, what goes around eventually comes around.

Cain related these things to Adam before taking one of his sisters to be his wife and departing the land. At that time, mankind's DNA had not yet degenerated to the point where siblings produced mutated offspring. Cain's life was riddled with trouble—especially from his wife. She learned well from her mother how to control men. Cain had to continuously come down hard on her to keep her in her place.

Eve had been bereaved of three of her children, but soon other children were born to them and they spread throughout the earth. These offspring quickly forgot about the Lord and soon the whole earth was filled with violence. With the violence, people turned away from God to worship false gods and sacrificed children to them. Unknowingly they worshiped Satan, much to his delight.

Even the animal world was soon filled with violence. Some animals that had formerly been herbivores became carnivorous and started preying on other animals. And some insects that were formerly benevolent, became a nuisance or even deadly, as did some plants and creatures of the sea. Many people learned the hard way about these deadly plants, insects and animals.

Cain settled in the land of Nod east of the land of Eden and built a city he called Enoch after his first born son. The sons of Cain turned away from God, but despite their wickedness, they proved highly inventive. Beginning with learning to control fire and experimenting with the effects of fire on different materials, they built great cities, developed agriculture, mined minerals and learned metallurgy that equals our present abilities. They invented music, art, and writing. They also learned physics and genetics and achieved a whole host of scientific, medical, and technological accomplishments that rivaled the twenty-first century. They also developed commerce and government that fueled their greed and lust for power.

About a year after Cain slew Abel, Seth was born to Adam and Eve, who were 130 years old at that time. The world Seth was born into bore very little resemblance to the world Adam had known after his creation. With the whole world chasing after false gods, Seth's children became the only ones to follow after God. Over the course of time, however, they too turned away from God, just as the sons of Cain had done. The degree of zeal that they formerly shown toward virtue shifted to a double degree of wickedness towards men.

But the greatest abomination occurred when the "sons of God," the fallen angels, lusted for the daughters of man. They disguised themselves as mighty men and abandoned their abode in the second heaven. They seduced the daughters of man and begat the Nephilim. These were giants among men who despised God to the utmost degree. They were men of renown who became great rulers of nations and made war with other nations. They developed aircraft and weapons of war capable of mass destruction. They learned to harness the power of the atom and built breeder reactors and nuclear weapons. With these they magnified the terror of war.

Nine hundred and some odd years after the earth's creation, Eve passed away. The heartbreak Adam felt was more than he could bear. As Adam neared the end of his life, he wrote down on clay tablets the creation account as God revealed it to him and the family history, which he passed down to Seth. As much as Adam was ashamed of the sins of his family, the Lord left him no choice but to include them, for they were the only way the world would understand the origin of death and suffering. As he lay dying, he gave his blessing to Seth and expressed how painful it was to lose his wife. But as painful as it was, it never came close to the grief of losing fellowship with God. His sin against God and its effects on the world were his single greatest regret. He sincerely wished that he could somehow go back and correct it. But it wasn't his to correct and the plan of redemption was already in motion.

Seth passed the tablets on to the faithful of his descendants whom the Lord had chosen beforehand to preserve His written Word. Each person in turn, wrote his part of the family history as the Lord directed. It was through this line that the Lord set aside His chosen few to be his witnesses to a wicked and perverse world, so that the world would be without excuse.

About fifteen hundred years after creation, God lamented the wickedness of mankind. But the abominations of the demonic offspring were what brought judgment upon mankind. Satan understood early on that only men of purely human genes were eligible for salvation. By diluting mankind with demonic genes, he hoped to make man ineligible for salvation and to be worshipped by them. When righteous Abel was murdered, Satan thought he had destroyed the line of men that the seed of the Messiah would come from. Then Seth had been born. Despite Satan's best efforts to corrupt the sons of Seth, one of his lines proved incorruptible. When every other line of man had been contaminated with the genes of demons, God vowed to wipe them off the face of the earth and decreed that 120 years of life be given them.

Of all the lines of men, only Seth's line remained pure through Noah, who found favor with God. Noah was commissioned to build an ark to save his family—and a pair of each kind of land animal that had the breath of life in it—from the coming world flood.

Chapter 4
Global Flood Catastrophe

1656 AC (Circa 2452 BC)

In my third dream, I was taken to the ark God had instructed Noah to build. There was a large gathering of animals but not as much human activity as I expected. I beheld Noah walking slowly toward a building as if carrying a heavy burden. He was tall with a full head of hair, thick beard, broad shoulders, and calloused hands. He looked like a man about sixty with streaks of grey in his hair and beard. Wearing a full length brown and white robe and sandals on his feet, he stopped briefly at the door of the building they called the meeting house and looked around. The only human activity within the compound surrounding the ark was that of a few servants going about their chores and his three sons still working on the ark.

Within the meeting house, the five remaining hired workers waited anxiously for Noah to return with their pay. They grumbled continuously at his apparent deliberate slowness. For nearly several decades they had labored on this foolish project of building the largest ship ever built. It was especially foolish in that it had been built in the middle of the Enochian hill country, a hundred leagues from the nearest open sea. And it had no means of propulsion or control. Hundreds of workers had started this project, happy to take the fools money. But over the years the workers gradually diminished in number as the ridicule they had to endure exponentially increased. Noah had to double, triple and finally quadruple their pay just to retain them—until only five remained. With their reputation and livelihoods in shambles, they were anxious to return to their homes to rebuild their lives.

Noah finally entered the building with five sacks of gold pieces. The only furniture was a single large table with the construction plans for the ark spread out on it. The plans were drawn on something resembling papyrus. Noah set the sacks before the five men on their floors mats, crouched on his ankles and said, "I understand the anxiety you must be feeling by the rejection of your people, but I implore you once again to repent. It is not yet too late. If you would just return to the Creator, believe that He is God, and obey His precepts, He will deliver you. There is more than enough room on the ark for you and your families."

"Your brain is addled, old man," Hanji retorted with a gravelly voice. "You've been breathing the fumes of pitch for too long. My own gods will see me through as they always have. Your God expects too much and is far too judgmental to suit me."

"You've always been a great architect and master craftsman, my friend, as this grand spectacle proves," Salias added as he adjusted his optical lenses affixed to his nose with a nose loop. "But you've gone over the edge. Our friendship is ended. I cannot believe in a God who would destroy the innocent with the wicked. That is not what a loving God would do. Only an evil God will do this."

"Your God has made my life a ruin and an object of derision," Barrack said belligerently in a deep baritone voice. "Now I must leave this land and go to another where I am not known and start over. Your beloved ship is near completion. I have had enough."

"I have neglected my family for too long," Dorma stated. "What wives remain have taken to loving each other in my absence—though I must confess that watching them is most titillating. Still, I must return before they decide I am no longer needed. As for your God, why should I sacrifice sensual pleasures just to please Him? What has He done for me?"

Galad shot to his feet in anger. "Salias is right. How can I believe in a God who will destroy innocent children and those who have done no wrong. What great sin have I committed that deserves death? A great war is raging around us. The sky-ships with their arrows of fire wreak havoc wherever they go. Great columns of fire rise up from the earth and boil over in the sky like a giant mushroom. Fierce winds of fire race outward and level entire cities. The peoples flesh melts off of them like wax. Countless thousands have been mercilessly slaughtered to satisfy the power-hungry egomaniacs who think they have the right to dictate to us how we ought to live, think and speak. Why does God not put a stop to this madness?"

"The purpose of the flood is to cleanse the earth of the corruption of mankind and the madness he has wrought," Noah responded.

"By killing everybody! How is God any different from the wicked?"

"There are none good, Galad. There are none who seek after God. All have turned away from God. Together they have become corrupt. There are none good, no not even one."

"Yet you are being saved. How do you rate?"

"I am as much a sinner as you are. Yet I have not turned away from God. I still seek after Him."

Galad spat on the ground. "You are the ultimate hypocrite,

and you expect me to believe!" He scooped up his bag of gold and stormed out the door. The others followed in agreement.

With a heavy heart, Noah joined his family for the evening meal.

His wife was quick to notice the sadness on his face. "Why has your countenance fallen, my husband?" she gently prodded.

He reflected on the years since construction of the ark had begun. The wickedness of mankind had increased exponentially and Noah was at a loss to explain it. Though there were many factors involved, it primarily had started when false teachings emerged about the origins of life and the age of the earth, teachings that essentially called God a liar and brought into question His very existence. Everybody knew that the earth wasn't millions or billions of years old. Everybody knew the facts of creation, but that didn't stop the scientists from reinterpreting the creation story and invented their own versions of evolution. The rebellious hearts of mankind desired to live free of God's moral laws, to escape accountability and the consequences of sin. People quickly seized on these false teachings as justification to deny God's existence and they threw out His perfect standard for a joyous and fruitful life.

To add to his sorrow, Noah's father, Lamech, passed away only a few years earlier. Lamech had been a chief help in designing and engineering the ark. And just last month, Noah buried his grandfather, Methuselah, the oldest man who had ever lived. Noah had been very close to his grandfather and had relied on him for encouragement. Without him, Noah would have despaired long ago and abandoned the ark. Methuselah helped him keep his eyes on God and His promises, rather than on the turmoil of the world and its growing hatred for those who followed after God.

Instead of pouring out his heart on these matters, Noah chose to focus on the issue at hand. "The last of the workers grew angry and left," he answered his wife. "They throw out the usual accusations and refuse to believe. My heart weeps for them."

"Only God can save them, my love. You have obeyed God's words and have given them warning. There is nothing more you can do. Yet we must continue to pray for them. There is still time."

Noah nodded. "You are correct, of course. Let us then give thanks for our meal and offer up intercession for our neighbors."

The next morning, Noah and his sons gathered together outside the meeting house to pray before beginning the days labor. People from the nearby villages were already gathering for the daily mocking. It was as if it had become the new national sport. Around the ark, the number of animals arriving from various places around the globe increased day by day. Only the land-dwelling and flying creatures that had the breathe of life in them were gathered. The insects and spiders, not having the breathe of life in them, were not gathered except for a few exceptions like the tarantula and scorpion kind. Most insects and arachnids would be able to survive by either stowing away on the ark, clinging to floating vegetation, or employing other strategies of survival.

While they prayed, a dragonfly with a two-foot wingspan occasionally circled them looking for insects to prey on. Its rapidly beating wings sounded like a continuous thunder. The giant dragonfly was the T. rex of the insect world in its day.

In the sky above them, aircraft, Galad's fearsome sky-ships, were occasionally seen competing for airspace with the pterosaurs. One such sky-ship, with a camera attached to its underside, roared above them as it buzzed the ark compound from two different directions. Shem watched the sky-ship wondering if anything was amiss. He was comforted that, despite anything men might do, God was in control and would not allow any harm to come to them.

Shem looked over at the gathering animals. Everyday there seemed to be a different kind of animal arriving. He had no idea where they were coming from. His thoughts turned to the past ninety eight years of his life. Shem was born when Noah was five hundred and two years old, two years after Japheth and two years before Ham. Sometime after they entered manhood, God commanded Noah to build the ark. Several large gopherwood trees brought in from the land of Cush were used to construct the ark. It was built in a prominent valley in the Enochian hill country, a hundred leagues east of the garden of Eden. Through this valley in the land of Assyria flowed the Tigris River. The valley was heavily forested except for the compound that had been cleared to build the ark. On each side of the valley was a high plateau, also heavily forested except for the land cleared for farming. The primary crop was fruit, grown from a numerous variety of orchards.

In the center of the valley at a major crossroads was a village supported by the commerce of those passing through it. It was through this shipping and trade business that Noah's forefathers had acquired their wealth. Relative to the big cities with their soaring towers, the village was a typical small community with four- or five-story structures built of baked bricks and wood. Some of the structures sported high domes and spires. The village had originally been founded by Seth, Adam's third son, and was one of the oldest villages around. Though they possessed advanced metallurgical skills, the village buildings had never been upgraded to steel and glass structures. They had been retrofitted, however, with glass windows, electricity and indoor plumbing. The electricity was generated on the other side of town by a turbine generator powered by the river.

The village was surrounded with high walls that shone brightly in the sun like polished silver. The walls weren't intended to keep out bandits and invading armies so much as to keep out the large dinosaurs that had no regard for human dwellings—particularly the long-necked sauropods with tails that swayed like cedar trees. They roamed the land in herds, trampling everything in their path. The bright light reflecting off the walls was intended to dazzle the eyes of the thundering herds of sauropods so that they veered away from the village.

Occasionally a herd of duck billed parasaurolophuses wandered through, their honking announcing their presence well in advance, but they didn't do as much damage as the sauropods. In the spring it wasn't uncommon to hear loud knocking sounds echoing through the valley. This was the sound of pachycephalosauruses butting heads during the mating season like the big horn sheep did in the mountains up north. These pachys were large bi-pedal dinosaurs with thick, domed skulls adorned with knobs and spines.

Most dinosaurs wisely stayed well clear of human settlements and lived in separate regions, but the sauropods were a particular menace during harvest time. It wasn't practical to construct walls around the orchards, so they had to be quick to harvest the fruit. Guards, armed with powerful firearms, were employed to keep the beasts away.

The sauropods always seemed to know when harvest time came, and they wanted their share of the bounty. Occasionally, a small herd of elephants also passed through wanting their share of the bounty.

The dinosaurs that did mingle with humans were mostly the small ones, and they did so mostly because of the scraps of food people kept wasting—or they were domesticated to haul heavy loads.

Velociraptors wandering the streets of small villages were a common sight, at least in the villages of the Enochian hill country. The three-foot-tall, six-foot-long raptors were marginally tolerated, but whenever they tried to make a meal of one of the dogs, they often became a meal themselves. It wasn't unusual to see someone throwing a head of cabbage or rotten tomatoes at them. Not that the raptors minded. They just ate the veggies, catching them in mid-flight and gulping them down in one swallow. They especially liked the melons that were thrown at them. If one didn't know better, one might be inclined to believe that they thought it was great sport, especially considering that they were a playful lot amongst themselves.

It is said, "From a distance, there is harmony," but despite appearances, there was no harmony among the people. On the high places within the surrounding hills, temples had been built. The people were devoted to worshiping and offering up sacrifices to false gods, the serpent-god being the most prominent. Many of them sacrificed small children to these false gods. A few housed male and female prostitutes devoted to their love goddesses. God never gave mankind permission to eat meat, but that didn't stop them from doing so, for they regularly ate meat sacrificed to idols.

The people went about their business during the day, but at night a strange transformation occurred. If the people weren't worshipping something, they were carousing in the streets in drunken debauchery, as drug abusers killed and robbed people to get more drugs. Rape and open sexual displays, both heterosexual and homosexual, were seen in the streets and city parks. And this was just a rural community. In the larger cities, organized crime and gangs ran the streets. The four super-nations themselves didn't get along and seemed to be at constant war with each other.

Rampant homosexuality and atheistic God-haters trampled society's moral standards. Interpreting the law according to relativistic morals rather than the letter of the law contributed significantly to the moral decay. Soon, mankind's view of right and wrong reversed itself; everything good became bad, and everything bad became good. They considered Adam's sin of eating from the Tree of the Knowledge of Good and Evil a blessing rather than a curse. Such was the world in Noah's time.

Shem looked over at the people assembling to mock them, and thought about the increasing wickedness of the people. He asked, "How much longer before the judgment, Father?"

"Soon, my son. Soon," Noah answered. "God has set the appointed time. In the mean time, we still have a few minor details to complete and then we must load the supplies."

"Do the women need to make any more trips to the market?" Japheth asked. "The people grow more hostile each day. It is no longer safe for them, even with our escort. You know what happened to one of the servant girls. Nobody raised a finger to help her. Some even joined in—right there in the middle of the street, no less. Does nobody have any shame? Does nobody care anymore?"

Noah shook his shaggy head. "The depravity of mankind continues to sink lower still. There seems to be no end to it." He sighed. "No, my son, it will no longer be necessary for the women to go to the market. We have all the supplies we need. And they have a host of preparations of their own to make." He looked at each of his sons and said, "Come. We must finish our work before the waters overtake us. The time of the flood has been decreed and God waits for no one."

Thus, for the next two to three months, the four continued to labor on the ark, completing the waste drainage and plumbing systems, the walls of the various rooms and stalls, as well as the cages for the smaller animals. The covering of the ark was also completed. By this time the last of the servants had departed from their midst.

Ham grumbled to Shem one day that he felt he was laboring in vain. "We are ordered about like servants, and to what purpose?"

"Father feels a great sense of urgency. Time is quickly closing in on us."

"Have you not heard what the experts are saying? Those whose job it is to know the earth say there is not enough water below our feet to cover the entire earth. If there is to be a devastating flood, it will only be a local one. They mock us and ask to what purpose are we building this ark, for the people will only seek higher ground and escape the flood."

"I do not put much faith in those so-called experts, brother. With God, nothing is impossible. If He can create the earth out of water, surely He can bring forth enough water to cover the earth. Remember, it is those so-called experts who say that the animals brought themselves into existence and turned themselves into different kinds of animals. They say that the earth, the sun and the stars all came about of their own accord. They call God a liar and deny His very existence. Then they turn right around and blame Him, the very One whose existence they deny, for all the bad things that happen to them. How can anybody listen to such people?"

Ham looked at the ark towering above them, seeming to stretch on forever before them. "Do you ever have doubts? Father fervently believes that God spoke to him and he is eager to obey His word. But God has not spoken to us. How do we know father heard God at all?"

"Look around you, Ham. God has confirmed His Word to us in a host of ways. Behold the animals and the signs the earth is giving us. Has not God given mankind one hundred and twenty years to live? It was a decree He declared twenty years before we were born, twenty years before God commanded our father to build the ark. Does not the end of the one hundred and twenty years draw nigh upon us? Take heed, my brother. Remember what God spoke to Cain. Sin crouches at the door, and its desire is for you. But you must master it. If you do what is right and obey God, will not your countenance be lifted up?"

Ham scoffed. "But to what purpose? Where does it get us? For we all must die."

Shem looked at the ark and back at Ham. He put his right hand on Ham's left shoulder, squeezed firmly and said, "It gets us salvation, my brother, for it is by faith that we are saved." He smiled reassuringly at him and then hoisted a large beam of wood upon his broad shoulder and carried it into the ark. He had to shoo away a deer standing by the door. The animal's shoulder was level with the top of his head, and sported a menacing-looking eighteen-point rack of antlers on its head.

Upon completing the ark the eight family members then embarked on the loading of provisions; food for both them and the animals for the next two to three years, thousands of bundles of hay and straw for the animals, seeds and seedlings of grain, vegetables, fruit tree saplings and grape vines for the growing of new crops and barrels of oil for the lamps and for cooking. And there were hundreds of barrels of fresh drinking water. Lastly, they brought aboard their personal effects.

During this time, the earth started trembling. At first the tremors were barely noticeable but they grew steadily in intensity. This was something nobody had ever experienced. It put the fear of God into the people, but instead of repenting and turning to the one true God for salvation, they offered sacrifices to their numerous false gods. One family even sacrificed all twelve of their children. In the eyes of God, sin is sin and all sin requires the payment of blood. But some sins are considered an abomination. The sacrifice and abuse of children of any age, born or unborn, is at the top of the list. It is difficult to determine if homosexuality, child sacrifice, or murder of the unborn topped the list of abominations. Killing the unborn was still murder, despite the people's attempt to justify those murders by calling the fetus a lump of flesh, something not yet human and thus having no value.

On the last day in their house, Noah and his sons offered up a sacrifice to the Lord for the temporary payment of their sins. Later, before the evening meal, they sang songs of praise and worship to the Lord and lifted up prayers of supplication for the people one last time. Ham saw this as an exercise in futility and only pretended to pray for them. The only heartfelt prayer he offered up was for the safekeeping of his family.

They ate their meal in silence, while outside the compound walls it sounded like a war was raging. The demons were gorging themselves on the souls of mankind. Unbeknownst to the people changes were occurring within the earth and the sky above them. The magnetic poles were starting to shift and massive amounts of static electricity was building up in the atmosphere. The earth shook mightily that night as bolts of lightning struck the earth continuously. Thousands died from the lightning strikes alone. Only the compound surrounding the ark was untouched. Still the people did not repent. The next morning they offered up even more children to their false gods.

That day God spoke to Noah, "Get thee and thy family and all the animals into the ark, for in seven days I will cover the earth with water. I will no longer strive with mankind for their corruption and wickedness increases day by day. I will wipe the people off the face of the earth and cleanse the earth of all their sins."

Noah wept for the people, especially the children. The little ones who had not yet reached the age of accountability were the ones being sacrificed to the false gods. This day, the little ones were no more.

Noah wasted no time in getting his family aboard the ark. It would take the next seven days to get all the animals aboard. Starting with the birds and smaller animals, Noah and his sons brought them aboard. They brought in the larger animals last. The birds and clean animals they brought in by seven pairs of each kind, a male and his female. The unclean animals came in by twos, a male and his female—two pairs of each kind, according to their own kind. Each one possessed all the genetic encoding for the hundreds of species within their kinds that would follow in future generations.

The ark was a very large barge-like vessel constructed of gopher wood. The gopher wood came from a massive tree that stood close to a thousand feet tall and measured over two hundred feet in diameter. A dozen of these trees provided all the wood necessary to build the ark.

As fossil fuels and coal were not available, the expensive specialized fuel the sky-ships used was not made available for general transport. For this reason, wooden sailing ships, some aided by steam power, still plied the seas, as opposed to the great steel behemoths of the present. Beasts of burden were still used to transport people and freight. For pulling heavy loads, the favored beast of burden was the elephant and ankylosaur. Ankylosaurs, built like battle tanks, weren't fast movers, but they were exceedingly strong.

The massive gopherwood trees were brought in from the land of Cush in the west, using scalar wave levitators. Ankylosaurs, herded by a few guiding hands, towed the massive, levitated trees. Since cutting such large trees with a huge, steel blade was not feasible, powerful CO^2 cutting lasers were used.

The keel beam of the ark, from which the ribs were attached, consisted of a single beam several feet thick, cut from the core of the tree. The remainder of the core was used for the bow stem and the stern post as well as for the primary corner and center rib beams. The rest of the tree was cut into huge wooden beams that formed the ribs, longerons, and cross beams with large thick planks secured to them. They were joined together by locking joints, and wooden pegs fit into holes a few thousandths of an inch smaller than the peg. The interference fit, plus the pitch sealant, ensured that the peg could never come back out. The planks were then covered with pitch, a tar-like substance, both inside and outside to make the vessel watertight.

The ark was designed to have three main decks that contained various-sized compartments and enclosures for the animals with ingenious waste-disposal systems under grated decks and bamboo pipes for distributing water. The upper deck was constructed ten feet from the top of the ark and was used for the storage of food, seeds and seedings. It also contained the enclosures for all the winged creatures and mouse and rabbit-sized animals. Noah's family also inhabited part of the upper deck. The middle deck was fifteen feet below the first and held the small and mid-sized animals. The lower deck was built twenty feet below the second and held the larger animals. The space between the lower deck and the bottom of the ark was used for water storage providing nearly fifty eight thousand gallons of drinking water that also served as ballast for stability. Hand pumps were used to distribute water to the various compartments and enclosures. Grating was built into the centers of the main decks to permit light and fresh air to flow through. Each deck had interconnecting ramps at each end and at the center of the ark. An elevator system was employed for the moving of food stuffs from one deck to another. It also came in handy for moving waste to the upper deck for disposal overboard.

The ark measured 300 cubits long, 50 cubits wide and 30 cubits high. A cubit was determined by dividing pi (3.14159) by six, which equalled 0.5236 meters, or 52.36 centimeters, which equalled 20.6 inches. This put the ark at about 515 feet (157.08 meters) long, 85.8 feet (26.18 meters) wide, and 51.5 feet (15.708 meters) high. The interior space measured about 2.2 million cubic feet. Each of the three main decks measured almost 43,775 square feet for a total of over 131,325 square feet.

Running the length of the ark along the top were ventilation coverings that could be removed. A single door was built into the side of the ark at the lower deck, with a single window above it at the upper deck, a cubit from the top. This window came in handy for waste disposal. The ark was mostly barge-shaped but the bow and stern were curved to a point and a large wooden wind-rudder was constructed atop the bow to keep the stern of the ark pointed toward the wind and the waves. A fixed rudder was attached to the stern to keep the ship from yawing and turning broadside to the waves. By keeping the bow pointed away from the waves instead of toward the waves, allowed the ark to surf the waves, permitting a more comfortable and less stressful ride.

On the last day, Noah stood in the door of the ark, looking out at the people that had gathered to mock him and God. There were even media camera crews broadcasting Noah's boarding the ark and his message around the world. Shem wondered why they were there when he heard one of the commentators saying it was now one hundred twenty years to the day since Noah issued his first warning. They didn't believe anything would happen and were there to mock them.

Noah implored them one last time, "Repent and believe in the Lord God almighty." Gesturing at the door where he stood he said, "Enter through the one and only door of salvation, and

God will forgive you of your sins. For it is by faith that you must be saved, not by works, lest anyone should boast."

The people, however, were offended at being called sinners. Those watching Noah's image broadcast into their homes or place of business laughed at him and shook their fists at him and God in defiance. Those present at the ark became angry and started throwing rotten vegetables and eggs at him. Some threw jagged rocks. They took Noah for a fool and regarded the things of God as foolishness. None of them believed his message or believed that anything would change. They foolishly believed that life would continue the way it always had.

A column of soldiers pushed their was through the throng of people intent on arresting Noah and his family. As they reached the compound wall, the officer in charge ordered Noah to surrender. They were being charged with treason, tax fraud, religious hate crimes and a host of political correctness violations, animal rights violations and environmental violations. As the soldiers busted through the gate, they fell flat on the ground as the earth shook mightily.

Huge fissures opened up in the earth and swallowed several people. Their mighty stone and steel structures were unable to stand under the earthquake's intensity and crumbled. In various places, sand geysers shot up hundreds of feet into the air. Geysers of superheated water shot up tens of thousands of feet through the fissures under great pressure. Then the sky darkened and rain fell in sheets. Never before had rain fallen in such massive torrents. But the people realized the error of their ways too late.

Those people gathered at the ark tried to scramble aboard the ark, but to their horror, the door seemed to move of its own accord. The unseen hand of God reached down from heaven, closed the door of the ark and sealed it. They wailed and shouted for another chance, but God's grace period of 120 years had ended suddenly and decisively. They had been warned repeatedly and had been given numerous chances to repent. Now the time to repent was past. They were without excuse. In Noah's six hundredth year, second month and seventeenth day, the fountains of the deep burst open.

In the following days of torrential rain, water poured through the valley, washing away everything before it, as hordes of people rushed to find higher ground. A surge of water crashed against the ark and prevailed upon it, lifting it free of the land. Inside the ark a great commotion rose when the ark lifted free of the land and rocked violently as it was carried forward by the waves. It was a sensation that none of the occupants of the ark had ever felt. Eventually the ark settled into a rocking motion that lulled and quieted the animals. Shortly afterward the Spirit of God hovered over the animals and placed most of them into a deep sleep.

On that last day, the earth shook to its very core, which triggered runaway volcanism that blew millions of tons of rock and ash into the atmosphere. The crust cracked like an eggshell and spewed trillions of gallons of water in the form of superheated steam under extreme pressure several miles into the atmosphere. Seen from space, the earth appeared to stagger in its orbit like a drunken sailor. The earth's shaking sent shock waves into the atmosphere, which were transmitted into space much like those given off by the sun, and they affected the other planets of the solar system. Mars also experienced catastrophic volcanism and flooding. The fifth planet became unstable and exploded to form the present-day asteroid belt. Even stable Venus tottered and experienced continuous volcanism, which continues to this day.

The water from the superheated steam cooled and fell to the earth as rain, which quickly covered the land with water. Over the course of forty days, the rain fell upon the earth, the mountains fell and the ocean floor swelled, pushing even more water over the land until all the mountains under the heavens were covered. The waters increased fifteen cubits higher and prevailed upon the earth for another one hundred and fifty days.

To the west, a large herd of dinosaurs was swept away by the raging floodwaters, intermingling several species. Another group of sauropods and theropods raced together, attempting to escape the floodwaters. People of large stature followed behind them, leaving their footprints in the mud with the dinosaur footprints. The surging water and sediment caught up with those that fled and swept them away. The sediment covered their tracks and preserved them. To the east, a group of protoceratops and velociraptors attempted to escape the surging floodwaters. They were swept up, intermingled and buried. One velociraptor was shoved into a protoceratops, impaling its chest on the other's neck frill. The velociraptor died instantly if it wasn't already dead. The two were buried together in such a manner that they appeared to be fighting each other. Large groups of mammals were swept up in like manner and buried in separate, successive layers. Vegetable matter was buried and squeezed between the sedimentary layers, producing coal seams. Whole cities were swept away and a few walled villages were buried among the vegetable matter that became coal.

The sedimentary layers were sorted out and laid in successive layers, but nowhere on earth were they laid down in the order assumed by charts developed in the mid to late nineteenth century AD, with their assigned dates of formation. Many of the assumed older layers lay on top of the assumed younger layers. Many layers were laid down out-of-order and some were missing completely. One whale was buried vertically, tail up, so that it crossed several sedimentary layers that supposedly took millions of years to form. Trees, stripped of their bark and branches by the surging water, were likewise buried vertically, crossing several sedimentary layers—and even several coal seams—that supposedly formed millions of years apart.

As the water increased over the land, the supercontinent Rodinia broke apart and rapidly separated. During the year the earth was covered with water, the continental plates moved across the face of the earth and reformed into the supercontinent Pangaea. It, in turn, rapidly separated once again, forming the present-day continents. The earth's magnetic field reversed itself several times during this period, which was recorded by the iron particles suspended in the lava spewing from the rifts of the mid-oceanic ridges following Pangaea's breakup. Before the sedimentary layers solidified, the movement of the continental plates deformed and bent the pliable sedimentary layers at sharp angles without cracking or breaking them. Great mountains were thrust up to magnificent heights and rifts opened, deforming the layers even further. Some rifts opened up and closed again, failing to properly form. At the same time, the ocean floors dropped to a great depth, with numerous volcanoes continuing to erupt and build to tremendous heights, forming numerous islands.

Of all the land-dwelling creatures that had breath in them, mankind was the last to succumb to the floodwaters. Very few were buried in the sediment. Of all the animals that died, very few were actually buried and fossilized. Most of the animals and people floated in the floodwaters with the vegetable matter and rotted before sinking. Their bones eventually dissolved without ever being buried. The air reeked for weeks from the rot of the dead animals, people and plants.

Once the rain stopped falling, the water prevailed on the earth for another 150 days. Following those days, God caused a great wind to pass over the earth and throughout the remainder of the year the waters subsided. As the lands lifted up and ocean basins dropped, the water flowed in great rivers and raced to the ocean in a mighty rush, carving out canyons and ravines along the way. The waters rushed to fill the lowered ocean basins. Even after the floodwaters receded, the mountains continued to build up in height, as the continental plates continued to move rapidly, gradually slowing down to their present rate of drift.

By the time the flood ended, the earth's tilt had changed from 11 degrees to 23.5 degrees and its equinox precession had been reset. Prior to the flood, the sun rose in the constellation of Leo during the spring equinox. Now it rose in the constellation of Taurus.

On the seventeenth day of the seventh month, the ark came to rest within the mountain range that became known as the mountains of Ararat in the region of Ararat as it was known in Moses' day. In the present day, the region is part of Iran. The volcano to the north that was destined to be called Mount Ararat was still relatively small and underwater at this time. The water continued to decrease steadily. On the first day of the tenth month, the tops of the mountains became visible.

When the rain stopped falling after forty days, Noah sent out a raven each day—until one day it failed to return. Then he sent out a dove, but finding no place to rest, she returned to the ark. He sent her out once a week until, one day, she returned with a freshly picked olive leaf in her beak. It was then that Noah knew the water was abating from the earth. The next day the ark grounded roughly on top of one of the mountains. When he sent the dove out a week later she didn't return. Then Noah opened the coverings of the ark. The fresh air felt like the breath of spring. A few months later, he beheld that the earth had dried up.

God ordered Noah to open the door of the ark. He and his family and all the animals that were with him disembarked from the ark. Noah built an altar and took one of every clean animal and bird, and offered up a burnt offering unto the Lord.

God took in the soothing aroma and said to Himself, "I will never again curse the ground on account of man, for the intent of his heart is evil from his youth; and I will never again destroy every living thing as I have done. While the earth remains, seedtime and harvest, cold and heat, summer and winter, and day and night, shall not cease." Then God blessed Noah and his sons and commanded them to go forth and multiply upon the earth.

God then handed down two laws. The first one gave mankind permission to eat meat for the first time, with the stipulation that they should not eat the blood of the animal, for the animal's life was in its blood. Noah and his sons didn't exactly find this palatable, but their children and grandchildren did.

The second law stated that whoever sheds the blood of mankind should have his own blood shed by the hand of man, for mankind was created in the image of God.

Finally, God made a covenant with Noah that He would never again cover the earth with water to destroy it. He then set a rainbow in the clouds as a sign of the covenant and a reminder for all successive generations.

Noah and his family were not yet aware of it, but the earth had just entered its one and only ice age, which would last about seven hundred years. During this period the animals would repopulate the entire planet. The dinosaurs, unable to adjust to the changed climate with lower oxygen levels and cooler temperatures, would eventually die off. Mankind, following his rebellion against God at the Tower of Babel, would also make it to the far corners of the earth. Unfortunately, mankind's evil nature never changed and would continue to corrupt the entire planet leading up to the present day, which remarkably resembles the days of Noah before the flood. God has kept His promise to never again flood the entire earth, though numerous local floods continue to occur. The next world judgment, however, is reserved for fire.

Chapter 5

Confusion at the Tower of Babel

1757 AC (Circa 2351 BC)

In my fourth dream, I found myself in the land of Midian, where Moses tended his father-in-law's flocks. It was another hot day in the northwest corner of the Arabian peninsula. In the city of Midian (present-day El-Bad), after spending the previous couple of weeks shepherding his father-in-law's sheep and goats near Mount Horeb, Moses relaxed as he perused the fruit of his labor over the last forty years. Whenever he thought back on how it had all began, he was amazed at how quickly fortunes could change.

Not more then forty years earlier, he had been a prince of Egypt, raised in the pharaohs court. He had received the best education anybody could get and led Egypt's army. Then he discovered he was a Hebrew, not an heir to the throne. He went to live among his people and found an Egyptian taskmaster beating one of them. Rushing to the mans defense, Moses ended up killing the taskmaster. At first he thought no one had seen the crime, for if he was caught, it meant the death penalty—even for a prince of Egypt. Then he noticed two of his fellow Hebrews fighting and tried to break it up. When one of them mentioned the Egyptian Moses killed, he realized that his crime had been witnessed. It was time to flee. He gathered his belongings, including the clay tablets that had been passed down from Adam all the way through Abraham and Joseph. One of the elders, a direct descendent of Joseph, had entrusted Moses with their care.

He walked south, a donkey in tow, in the wilderness of Egypt (Sinai Peninsula) along the coast of the western arm of the Red Sea (the Gulf of Suez). When he reached the southernmost tip, he proceeded northeast along the coast of the eastern arm of the Red Sea (the Gulf of Aqaba) until he found his way blocked by high mountains. Looking across the Strait of Tiran he could see the land of Midian. He needed to get across and out of Egypt. When he disembarked from the fishing boat he hired to take him across, he was a free man.

As he drew near to the city of Midian he came upon a well and stopped to rest. As he rested, seven daughters of the priest of Midian came to water their flocks, but the other shepherds drove them off. Moses, furious at the injustice of the shepherds' actions, drove them off and drew water for the women to water their flock. They were astonished that an Egyptian would stoop to help them. When the women returned to their home, their father, Jethro, was surprised that they had returned so soon. When they told him what had happened, he chastised them for leaving the man behind. He invited Moses to dine with them and gave him his oldest daughter, Zipporah, for his wife. Moses had been tending his father-in-law's flocks ever since—a large flock that included sheep and goats. At the time, the size of the flock indicated a true measure of wealth.

Besides his time in the field with the flock, Moses worked

at transliterating the clay tablets that had been handed down to him. After the confusion of mankind's languages, Shem had translated the original tablets into Chaldean before passing them on to Terah, who in turn, passed them on to his son, Abraham. The original tablets had then been destroyed to prevent anyone—especially Nimrod—from learning the original language and perhaps reuniting mankind with it.

Moses found the descendants of Esau in the land of Edom just north of the land of Midian and convinced them to sell Esau's tablet to him. He did the same with the descendants of Ishmael at Beersheba in the Negev desert. A total of eleven tablets plus Joseph's papyrus scroll were transliterated and combined into a single scroll. Now, forty years later, the work was complete. The completed work was titled *Genesis*. It was the first of five books Moses would write. These five books became known as the Torah. He read through the scroll one more time to ensure its accuracy. Upon reading the account of the worldwide flood and the Tower of Babel, he reflected on how much the world had changed since then.

When Shem disembarked from the ark with his father and brothers, they looked out upon a world that was anything but balmy and serene. In fact, it was cool, windy, and oftentimes, stormy. Earthquakes were quite frequent, as the fractured continental plates shifted and shoved against each other, pushing mountain peaks ever higher into the sky.

For the next hundred years, the sun was seen only as a blurry orb in the sky through the volcanic dust and aerosols that continuously spewed into the atmosphere. This resulted in cool land masses and warm oceans that produced continent sized hypercanes over the oceans, which lasted for weeks as they ravaged the coastal lands. Large quantities of rain fell in the temperate regions, while massive amounts of snow fell in the polar regions.

With no opportunity to melt, the snow kept piling up to form great ice sheets that spread over North America, Europe, parts of Asia, Greenland and Antarctica. The earth had just entered the first stage of its one and only ice age. Surprisingly, throughout the first stage of the ice age, Siberia and most of Alaska remained free of snow and ice. Bordered by a warm Arctic ocean, they were covered with rich, grassy plains that supported large herds of mammoths and a vast variety of other animals.

Unlike people, the animals spread rapidly over the earth. The dinosaurs, however, had a difficult time adapting to the continuous climate changes and eventually died out, though a few managed to hang on well into the seventeenth century AD. In the sea, a great many creatures were unable to adapt to an ocean that became salty during the flood and subsequent runoffs. The large reptiles and a few of the mammals and fish became extinct because of their inability to adapt to salt water. Of all the reptiles that roamed the sea, only the sea turtle and some sea snakes were able to survive the change.

After Noah made a sacrifice to the Lord, he moved his family to a sheltered valley to the south on the western slopes of the mountain range the ark came to rest on. Moses knew these peaks as the mountains of Ararat in the region of Ararat (previously known as Urartu. The mountains of Ararat run from the northern end of the Persian Gulf northwest through present day Iran and into eastern Turkey and Armenia.

Noah and his sons took with them provisions and their flock of domesticated animals. In the valley they built a house for themselves and an enclosure for the animals, all from the wood they salvaged from the ark. Shem's first son, Arpachshad, was born two years later.

The earth continued to shake from time to time. To the northwest, a great volcano kept erupting and eventually grew to great heights. So violent were some of those eruptions that if anything manmade had been sitting on its slopes, it would have been utterly destroyed. Such would have been the fate of the ark if it came to rest on an active volcano. Today, that volcano is an extinct volcano known as Mount Ararat.

In the sheltered valley of the mountains of Ararat, Noah and his sons planted crops and a vineyard that would later cause trouble for Ham. The grapes were made into a wine, of which Noah had a little too much of one night and lay exposed while he slept. Ham saw Noah's nakedness and reported it to Shem and Japheth. They took a covering and laid in over their father, while walking backwards and keeping their faces turned away to keep from looking at his nakedness. It isn't known for certain, but it is widely speculated that Ham and his son Canaan may have done something indecent to Noah. Whatever they did, Noah was aware of it and cursed them for it.

It seemed that Ham's descendants were destined to follow a path of evil—at least more so than the others—for Nimrod, the son of Cush, the son of Ham, would rise up and become the first world dictator. By his wickedness, the people were led astray to worship false gods. About a hundred years after the ark landed on the mountains of Ararat, the people, now numbering over a thousand, were still living in the sheltered valley.

They seemed content to remain within the relative protection of the mountain valleys, but the valleys were not enough for Nimrod. Nimrod was ambitious and, above all, desired power. He disliked following other people's rules. He wanted to be the leader and the god of the people. He was a mighty hunter and a natural leader who gathered faithful followers. While the people thought he was favored by the Lord, he actually stood in opposition to the Lord.

Nimrod earned his reputation as a mighty hunter before

the Lord by bringing down a ferocious dinosaur that was preying on their livestock. He and a few other men followed the tracks it had left behind and happened upon a midsize allosaur. Nimrod faced the dinosaur with only two large, obsidian-tipped spears. He threw one spear, which impaled the creatures chest. Instead of being killed, it only became enraged. Nimrod ran and leaped up on some rock outcroppings. Taking the high ground, he turned to face the roaring beast. He threw his second spear into the charging allosaur's gaping mouth, which pierced straight into its brain. The dinosaur fell in a cloud of dust at Nimrod's feet. The men with him circled the dead dinosaur and praised Nimrod for his heroics. They followed him on other successful hunting parties and killed every dinosaur they could find.

Like Nimrod, these men became boastful and thought themselves greater than they were. While on these expeditions, Nimrod convinced the men that their happiness could only be procured through their own courage and that they should convince the rest of the people of the same. He also shared with them his vision of a kingdom centered around a great tower that would make a name for themselves. Also, because they had dismantled the ark, they no longer had a place of refuge in case the Lord came to a state of mind to flood the world again. This great tower would serve as their new place of refuge.

Nimrod made the mistake of thinking God was like men. In his pride and arrogance, Nimrod became so contemptuous of God that he vowed revenge on God if He flooded the earth again. He was already beginning to think of himself as a god with the same power as God.

While most of the people were convinced of Nimrod's words, some level heads prevailed. They reasoned, "Why build a tower? Why not just go to the mountain tops?" They knew, that even with the technology and knowledge Noah brought with him, they couldn't build a tower taller than the mountains. As often happens when evil men don't get their way or if someone dares to oppose them, Nimrod turned to tyranny. In his anger, he violently bullied the people into turning away from the fear of God. Those who didn't do as he demanded were beaten to a pulp or killed as an object lesson. Since people seldom stood together to oppose evil and defend each other, Nimrod's thugs found it easy to bully them into compliance. He then forced the people to remain together instead of spreading over the face of the earth. One family that tried to leave didn't get very far before being slaughtered. This put fear into anyone else with a mind to leave. Finding the valley unsuitable for his kingdom, he led the people from the region of Ararat to look for suitable land to build a city.

From out of the east (not the north) they came to the land of Shinar (Babylonia). There they found a fertile plain perfect for farming and raising livestock. Two great rivers flowed through the plain, which they called 'Euphrates' and 'Tigris' after two of the rivers that once flowed from the garden of Eden. The regions they flowed through were named Assyria to the north and Shinar to the south. Near the Euphrates river, Nimrod built the city of Babel. Babel, however, wasn't the name he originally intended to give it. He envisioned something much grander, something fitting for a grand city that spoke of the people's greatness.

It isn't known if Noah and his sons accompanied the people to the land of Shinar, but the people took much of the knowledge and technology he carried with him on the ark. Including the engineering skills required to build different types of structures. They also possessed knowledge of metallurgy, farming, medicine, and a host of other skills that had long since been forgotten and only relatively recently rediscovered—like chemically generated electricity.

When they reached the junction of the rivers, some of the people took up farming while others became shepherds or raised beasts of burden. A few built boats and became fishermen. Most of the people, however, gathered together and built houses for themselves. At first the city that Nimrod wanted to build started out as a loose collection of homes near the river bank which the people combined with shops to ply their trade. Some made musical instruments and still others made pottery. Some made fabric for clothing or various wood products.

Normally a city would have been built with walls surrounding it, but there were no enemies at the time to defend against. The few large dinosaurs that remained in the land of Shinar were few and far between. They rarely wandered anywhere near human habitation. Those that did, didn't live long. Only the small dinosaurs were bold enough to come near them, like the chicken-sized compsognathus that preyed mostly on lizards and rodents. At first they weren't a concern, and the people gave them no mind, but they bred quickly and soon overran the place. Even the cats couldn't compete with them. The compies, which made a mess of everything, had to go. Soon the compies and their eggs filled everybody's cooking pot. Over the course of a few years, they were all killed off, and chickens took their place in the pot.

Shem's great-grandson, Eber, was born at about the time the people journeyed out of the east. Construction of the city of Babel began when he was just a small boy. He grew up learning how to make bricks and later, as a young man, he learned to use them to build structures. Once the foundation for a massive tower was laid, he was recruited to begin building the tower.

The tower was to be the crowning jewel of the city—a monument to the people's greatness. The tower was also to be a symbolic gateway into heaven for the gods to come down to earth—Satan's counterfeit mountain of God. Because of Nimrod, most of the people rejected God completely and invented new gods in their own image to replace Him. They worshipped the stars and the moon, thinking they influenced the lives of men. But chief among their gods was one called Marduk. It took the shape of a bull with a sun disk between its horns and was associated with Nimrod himself. Nimrod was often pictured on reliefs as part-bull with wings. His throne was to be set at the pinnacle of the tower, where they intended to make their sacrifices.

The people in their pride intended to build the tower high enough to reach into heaven. They built it, not just to make a name for themselves and to escape any potential future floods, but also to commune with their false gods. Possibly they even hoped to become gods themselves.

Because of the tower's great size, a great deal of weight would be resting on the lower levels. Simple clay-and-straw bricks were simply not strong enough to bear that kind of weight. Instead, they mixed limestone and other elements together to form bricks and baked them in an oven to make them as strong as concrete. These bricks were by no means small. Rather, they were huge blocks weighing thousands of pounds. One of the technological items Noah had brought with him on the ark was a scalar wave levitator. This levitator was used to place these heavy bricks into place. The bricks were so heavy that they didn't need mortar to cement them together. The tower was built with a number of cavernous rooms or temples for worshiping their various gods. Nimrod planned to have thirteen levels. Stepped ramps were built into the sides of the tower to reach the upper levels.

While the people were busy about their labors, God took notice of their work and the unity they had forged between them. The Lord said, "Behold, they are one people and they all have the same language. This is what they have begun to do, and now nothing that they purpose to do will be impossible for them. Come, let Us go down and confuse their language that they may not understand one another's speech."

The people were constructing the third level when a great storm blew in from the west and prevailed upon the tower. Immensely powerful whirlwinds and lightning bolts continuously struck the tower. A great earthquake shook the tower as the people scattered and cowered in fear. Nimrod bravely stood on top of the partially built tower and, thinking he was a god, tried to rebuke the storm. Instead, he was greatly humiliated by the destruction of his tower. Nimrod emerged from the ruins of the tower, looking worst for the wear but suffering only minor injuries.

When the storm passed, pandemonium broke out in the city as each family found that they were unable to understand the languages of their neighbors. The languages were divided according to families rather than individuals, to preserve the family unit.

Work on the tower immediately ceased. Nimrod wasn't about to let construction of the tower stop just because their language was now different. He insisted that the tower was to be rebuilt, no matter the cost, but it was an exercise in futility. He gathered the heads of the various families and attempted to communicate with them and learn each other's language, but it was to no avail. They simply had no common reference to work from. No one, with the exception of Noah and his sons, remembered how to speak the original language, nor how to read or write it. Noah and his sons were not affected by the judgement and they understood this was God's judgment on the people. They refused to help Nimrod relearn the original language so he could teach others.

Slowly the families started leaving the city to settle in their own lands. Most of Shem's descendants went east while Ham's descendants went into Africa where Mizraim became the father of the Egyptians, Japheth's descendants went north and west. A few of each, however, remained in the Mesopotamian area.

Over the course of a few years, the city's population dwindled to a few dozen. A few generations later, those who settled in Egypt, west China and Mexico built pyramids that were inspired by the Tower of Babel. Some had sloped sides while others had stepped sides. In Shinar, however, the tower would never be rebuilt and it remained a ruined heap of limestone bricks. Nimrod would still get his kingdom, but he would never have complete control of the whole world. Over the years, he watched sadly as small groups of people left, but he remained undaunted in his plans.

As the Mesopotamian population grew, Nimrod built the cities of Erech, Accad, and Calnah in the land of Shinar. Later he expanded his kingdom north into Assyria and built the cities of Nineveh, Rehoboth-Ir and Calah. Between Nineveh and Calah he built his last city; Resen. Resen became the greatest city of them all, and for a time it was the seat of the Assyrian government. Nimrod lived to be over four hundred years old before he died. He learned the hard way he was not a god after all. By that time the population had grown to well over ten thousand.

Though no one knew how Nimrod died, word was out that Nimrod hadn't died of natural causes. What *was* known was that Nimrod's sorcerous mother, Semiramis, Queen of Assyria, who was also his pregnant wife, feared loosing her position of power when Nimrod's successor appointed a new queen. When her child was born she named him Tammuz and declared to the people that he had no human father and was Nimrod himself returned to life. Thus began the reincarnation idea that would become a pillar of faith among the occult and far eastern religions. Semiramis was elevated to the status of goddess and was regarded as the "Queen of Heaven". She was portrayed among a number of statues and reliefs as a mother holding her child similar to the Mary statues in todays Catholic churches. People worshipped these images by kissing the feet and praying to them. When Semiramis died, legend had it that she returned each spring from an egg that fell from the sky and landed among some wicker weeds. They called her Ishtar (pronounced Easter). Each spring the people would put on their finest clothing and go out hunting for the egg of Ishtar.

In those days, men were judged by who their father was. Tammuz strove in vain to be like his father and to live up to his reputation as a mighty hunter. At the age of forty he went out hunting and was killed by a wild boar. The people mourned for him for forty days, a day for each year of his life.

Shortly before the languages were confused, Eber's wife gave birth to his first son, whom he named Peleg. His name, which means division, was chosen prophetically, for it was in his lifetime that the nations of the earth were divided. After the nations divided, Eber, son of Shelah, son of Arpachshad, son of Shem, chose to keep his family in the land of Shinar. He relocated south in Sumer and extended his craft into stone masonry while Peleg took to raising goats. Peleg's wealth grew as his goat herd grew and he eventually took to raising sheep as well.

One of Peleg's descendants, Nahor, and his family of shepherds, relocated to Ur of the Chaldeans. There, his son Terah had three sons named Nahor, Abram and Haran. Abram took his half sister, Sarai as his wife. When Abram's brother Haran died, his father Terah took Abram, his other brother Nahor, their wives and Haran's son Lot up the Euphrates river. In the land of Assyria, he founded a city called Haran named after his son. Haran was built near the Euphrates River. It was surrounded by green land suitable for grazing sheep and goats and for growing crops.

When Abram was fifty-eight years old and living in Haran, the world mourned Noah's death. Noah was 950 years old when he died. In Abram's seventy-fifth year, the Lord directed him south into Canaan where He would establish Abram as a great nation. The Lord later renamed him Abraham and his wife Sarai was renamed Sarah. His nephew Lot accompanied him to Canaan.

During one of the famines that struck the land of Canaan, Abraham sojourned in Egypt for a short time. During that time he taught the Egyptians mathematics and astronomy. After returning to Canaan, Abraham's flock and herdsmen grew into a great company, as did Lot's. Whenever a new well was dug, the herdsmen argued over who it belonged to. Abraham and Lot decided to separate. Lot settled in the Jordan River valley near Sodom, while Abraham's flock and herdsmen remained in the hill country.

At some point Lot acquired a house in Sodom. He later lost everything when Sodom and Gomorra were destroyed for their excessive wickedness and abusive homosexual lifestyle. Of all the people living in the five cities in the Jordan River valley, only one righteous man was found. Lot escaped the destruction of Sodom and Gomorra with only his two daughters. His wife died when she disobeyed the angel of the Lord's command not to look back, and was turned into a pillar of salt.

A year after Sodom and Gomorra's destruction, when Abraham was one hundred years old, his son Isaac was born. Isaac was the son of promise, but he wasn't the first born son. Because Sarah was barren, and grew impatient with the Lord's promise for a son, she gave Abraham her Egyptian handmaiden, Hagar, as a wife. Through Hagar, Sarah hoped to have a son. Hagar conceived and gave birth to Ishmael. Though Ishmael was Abraham's firstborn son, he was not the son of promise.

After Isaac was born, Hagar and Ishmael were sent away and resided in Beersheba. Eventually, Abraham settled in Hebron, where his people became known as Hebrews. After Sarah died, Abraham took another wife and had several more children. He died at the age of 175 years. Noah's son Shem, died thirty-five years later, the same year his son, Arpachshad died, and about the same time period Nimrod died.

During Abraham's lifetime, the ice age was at its midpoint and the climate was undergoing another change. The Arctic Ocean had cooled off to the point where it was no longer keeping Siberia and Alaska warm and the land was starting to ice over. The jet-stream shifted north from the equatorial latitudes to the mid-latitudes, bringing with it hot dry air. This caused the rivers of the Sahara and the water sources of Canaan and Mesopotamia to dry up. The lush savannas of the Sahara died and gave way to the Sahara desert. The fertile plains of Mesopotamia gave way to the Arabian desert. The strong winds blew away the topsoil and carried it all eastward.

To make matters worse, the North American super-volcano Yellowstone erupted three times during the ice age as the continent continued to move west. This movement put pressure on the Yellowstone magma plume and squeezed it until it erupted violently. Yellowstone wasn't the only super-volcano to erupt in these times. About a dozen other super-volcanoes around the earth erupted for much the same reason. The millions of tons of dust and ash they threw into the atmosphere blotted out the sun for years, reducing the mean temperature significantly, causing a resurgence of the ice sheets. The lower temperatures and lack of sunlight caused crop failures throughout Europe, Africa and the Middle East bringing famine and disease. Toward the end of the ice age, the continuous dust storms over North America led to the extinction of a host of animals, including the mammoth.

During this time, Isaac's wife, Rebecca gave birth to twin sons, Esau and Jacob. Esau was the oldest but Jacob tricked him out of his birthright and tricked his father into giving his blessing to him instead of Esau. Jacob fled to Haran to take a wife from his relatives and ended up with four wives. Through them he had twelve sons who became the patriarchs of the twelve tribes of Israel. Esau, in the mean time took wives from the neighboring peoples. When Jacob returned to Hebron with his family and a large flock of sheep and goats, he expected a fight with Esau. Instead Esau forgave him and welcomed him back. Later Esau moved his family across the Jordan River and became the father of the Edomites.

Jacob found favor with God, Who renamed him Israel. Israel's favorite son was Joseph for whom he made a coat of many colors. Ten of his brothers became jealous of him and when Joseph showed them the coat, they sold him into slavery and lied to their father about his alleged demise. They intended this for harm to Joseph but it was done as the Lord intended to preserve them.

While a slave in Egypt, Joseph was cast into prison for a crime he had not committed. In prison, Joseph acquired a reputation for being able to interpret dreams. He was summoned by Pharaoh Sesostris III to interpret his very troubling dream, which foretold of a seven year severe drought that would follow seven fruitful years.

Joseph was made Vizier of Egypt to prepare for the coming drought and resultant famine. Following the seven fruitful years, one of the super-volcanoes erupted and caused a severe drought in the eastern Mediterranean. When Israel learned Egypt had food, he sent his sons there to buy grain. On their second visit Joseph revealed himself to his brothers and insisted they return with their father and settle in Egypt. With Pharaoh's approval, Joseph settled his family in the land of Goshen in the eastern Nile delta. With Israel came a total of seventy people.

During the seven-year famine, the strength of the government grew as it took ownership of most everything. Even the hereditary monarchs lost rulership of their provinces as they ceded everything to Pharaoh in exchange for food. The Hebrews, in the meantime, prospered and built cities in Goshen. The city of Avaris—called Zoan in the Bible and later called Tanis—became their capital.

Toward the close of the twelfth dynasty, Egypt began to crumble and the Hebrews moved into a position of power. These Asiatics from Palestine, called the Hyksos, ruled Egypt for the next three hundred or so years. While the Hebrews resided in Egypt, the descendants of Ishmael prospered in the land of Canaan and became a great nation. In Egypt, a number of pharaohs reigned during the thirteenth through the seventeenth dynasties, however, the Hyksos ruled the land until Pharaoh Ahmoses I ascended to the throne. Ahmoses I did not know Joseph. He forcibly removed the Hyksos from power and reunited Egypt. At his death, his son, Amuntotep I, assumed the throne.

Egypt was at war with Syria at that time. The Hebrews were a vary large company that out- numbered the Egyptians. Pharaoh Amuntotep I feared the Hebrews would join forces with the Syrians and overthrow the government. Thus he placed them in bondage and forced them into hard labor. Because they were scattered all across Egypt, they were also required to relocate back to Goshen where they could be controlled. Not all the families did so, however. Some were permitted to remain where they were to work as bond-slaves to the government. Those in Goshen were forced to build the storage cities of Pithom and Raamses.

Throughout their years in Egypt, they forgot about their God and worshipped the Egyptian gods, primarily the sun god Ra. Ra was depicted as a bull or calf with a sun disk between his horns similar to Marduk. Under their bondage the Hebrews remembered their true God and cried out for deliverance.

Pharaoh hoped to reduce their numbers under the hard labor of building canals, but the more the Hebrews labored, the more they multiplied. When Thutmoses I became pharaoh, he intensified the oppressive measures, but the Hebrews' numbers kept increasing. He ordered the death of all male Hebrew babies, which resulted in baby Moses being placed in a basket made of bulrushes and sent floating down the Nile while his sister followed it. Moses' family was one of those employed outside Goshen and lived in a town twenty miles south of Memphis.

A few miles downstream, in the capital city of Memphis, fifteen-year-old Hatshepsut, the daughter of Thutmoses I, came down to the Nile to bath. She found the basket with the baby crying inside. She fell in love with the baby as she held him. She tried to feed him but he wouldn't suckle, nor would he do so for the other women of her court. At Moses' sister's suggestion, Hatshepsut hired the baby's own mother to nurse him. Only then did he suckle. When he was older and was brought into the house of Pharaoh, Hatshepsut named him Moses because she had drawn him from the Nile, thinking he was a gift from her god.

Growing up in the house of Pharaoh, Moses displayed extraordinary intelligence and was the most beautiful child anyone had ever seen. At the death of Hatshepsut's father, she was forced to marry her half brother Thutmoses II so he could legitimize his claim to the throne. Since Moses had grown large in stature and displayed exceptional skill in administration and speech, Thutmoses II gave him charge of the army to invade Ethiopia, whose forces were invading their southern border and taking Egyptians into slavery. Under Moses' leadership, the Egyptian army overwhelmed the Ethiopians. After a long siege of the Ethiopian capital, peace was made when Moses agreed to take the Ethiopian king's daughter as his wife. She remained in Ethiopia, however, and he never had relations with her. He returned to Memphis victorious and the Egyptians began to fear that he would lead the Hebrews against them.

Thutmoses II reigned only thirteen years and died a year before Moses fled from Egypt. Hatshepsut became the next pharaoh, the female king of Egypt. Unlike the European kings, an Egyptian king was considered an office of rulership that had no bearing on the gender of the person holding the office. Hatshepsut wasn't the first female Egyptian king, nor was she the last. She shared a co-regency with her step-son Thutmoses III who was given command of the army while she ruled Egypt. Under her rule, Egypt was at peace with its neighbors and it prospered.

Around that time, Moses began to associate more with his own people and refused to be called the son of Hatshepsut. She had intended him to succeed her as the next pharaoh, but she considered this an act of betrayal that seemed to bolster the people's fear of him. When Moses killed an Egyptian taskmaster for beating a fellow Hebrew, that was the excuse needed to order his death. The order was sent out, but by then, Moses had already packed his personal effects and fled to the land of Midian.

Now forty years later, Moses thought about the sons of Israel's plight and remembered that God had told Abraham that the Hebrews would live for four hundred years in a strange land. He understood that to mean four generations of approximately one hundred to one hundred and twenty years each, which at the time the prophecy was given, was a man's average lifespan. It had now been almost four hundred and thirty years. Moses wondered when God would deliver them from Egypt and by what means. Never in his wildest imagination did he ever think that God would chose him—a fugitive and criminal who developed a stuttering problem—to lead the people out. Hatshepsut's reign lasted nearly twenty-two years. At her death, Thutmoses III became the next pharaoh. Between Moses' betrayal of Hatshepsut and the hatred Thutmoses III felt for him, Moses was under no illusion that he would be allowed to return.

Moses finished proofreading the scroll before rolling it up. The next morning, he rose to tend the sheep. He took them to the wilderness of Shur and came to Mount Horeb, the mountain of God, also called Mount Sinai. At the base of the mountain, the Lord appeared to him within a burning bush. Though the bush was on fire, it was not consumed by the fire. Moses marveled at it and turned aside to see this burning bush.

As he approached, the Lord spoke to Him from the midst of the bush. "Moses, Moses," He said.

"I am here," Moses replied.

"Do not come near here. Remove your sandals, for the ground you are standing on is holy ground. I am the God of your father, the God of Abraham, the God of Isaac, and the God of Jacob." Upon hearing this, Moses turned his face, in fear of looking at the Lord. The Lord continued speaking saying that he had heard the cry of His people and had seen their affliction. He then stated His intention to deliver them from Egypt and bring them to the Promised Land that flowed with milk and honey. He then added, "Therefore, come now, and I will send you to Pharaoh so that you may bring My people, the sons of Israel, out of Egypt."

Moses, in fear of Pharaoh's wrath, answered, "Who am I, that I should go to Pharaoh, and that I should bring the sons of Israel out of Egypt?"

The Lord assured Moses that He would be with him and He instructed him to bring His people to this very mountain to worship Him.

Moses objected saying, "Behold I go to the sons of Israel.

Suppose they don't believe me and ask who sent me. What is His name?"

The Lord replied, "I AM WHO I AM. Tell them I AM sent you." The Hebrew word for "I am" is *YWYH*. It is the Israelites' holiest name for God and they won't speak it for fear of mispronouncing it. Instead, they refer to Him simply as Lord. The name Jehovah is not found in the original Hebrew. It is derived from Iehouah, the Latin translation of YWYH (Yahweh).

Moses objected further, and the Lord gave him certain powers to perform. But Moses wasn't impressed with these powers for he had seen the Egyptian priests perform these same powers to amaze and control the people. He continued to raise objections saying he was slow of speech, as he kept trying to get out of going to Pharaoh. Finally the Lord became angry with Moses and sent him away, saying that He would send Moses' brother Aaron to meet him and speak for him.

Moses packed his belongings and brought his wife and two sons with him. Along the way, the Lord became angry with Moses because his two sons had never been circumcised as God's covenant with Abraham required. In anger, Zipporah circumcised the two young men and averted God's wrath on them.

As Moses approached the land of Goshen, Aaron came to meet him, just as the Lord had said he would. Aaron took Moses directly to the elders. Using the powers God had given him, Moses persuaded the elders to believe that God had sent him to lead them out of Egypt to the Promised Land.

When Moses and Aaron went before Pharaoh and demanded that he let the sons of Israel go to worship the Lord, Pharaoh laughed at them saying, "Who is God that I should let your people go?" Pharaoh sent Moses away and issued a decree that the sons of Israel were to find their own straw to make bricks—without reducing their quota.

Upon hearing the decree. the Hebrews became angry with Moses and cursed him. After beseeching the Lord, Moses met with the elders and repeated what the Lord had said to him, saying that Pharaoh would release them under compulsion.

Again Moses went before Pharaoh and demanded that he let the people go, but Pharaoh refused. Moses then performed the signs God had given him to perform, throwing down his rod, which became a large snake. Pharaoh wasn't impressed as his chief priests only duplicated what Moses did with their own secret arts. Their rods likewise turned to snakes, but Moses' snake swallowed up their snakes. Moses then picked up his snake, which turned back into a rod. But Pharaoh only sent him away and refused to let the people go.

The next morning, Moses met Pharaoh at the shores of the Nile and repeated his demand. This time Aaron touched the Nile with his rod, and the Nile turned to blood. Again Pharaoh wasn't impressed as his priests duplicated the feat.

The following day, the Lord sent Moses back to Pharaoh and repeated his demand. When Pharaoh refused, Aaron stretched his hand over the waters of Egypt and frogs came out of it. Once again, Pharaoh wasn't impressed, as his priests did the same. But they couldn't get rid of the frogs. They were everywhere—in there houses, their beds, and even their ovens and kneading bowls. In Goshen, however, their were no frogs. Several days passed before the people demanded that something be done about the frogs. Pharaoh begged Moses to get rid of them promising to let his people go. When the frogs were gone, Pharaoh changed his mind and refused to let the people go.

This time, Aaron struck the dust of the earth, and gnats covered everything, including man and beast. The priests were not able to duplicate the gnats with their secret arts and admitted that this was the hand of God. The previous works of God had been duplicated by the priests, but it wasn't so much that the priests were duplicating God's work as that God was actually duplicating *their* works. In essence, God was mocking them. When they couldn't bring forth gnats themselves, they knew that this was the judgement of God and they were humbled before Him.

As before, Pharaoh hardened his heart and refused to let God's people go. So God brought forth insects that covered the land and devastated their crops. Only in Goshen were there no insects. Pharaoh agreed to let the sons of Israel make their sacrifice to God but insisted that they do it within the land. Moses refused, because what they needed to sacrifice was considered an abomination to the Egyptians. Pharaoh agreed to let the people go, but when the insects departed the land the next day, he once again hardened his heart and didn't let the people go.

The next judgment was even more severe, as pestilence swept over the land and struck down their livestock. All their horses, donkeys, camels, sheep and goats died of the pestilence. But the livestock of the sons of Israel were not affected and not a single one died. The gold of the Egyptians began to flow into the land of Goshen as they purchased livestock and food from the Hebrews. Pharaoh, however, continued to harden his heart and wouldn't let the people go.

The Lord then instructed Moses to take ash from the kiln, stand before Pharaoh, and throw the dust into the air. The ash spread over the land and produced boils on the Egyptians and the beasts of the field. Pharaoh still would not let the sons of Israel go, so the Lord brought a plague of hail upon the land, from which the people and the livestock had to take shelter.

A severe storm arose and battered the land with lightning and large hailstones. Flashes of fire erupted from the hailstones as if they were made of frozen methane. Every man and beast in the field was killed by the hail and the lightning. Every plant was destroyed, and every tree was shattered. The barley and flax were ruined. The wheat and spelt, however, were not ruined, for it was not yet the season for them. Never before or since has the land of Egypt seen a storm this severe, yet in the land of Goshen, there was no hail. When the hail and lightning and rain ceased, Pharaoh once again hardened his heart and would not let the people go.

More gold flowed into the land of Goshen, as the Egyptians bought food and livestock from the Hebrews. Some months later when the winter had passed and the wheat was in season, Moses once again went before Pharaoh and asked, "How long will you continue to refuse to humble yourself before God and let His people go? Tomorrow a plague of locusts will cover the land and consume everything that survived the hail."

The locust covered every square inch of the land so that not a spot of land could be seen. They ate everything that grew in the field and the sprouts of every tree. Even the houses were filled with them. In the land of Goshen, however, there were no locusts. Pharaoh humbled himself and asked Moses to beseech the Lord to remove the locusts. The Lord shifted the wind so that a strong west wind blew over the land and carried every locust into the Red Sea. As before, Pharaoh hardened his heart once the locusts were gone.

Then darkness fell over the land for three days, but in Goshen there was light. This was no eclipse of the sun, for eclipses don't last for three days. Nor do they cast darkness over the whole land and leave one spot in the middle with light. This darkness was so oppressive, it could be felt. Pharaoh's heart continued to be hardened, and he would not let the people go. He even threatened Moses that if he saw his face again, Moses would die.

The Lord had one more judgement in store for Egypt—the worst one by far—in which every firstborn man, woman or child would die. Even the firstborn of the cattle would die. To prepare for this judgement, the sons of Israel were instructed to take an unblemished lamb—either from a sheep or a goat—and keep it until the fourteenth day of the month. Those families that were too small to eat a whole lamb, were to share a lamb with their neighbors. At twilight they were to sacrifice the lamb and spread the blood over the doorpost and lintel of their houses. They were then to roast the lamb and eat it at midnight with unleavened bread. These were the Passover Lamb and the Feast of Unleavened Bread.

At midnight on that first Passover, the angel of death swept over the land. In each house that did not have blood of the lamb on the doorpost and lintel, the firstborn of that household died. Throughout the land, there was weeping and wailing—even in the house of Pharaoh.

Pharaoh himself did not die, for he was not his father's firstborn child. Princess Neferura, Hatshepsut's eldest daughter was the firstborn. She had died while in her late teens, before Moses fled Egypt. Thutmoses III was born after Neferura. He was Thutmoses II's second child, the son of a concubine. When he became Pharaoh, he took Hatshepsut's second daughter, Merira-Hatshepsut, as his wife to legitimize his claim to the throne.

The Egyptians pled desperately with their false gods for help but to no avail. They were powerless before the one true God. At the death of Pharaoh's firstborn son, the heir to his throne, his heart was finally broken. The next day, Israel was all but driven from the land. The Egyptians gave them what remained of their gold and silver and begged them to leave while Pharaoh commanded them to leave. There was now no doubt among the Egyptians who God was and that He was the one and only true God—the God of gods, the Lord of Lords and the King of Kings.

After nearly a year of enduring ten plagues, the Egyptians

drove out the Hebrews. Along with all their possessions, their cattle and sheep, they were led into the wilderness of Egypt and down the eastern coast of the Gulf of Suez. The Lord went before them in a pillar of fire by night and a cloud by day.

Upon arriving at the southernmost point, they turned northeast and followed the coast of the Gulf of Aqaba to Etham. There they had to turn back, for they were shut in by the mountains. The Lord took them there to show them that, with the mountains before them and the sea behind them, they had nowhere to go. Only God could provide for their salvation. They thus camped at Pi-hahiroth (present-day Strait of Tiran) for eight days and waited to see what the Lord would do. It was the first test of their patience and their faith. Both would prove to be in short supply.

When word reached Pharaoh that the Hebrews were just wandering aimlessly in the wilderness, he had a change of heart and sent his army to bring them back. He took several thousand calvary soldiers and six hundred select chariots with officers over them and pursued the Hebrews. The Hebrews saw them approaching and cried out to Moses, who had no idea what the Lord was going to do. The last time he had been here, he took a boat across the Strait of Tiran, but with nearly two million people, it could take weeks to ferry people across. With all the boats they would need, they would be better off using them as pontoons and building a floating bridge. But that wasn't the Lord's plan. He had a powerful demonstration in mind for the Hebrews that they might know that He alone was God and there were no others.

God commanded Moses to stretch out his hands over the sea and a strong east wind blew on the waters of the Strait of Tiran throughout the night. The Strait of Tiran was about eleven miles wide with a natural underwater bridge about 670 feet below the surface. On either side of the underwater bridge the sea drops to a depth of 1400 to 1500 feet. The wind concentrated on a single strip of water forming a channel over the underwater bridge, while water piled up on either side. It continued blowing throughout the night until the channel reached the bottom, which was dried by the wind. Once the channel had been created, the water was supernaturally held back.

By sunrise the water was completely parted providing dry land to walk on. As the Egyptian army approached, the Lord stood between them and His people causing confusion among the army. Moses, in the mean time, led the sons of Israel down the steep embankment through the parted waters. The waters rose up on each side of them almost seven hundred feet high. About three hours later, Moses climbed the embankment on the other side into the land of Midian. It took the rest of the day for the remainder of the sons of Israel and their families to pass through the parted waters.

At sunrise the next day, as soon as the Hebrews were across, the Lord permitted the Egyptians to pursue them. Pharaoh, however, remained behind with his body guards. On the other side, God commanded Moses to stretch out his hands over the sea and the sea closed on top of Pharaoh's army and swept them off the bridge into the deep. Horses and riders, along with the senior officers in their chariots of gold, were cast into the sea and drowned in the depths. Not even one remained. Thousands of dead soldiers were seen floating in the sea.

In the land of Midian, the sons of Israel rejoiced while proud Pharaoh Thutmoses III, shocked at the loss of his army, returned to Memphis with only his bodyguards. After seventeen years, his annual campaigns against Canaan and Syria came to an abrupt end. Upon his return, he sought revenge against Moses by attempting to wipe out every trace of his existence from the official records. Moses' adoptive mother's statues and tomb near Thebes—including those of Senenmut, her vizier and strongest supporter—were defaced and wrecked. (Curiously, Senenmut disappeared the same year Moses fled Egypt. His tomb was never finished, nor was his burial site ever found. There were a great many parallels between Senenmut and Moses. They may or may not have been the same person.) Pharaoh even removed Hatshepsut's body from her tomb and buried her in an unknown location. Sometime, thereafter, the political seat was moved from Memphis to Thebes where it remained until the twentieth dynasty. The Hebrew's Goshen capital of Avaris was converted into a fort and soldiers graveyard. At Pharaoh's death, his second-born son who took the name Amenhotep II, succeeded him to the throne.

About the time of the exodus, the ice age was also coming to an end. The earth, however, was a long way from recovering from the flood, as climate changes continued with intermittent periods of global cooling and global warming continuing to the present day. These global cooling and warming cycles were mostly driven by geothermal and solar sunspot activity. The polar ice caps would wax and wane accordingly and the polar bears, which adapted to the extreme polar climate, unlike the original bear kind, were never in danger of dying out. Unfortunately, the same could not be said for other species that did die out as a result of the earth's naturally occurring climate fluctuations.

The sons of Israel, in the meantime, underwent a period of testing in which they failed miserably. They were not permitted to enter the Promised Land because of their rebellion against God and for their continuous obstinance. For forty years they wandered around in the wilderness of Zin (present-day central Jordan) between the land of Moab and Edom. Moses was not permitted to enter the land because of his disobedience when the Hebrews complained for the second time about not having water. The first time, Moses had been instructed to strike a rock with his rod, and water came out of it. The second time, he was instructed to speak to the rock, but he chastised the people instead and struck the rock. Water came out of it as before, but for his disobedience he was only permitted to see the land, and not enter it. At the foot of Mount Sinai (present-day Al-Lawz), while Moses was gone for a year on the mountain, conversing with God, the people grew impatient. They rebelled against God and worshipped a golden calf. Several thousand died for their rebellion against God.

Even after that, they still didn't learn their lesson and were condemned to wander in the wilderness until that generation died out. Only Joshua and Caleb were permitted to enter the land because of their faithfulness to God. Once the rebellious generation had died off, Moses turned over command of the people to Joshua and then proceeded alone to a high mountain. On this mountain, from which he could see the Promised Land, he died at the age of 120 years old. The Lord Himself buried Moses in a secret location so the people wouldn't try to retrieve and lift his body to worship him. Satan, however, tried to claim it and had to battle Michael the Archangel for it. Naturally, he lost. For all his boasted power, Satan was not able to defeat the archangel.

At about sixty years of age, Joshua led Israel into the Promised Land and drove out the inhabitants. The sons of Ishmael were also wiped out. Just prior to Joshua leading Israel across the Jordan River and laying siege to Jericho, Amenhotep II invaded Canaan, carrying away over one hundred thousand slaves, making it that much easier for Joshua to conquer Canaan. After taking possession of the land God had promised them, the Israelites were in constant contention—with their neighbors and among themselves. They went through continuous cycles of rebellion against God, followed by judgment, repentance, and God's deliverance. During that time, Israel was ruled by judges appointed by God. About four hundred years after the Exodus, the people rebelled against God yet again and demanded a king like their neighbors had.

Saul was chosen to be their first king but when he disobeyed God, his kingdom was transferred to David. King David earned his fame when he killed Goliath, a Philistine giant with six fingers and toes on each hand and foot, when no one else would accept his challenge to fight him. Goliath laughed at little David, but he wasn't laughing when David flung a stone into his forehead and knocked him out. David took Goliath's own sword and cut his head off with it. After Saul's death, David was crowned king in his place. King David was—and still is—revered as the greatest king in Israel's history.

At King David's death, the kingdom passed on to his son Solomon. Solomon became known as the wisest man who ever lived and he amassed great wealth for Israel. Because King David had been a warrior, God instead chose Solomon to build the first temple of God. In the fourth year of Solomon's reign, 480 years after the exodus from Egypt, he started construction on the temple of God. Following the death of King Solomon, because he had worshipped false gods to appease his numerous wives, Israel was split into two nations; Israel to the north and Judah to the south. Even then, their rebellion continued and they continuously fought with each other. It all culminated with Israel's exile into Assyria. A hundred years later, Judah was exiled into Babylon.

While in Babylon, Daniel the prophet wrote this prophecy:

> Seventy weeks have been decreed for your people and your holy city, to finish the transgression, to make an end to sin, to make atonement for iniquity, to bring in everlasting righteousness, to seal up vision and prophecy, and to anoint the most holy place. So you are to know and discern that from the issuing of a decree to restore and

rebuild Jerusalem until Messiah the Prince, there will be seven weeks and sixty-two weeks; it will be built again, with plaza and moat, even in times of distress. Then after the sixty-two weeks the Messiah will be cut off and have nothing, and the people of the prince who is to come will destroy the city and the sanctuary. And its end will come with a flood; even to the end there will be war; desolations are determined. And he will make a firm covenant with the many for one week, but in the middle of the week he will put a stop to sacrifice and grain offering; and on the wing of abominations will come one who makes desolate, even until a complete destruction, one that is decreed, is poured out on the one who makes desolate. (Daniel 9:24–27)

After seventy years in exile, Nehemiah, the cup bearer of King Artaxerxes, petitioned the king for permission rebuild the walls of Jerusalem. The king granted Nehemiah's petition and issued the prophesied decree. As was also prophesied, there was a great deal of opposition to rebuilding the walls of Jerusalem. The job was completed in forty-nine years, and then followed 434 years of relative peace.

Alexander the Great conquered Persia and after his death, his kingdom was divided among his four generals.

During the reign of Antiochus IV, the Jewish Maccabees rebelled against him. This led to his erecting a statue of Zeus in the Jewish temple. He sacrificed a pig on the altar and put an end to Jewish religious practices. Antiochus was not the Antichrist, as many presume. This was just another attempt by Satan to counterfeit the fulfillment of prophecy and cause confusion.

During the reign of Herod the Great, Jesus Christ was born.

Sixty-nine weeks of years after the decree to restore and rebuild Jerusalem was issued—to the day—the Messiah, Jesus Christ, was rejected. Five days later, He was crucified. One more week of years remains for Israel to fulfill the prophecy in which the Antichrist will bring desolation.

Chapter 6

The First Coming
of Jesus Christ

8 BC

In my fifth dream, I found myself in a dark and dusty carpenters shop. Somehow I knew I was in the village of Nazareth. It was the year of our Lord and Savior's birth. Joseph, son of Jacob and descendant of the line of David, king of Israel, blew out the oil lamps in his shop and closed the doors. Putting on a cloak, he walked out the back door into the cold January night. He proceeded through the courtyard to his house, lit a fire for heat, and ate a late supper. He looked around his house and mourned. This should have been a joyous day, for he had spent the last two years building this house in preparation for his wedding.

He had been ready to talk to his best man about the timing of the wedding when Mary's father, Eli, had informed him of her miraculous pregnancy. Eli found the story of her conception hard to believe. How did one get pregnant without knowing a man? Despite his love for his daughter, he wanted to have her stoned for bringing this shame to her family. But since she was betrothed to

Joseph, he felt it was Joseph's duty to bring her before the court. Joseph was grieved when he heard the news, but he wasn't so quick to pass judgment. He only said that he would consult the Lord about it.

Joseph dearly loved Mary but feared what the people would do when they learned of Mary's pregnancy. He had been looking forward to this marriage since his parents had arranged this betrothal two years earlier. He was also a righteous man and sought to keep the law of Moses as much as humanly possible. The penalty for adultery was death by stoning and when the people of his village found out, they would certainly demand it. Because of his love for her, he couldn't bear the thought of bringing harm to her. The only thing he could think to do was to send her away secretly.

He worked later than usual that night hoping an answer to his dilemma would present itself while he worked. But nothing came to him. That evening he stood at the foot of his bed and prayed that the Lord would give him guidance, a sign of some sort that would show him what he should do.

He tossed and turned for quite some time before finally falling asleep. In a dream, an angel of the Lord appeared to him saying, "Joseph, son of David, do not be afraid to take Mary as your wife; for that which has been conceived in her is of the Holy Spirit. And she shall bear a Son; and you shall call His name Jesus (Yeshua in Hebrew), for it is He who will save His people from their sins."

Joseph awoke that morning and immediately called for Eli. Upon informing him of what the angel had told him, they agreed to keep the pregnancy a secret. Since it had been only three days since Mary conceived, they reasoned, that if they married in the next couple of days, no one would be the wiser.

That evening, Joseph informed his father and his best man that the time had come. At midnight Joseph and his best man arrived at Eli's house unannounced. When they reached the door, his best man blew a horn seven times and called out in a loud voice, "Behold the bridegroom has come."

At his proclamation, Joseph also called out with a loud voice, "Mary, come out hither."

Mary, who had been anxiously awaiting this moment for the last two years with her bags packed the entire time, rushed out to meet him. Joseph then led Mary to his father's house where the ceremony was conducted.

Mary had three sisters. The oldest of the three, serving as her bridesmaid, carried her bags for her. The whole town, aroused by the horn, followed behind them, forming a great wedding procession. After the ceremony, there followed a celebration and a marriage feast that lasted throughout the night and the entire next day until sunset.

When the sun sank below the horizon, Joseph took his bride to his house for their seven-day honeymoon. But he kept her a virgin until she gave birth. About a month after their marriage, he announced Mary's pregnancy. There was great rejoicing among the people, and no one was aware of the timing of her conception. No one suspected that Joseph was not the father of her child. Even her siblings didn't know, for her parents kept it a tightly guarded secret.

When the angel Gabriel appeared to Mary to inform her of her miraculous conception, he also told her of Elizabeth's pregnancy in her old age. Elizabeth, who was already in her sixth month, was a relative of Mary and lived in the hill country near Jerusalem. When Mary heard this news, she was determined to visit Elizabeth.

Joseph was at first hesitant to let her go, fearing for her safety because of her pregnancy. Mary was a strong, healthy, sixteen-year-old, but he was still concerned for her. After much cajoling from her, he changed his mind and let her go. She was in her fourth week of pregnancy when he packed her bags on a donkey and sent her off with a convoy en route to Jerusalem. The convoy would be passing near Elizabeth's home. Joseph sent a courier to Elizabeth to inform her of Mary's arrival.

Mary found Elizabeth waiting for her in her courtyard. When Mary greeted her, the baby in Elizabeth's womb leaped for joy and she was immediately filled with the Holy Spirit. She cried out with a loud voice, saying, "Blessed are you among women, and blessed is the fruit of your womb. How has it happened that the mother of my Lord has come to me?"

Mary replied, "My soul exalts the Lord, and my spirit has rejoiced in God my Savior. For He has had regard for the humble state of His bondservant. Behold, from this time on, all generations will call me blessed. For the Mighty One has done great things for me and holy is His name."

Mary remained two months until Elizabeth gave birth to her baby. Elizabeth's husband, who had been struck dumb because he would not believe the message he received from an angel, named the baby John. Immediately his tongue was loosed and he shouted for joy. Everyone present was amazed. John was later known as John the Baptist, who had been sent to prepare the way for Jesus and to declare Him the long-awaited Messiah. John was given the spirit of Elijah to make straight the way of the Lord. Jesus' birth was six months away.

Mary returned to Nazareth where Joseph anxiously awaited her. He was overjoyed when she finally returned to him safely, but her stay in Nazareth would be a brief one.

Several months earlier in Rome, it had entered into Caesar Augustus' mind to take a census of all the inhabitants of Rome and its occupied lands, a census that took two years to complete. This census was a general census of the Roman Empire that was taken every fourteen years. The job of conducting the census in Palestine was given to Quirinius, who was the military procurator of Syria at the time. As the current governor was inept, Quirinius assumed many of the governor's duties. This was the first census he conducted in Palestine and ordered everyone to register for the census in the cities of their birth in accordance with Roman requirements. Herod the Great, elected by the Roman senate to rule Palestine in 40 BC, offered no objection to it, for he wanted to know himself what the numbers were.

For Joseph, the census requirements meant traveling to Bethlehem with his pregnant wife. By the time he received word of the census, Mary was in her third trimester. With fear and uncertainty of the future, he put Mary on a donkey and traveled with a caravan to Jerusalem along with other members of his and Mary's family. From Jerusalem they made the short journey south to Bethlehem on a well-traveled road.

The Roman officials taking the census asked numerous questions relating to their family, ancestry, and property. Afterwards, they proceeded to their ancestral home in Bethlehem. Both Joseph and Mary were descended from the line of King David whose grandfather was Boaz. Boaz owned a threshing floor in Bethlehem which had been handed down to successive generations within the line of David. By the time of Jesus' birth, Boaz's home had been converted into an inn.

As Joseph and Mary reached the inn, Mary's water broke and she issued blood. According to the Torah, a woman who had an issue of blood for any reason, including childbirth, was considered ritually unclean. To keep from defiling the rest of the people in her household, she was to be separated from them. Because Mary was issuing blood, no room was available for them at the inn. A separate room, detached from the house, was set aside for this purpose, but it too was occupied. The mistress of the inn, one of their distant cousins, took Mary to Migdal Eder (Tower of the Flock) a short distance north of town and sent for a midwife. Mary's mother and sisters went with them while the others remained in town to look for lodging.

Bethlehem was a small town in the hill country about five miles south of Jerusalem. Between Jerusalem and Bethlehem and all around Bethlehem, thousands of sheep grazed in the hills. But these were no ordinary sheep. The lambs of these sheep were destined to be offered up as a continual sacrifice in the temple of God. This required the lambs to be perfect in every way, without spot or blemish. In between Jerusalem and Bethlehem was Migdal Eber, where Jacob had buried his wife Rachel after she died giving birth to Benjamin, his youngest son. A two-story watch tower had been built there for the chief shepherd to keep watch over the flock. Other shepherds were in the fields along with the sheep, to keep them from harm. So important were these sheep that, if necessary, the shepherds would give their lives to protect them.

During the lambing season, the sheep were brought to the watch tower. At the base of the watch tower was a cave that served as a lambing station. Because of the importance of these lambs, the lambing station was kept as clean as any hospital. When the lambs were born they were wrapped in swaddling cloths. Swaddling cloths were not birthing cloths. They were used to keep the lambs from harming themselves. They were then laid in a manger—a hewn depression in the rock that also served as a feed trough—until they calmed down and could be inspected for blemishes.

Mary was taken to the lambing station, where she gave birth to Jesus. The midwife wrapped the baby in swaddling cloths to protect Him and gave Him to Mary to hold. As Mary held Him and looked at Him, she was looking at the face of God. It is no small wonder that God loved mankind so much that He chose to step down from His throne and become a man. While He became a man, He never laid aside His divinity. He was still God, for only God can forgive sins and pay a substitutionary price for mankind's sins. Did Mary understand this as she held Him? When she kissed Him, did she know she was kissing God? Did Joseph understand this when he held Him? Joseph looked at Him with joy and wonder before laying Him in the manger. Mary lay beside Him in the straw to rest, while Joseph stood nearby, keeping watch over them. By this time, Eli and Joseph's parents joined them.

While the Feast of Tabernacles was celebrated in Jerusalem, shepherds in the field were keeping watch over their sheep through the early fall night. The autumn nights were growing chilly, but they had not yet brought the sheep in for the winter to protect them from the cold. This was generally done about the end of October to early November. Suddenly an angel of the Lord appeared before them, shining all about them with the glory of the Lord. His appearance filled them with a terrible fright.

The angel said to them, "Do not be afraid, for behold, I bring you good news of a great joy which shall be for all the people; for today in the city of David there has been born for you a Savior, who is Christ the Lord. And this will be a sign for you; you will find a baby wrapped in swaddling cloths, and lying in a manger."

Suddenly a multitude of angels filled the night sky, praising God and saying, "Glory to God in the highest, and on earth peace among men with whom He is pleased."

When the angels departed, the shepherds said among themselves, "Let us go then to Bethlehem and see this thing that has happened which the Lord has made know to us."

The shepherds were intimately familiar with birthing lambs. By the signs the angel told them to look for, they knew precisely where to look for the baby. Though they wondered why a baby would be born in a lambing station. When they reached the watchtower, they found Mary lying in the straw next to the manger where Jesus was laying. Joseph was sitting next to her watching over her and the baby. When the shepherds entered, he rose and met them at the door. "What do you seek?" he asked.

They told him what the angels had said and stated, "We're looking for the Savior who was born this night."

Joseph smiled and said, "Come and see."

To everyone present, they repeated what the angel had said about this child. Everyone wondered what these things meant, but Mary treasured them up and pondered them in her heart. The shepherds later returned to their flocks glorifying and praising God for all that they had seen and heard.

It wasn't by chance or trick of fate that Jesus had been born in a lambing station. This location had been specifically chosen by the Father at the moment Adam had sinned. At the very mention of Bethlehem, everybody pictured, sacrificial lambs. Two lambs were required to be sacrificed each day as a continual sacrifice to the Lord—one in the morning for the first sacrifice of the day, and one in the evening as the last sacrifice of the day. Jesus, who was to be the sacrificial Lamb of God as the permanent atonement for the sins of mankind, was born in the same location and manner as the sacrificial lambs that were offered up as a temporary atonement for the sins of Israel. Jesus' crucifixion corresponded to the last sacrifice of the day. He was the final sacrifice for the payment of all of mankind's sins, both past and future. In this manner, Micah's prophecy of the coming Messiah was fulfilled to the letter.

The next day, they moved to a house Joseph's parents had found among their kinfolk. After eight days passed, the baby was circumcised and given the name Jesus (Yeshua). After the days of purification were complete according to the law of Moses, Mary and Joseph presented Jesus at the temple in Jerusalem and offered up two turtledoves as an offering to the Lord. At that time both Mary and baby Jesus were declared ritually clean.

As they were about to leave an elderly man named Simeon approached. He had been promised by God that he would not die without seeing the Christ. He had been led by the Holy Spirit to come to the temple, where he beheld the child. He took the child in his arms and blessed Him, saying, "Now, Lord, Thou dost let Thy bondservant depart in peace, according to Thy word; for my eyes have seen Thy salvation, which Thou hast prepared in the presence of all people, a light for revelation to the gentiles, and the glory of Thy people Israel."

Both Mary and Joseph were amazed at the things he said about the child. Simeon gave the child back to Mary and said, "Behold, this child is appointed for the fall and rise of many in Israel, and for a sign to be opposed. And a sword will pierce even your own soul to the end that thoughts from many hearts may be revealed."

An eighty-four-year-old widow named Anna, who served in the temple day and night in fasting and prayer, walked up giving thanks to God. She continued to speak of Him to all those looking for the redemption of Israel. Joseph wondered about these things, but Mary treasured them in her heart.

Afterwards instead of returning to Nazareth with the rest of their family, Joseph and Mary remained in the house and worked in Bethlehem for a couple of years. While in this house, surprise visitors showed up at their door, bearing gifts for the child.

Several magi from the east, Babylonian star-worshipers who carefully monitored the movement of the stars, first arrived in Jerusalem. They inquired of Herod the Great, asking, "Where is He who has been born king of the Jews? For we saw His star in the east and have come to worship Him."

When Herod heard this from the magi, he was greatly troubled. The last thing he wanted was to share his throne with another king. His pride was also greatly wounded that so many magi had come all this way, not to see him but to see a newborn king. He called the chief priests and scribes to inquire where the child was to be born. When they heard of the Messiah's birth, they too were greatly troubled. Though they had been looking for the Messiah, they weren't at all willing to submit to Him. Like Herod, they viewed Him as a threat to their power and authority. Reluctantly, they informed Herod that, according to the prophet Micah, He was to be born in Bethlehem. Herod passed this information to the magi, instructing them to return and let him know where the child was living. He did so, not that he might go to worship the child as he told the magi, but that he might use the magi to locate the child and destroy Him.

For the last two or three hundred years, the Pharisees had taught the people that the prophecies of Scripture were not to be interpreted literally but rather spiritually. They failed to understand that the Scriptures could not be understood by personal interpretation but rather by the context in which it was written just as any other written materials were understood. Interpreting the prophecies allegorically or spiritually made absolute nonsense out of them. The result was that the people no longer knew the signs or the time of the Messiah's coming; they only knew that He was coming.

But the Messiah they were looking for was not the one that was born to them. They were looking for a conquering Messiah to deliver them from their enemies, not a suffering Messiah as prophesied by Isaiah. They didn't understand that He first had to suffer and die for their sins. Then He would return to conquer their enemies. Nor did they understand that He would be God Himself. Because of this misunderstanding and unwillingness to submit to Him, He became an offensive rock of stumbling for them, which continues to the present day.

The magi, on the other hand, held Daniel's prophecies of the coming Messiah in very high regard, for it was his interpretation of King Nebuchadnezzar's forgotten dream that had saved their forefather's lives. They had interpreted the prophecies literally, as they were meant to be. They knew exactly when to expect the Messiah and they knew the signs of His coming. They had been counting the days and knew that the time of His birth was getting close. When they observed His star rising for the first time in the constellation they associated with Israel, they knew the time had come. Thus they came to Jerusalem, looking for the Messiah who was born the King of the Jews. In faith they had come a long distance just to worship the boy Messiah.

The magi continued to follow the star to Bethlehem. Stars were symbolic of the angels. This star was an angel of the Lord that shone like a star. He had been sent to guide the magi to the Messiah. No celestial object could do the things this angel did. In Bethlehem, he stood over the house where the child was and illuminated it. Stars don't stand in one place and shine on one location.

About a year or two after the birth of Jesus, the magi entered the house and saw the child with Mary. They rejoiced exceedingly and fell down in worship of Him. They then offered Him gifts of gold, frankincense and myrrh. That evening several of Joseph and Mary's kinfolk joined them in a feast to hear the purpose of the magi's visit. But none of them understood the significance of what these men said.

Following the feast, some of the magi bedded down in the main room of the house. The other magi slept out in the court yard due to lack of room in the house. As the magi slept that night, they were warned in a dream of Herod's intentions. The next day they returned to their own country by a different way from which they had come. Joseph was also warned in a dream and was told to take the child to Egypt.

When Herod heard of the magi's trickery, he became enraged and sent his solders to Bethlehem to kill every male child two years old and under. There was great trepidation and mourning in Bethlehem that day. The women wept for their children and would not be comforted.

So great was the number of people Herod had killed in his lifetime that this slaughter went largely unnoticed in Judaea. It seemed hardly a day passed when someone wasn't killed at Herod's orders. In 4 BC, Herod's killing came to an end at his own agonizing death.

Joseph and Mary remained in Egypt for almost two years before Joseph was informed in a dream of Herod's death and instructed him to return to Israel. When Joseph learned that Archelaus was made ethnarch of Judaea in his father's place, he became fearful, for Archelaus had as much blood on his hands as his father did.

Instead of returning to Judaea, Joseph took his family to Galilee, back to his former home in Nazareth. Upon their return, they learned that Mary's sister Salome was betrothed to Zebedee of Capernaum. Zebedee was a Pharisee who owned a fishing business.

Each year thereafter, Joseph took his family to Jerusalem for the Feast of the Passover. When Jesus was twelve, His family was returning home following the Feast of First-fruits, but Mary and Joseph didn't know that Jesus remained behind. Supposing that He was with relatives or acquaintances, they didn't discover He was missing until a day later. They left their other children with their relatives and returned to Jerusalem.

Among those other children were James and Jude, two of

Jesus's half brothers who were destined to become two of His disciples. They became apostles themselves, but they weren't counted among the original twelve apostles. Among the relatives were Zebedee and Salome. Salome was a couple of months pregnant with John on this Passover journey. Both he and his older brother James were destined to become two of the original twelve apostles of Jesus.

In Jerusalem, Mary and Joseph searched for three days until they found Jesus in the temple of God. He was sitting among the teachers, listening to them and asking questions. They were all amazed at His understanding. Mary was astonished and asked Him, "Son, why have You treated us this way. Behold, Your father and I have been anxiously looking for You."

Jesus answered, "Why is it that you were looking for Me? Did you not know that I had to be in My Father's house?" By this statement, He indicated from an early age that He fully understood who He was and His purpose for coming.

Neither of His parents understood His answer, but Mary treasured the words in her heart. He then submitted to them and returned to Nazareth. Each year thereafter, following the journey to Jerusalem for the Passover, Jesus returned to Nazareth with His parents. As prophecy had foretold, Jesus was known as a Nazarene.

There Jesus lived, as He grew in wisdom and stature and favor with God and with men. He worked with Joseph as a carpenter, a handyman, a common laborer who worked with his hands, until He departed to begin His ministry. Sometime before Jesus began His ministry, Joseph passed away.

Jesus had to wait until He was at least thirty years old before He would be recognized as a rabbi. The Jewish people would never accept Him as their Messiah at a younger age. But before He could begin His ministry He first had to be baptized. He found John the Baptist preaching a message of repentance and baptizing people in the Jordan River. He was the one spoken of by the prophet Isaiah as, "the voice of one crying in the wilderness, 'Make ready the way of the Lord.'" John baptized Jesus and testified that He was the Messiah. As John did so, the Holy Spirit came upon Jesus in the form of a dove and the Father spoke from heaven, "This is My beloved Son. In whom I am well pleased." This was followed by forty days of fasting and testing for Jesus in the wilderness east of the Jordan River.

Jesus told Satan where he could get off and, upon John the Baptist's arrest, He took up where John left off. In 29 AD, Jesus began His three-and-a-half-year ministry. He first went to Nazareth, where He informed the people that the Prophecy of Isaiah has been fulfilled. They rejected Him and tried to kill Him. It wasn't yet His time, however, and He walked away safely from among them. He came to Capernaum in Galilee, preaching and performing miracles. There, five of His disciples were called to follow Him. They included Andrew who had been present at Jesus' baptism and his brother Peter; the sons of Zebedee, James and John; and an Israelite named Phillip. Following a wedding feast where He turned water into wine, He set out in search of the rest of His disciples.

For the next three and a half years He preached the gospel to the poor, healed the sick, cleansed the lepers, made the lame and paralyzed to walk, the dumb to speak, and the blind to see. He cast out demons and on at least one occasion, raised the dead. These works were done as prophecy foretold as proof that He was the Messiah. But the religious leaders of the day were not willing to accept Him as the promised Messiah. Because Jesus claimed He was one with the Father, the Sanhedrin accused Him of blasphemy and sought to put Him to death as prophesied by Isaiah. On the last day of the sixty-ninth week of years, as prophesied by Daniel hundreds of years earlier, the Messiah was rejected and cut off. In the manner prophesied in detail by King David in the Psalms, Jesus was crucified on a Roman cross between two thieves.

Chapter 7
The Passion of Christ on the Cross of Redemption

33 AD

In my sixth dream, I found myself standing outside a village on a hill northeast of Jerusalem. In the valley, I beheld our Lord Jesus Christ and His disciples approaching. Friday, March 27, 33 AD, was a balmy spring day, as Jesus and His disciples arrived at Bethany. They had journeyed from Jericho to Jerusalem after sojourning in the city of Ephraim for a few weeks. Ephraim was near the wilderness were Jesus had spent forty days fasting prior to the start of His ministry. It was necessary for Him to retire there again after raising Lazarus from the dead, for on account of that miracle, the people were following after Jesus. The Sanhedrin and chief priests felt that this was a threat to their power and sought to put Jesus to death. They had even issued orders for anyone who knew of His whereabouts to report it to them.

Upon leaving Ephraim, Jesus explained to His disciple why it was necessary to go to Jerusalem; that He would be delivered to the Pharisees and crucified, but in three days He would rise again. None of the disciples seemed to understand what He meant.

On the way to Bethany, Jesus passed through Jericho where He healed the blindness of several people. While in Jericho, He stayed at the house of Zaccheus, a chief tax collector. Zaccheus, being a man of small stature, wanted to see Jesus but couldn't see over everybody's heads. So he climbed a tree to see over them. When Jesus passed by the tree, He looked up and called Zaccheus down, saying that He desired to dine with him in his home. That night, Zaccheus believed in Jesus unto salvation.

Jesus declared, "Today salvation has come to this house because he too is a son of Abraham. For the Son of Man has come to seek and to save that which was lost." In this statement, Jesus declared His whole purpose for coming to earth; to diligently seek out and redeem those who are lost, and to restore their relationship with the Father.

The following Friday afternoon Jesus and his disciples reached the villages of Bethany and Bethphage near the Mount of Olives outside of Jerusalem. In Bethany He came to the house of Lazarus. Mary, Lazarus' sister, was overjoyed at His arrival and delighted at hearing His teaching. The last time Jesus had dined with them, Mary sat at his feet listening to His teaching while Martha fussed with preparing the meal. Martha complained that Mary wasn't helping her, but Jesus rebuked her saying that Mary had chosen the better part and it would not be denied her. That afternoon, however, they were busy preparing the Sabbath meals.

Saturday, March 28, the Sabbath day progressed quietly. The evening meal was a festive occasion as they reclined at the table with Jesus. The house was filled with laughter when Mary, without any preamble, took a pound of very costly perfume of pure nard and anointed the feet of Jesus with it. As the house filled with the fragrance of the perfume, the others became quiet at the solemnness of the deed. Then, in all humility, she wiped His feet with her hair and kissed them.

Judas Iscariot saw this as a repugnant display of waste and said, "Why was not this perfume sold for three hundred denarii and given to the poor?" Judas, however, wasn't the least bit concerned about the poor. He was a thief, and since he kept the money box, he often pilfered from it.

Jesus said to him, "Leave her alone that she may keep it for the day of My burial. For the poor you always have with you, but you do not always have Me."

Following the evening meal, other people of the village learned that Jesus was at the house of Lazarus and gathered at the house to see Him. He preached from the Scriptures and healed many of their infirmities. It was quite late when they finally returned to their homes.

The Pharisees hated it that Jesus healed on the Sabbath. They considered it a violation of the law of Moses, not understanding that He was Lord of the Sabbath. The Pharisees were the ultimate hypocrites, who had their priorities completely backwards. They believed it was okay to rescue distressed animals, but it was not okay to heal people.

Jesus rose early in the morning on Sunday, March 29 for His morning prayers. Though He was himself God and equal with the Father, He was still subordinate to the Father and yielded to His will. Thus He still needed to commune with the Father every day.

Following the morning meal, He sent two of His disciples to the village of Bethphage. Before they left, He told them that as they entered the village they would find a donkey tied to a door along with her colt on which no one had yet sat. The disciples were to bring the animals to Him to ride into Jerusalem. The two disciples went to Bethphage and found the donkeys just as Jesus said they would. When they untied the donkeys, the owners challenged the disciples asking why they were untying them. They said that the Lord had need of them. The owners, being disciples of Jesus, knew who they were referring to and immediately gave them permission to take them.

Upon returning to Bethany, the disciples put garments on the donkeys. Jesus chose to ride the colt, which submitted to Him without bucking. As they were approaching Jerusalem, many believers cut leafy palm branches from trees in the field and laid them on the road before Jesus, while others laid garments on the road. They went before Him and followed after Him proclaiming in loud voices, "Hosanna to the Son of David! Blessed is He who comes in the name of the Lord. Hosanna in the highest!"

As Jesus approached Jerusalem, He wept over it, saying, "If only you had know in this day, even you, the things that make for peace! But now they have been hidden from your eyes. For the days shall come upon you when your enemies will throw up a bank against you and surround you, and hem you in on every side, and will level you to the ground and your children within you, and they will not leave in you one stone upon another, because you did not recognize the time of your visitation."

When they entered Jerusalem, the chief priests demanded that Jesus rebuke his followers, but He answered, "If these were to be silent, the stones would cry out." With that proclamation, the whole city was stirred up and asking, "Who is this?" The believing multitude answered, "This is the prophet Jesus, from Nazareth in Galilee."

Some asked, "Can anything good come from Nazareth?" The region around Nazareth had a reputation of being the home of the dregs of the earth. They were the type of people, the low and destitute, that Jesus associated with—not the high and mighty, the proud and the haughty. This was another matter that the Pharisees and Sanhedrin hated. They never considered themselves sinners, but they considered those Nazarene sinners unworthy of Jesus' stature. They hated that Jesus gave special attention to such lowly people rather than to themselves.

It was already afternoon when Jesus dismounted the colt and told the same two disciples to return the donkeys to their owners. Upon His triumphal entry into Jerusalem, sixty-nine weeks of years had passed, to the day, since the decree to rebuild Jerusalem was issued—just as Daniel prophesied. Jesus then proceeded to the Temple where He sat and watched the people come and go about their business. There wasn't much activity at the temple and nobody paid Him any mind until the children began crying out "Hosanna to the Son of David!"

The self-righteous chief priests became indignant and said to Him, "Do you not hear what they are saying?"

Jesus answered, "Have you never read that 'out of the mouth of infants and nursing babes Thou has prepared praise for Thyself'?"

As He sat there, some Greeks who had come to worship at the feast approached the disciples and asked to see Jesus. When the disciples told Jesus of their request, He answered, "The hour has come for the Son of Man to be glorified. Truly, truly, I say to you, unless a grain of wheat falls to the earth and dies, it remains by itself alone; but if it dies, it bears much fruit. He who loves his life loses it; and he who hates his life in this world shall keep it to life eternal. If anyone serves Me, the Father will honor him. Now My soul has become troubled; and what shall I say, 'Father, save Me from this hour'? But for this purpose I came to this hour. Father, glorify Thy name."

As soon as He said this, a voice came from heaven saying, "I have both glorified it and will glorify it again." The multitude standing around heard only thunder, while others said an angel spoke to Him.

Jesus said to them, "This voice has not come for My sake, but for your sake. Now judgment is upon this world. Now the ruler of the world shall be cast out and I will be lifted up from the earth and will draw all men to Myself."

These words were spoken, indicating how He would die. He encouraged them to seek the light (Jesus Christ) that they might be called sons of light, lest the darkness overtake them. But even with the signs He had performed, they would not believe. Because of their rejection of Him, Israel's prophetic clock stopped with one week of years remaining. He then withdrew from the temple and returned to Bethany to lodge for the night.

Monday morning, March 30th Jesus returned to Jerusalem. As He was going, He became hungry and saw a fig tree in leaf in the distance. Though it was not the season for figs, He went to see if any fruit were upon it. When He found nothing except leaves He cursed the tree saying, "No longer shall there ever be any fruit from you." Immediately the tree began to wither.

Upon entering the temple, He was greeted with the sights and sounds of people buying and selling animals for the Passover sacrifice. Filled with anger, He rampaged through the temple, turning over the tables of the moneychangers and the seats of those selling doves. He chased them out of the temple and would not permit anyone to carry goods through the temple, saying "Is it not written, 'My house shall be called a house of prayer for all the nations'? But you have made it a robbers' den." He had done the same thing at least once before, yet here they were again. The high priests grew angry with Him for they received kickbacks from the sellers.

Jesus spent the rest of the day teaching the multitude and healing the sick. The chief priests and the scribes became afraid of Him for the multitude was following after Him instead of obeying them. They whispered to each other that somehow this man needed to be eliminated.

As Jesus was about to leave the temple, He lamented, "O Jerusalem, Jerusalem, who kills the prophets and stones those who are sent to her! How often I wanted to gather your children together, the way a hen gathers her chicks under her wings, and you were not willing. Behold, your house is being left to you desolate! For I say to you, from now on you shall not see Me until you say, 'Blessed is He who comes in the name of the Lord!'" This was said in reference to His prophesied second coming at the end of Israel's seventieth week of years.

Tuesday morning, March 31st Jesus returned to Jerusalem. When they passed the cursed fig tree, the disciples marveled that the tree was completely dried up. Peter asked how this was possible.

Jesus said to them, "Truly, I say to you, if you have faith and do not doubt, you shall not only do what was done to the fig tree, but even if you say to this mountain, 'Be taken up and cast into the sea,' it will happen. And all things you ask in prayer, believing, you shall receive. And when you stand praying, forgive if you have anything against anyone, so that your Father also who is in heaven may forgive you your transgressions."

Upon entering Jerusalem He proceeded to the temple, where He was confronted by the chief priests and elders of the people challenging Him, "By what authority do you do these things and who gave you this authority?"

Jesus replied, "I will ask you one thing, and if you tell Me, I will also tell you by what authority I do these things. The baptism of John was from what source, from heaven or from men?"

They gathered together and began reasoning between themselves, "If we say that John's baptism was from heaven, He will say, 'Why then, did you not believe him?' But if we say it was from men, we fear the multitude, for they regard John as a prophet." They reached a consensus and returned to Jesus, saying, "We do not know."

And Jesus said, "Neither will I tell you by what authority I do these things." He then told them the parable of the vine growers that was also a prophecy. It illustrated how the Father was the owner of the vineyard (Israel), the Jews were the vine-growers who rented the vineyard, the slaves sent to collect the rent were the prophets they killed and Jesus was the Son they put to death. For this they will be cast out of the land.

The parable seemed lost on the Sadducees and Pharisees as they asked Him a number of questions, seeking to trap Him in a statement that they might use to discredit Him and expose Him as a fraud. Because He answered them truthfully, they were unable to rebuke Him. But Jesus rebuked the Pharisees for their hypocrisy, for forcing the people to follow the traditions of men rather than the Word of God, and for requiring the people to live to a standard higher than they themselves were willing to follow.

The expectations of the Pharisees are the very definition of hypocrisy. These double standards blinded them to the fact that they—not the ones they were accusing—were the true hypocrites. Seven woes of condemnation were pronounced upon the Pharisees. So scathing were these rebukes that they retreated in shame.

Prior to departing the temple, Jesus sat opposite the treasury and observed the people putting money in the offering. The wealthy put large sums of money into the offering and often made a show of it, but one poor widow woman put in only two small copper mites. Jesus remarked to his disciples, "Truly, I say to you. This poor widow put in more than all the contributors to the treasury. For they all put in out of their surplus, but she, out of her poverty, put in all she owned, all she had to live on."

As evening drew near, Jesus departed from the temple. His disciples pointed out the temple buildings to Him, in obvious pride, as though He had never seen them before. He said to them, "Do you not see these things? Truly I say to you, not one stone here shall be left upon another, which will not be torn down." They quietly contemplated this prophecy, which was later fulfilled in 70 AD, as they retired to Bethany where they spent the night. While they were resting on the Mount of Olives opposite the temple, the disciples came to Him privately and asked what would be the signs of His second coming and the end of the age.

Jesus answered, "See to it that no one misleads you. For many will come in My name saying, 'I am the Christ,' and will mislead many. And you will hear of wars and rumors of wars. See that you are not frightened, for those things must take place, but that is not yet the end. For nation will rise up against nation, and kingdom against kingdom, and in various places there will be famines and earthquakes. But these are merely the beginning of birth pangs. Then they will deliver you to tribulation and will kill you, and you will be hated by all nations on account of My name. And at that time, many will fall away and will deliver up one another and hate one another. And many false prophets will arise and mislead many. And because lawlessness is increased, most people's love will grow cold. But the one who endures to the end, he shall be saved. And this gospel of the kingdom shall be preached in all the world for a witness to all the nations, and then the end shall come." Notice that Jesus did not say that the whole world would become believers before His second coming, as the Christian Dominionists insist, but only that His gospel will be preached in all the world.

Jesus related to them the parable of the fig tree. The fig tree He had cursed earlier was not cursed out of vengeance for not having any fruit on it. It was cursed as a visual prophecy of

Israel's condition. Israel has always been symbolized by the fig tree. The fig tree Jesus cursed had leaves on it but no fruit. Israel, likewise, had the appearance of life, but it was spiritually dead. The withered fig tree indicated that Israel would lose even the appearance of life and be cast into exile. At the appointed time, the tree would once again sprout leaves, giving the appearance of life, but it would remain spiritually dead. By this the world would know that summer was near and the time of the end was at hand. The parable of the fig tree was fulfilled at Israel's rebirth on May 28, 1948. To this day, Israel remains spiritually dead.

Jesus continued to tell His disciples of the perilous times and tribulations to come. He then told of His glorious return to end the madness for the elects sake, lest there be none left alive and the earth be rendered uninhabitable.

The disciples contemplated all this as they continued on to Bethany. As if what He'd said earlier wasn't enough to think about, He revealed more to them. "You know that after two days the Passover is coming, and the Son of Man is to be delivered up for crucifixion." After three years with Jesus, the disciples still did not understand what He meant by this.

Wednesday, April 1ˢᵗ they spent the day at the home of Simon the leper. Come evening, as they reclined at the table, a woman came to Jesus with an alabaster vial of very costly perfume and poured it out on His head.

As when Lazarus' sister, Mary had washed Jesus' feet with pure nard, Judas Iscariot became indignant and said, "Why this waste? This perfume might have been sold for a high price and the money given to the poor." Apparently, what Jesus said the first time hadn't sunk in.

Jesus repeated His previous rebuke, saying, "Why do you bother the woman? She has done a good deed for Me. The poor you have with you always but you do not always have Me. When she poured this perfume upon My body, she did it to prepare Me for burial. Truly I say to you, wherever this gospel is preached in the whole world, what this woman has done shall also be spoken of in memory of her."

Jesus' rebuke didn't sit well with Judas. Later that night he slipped out and consulted with the chief priests about delivering Him up to them. They agreed to a payment of thirty pieces of silver, the price they considered the value of a man's life. From then on, Judas began looking for an opportunity to betray Jesus.

Jesus remained in Bethany throughout the day of Thursday, Apr. 2nd hiding Himself from those who wished to put Him to death, for His hour was not yet at hand. At sunset on Thursday evening the Passover began. Passover does not occur on the same day each year. That year it occurred on Friday. That Thursday was also the preparation day for the Feast of Unleavened Bread when the Passover lamb was to be sacrificed. Earlier that afternoon, the disciples came to Jesus and asked where He wanted them to prepare the Passover meal.

He sent Peter and John, telling them, "Go into the city, and a man carrying a pitcher of water will meet you. Follow him and wherever he enters, say to the owner of the house, 'The Teacher says, "Where is My guest room in which I may eat the Passover meal with My disciples?"' And he himself will show you a large upper room, furnished and ready. Prepare for us there."

They went to Jerusalem and found the man carrying a pitcher of water. It wasn't hard to find him, since such work was considered women's work. Men simply didn't do women's work unless they had no other choice. They followed the man to his master's house and inquired of the upper room as Jesus had instructed.

That evening, Jesus met them there, knowing that the hour of His departure was upon Him and that He would soon return to the Father. In the upper room, He reclined at the table with

His disciples, having loved His own that were in the world to the very end. During supper, it grieved Him that Satan had already put into Judas' heart to betray Him that night.

After supper, Jesus rose from the table, removed His garments and girded Himself with a towel. He filled a basin with water, washed the disciples feet and dried them with the towel He had girded Himself with.

When Jesus came to Peter, he said, "Lord, do you wash my feet?"

Jesus answered, "What I do you do not realize now, but you shall understand hereafter."

"Lord, never shall you wash my feet."

"If I do not wash you, you have no part of Me."

Peter repented and said, "Lord, not my feet only, but my hands and my head."

"He who has bathed needs only to wash his feet, and he is completely clean. And you are clean." Referring to Judas, He added, "But not all of you."

Jesus then dressed Himself and returned to the table. He explained to them what He had just done and why. He did this as an example for all to follow. For all of His disciples, not just the twelve, were to keep each other accountable and free from sin.

He said to them, "I do not speak of all of you. I know the ones I have chosen. But that the Scriptures may be fulfilled, 'He who eats My bread has lifted his heel against Me.'" After saying this, He became troubled in spirit and said, "Truly, truly, I say to you that one of you will betray me."

The twelve looked at each other grieving and said one by one, "Surely not I, Lord?" Even Judas Iscariot was bewildered, for he thought he was going to force Jesus to bring in His kingdom and defeat Israel's enemy, not deliver Him up to death.

John, who had become a very close friend with Jesus, was

leaning against His breast when Peter gestured to him "Tell us of whom He is speaking."

John asked Jesus, "Lord, who is it?"

Jesus replied quietly, "That is the one for whom I shall dip the morsel and give it to him." He then dipped the morsel and gave it to Judas and said, "What you do, do quickly." Only John knew why Jesus said this to him. The others assumed he was sent on a mission of mercy.

After Judas departed, Jesus took some bread, broke it and gave it to His disciples and said, "Take, eat. This is My body which is given for you. Do this in remembrance of Me." Then He took a cup of wine, and giving thanks, gave it to them saying, "Drink from it, all of you, for this is blood of the new covenant, which is poured out for many for forgiveness of sins." When the cup had gone around, Jesus said, "Now is the Son of Man glorified, and God is glorified in Him. Little children, I am with you a little while longer. You shall seek Me and as I said to the Jews, I now say to you also, 'Where I am going you cannot come.'"

Peter asked, "Lord, where are You going?"

"Where I go, you cannot follow Me now, but you shall follow later."

"Lord, why can I not follow You right now? I will lay down my life for you."

"Will you lay down your life for Me? Truly, truly, I say to you, a cock shall not crow until you deny Me three times." Peter was shocked that He said this to him. "Let not your heart be troubled; if you believe in God, believe also in Me. In My Father's house are many dwelling places; if it were not so, I would have told you. I go to prepare a place for you and if I go and prepare a place for you, I will come again, and receive you to Myself that where I am, there you will be also. And you know the way where I am going."

Thomas remained confused. He didn't understanding where Jesus was going and asked how he was to know way.

Jesus said, "I am the way, the truth, and the life; no one comes to the Father but through Me. If you had known Me, you would have known the Father also. From now on, you know Him and have seen Him."

Phillip said, "Lord, show us the Father, and it is enough for us."

Jesus said, "Have I been so long with you, and yet you have not come to know Me, Phillip? He who has seen Me has seen the Father. How do you say, 'Show us the Father'? Do you not believe that I am in the Father, and the Father is in Me? The words that I say to you I do not speak of My own initiative, but the Father abiding in Me does His works. Believe Me that I am in the Father, and the Father in Me." He continued to comfort them saying that He would not leave them orphaned but would send another helper, the Holy Spirit.

Judas (not Iscariot) asked, "Lord, what has happened that You are going to disclose Yourself to us, and not the world?"

"If anyone loves Me, he will keep My word, and My Father will love him, and We will come to him, and make Our abode with him. He who does not love Me does not keep My words; and the word which you hear is not Mine, but the Father's who sent Me. These things I have spoken to you while abiding with you. But the helper, the Holy Spirit whom the Father will send in My name, He will teach you all things, and bring to your remembrance all that I said to you. Peace I leave with you; My peace I give to you. Not as the world gives do I give to you. Let not your heart be troubled, nor let it be fearful." The peace that Jesus gives is not the kind of peace the world is capable of giving. It is a peace that cannot be counterfeited and surpasses all understanding that all true believers in Jesus Christ experience.

Jesus continued His teaching, saying that He was the vine and that the followers were the branches. A branch cannot bear fruit unless it abides in the vine. A branch that does not bear fruit is trimmed and cast into the fire. A branch that does bear fruit is pruned that it may bear more fruit. "If you keep My commandments, you will abide in My love, just as I have kept My Father's commandments, and abide in His love. These things I have spoken to you, that My joy may be in you, and that your joy may be made full. This is My command; that you love one another, just as I have loved you."

Before departing, He warned them of things to come, saying that the world would hate them because they first hated Him. The disciples would be cast out and killed by those who thought they were doing service to God. Concerning the Holy Spirit, He told them, "But I tell you the truth; it is to your advantage that I go away. For if I do not go away, the Helper shall not come to you; but if I go, I will send Him to you. And He, when He comes, will convict the world concerning sin and righteousness and judgment; concerning sin, because they do not believe in Me; and concerning righteousness, because I go to the Father and you no longer behold Me; and concerning judgment, because the ruler of this world has been judged. I have many more things to say to you, but you cannot bear them now. But when He, the Spirit of truth, comes, He will guide you into all the truth, for He will not speak of His own initiative, but what He hears He will speak, and He will disclose to you what is to come. He shall glorify Me, for He shall take of Mine and shall disclose it to you. All things that the Father has are Mine; therefore I said, that He takes of Mine, and will disclose it to you." He then told them of His crucifixion and resurrection explaining that He was leaving the world now and returning to the Father.

The disciples said, "Now you speak plainly. Now we know

that You know all things, and have no need for anyone to question you. By this we believe that You came from the Father."

He said to them, "Do you now believe? Behold, an hour is coming, and has already come for you to be scattered, each to his own home, and to leave Me alone; and yet I am not alone, because the Father is with Me. These things I have spoken to you that in Me you may have peace. In the world you have tribulation, but take courage; I have overcome the world."

He then offered up a prayer for them to the Father. After singing a hymn, He led them out to the Mount of Olives to a garden called Gethsemane. He said to them, "Sit here until I have prayed. Pray that you may not enter into temptation." He left them there taking with Him Peter and the two sons of Zebedee, John and James. When they had walked a little farther He became distressed and said to them, "My soul is deeply grieved to the point of death. Remain here and keep watch."

He went a short distance beyond them and fell to the ground, praying, "Abba, Father! All things are possible for Thee. If Thou art willing, remove this cup from Me; yet not My will, but Thine be done." Being in agony, He prayed so fervently that the capillaries in His forehead burst. The blood mingled with His sweat that became drops of blood falling to the ground. An angel from heaven then appeared to Him and strengthened Him.

He returned to the three and found them sleeping. He said to Peter, "Simon, are you asleep? Could you not keep watch for one hour? Rise and pray that you may not enter into temptation." He departed them a second time and repeated His prayer. He returned to them and found them sleeping once again and they didn't know how to answer Him. He departed to pray some more and when He returned a third time, He said to them, "Are you still sleeping and taking your rest? It is enough; the hour has come. Behold, the Son of Man is being betrayed into the hands of sinners. Arise, let us be going. Behold, the one who betrays Me is at hand."

As He was speaking, Judas Iscariot, leading a multitude carrying swords and clubs, approached Him, saying, "Hail, Rabbi!" and kissed Him. For that was the signal for the multitude to arrest and lead Him away under guard.

Jesus said, "Judas, are you betraying the Son of Man with a kiss?"

One of the twelve drew his sword and struck the slave of the high priest, slicing off his right ear.

Jesus said to him, "Put your sword back into its place, for all those who take up the sword shall perish by the sword. Or do you think that I cannot appeal to My Father and He will at once put at My disposal more than twelve legions of angels? How then shall the Scriptures be fulfilled, that it must happen this way?" After picking up the slaves ear and healing the man, Jesus turned to the multitude and asked "Whom do you seek?"

They answered Him, "Jesus of Nazareth."

"I am He." When He said this, they all drew back and noisily fell to the ground. Once they had picked themselves up, swords and shields clattering, Jesus once again asked, "Whom do you seek?"

Again they answered, "Jesus of Nazareth."

"I told you that I am He. Have you come out with swords and clubs to arrest Me as you would a robber? Every day I used to sit in the temple, teaching and you did not seize Me. But all this has taken place that the Scriptures of the prophets may be fulfilled."

As the soldiers seized Him, all the disciples fled from Him except John. Peter, however, didn't go far. Jesus was led away to the high priest Caiaphas, where the elders and scribes were already waiting. Peter followed from a short distance but wasn't allowed inside. John, however, being the son of Zebedee who was a Pharisee, was permitted to enter the council chambers. John noticed Peter standing outside and brought him into the courtyard. There he waited with the officers to see the outcome.

As Jesus stood before Caiaphas, several false witnesses were brought forth but none of them offered consistent testimony until two of them stated, "We heard Him say, 'Destroy this temple, and in three days I will raise it up again.'"

Caiaphas seized on this and said to Jesus, "What is this they are saying? Do You not answer?" But Jesus kept silent. In frustration, Caiaphas said to Him, "I adjure You by the living God that You tell us whether You are the Christ, the Son of God."

Jesus then answered him, "You have said it yourself. Nevertheless I tell you that hereafter you shall see the Son of Man sitting at the right hand of power and coming on the clouds of heaven."

Caiaphas tore his robes and cried out, "He has blasphemed. What further need do we have of witnesses? Behold you have heard the blaspheme. What do you think?"

They all said with one voice, "He is deserving of death."

And they spat on Him and beat Him with their fists. Others slapped Him and said, "Prophecy You Christ. Who is the one who hit You?"

In the mean time, Peter was outside, sitting in the courtyard and trying to stay warm, when a certain servant girl said to him, "You too were with Jesus the Galilean."

But he denied it saying, "Girl, I do not know what you are talking about," and then he departed.

As he went out the gateway another servant girl said, "This man was with Jesus of Nazareth."

But Peter denied it with an oath, "I do not know this man."

A little while later, bystanders came up and said to Peter,

"Surely you too were one of them, for the way you talk gives you away."

He began to curse and swear, saying, "I do not know the man." Immediately a cock crowed, and he remembered what Jesus said to him, "Before a cock crows, you will deny Me three times." He ran out and wept bitterly.

The sun was just rising on Friday, April 3rd the day of Passover, when the chief priests and the elders counseled together to put Jesus to death. But they didn't have the authority to do so. They bound Him and led Him out to Pontius Pilate, the prefect of Judaea.

When Judas Iscariot heard that Jesus had been condemned, he felt remorse for betraying Him. He went to the chief priests and elders and said to them, "I have sinned by betraying innocent blood."

They answered him, "What is that to us? See to it yourself."

Judas cast the thirty pieces of silver on the sanctuary floor and departed. He went out of the city and upon finding a tree extending over a cliff, he hung himself. For several days his body hung there until the tree broke. Then he fell onto the rocks below, bursting his bloated body open and spilling his innards on the ground.

The chief priests collected the silver pieces and said, "It is not lawful for us to return it to the treasury for it is blood money." And they counseled together and bought the potter's field for a burial ground for strangers. From that point on, the field was known as the Field of Blood.

At sunrise Jesus was led to the praetorium, but Caiaphas and the elders would not enter, that they might not be defiled for the Passover meal. Pontius Pilate came out to them and asked what they were accusing Jesus of.

They said, "We found this man misleading our nation, and

forbidding people to pay taxes to Caesar and saying that He Himself is Christ, the King."

Pilate answered, "Take Him yourselves, and judge according to your law."

They replied, "We are not permitted to put anyone to death."

Pilate couldn't understand how any of these things justified putting a man to death. He went back inside and summoned Jesus to him. "Do you hear what Your accusers are saying?" He was amazed that Jesus remained silent. "Are You the King of the Jews?"

"Are you saying this on your own initiative or did others tell you of Me?

"I am not a Jew, am I? Your own nation and chief priests delivered You to me. What have You done?"

"My kingdom is not of this world. If My kingdom were of this world, then My servants would be fighting that I might not be delivered up to the Jews. But as it is, My kingdom is not of this realm."

"So You are a king?"

"You say correctly that I am a king. For this I have been born, and for this I have come into this world; to bear witness to the truth. Everyone who is of the truth hears My voice."

Pilate asked, "What is truth?" Finding nothing treasonous toward Rome in Jesus' actions, he went out to the Jews and said, "I find no guilt in Him."

But the Jews kept insisting, "He stirs up the people, teaching all over Judaea, starting in Galilee, even as far as this place."

When Pilate learned that Jesus was a Galilean, he sent Him to Herod Antipas who himself was in Jerusalem at that time for the Passover.

Herod was glad when Jesus was brought to him, for he had

been wanting to see Him for a long time. He had heard much about Him and was hoping Jesus would perform some sign for him. He questioned Him at length, but Jesus remained silent. The chief priests and elders kept accusing Him vehemently. In his disappointment, Herod and his soldiers treated Jesus with contempt, put a purple robe on Him and sent Him back to Pilate.

Pilate again came out to them and said, "I have questioned Him and found no guilt concerning these things you accuse Him of. Neither does Herod for he sent Him back to me. Therefore I will order that He be punished and then release Him."

The chief priests shouted out, "No! Release for us Barabbas."

During the festival, the prefect was accustomed to releasing one prisoner, whomever the multitude chose. At that time there was being held a notorious prisoner called Barabbas, a thief and a murderer. Pilate sought to release Jesus but the chief priests had whipped up the multitude into a frenzy and they kept calling for him to release Barabbas instead. Pilate asked, "What then shall I do with Jesus who is called Christ?"

"Let Him be crucified," they called out.

"Why? What evil has He done?"

But they shouted out all the more, "Let Him be crucified."

Pilate saw that he wasn't getting anywhere and that a riot was about to break out. He took water and washed his hands in front of them saying, "I am innocent of this man's blood. See to that yourself."

The crowd answered, "His blood be on us and on our children."

Pilate therefore released Barabbas and ordered Jesus scourged.

Jesus was led into the praetorium, where the Roman cohort

stripped Him and gave Him forty lashes with a cat-o'-nine-tails. This was a short whip made up of a dozen strands of leather with a sharp piece of iron barb tied to the ends. When these iron barbs dug into His skin, they tore off strips of flesh as they were pulled out. So much flesh was torn off that His back resembled a plowed field. In places, the bones of His ribs were visible. The average man would have died long before the count of forty was reached. But Jesus somehow survived. Amazed that He was still alive, the guards pulled Him up on His feet. The Roman cohort put a scarlet robe on Him and gave Him a cane as His scepter. They then wove a crown of thorns and pressed it into His skull. They mocked Him and pretended to worship Him, saying, "Hail, King of the Jews." They then took the cane from Him and beat Him over the head with it. When they returned Him to Pilate, he was aghast at the sight of Him.

Pilate once again came out before the crowd, saying, "Behold, I am bringing Jesus out to you, that you may know that I find no guilt in Him."

Jesus, therefore, was brought out, wearing the scarlet robe and crown of thorns. His face was all bruised and puffy from the beating. Blood streamed off His back and down His legs. Pilate said, "Behold the man."

The chief priests and elders cried out, "Crucify, crucify!"

Pilate said to them, "Take Him yourself and crucify Him, for I find no guilt in Him."

The chief priests said to him, "We have a law that He ought to die because He made Himself out to be the Son of God."

Pilate became more afraid when he heard this and asked Jesus, "Where are You from?" But Jesus remained silent. "You do not speak to me? Do You not know that I have authority to release You and I have authority to have You crucified?"

"You would have no authority if it had not been given from

above. For this reason, he who delivered Me to you has the greater sin."

Pilate again made efforts to release Him, but the Jews cried out, "If you release Him, you are no friend of Caesar. Everyone who makes himself out to be a king opposes Caesar."

Pilate took his seat on the judgment seat at the place called The Pavement. It was already late in the morning when he said to the Jews, "Behold, your king."

They cried out, "Away with Him, away with Him. Crucify Him."

"Shall I crucify your King?"

"We have no king but Caesar."

Exasperated, Pilate reluctantly ordered Jesus' crucifixion. Jesus was taken out, and a cross was placed upon His back. He was led through the streets of Jerusalem carrying His own cross to a place called the "place of a skull." Two thieves proceeded Him, also carrying their own crosses. Along the way, being severely weakened by His loss of blood, Jesus fell several times, bruising His heart in the process. At one point He became so weak that He could proceed no further. In the crowd was a man from the country called Simon of Cyrene, who was forced to carry Jesus' cross for Him. A multitude of people followed behind Him and the women were mourning and lamenting Him.

When they reached the place of a skull, Jesus was stripped of His garments, ripping anew the scabs on His back. He was then placed on His cross and huge spikes were driven through His hands and feet. The two thieves, who were also held to their crosses with spikes in their hands and feet, were placed on each side of Him. Pilot ordered a sign hung above Jesus' head saying "king of the Jews," in three different languages. The chief priests objected to it, but Pilot ordered it to remain.

As Jesus hung there, inhaling was relatively easy but exhaling was very difficult. To exhale, He had to pull or push Himself up. The spikes where driven through the bases of His hands, through the carpal tunnel where the nerves ran through. The nerves rubbed against the spikes making it excruciatingly painful to pull Himself up to exhale. It was just as painful to push Himself up with His feet.

The pain of exhaling also made it hard to speak, but He somehow made His words clear enough to be understood. Looking down at the crowd, He said, "Father, forgive them, for they know not what they are doing."

The soldiers, who were casting lots to divide His garments, looked up, amazed that He would say such a thing. If they had been hanging there, they would have been cursing everyone in final defiance. In fact, one of the thieves was doing just that. He was also mocking Jesus saying, "If You are the Son of God, save Yourself and us and come down from the cross."

The other thief rebuked him saying, "Do you not fear God, being under the same sentence of condemnation? And we justly, for we are receiving what we deserve. But this man has done nothing wrong." To Jesus he said, 'Remember me when You come to Your kingdom."

Jesus answered, "I say to you, this day you will be with Me in paradise."

At the foot of the cross stood Jesus' mother, her sister Salome, and Mary Magdalene. John was also standing nearby. Jesus said to His mother. "Woman, behold your son." And to John He said, "Behold your mother." From that point on, John took care of Mary as his own mother until the day she died.

At about noon, a sudden darkness fell on the land for a period of three hours. It was a supernatural eclipse of the sun that was observed and recorded in many parts of Europe and Africa. It wasn't the kind that normally occurs when the moon passes in front of the sun, for the moon was on the opposite side of the earth at that time, being a full moon. While the sun was obscured the sins of the world were poured out on Jesus. For three hours He endured this torment. While the sins of the world were placed on His shoulders, the Father turned His back on the Son. This was the first and only time the Son was separated from the Father. This was the greatest torment He endured on our behalf.

Going to the cross, Jesus was prepared for everything. Everything, that is, but one. This separation from the Father was the one thing He was not prepared for. Though He knew it was coming, even He didn't fully know what it truly meant to be separated from the Father. In anguish from this separation, He cried out, *"Eli, Eli, lama sabachtani?"* That is, "My God, My God, why hast Thou forsaken Me?"

With this statement, the darkness lifted just as suddenly as it had fallen. When those standing around heard Jesus' last words, they thought He was calling for Elijah. One of them went and filled a sponge with sour wine mixed with gall and lifted it to Him on a reed to drink. The others mocked, saying, "Let us see if Elijah will come and save Him."

Jesus sipped of the sour wine and then, with a loud raspy voice cried out, "It is finished." He struggled to pull Himself up one last time. "Father, into Thy hands I commit My spirit." At that time His bruised heart ruptured, the blood mixing with water from the bruising that accumulated in the sack surrounding the heart. It wasn't by asphyxiation that He died as indicated by His ability to talk while hanging on the cross. He died, rather, by a ruptured heart—or literally by a broken heart.

At about forty years of age, Jesus breathed His last, fulfilling the law of Moses for the redemption of mankind. At the very moment of His death, the veil of the temple at the entrance to the Holy of Holies, a barrier which measured about four inches thick and weighed several hundred pounds, was torn asunder as though it were rice paper. Symbolically, the torn veil demonstrated that there was now nothing separating us from the Father. A great earthquake also shook the land, splitting the rocks and crumbling buildings. The earthquake was also felt throughout Greece and Egypt.

The centurion, seeing how Jesus died, said, "Truly this man was the Son of God."

As evening approached, Joseph of Arimathea, a man of considerable wealth and a disciple of Jesus, approached Pilate to request the body of Jesus. Pilate, surprised that Jesus was already dead, ordered it so. Because of the high Sabbath, which began that evening, the soldiers broke the legs of the two thieves. The chief priests requested this so they would die more quickly and not be left hanging there on the Sabbath day. When they came to Jesus, they knew that He was already dead and saw no need to break His legs, fulfilling another prophecy that none of His bones would be broken. One of the soldiers thrust his spear into Jesus' left side and pierced His heart. The blood mixed with the water in the heart sack poured out through the wound.

Joseph of Arimathea had Jesus' body lowered from the cross. He wrapped Jesus in a linen cloth and laid Him in a new tomb that he had prepared ahead of time for himself. A massive stone was then rolled in front of the tomb entrance. Sometime during the night, the two thieves died and were buried.

While the Jews prepared to celebrate the Feast of First-fruits, Jesus descended into paradise, also known as Abraham's Bosom and Sheol. He was accompanied by the thief He had promised would be with Him in paradise. The thief who mocked Jesus descended into Hades. While in paradise, Jesus set the captives free. These were the faithful who were temporarily held there in comfort until provision was made for their sins. When Jesus rose from the dead, the tombs of the faithful were opened, and they were resurrected with Him. Many thousands were seen walking about the city for the next few weeks.

Sheol consisted of two parts separated by an impassable barrier. On the other side of the barrier was the place known as Hades, which later became known as Hell. The unfaithful and unbelievers remained there in fiery torment until the day of their release for the judgment. Today, paradise is empty, as all believers now go straight to heaven upon their death. Hades, on the other hand, is more crowded than ever and will get even more crowded before judgment day arrives.

While Jesus was in paradise, the chief priests remembered what He had said about rising from the dead. They ordered His tomb sealed and stationed two elite guards to watch it, in case His disciples tried to steal the body. They reasoned that the second deception would be worst than the first. But these precautions were useless. On Sunday morning before sunrise, the day of the Feast of First-fruits, Jesus rose from the dead, being the first fruit of the resurrected. At His resurrection, fellowship was restored with the Father, and was never again to be separated from Him. Without this resurrection, mankind could not have been restored to fellowship with the Father. Without this resurrection, Jesus' sacrifice on the cross would have been done in vain. This resurrection dealt a severe blow to Satan. Jesus was bruised on the heel, but Satan was bruised on the head.

Early Sunday morning, April 5th while it was still dark, Mary Magdalene, Mary the mother of Jesus, and Salome the mother of John—all of whom had ministered to Jesus and His disciples—came to His tomb, carrying spices they had prepared during the preparation day for His embalming. They were discussing how they were going to move the stone, when a severe earthquake occurred and two angels descended from heaven to roll away the stone. The angels' appearance was like lightning and their garments were as white as snow. The guards, the elite of the Roman cohort, shook for fear of them and promptly fainted.

One of the angels said to the women, "Do not be afraid, for I know that you are looking for Jesus, who has been crucified. He is not here, for He has risen. Come, see the place where He was lying. Then go quickly and tell His disciples that He has risen from the dead. Behold, He is going before you into Galilee. There you will see Him. Behold, I have told you."

The other two women quickly departed, but Mary Magdalene, perplexed by the angel's words, remained behind. When at last she turned to leave she saw a man whom she supposed was a gardener. She asked Him where they had taken the body of Jesus.

When He spoke her name, her eyes were opened and she immediately recognized Him. She tried to wrap her arms around Him in excitement, but He said, "Woman, do not lay hold of Me, for I have not yet been glorified. But go to Jerusalem and report all that you have seen to My disciples."

The women ran back to Jerusalem to the upper room where the disciples were hiding for fear of the Jews. When the women reported what they had seen, their words sounded like nonsense to the men. Mary Magdalene arrived and reported seeing Jesus alive. The disciples were incredulous that Jesus would appear first to her instead of to them. Peter and John, therefore, went to see for themselves. John ran ahead and stopped at the tomb entrance, but Peter entered the tomb and saw the linen wrappings laying where Jesus had lain. The head covering was folded neatly near the wrapping, but the wrapping was just an empty shell.

Later that evening, two of the lesser disciples came to them in the upper room, reporting that Jesus had appeared to them on the road to Emmaus and had explained the scriptures to them beginning with Moses and then the prophets. They didn't recognize Him at first—until He broke bread with them and then vanished from their sight.

As they were speaking, Jesus suddenly appeared in their midst. At first they thought they were seeing a ghost, but Jesus said, "Why are you troubled and why do doubts arise in your hearts? See My hands and My feet, that it is I Myself. Touch Me and see, for a ghost does not have flesh and bones as you see that I have." They still were unable to believe and were afraid to touch Him. He asked them. "Do you have anything here to eat?" They gave Him some broiled fish, which He ate, proving that He was not a ghost.

Then they believed Him, but Thomas was not with them. Later, when they told Thomas of these things, he said he would not believe until he had put his hand in Jesus' side and felt the holes of the spikes. He became known from then on as "doubting Thomas".

Eight days later, Jesus appeared to them again. This time, Thomas was with them. "Peace be with you," He said to them. To Thomas He said, "Reach here your finger and see My hands. And reach here your hand and put it into my side, and be not unbelieving, but believing."

Thomas therefore answered, "My Lord and my God!"

"Because you have seen Me, have you believed? Blessed are they who have not seen, and yet believed."

As instructed, they went to Galilee, where Jesus met them by the Sea of Tiberias. While they were having breakfast Jesus said to Peter, "Simon, son of John, do you love Me more than these?"

"Lord, You know that I love You."

"Tend My lambs." Jesus then asked him a second time, "Simon, son of John, do you love Me?"

"Yes Lord, You know that I love You."

"Shepherd My sheep." Then Jesus said to him a third time, "Do you love Me?"

Peter was troubled when Jesus asked a third time if he loved Him. "Lord, You know all things. You know that I love You."

Jesus said, "Tend My sheep."

Three times Peter had denied that he knew Jesus. Three times Jesus asked him if he loved Him and commanded him to take care of His church, signifying that all was forgiven and reestablishing His promise that upon Peter, "the rock", Jesus would build His church.

Forty days after the day of His resurrection, Jesus met with His disciples one last time on the Mount of Olives. Aside from the original eleven, there were over five hundred people with them, not counting the women and children.

Jesus said to them, "All authority has been given to Me in heaven and on earth. Go therefore and make disciples of all the nations, baptizing them in the name of the Father, and the Son, and the Holy Spirit, teaching them to observe all that I commanded you. And lo, I am with you always, even to the end of the age."

Jesus then lifted up His hands and blessed them. As He did so a cloud lifted Him up into heaven. The thousands of faithful Old Testament saints who had been resurrected with Him also ascended into heaven. While His disciples gazed up into the sky, two angels in white clothing appeared beside them saying, "Men of Galilee, why do you stand looking up into the sky? This Jesus, who has been taken up from you into heaven, will come in just the same way as you have watched Him go into heaven."

Ten days later the disciples were gathered in the upper room. While praying, the Holy Spirit came upon them as tongues of fire that rested upon each of them, just as Jesus had promised. The pouring out of the Holy Spirit upon the newborn church marked the miraculous beginning of the age of the Gentiles.

The apostles went out and boldly proclaimed the gospel of Jesus Christ to those in the city. That day three thousand new believers were added to their number. Afterwards, they went into all the world, as Jesus had commanded, starting in Jerusalem, then Judaea and Samaria, then going to the rest of the world.

By the indwelling power of the Holy Spirit, they preached the sacred and imperishable proclamation of eternal salvation by faith in Jesus Christ. Not by good works, or by repeatedly chanting endless prayers does one obtain eternal life, but by faith in Jesus Christ alone. No one perishes eternally because of their sins, for Jesus paid for them on the cross. Rather, they perish eternally for their refusal to believe in the name of the Son of God. For there is no other name under heaven, given to men, by which mankind must be saved.

Chapter 8

John of Patmos

AD 98

*I*n my seventh dream, I found myself standing on an irregularly shaped, picturesque island of volcanic origin. Numerous coves with rocky and sandy beaches dotted the shoreline. The island was mostly covered with low shrubs, with a few clumps of trees scattered about. It consisted of three sections, each connected to the other by a narrow isthmus. Between the northeastern and center sections, a port village lay near the entrance of a natural harbor. The northeastern section was the largest section, while the southern section was about half the size of the center section.

This was the island of Patmos where the apostle John was exiled. Patmos was located on the eastern side of the Aegean Sea near Phrygia (present-day western Turkey). John's hill was the highest point of the island in the middle of the center section. From the top of the hill, I could see the entire island with the sea all around. Though Patmos was one of the northernmost islands of the Dodecanese Islands, only a few small islands around Patmos could be seen.

For some reason, I'd always pictured Patmos as a barren,

lifeless island where prisoners made little rocks out of big rocks. I saw no such activity here. There was plenty of other activity, though. Patmos was the place where political prisoners were exiled, not hardened criminals. In the harbor prisoners unloaded a supply ship. I stood atop the highest hill, taking in the view, when my attention was drawn eastward as someone ascended the hill.

An elderly man was climbing to the top of the hill. He wore a full-length brown robe and sandals. His weathered face and long gray beard gave him a haggard look. His abode was a mere cave on the east side of the hill.

John the Apostle reached the top of the hill and sat on a rock, contemplating the disturbing news he had received not long ago. It wasn't even seventy years after Christ's crucifixion and already the church was going astray. How did it get that way and what did this mean for the future? His thoughts drifted to the past.

John is called the "apostle of love" and is often pictured as having an effeminate appearance. There was nothing effeminate about John. Nor was he always loving. Quite the opposite, actually. It wasn't for nothing that Jesus called him and his brother James the "sons of thunder." When the two brothers first followed Jesus, they were both ambitious, zealous, intolerant and quick to judge. For them everything was black-and-white. It was either right or wrong — no *ifs, ands,* or *buts.* These were traits Jesus needed for them to have, but they needed to be tempered with love and humility.

John was the son of Zebedee and Salome. Zebedee was a Pharisee who owned a prosperous fishing fleet in Galilee. Salome was the sister of Mary the mother of Jesus. John and James were cousins of Jesus, but they didn't grow up with Him. They both worked with their father until Andrew told them about Jesus. Andrew was the brother of Peter, with whom James and John were partners. Andrew was also a disciple of John the Baptist and was present when Jesus came to John for baptism.

John the Baptist saw Jesus coming to him and said of Him, "Behold the Lamb of God who takes away the sin of the world! This is He on behalf of whom I said, 'After me comes a man who has a higher rank than I, for He existed before me.' And I did not recognize Him, but in order that He might be manifested to Israel, I came baptizing in water." John baptized Jesus and as Jesus walked out of the water, the Holy Spirit came down in the form of a dove and rested upon Him. John testified, "And I did not recognize Him, but He who sent me to baptize in water said to me, 'He upon whom you see the Spirit descending and remaining upon Him, this is the one who baptizes in the Holy Spirit.' And I have seen and have borne witness that this is the Son of God."

Immediately afterward the voice of the Father was heard from heaven saying, "This is My beloved Son, in whom I am well pleased."

Jesus then departed for the wilderness to be tested. Andrew and one of the other disciples of John followed Jesus and spent the night with Him. The following day, Andrew returned to Capernaum and told Peter, James and John about Jesus. About a month and a half later, in the fall of AD 29, Jesus began His ministry in Galilee, healing those who were afflicted with various diseases, demoniacs, epileptics, and paralytics. He came to Capernaum and preached to the multitudes by the sea. Peter and Andrew were in their boat mending their nets when Jesus asked them to put the boat into the water. Seated in the boat Jesus continued preaching. He then turned to Peter and told him to cast his net into the water.

Peter objected saying, "Master, we have been fishing all day and caught nothing. But as You commanded it, I will do so." Immediately the net was so full of fish that it was about to tear.

James and John were nearby, mending their nets, when Peter asked them to come help. Both boats were so full of fish that they nearly sank. Peter said to Jesus, "Lord, depart from me for I am a sinful man."

Jesus replied, "Come, follow Me, and I will make you fishers of men." Peter and Andrew, after tending their boats, followed Jesus. James and John also followed Him, leaving their father and his servants to tend the boats.

Andrew later found Phillip (Nathaniel) sitting under a tree and told him about Jesus. Phillip asked, "Can anything good come out of Nazareth?"

Andrew answered, "Come and see."

When Jesus saw Phillip, He said of him, "Behold, an Israelite indeed in whom is no guile." Phillip then believed and followed Jesus.

In addition to Peter, Andrew, James, John and Phillip, seven others were specifically called to be His primary disciples; Matthew (Levi) the tax collector, Bartholomew, Thomas, James the son of Alphaeus and his son Judas (also known as Jude and Thaddaeus), Simon the zealot and Judas Iscariot. Jesus had many followers including seventy lessor disciples. About a year into His ministry, He sent them out throughout Judaea, Samaria and Gallee. His half brothers, James and Jude were among the seventy. For the next three and a half years, Jesus taught them His precepts and molded them to be the men of God He needed them to be. He loved them to the end and had to rebuke them a number of times for their errors.

One instance for John and James was when they sought a place to spend the night in a town in Samaria. The towns folk refused to permit them to stay because they were heading for Jerusalem. John and James became angry with them and asked Jesus if they could call down fire from heaven to consume them.

Jesus answered them, "You do not know what kind of spirit you are of; for the Son of Man did not come to destroy men's lives but to save them." It was then that Jesus referred to them as the "sons of thunder."

The brothers demonstrated their ambition and zeal when they convinced their mother to ask Jesus to grant them the right to sit on His right and left sides when they entered His kingdom. They figured that surely He wouldn't refuse His aunt's request. Jesus replied, "You do not know what you are asking. Are you able to drink the cup that I drink or to be baptized with the baptism with which I am baptized?" The brothers stated that they were able and Jesus answered, "The cup that I drink, you shall drink; and you shall be baptized with the baptism with which I am baptized. But to sit on My right, or on My left, this is not Mine to give, but it is for those for whom it has been prepared." In the coming years, the brothers learned to be careful what they wished for.

At the mountain of transformation, Peter, John and James, who formed the inner circle of the disciples, witnessed Jesus talking with Elijah and Moses. There they saw Jesus in His full glory. They heard the Father speak from heaven saying, "This is My Son, My chosen one. Listen to Him." This was the second of three times the Father spoke from heaven.

Afterwards on the way to Capernaum, the disciples were discussing who was greatest among them. When Jesus asked about it, they became ashamed of their frivolous discussion and remained silent. Jesus said, "If anyone wants to be first, he shall be last of all and servant of all." This was the very definition of humility. One was not to merely think of his own needs but to consider the needs of others as more important. Jesus set a child before Himself and added, "Whoever receives one child like this in My name receives Me; and whoever receives Me does not receive Me but Him who sent Me."

Humbled, John confessed that they saw a man casting out demons and tried to stop him because he wasn't following them. Jesus said to him, "Do not hinder him, for there is no one who shall perform a miracle in My name, and be able soon afterward to speak evil of Me. For he who is not against us, is for us. Whoever gives you a cup of water to drink because of your name as followers of Christ, truly I say to you, he shall not lose his reward. And whoever causes one of these little ones who believe to stumble, it would be better for him if, with a heavy millstone hung around his neck, he had been cast into the sea."

John then began to learn to become more tolerant for those who also believed but weren't part of his group. And by watching Jesus' example, he matured in his love for others. In time he learned humility while still retaining his zeal for the truth of Jesus Christ and intolerance for sin and falsehoods. His love for Jesus grew stronger and he became closer to Him than the others did. He learned that not building a life on Jesus and His love was like building a house on shifting sand.

When Jesus was arrested in the garden of Gethsemane, John was the only one who didn't abandon Him. At His crucifixion John stood at the foot of the cross with his mother Salome, Mary the mother of Jesus, and Mary Magdalene. Seven demons were cast out of Mary Magdalene and she followed Jesus along with Salome, Mary and a few other women who ministered to Jesus and the disciples. Prior to Jesus yielding His spirit to the Father, He placed His mother in John's care. In caring for Mary, John learned even more about the love of Christ.

Following Pentecost, the fledgling church grew in strength and numbers, and so did opposition from the religious leaders. Peter and John were the first to feel that opposition when they were preaching in the temple. They were both arrested by the temple guard and brought before the high priests. The priests noted these two were uneducated men and observed that their confidence came from having been with Jesus. They ordered the apostles to no longer preach in Jesus' name. They answered, "Whether it is right in the sight of God to give heed to you rather than God, you be the judge; for we cannot stop speaking what we have seen and heard."

As the number of believers grew, so did Peter's stature. People from all over were bringing their sick to him to be healed. They even laid them in the street where Peter walked that his shadow might pass over them. Jealous, the Sadducees arrested Peter. That night, while the saints prayed, an angel of the Lord released Peter from prison. The prison guards were at a loss to explain what had become of Peter and were executed. The next day, while Peter and the other apostles were preaching in the temple, they were all arrested.

The high priest said, "We gave you strict orders not to continue teaching in this name, and behold, you have filled Jerusalem with your teaching, and intend to bring this man's blood upon us."

The Apostles answered, "We must obey God rather than man. The God of our fathers raised up Jesus, whom you had put to death by hanging Him on a cross. He is the one whom God exalted to His right hand as a prince and a Savior, to grant repentance to Israel and forgiveness of sins. We are witnesses of these things and so is the Holy Spirit, whom God has given to those who obey Him."

The council was angered by these words and sought to put the disciples to death. However, a teacher of the law called Gamaliel urged restraint saying that if this was the work of men, it would be overthrown, but if it was the work of God, they would find themselves fighting against God. The apostles were instead flogged and released. They rejoiced at being considered worthy to suffer for Christ's sake.

They kept on preaching in the name of Jesus and more believers were added to their numbers. One of those new believers, Stephen, was filled with the Holy Spirit and started preaching the gospel. He was arrested and brought before the council. During his defense, he preached the history of Israel and rebuked the authorities for resisting the Holy Spirit and murdering the prophets sent to them. In their anger, they carried him outside the city walls and stoned him to death. He had the honor of being the first martyr for Jesus Christ.

That day a great persecution rose against the church. A young man named Saul, a Pharisee, started going from house to house with the temple guard, dragging believers to prison. The believers scattered throughout Judaea and Samaria, preaching the gospel wherever they went. The more the church was persecuted, the stronger and larger it became. It was like throwing water on an oil fire; it just spread the fire further. This fire spread into Asia minor, Africa and Europe, and it could not be put out.

The apostles, likewise, scattered throughout Israel, but Peter, John, and James remained in Jerusalem. Saul, on his way to Damascus to search for believers to arrest, had a miraculous conversion when Jesus appeared to him. Jesus said to him, "Saul, Saul, why are you persecuting Me?" He later spent three years in the wilderness where Jesus had been tempted, learning Christ's precepts. Thereafter, he was known as Paul and became the greatest of the apostles, though he considered himself the least. He did more than all of the others to spread the gospel into Europe.

While Stephen was the first Christian martyr, John's brother James was the first apostle to be martyred. He was beheaded by Herod Antipas. Seeing how this pleased the crowd, Antipas sought to put more believers to death. Instead, he was eaten by worms from the inside out and died.

Phillip, after leading an Ethiopian official to Jesus Christ was supernaturally teleported to Phrygia. There he preached the gospel and was crucified for his testimony of Christ. Matthew, the tax collector, was preaching in Parthia and Ethiopia where he was slain by a halberd (a pike with an axe head at one end and a spear on the other). James, the half-brother of Jesus was still preaching the gospel at the age of ninety-four, when he was beaten and stoned by the Jews. Matthias, who replaced Judas Iscariot, was stoned and beheaded in Jerusalem. Andrew was crucified in Edessa. His cross was fixed transversely with two ends in the ground forming an X. It became known as St. Andrews' cross. Mark, who wrote the gospel of Mark, was converted by Peter. He accompanied Paul on one of his missionary journeys and was later dragged to pieces by the people of Alexandria.

The emperor Nero instigated the first great persecution of Christians outside Jerusalem. He used all sorts of unspeakable horrors to put Christians to death. He had Peter crucified, who requested to be hung upside-down. He didn't think he was worthy to be crucified the way Jesus had been. Nero also had Paul beheaded with a sword. This persecution, like all the other persecutions only made the church stronger as the gospel was spread even further. Seeing how the Christians were put to death, many people took pity on them and marveled that they considered the truth of Jesus Christ worth dying for.

Jude, another half-brother of Jesus, was crucified in Edessa. Bartholomew reached India where he translated the gospel of Matthew into the Indian language. He was later beaten and crucified by idolaters. Thomas, known as Doubting Thomas, also reached India where he enraged the pagan priests and was thrust through with a spear. Luke, the historian who wrote the Gospel of Luke and Acts, traveled with Paul. He was hanged on an olive tree by idolatrous Greek priests. Simon the Zealot took the gospel to Mauritania, Africa and even made it to Britain where he was crucified. Timothy, a disciple of Paul and first elder of the church in Ephesus, was beaten with clubs by idolators.

After Mary, the mother of Jesus, died, John preached in Phrygia. Tradition has it that Mary Magdelene was betrothed to him and accompanied him to Ephesus. While in Ephesus, the Romans annexed Israel, ran the Jews out of Jerusalem and destroyed the temple in AD 70. Not one stone was left atop another just as Jesus had prophesied. Two years later, the Roman governor Flavius Silva defeated the last remaining zealots taking refuge at Masada.

In AD 81 Domitian became the emperor of Rome. About the mid-nineties, he instigated the second great persecution against the Christians for refusing to worship him as a god. Whenever something bad happened—like famine, pestilence, or an earthquake—he blamed it on the Christians. While John was residing in Ephesus, Domitian had him arrested and brought to Rome. He tried to deep-fry John alive by dunking him in a cauldron of boiling oil. Oil boils at six times the temperature of water. Like Shadrach, Meshach, and Abed-nego, who were delivered from the fiery furnace unhurt, John likewise emerged unhurt. Thousands believed in Christ after that. After John survived the boiling oil, Domitian exiled him to the island of Patmos.

John wasn't forced to do hard labor like the other political prisoners. Instead, being advanced in age, he was given free run of the island. He was only required to periodically check in with the centurion in charge and receive his allotment of food. John had been on the island only a few months when he received word that the prophecy Paul had given to the Ephesians was being fulfilled.

During his last visit to Ephesus on his way to Jerusalem, Paul had admonished the overseers to be on guard. He said to them,

"Be on guard for yourselves and for all the flock, among which the Holy Spirit has made you overseers to shepherd the church of God which He purchased with His own blood. I know that after my departure savage wolves will come in among you, not sparing the flock; and from among your own selves men will arise, speaking perverse things, to draw away the disciples after them. Therefore, be on the alert, remembering that night and day I did not cease to admonish each one with tears."

Some four decades later false teachers did arise as Paul had warned. Gnosticism began to take root and started infiltrating the church. Gnostics questioned the fundamentals of Christianity and the relationship between God and the humanity of Jesus. Seeking inclusivity, they questioned who was really is a Christian and sought to widen the definition.

While sitting on top of the hill John contemplated these things and prayed for the church. For the next week, he prayed every day. While in prayer on the Lord's day, Jesus appeared to him. This was the reason John's life had been spared from the boiling oil; to receive the revelation of Jesus Christ prophesying the end-times that precede the return of Jesus Christ. This revelation has been troubling mankind ever since.

While in prayer, John heard a loud voice behind him, telling him to write in a book all that he was about to see. The book was then to be sent to the seven churches in Asia—the churches of Ephesus, Smyrna, Pergamum, Thyatira, Sardis, Philadelphia and Laodicea. John turned and saw Jesus standing among seven golden lampstands. He wore a white robe that reached to His feet and a golden girdle about His chest. His hair was white as snow; His eyes burned like fire, and His skin glowed like the noonday sun. His voice sounded like the thunderous rush of a waterfall and out of His mouth came the Word of God like a sharp, two-edged sword. In His right hand he held seven stars.

This was the One of whom John testified—the faithful witness, the firstborn of the dead, and the ruler of the kings of the earth. He was the One who loved us and was pierced, who released us from the bondage of sin by His blood. He was the One who would be returning in the clouds, whom every eye of every nation would see. Even those who had gone down to Hades would see His coming and mourn. This was Yeshua (or Yehoshua; "the Lord is salvation"), the only express image of the Father. He would be called Wonderful, Counsellor, the Almighty God, Father and the Prince of Peace.

When John saw Him, he didn't immediately recognize Him and he fell at Jesus' feet in great fear. In the flesh, Jesus had been a Jew with Jewish features. Now He no longer bore any resemblance to His flesh. He was God and now appeared in all His glory.

Jesus laid his right hand on John and said, "Do not be afraid, I am the first and the last, the living One. I was dead, and behold, I am alive forevermore." These were names that only applied to the eternal almighty God. Jesus was God and was one with the Father. He was the risen Christ who had died for the forgiveness of sins and had risen from the dead as only God could do. He was the Christ who had been given all authority in heaven and on earth. "And I have the keys of death and of Hades," He said to John, "Write therefore the things you have seen, and the things that are and the things that will take place after these things."

Jesus went on to explain that the lampstands surrounding Him represented the seven churches. The seven stars were the angels of those churches, empowered to carry out God's will within each church. Each of the seven churches received a message. These churches were chosen to represent the seven church types of the church age until Christ returned for His church. The messages given to the seven churches were addressed to the angels of those churches. They weren't solely meant for the church members as warnings and encouragement; they also served as instructions to the angels given charge over those churches to fulfill Scripture as written.

Ephesus represented the first church type. It was known as the apostolic church and it enjoyed a close relationship with Jesus Christ, working diligently and patiently in full expectation of Christ's return. They were a discerning church that put to the test the teachings of those who claimed to be disciples of Christ. Lies were exposed and false teachers and prophets were cast out. At the time John was exiled to Patmos, the love this first church had exhibited was beginning to grow cold. With the passing away of the apostles and first Christians, the heresy of the Gnostics was beginning to take root within the church just as Paul had warned.

The church members were warned to return to their first love, to repent and do the first works. Jesus promised that those who overcame would eat of the Tree of Life. A few individuals chose to heed the warning, but as a church they chose not to obey. They gave in to the lust of the body and established a special priesthood, which Scripture did not support. Their lampstand was subsequently removed from its place, and they passed into history.

Throughout the church age, the overcomers were the only members of the church who were considered washed in the blood of the Lamb. They were members of the body of Christ and lived by the power of the Holy Spirit. They were not saved by their works but by their faith in Jesus Christ. The other church members only paid lip service, trying to earn their salvation. They were not true believers or considered part of the body of Christ.

Smyrna represented the second church type and was known as the persecuted church. Each year in Smyrna, Roman citizens had to burn incense on the alter of the Roman goddess Dea Roman. Christians and others who refused to do so were burned at the stake. Some were put in the arena and killed by wild beasts as entertainment. Despite their persecution and poverty, they continued the work of Christ. Jesus considered them rich spiritually. Jews who rejected their Messiah sought to put Jewish believers to death. These unbelieving Jews were not considered Jews but were of the synagogue of Satan. Jesus said not to fear the coming tribulations, which would last for ten days. Those who remained faithful until death were promised the crown of life.

Throughout the first three hundred years, the church suffered persecution from ten different Roman emperors. Nero was the first; then came Domitian during John's later years, followed by Trajan, Marcus Aurelius, Severus, Maximinus, Decius, Valerian, Aurelian and Diocletian. It wasn't until Constantine converted to Christianity and legalized Christianity in Rome in AD 312 that the persecutions stopped. Unable to destroy the church through persecution, Satan started a new strategy of corrupting the church from within by joining it to the pagan world political system.

Pergamum represented the third church type and was known as the church that committed adultery with the world political system. Pergamum was the location of Satan's throne and was considered the birthplace of Zeus. Zeus and Aesculapius were actively worshipped there. Zeus' alter was built on a foundation 115 feet high. Satan's throne was relocated to Pergamum when Cyrus conquered Babylon. The Babylonian priesthood that relocated here can be traced back to Nimrod, who founded the Babylonian religion. This religion included the worship of Nimrod's mother/wife Semiramis and their son Tammuz. Semiramis was considered the "Queen of Heaven" and was known in Phoenicia as Ashtoreth. It was Israel's worship of Ashtoreth and Tammuz, and their refusal to repent that led to their first exile. In Egypt, Semiramis and

Tammuz were known as Isis and Horus. In Greece they were known as Aphrodite and Eros. In Rome they were known as Venus and Cupid. Under Roman rule, Pergamum became the center of emperor worship. This Roman religion absorbed the Babylonian religion. In AD 378 under Damasus, the bishop of Rome, the Babylonian religion was transferred into the Roman church. The Roman gods were given the names of the apostles and the names of Venus and Cupid were changed to Mary and Jesus.

Jesus praised the Pergamum Christians for holding fast to their faith, even while dwelling where Satan's seat was. But Jesus chastised them for holding to the teachings of Balaam and Gnosticism, which He hated. Balaam was a prophet-for-hire who taught Balak how to put a stumbling block before Israel to get God to curse them; by using women to entice the Israelites to commit fornication and intermarry. Then they would worship the women's pagan gods and corrupt Israel from within. Gnosticism taught Christians that it was okay to commit sin with the world. This fornication with the world, holding to the doctrines of Gnosticism, and the infiltration of the Babylonian religion, caused a spiritual disaster. Jesus warned the church to repent or He would wage war with them by the sword of His mouth, the Word of God.

During this period, the canon of Scripture was accepted and the doctrines of Gnosticism were declared heretical. Unfortunately, this church continued to play the spiritual harlot, and the Babylonian practices became doctrine. This doctrine included prayers for the dead, adoration of saints and angels, worship of Mary with child and praying to her instead of God. Mass and worship were conducted in Latin, and hell was replaced with a purgatory. Jesus promised that the overcomers would eat of the hidden manna that is the Bread of Life and would be given a white stone of innocence with a new name written upon it. Under the Roman justice system jurors were each given a white stone and a black stone. A white stone was cast if the defendant was deemed innocent.

Thyatira represented the fourth church type and was known as the church that committed adultery with the satanic religion of Babylon. The name *Thyatira* was derived from two words meaning "sacrifice" and "continual". It is the same meaning of the name given to the sacrifice offered during the Roman Catholic mass. As in Pergamum, Thyatira practiced the Babylonian religion and the worship of Zeus. The priests who interpreted the Babylonian doctrines were called Peter. Each "Peter" wore the insignia of the gods Janus and Cybele, which consisted of two keys that represented spiritual authority. It was for this reason that Saint Peter is erroneously thought to control the gates of heaven, determining who goes in and who doesn't.

Like Thyatira, this church absorbed the Babylonian doctrines, out of which came the first institutionalized church called the Roman Catholic Church. Jesus praised the church in Thyatira for their love, faith, service and perseverance. These are the things the Catholic church excels at and it continues to be a stalwart — at least officially — against birth control, homosexuality, the feminization of the church, and the abomination of abortion. It is also active in providing humanitarian aid and caring for orphaned children.

These things aside, the church in Thyatira tolerated the teachings of a woman Jesus called Jezebel, who was a false prophetess who led the faithful astray by committing acts of immorality and eating things sacrificed to idols. Historically, Jezebel had been a wicked queen who married the king of Israel after northern Israel separated from Judah. She worshiped the Babylonian gods and sought to kill all of God's prophets. The woman whom Jesus later called Jezebel represented the false pagan, "dark things of Satan" that were adopted or tolerated by the church. This the Catholic Church has done, and like Jezebel, it is responsible for killing a great many of God's people. It has been given room to repent (1,400 years and counting), but it shows no inclination or desire to do so.

Unlike the previous three church types that passed into history, the Thyatira church type continues to the present. The Catholic Church is destined to increase in power until her final destruction and the death of her offspring during the tribulation period. To the overcomers of this church, who have not partaken of pagan practices during the tribulation, Jesus has promised authority and rule over the nations with a rod of iron when He returns.

The fifth church type was represented by Sardis. It was known as the spiritually dead, carnal church. This was the institutionalized Protestant church that formed after Martin Luther broke from the Catholic Church in AD 1517. This church will continue until its completion during the tribulation. Jesus chastised this church for claiming to be Christian, giving the appearance of having spiritual life when they were really dead. They had never been born of the Holy Spirit. They think, because they attend church, do good deeds or were born into a Christian family that they are saved. Martin Luther broke from the Catholic church to begin cleaning up the heresy of the Catholic church, but the process was never completed. Many Protestant churches have instead fallen back into the same heresy of the Catholic church. Their memberships are declining and losing their youth, yet they can't understand why. To attract new members, these churches have compromised with those who flaunt their sinful lifestyles. They have adopted humanistic beliefs and have even become hostile towards biblical truth. There are those within this church who are still faithful, however, and they are encouraged to be watchful and to strengthen what remains. These few faithful have not defiled their garments and will walk with Christ in white, for they are worthy. To those who refuse to be watchful, Jesus has promised to come like a thief in the night at an hour they will not expect. They will be left behind to endure the terror of Satan's reign during the tribulation. Those who overcome and believe in Jesus Christ unto salvation will be clothed with white garments and their names will not be blotted out of the Book of Life.

The church in Philadelphia, known as the church of brotherly love, represented the sixth church type. This church was the great missionary and evangelical church that came out of the Sardis church in the early eighteenth century. It will remain until the rapture. It started with the great western revivals shortly before the birth of the United States of America. Many of the faithful came to the United States, fleeing the oppression of the state-sponsored protestant churches of Europe. The overcomers of the Sardis church held fast to the truth of the Scriptures and took the good news of God's grace to all the nations. They restored the authority of the Scriptures and brought back the teachings of the imminent return of Jesus Christ and His millennial reign on earth.

Just as Enoch walked with God in faithfulness and was taken up without seeing death after three hundred years had passed (365 years to be exact), so too the church of Philadelphia will be taken up in the rapture about three hundred years after her walk with God began. To the Jews who converted to Christianity and were ostracized by their families, Jesus has promised that those of the synagogue of Satan will bow down at their feet and know that Jesus loved them. To this church, because they have kept the word of His perseverance, He has promised to keep them from the hour of testing that will come upon the whole world. The overcomers in this church will be made the pillars of the temple of God in the New Jerusalem. Upon these pillars of the temple, He will write a new name. They will be given new identities just as Jesus changed Simon's name to Peter.

The final church was Laodicea, known as the materially rich, apostate church. This church type applies to the apostate church that began to come into prominence around AD 1900 and will continue into the tribulation. It represents materially rich churches that are spiritually poor. The city of Laodicea in John's day was a very wealthy city of merchants, bankers and industry. It was known for the lukewarm water brought in by aqueduct from the hot springs of Hierapolis. The city had a famous school of medicine known for its eye ointment. Within the ruins of the city have been found a gymnasium, a large racetrack, three lavish theaters and several bathhouses, indicating that the people liked to be entertained. The city was so wealthy, and lacking nothing, that when it suffered a devastating earthquake, it turned down Rome's offer for aid. They asked for nothing and received nothing in return. The church in the city had a large building, but nothing was known of its ministry. By all appearances, the church was most likely wealthy, self-centered, and liked to be entertained. They added very little to the evangelism and missionary efforts of the early church.

The apostate church of the twentieth and twenty-first centuries mirrors Laodicea exactly. It emerged from the Sardis protestant churches that adopted the theory of evolution, which caused the church leaders to question the authority of the book of Genesis. They gave science a higher authority than God and started reinterpreting the creation account and the world flood to fit the evolutionary consensus. Protestant seminaries started questioning the basic foundations of Christian truth and produced lukewarm church leaders who doubted the Scriptures. These church leaders taught the doctrines of secular humanism and satanic psychology from their pulpits. The congregation soon became indifferent to the foundations of Christianity.

The emergence of the seeker-friendly purpose-driven life and "emergent" churches turned churches into social clubs that appealed to people's emotions and desires rather than their spiritual needs. The leaders of these churches became rich, living extravagant lifestyles through the offerings fleeced from their congregation. The members were deceived into thinking that the Scriptures could not be understood literally and they condemned those who held to the literal interpretation of the Scriptures. They embraced the social cancer of political correctness, claiming it was hateful to remind people of their sinfulness. They considered it harmful to say that people were bound for hell if they didn't believe in Jesus Christ. They mixed in the teaching of new-age pagan theology, eastern mysticism spirituality (something they're calling Spiritual Formation) and the doctines of Satan. Some even tried to mix Islam and Christianity into something they called *Chrislam,* thinking it would promote peace between the two diametrically opposed religions.

The people of this apostate Laodicean church, thinking they had become wise, became fools. Thinking that they were spiritually rich and enlightened, they asked for nothing and became spiritually bankrupt and blind. What they did ask for, they requested for the wrong reasons, expecting God to grant their every wish, like a magic genie in a lamp. They thought they lacked nothing, but they were naked and didn't know it.

Because this church became lukewarm, Jesus said he would spew them out of His mouth. Jesus implored these people to buy from Him "gold refined by fire" that they might be truly rich, to buy white garments to cover the shame of their nakedness and eye salve for their eyes that they might see. He stated that

He rebukes and chastises those He loves, imploring that they be zealous therefore and repent.

Jesus is standing at the door knocking. If anyone opens the door, Jesus will come in and dine with him, and he with Jesus. This church is destined to be left behind in the rapture and will endure the terrors of the tribulation. To those who overcome in the tribulation, either losing their lives for His sake or enduring to the end, He will grant the right to sit with Him on His throne. Though they be left behind in the rapture, those who believe in Jesus Christ during the tribulation will still be just as much a part of the bride of Christ as those taken up in the rapture.

After the seven messages were given to the churches, John was taken up to be shown what must take place afterwards, but he wasn't shown the events leading up to those things. However, in my dream I was given the privilege of seeing them.

According to the prophet Daniel, there would be seven world empires. At the time of Daniel's life, three empires had already passed into history; the Hittite, Egyptian, and Assyrian empires. Babylon was the current world empire and three were yet to come; the Medo-Persian empire, the Greek empire, and the Roman Empire. The Roman Empire was divided into two and eventually dissolved, but it never truly faded away. In the last days, the Roman Empire will be revived in a loose confederacy of ten supernations.

The ten-nation confederacy of the revived Roman Empire won't just happen. It will require three world wars to bring it about. As the church of Philadelphia and the United States rose to prominence, Satan embarked on a new strategy to destroy the Jews and Christians and to establish his last world empire. He devised a two pronged attack to destroy the spiritual will of the people and to control the governments of the world.

The first prong started with the theory of evolution. Charles

Darwin proved to be a willing accomplice. His work provided the vehicle that atheists were looking for to deny God's existence on scientific grounds, thinking they were going to escape accountability. The spread of evolution caused confusion within the church and led many to doubt the authority of the Scriptures. This eventually led to the rise of the Laodicean apostate church. Karl Marx and Nietzsche also proved willing accomplices in establishing atheistic communism and socialism using evolution as justification. Many members of President Abraham Lincoln's administration promoted the teachings of Karl Marx.

The other prong started with the establishment of the ultrasecret Illuminati. It was comprised of thirteen prominent families and a few lesser ones. Through them Satan controlled industry, the media and governments. They infiltrated various secret societies and academia, and they established various political organizations to establish international policy. The Illuminati didn't use *ad hoc* methods to bring in the new world empire they called the New World Order. They drew up a blueprint called "The Protocols of the Learned Elders of Zion". Knowing that this would eventually become known and cause an uprising, they established a front man to take the fall and made it look like the Illuminati had become a thing of the past. Through him, they leaked the Protocols and intentionally made it look like a Jewish conspiracy to take over the world. Of course, there was never a Jewish conspiracy to take over the world, but the world didn't know that. An uprising occurred and great sums of money were spent by the Jews to discredit and dismiss the Protocols as a fraud. The public was eventually convinced that it was a fraud and it passed out of public consciousness. To this day it's still believed to be a fraud and those who claim otherwise are ridiculed. The Illuminati was then free to follow the Protocols without anyone the wiser for it.

Three world wars were planned to bring about the New World Order. Before the concept of communism and Nazism were known, they had been planned for well ahead of time. The first world war was fought to destroy the Russian Czars and establish Russia as a stronghold for atheistic communism. Differences between the British and German empires were used to start the war. The second world war was started using the controversies between Nazi fascism and political Zionism. It was fought to strengthen communism and to keep Christianity in check until the final required social cataclysm. It was also a catalyst for reestablishing the nation of Israel. The third world war was planned to start over the controversies of political Zionism and Islam. The plan was for them to completely destroy each other while the rest of the nations fight each other into a state of complete physical, mental, spiritual and economic exhaustion. The stage will then be set to establish a one-world government.

In the decades leading up to the third world war, social policies were put into place as planned in the Protocols to condition the world to accept the New World Order. Political correctness was invented to control how people thought, spoke and acted. The drug wars, public school shootings, and the war on terror were instigated to justify restricting the rights of the people, disarming the public and establishing a police state in the name of national security. In my dream, I saw that climate change, overpopulation and industrial environmental abuse seemed to justify the Agenda 21 agreement to override government sovereignty, and control resources and land use. Students had been brainwashed with a revised history, and the puppet liberal media had brainwashed the public into thinking that progressive socialism was the direction the world needed to go for mankind to evolve. Due to Islamic influence, the United Nations determined that Israel was a threat to world peace and used the puppet liberal media to stir up the nations against Israel.

In Israel there had already been limited fighting. Eight times now, Israel's neighbors had tried to destroy her. World War III is now staring us in the face with the possible fulfillment of the Psalm 83 prayer of Asaph. Psalm 83 was more of a prayer than a prophecy. Nowhere in this prayer does God state anything in the prayer will come about. But we know God answers all prayer, though not necessarily how we would like them to be answer. Sometimes "no" is answer, and sometimes "wait" or "not yet" is an answer. This is one prayer that has yet to be answered.

In my dream, WWIII was the answer to that prayer. This dream didn't actually show me what started the war, but I was given the impression it had something to do with the Temple Mount in which the Muslims launched a flagitious, false flag operation in which thousands of their own people were sacrificed. The nature of the attack automatically put the blame on Israel and justified a retaliatory invasion. The destruction of the Muslim's third holiest site, united the Arabs against Israel more than anything else could have. But an Iranian attack on the middle-east oil fields divided the Arab forces leaving Israel's nearest neighbors to continue the war without full Arab backing. The sinking of a US aircraft carrier in the Persian Gulf dragged the US into the middle-east war. As Israel fought for her life, Arab and US forces fought Iran and Russia for control of the Persian Gulf region.

However WWIII starts, it will surely be a nuclear war. In my dreams, I saw this war as the fulfillment of Damascus' prophesied destruction. The Muslim Brotherhood controlled Syrian government had just launched a barrage of missiles carrying chemical weapons at Israel in retaliation for the destruction of the Temple Mount. Israel, in turn, carried out its promise to reduce Damascus to a pile of rubble.

It was a typical early-winter sunset over the city of Damascus, Syria. The call for maghrib salat, the fourth prayer at sunset, was heard throughout the city as people gathered at the mosques. The Syrian military radar operators, monitoring hundreds of aircraft in the air, noticed several targets appear out of nowhere. They flew at a speed of Mach 5 and followed a direct path toward Damascus. Syrian anti-missile and anti-aircraft batteries were unable to stop the ones that mattered. Most of the incoming missiles were decoys. A few were not. Twelve made it through. Twelve was more than enough.

At a thousand feet above the ground, the first missile detonated directly over the Al Manshieh garden, a flash of extremely bright light illuminated the valley for several seconds. Several more detonations occurred around the city. The light from these detonations was so bright it made the sun appear dark. When the light dimmed, several fireballs about 3,600 feet wide rose skyward above the city. With temperatures within each fireball reaching tens of millions of degrees, every person and structure within a half-mile radius of each blast was instantly incinerated. The intense heat instantly ignited every combustible material within a three-mile radius.

While the fireballs rose skyward, a shockwave having a density of thousands of pounds per square inch separated from the fireballs and raced outward at speeds several times the speed of sound. As it spread outward, it swept up everything not tied down. The overpressure from the shockwaves collapsed people's lungs and ruptured eardrums. Buildings imploded as structures were crushed and ripped from their foundations. Past the three-mile mark, the shockwaves slowed to the speed of sound and lost density as they spread out. Immediately behind the shockwaves came a wall of thermal radiation, with wind speeds near five hundred miles per hour. The heat of this wall of fire ignited ruptured fuel tanks, gas lines, and combustible material. Trees were scorched and stripped of their branches. People who survived the crushing shockwave suffered fifth-degree burns, as their flesh was torn from their bodies like melted wax.

The fireballs rose skyward and expanded, producing a vacuum below them. The air and dust that were pushed away by the initial blasts, now rushing toward the fireballs and following them upward, forming the stem of the mushroom clouds. The clouds continued to expand upward and outward like an opening parasol, reaching heights of sixty thousand to seventy thousand feet. The expanding clouds, glowing in the failing evening light, lingered for hours.

When the blasts dissipated, all that was left of Damascus was a smoking, radioactive wasteland. In an area outward to about three miles from ground zero of each blast the land was littered with the skeletal remains of thousands of people, and the debris of blown-apart buildings and vehicles. All that remained standing were the twisted steel frameworks of dozens of high-rise buildings, a few thick stone walls and blackened bare tree trunks.

Damascus had been the worlds oldest continuously inhabited city in which 2.5 million people lived. With twelve one-megaton, near-surface explosions, the city was virtually destroyed, and almost two million people lost their lives. Hundreds of thousands more died in the following weeks from nuclear radiation sickness. The radioactive fallout rendered the entire valley uninhabitable.

Come morning, nothing living moved among the ruins. Years would pass before the radio-active debris would be removed and new plant growth could be seen. After the attack on Damascus, the rest of the world was pulled into the war. A North Korean and Chinese nuclear electromagnetic pulse (EMP) strike against the United States and the resultant US retaliatory strikes plunged half the world into darkness. As planned, the nations fought each other into a state of economic, physical and spiritual exhaustion.

By the end of the war, Israel remained standing and occupied half of Syria, Lebanon, Jordan, and all the Palestinian lands. The Palestinians ceased to be a distinct people (not that they ever were one), and the Muslims were reduced to insignificance. Egypt was not included in Asaph's prayer but it still joined the attack on Israel. Though it was defeated, it was not destroyed or occupied like Israel's other neighboring nations. The destruction of Israel's neighbors brought peace to Israel for the first time since its rebirth and lulled Israel into a false sense of security. Out of the ashes of the nuclear war, a loose ten-nation confederacy arose and the worlds religious institutions merged into a one world religion, thinking this would guarantee world peace.

Currently, the world sees the true Christian church as a threat to their power base, and seeks to destroy her. Before the rapture, she endures increasing persecution, which strengthens the believers, and exposes the pretenders. To save their own skins, the pretenders readily deny their faith in Jesus Christ. It also endures the horrors of World War III and witnesses the rise of the ten-nation confederacy. As God promised the church of Philadelphia, it will not go through the time of testing in the tribulation. The rapture, however, is not an imminent event. There is no event that must proceed it and can happen at any time when the people least expect it.

In the blink of an eye, millions of true believers in Jesus Christ around the world vanished from the earth. The graves of the believers opened, the earth yielded the ashes of the cremated believers and the sea gave up their dissolved bodies. The dead in Christ rose up first and their souls were reunited with their resurrected bodies. An instant later, the still-living believers in Christ were caught up in the air with them. They left behind their clothing, electronics and accessories. The handicapped left behind their wheel chairs and prosthetics. Both the living and the dead arrived in the clouds wearing gloriously white linen garments with whole and perfect bodies. Of the adults, regardless of their age, they all appeared to be in their mid-thirties and they glowed with an inner beauty.

These were then taken into heaven where their works were judged by fire. The good works emerged purified like gold and silver while the bad works burned up like wood and straw. What remained was then presented to Jesus who rewarded them accordingly. No one was denied entry into the kingdom of God regardless of how few works they had, for salvation is guaranteed to those who believe in Jesus Christ by faith alone, not by works.

On earth, pandemonium wreaked havoc on the world as true Christians who were driving cars or trucks, flying aircraft, controlling air traffic, operating or repairing machinery, fighting fires, delivering babies or working in their offices suddenly disappeared. People freaked out as the believers they were talking to or the young children they were holding disappeared before their very eyes.

In the aftermath thousands died as pilotless aircraft fall from the sky and driverless vehicles plow into other vehicles, structures or power poles knocking out the power grid. Chaos broke out in every hospital, as every baby disappeared into thin air—some while still in the womb. Families were bereaved of their children, as every child under the age of accountability also disappeared. By the end of the week, the world's stock markets plummeted thousands of points, as insurance premiums skyrocketed and the industrial world came to a grinding halt. But that was just the start of it. The repercussions were felt for months and years to come.

Once the initial shock of the disappearances wore off, the trauma of the aftermath and the mourning for the missing began.

Among the social and political psyches, there was mixed reaction. Some were gripped by panic, thinking that aliens from another planet have attacked. Others rejoiced thinking that those same aliens finally came to remove the malcontents so mankind could evolve to the next spiritual level. Most people were in between these extremes and, having no understanding of what had just happened, fell into a state of confusion and despair. For many, time itself came to a standstill, as they wondered what might happen next. Even in places where very few disappeared, the ripple effects of the rapture were felt.

Regardless of what people choose to believe, the true cause was immediately rejected. To believe that Jesus came and raptured His church required people to believe that God existed after all. This required them to acknowledge that they were accountable for their sins. This intolerable condition lead the world to ridicule those who espoused the rapture. Many of those who put their faith in Jesus after the rapture were beaten and killed for daring to suggest that Jesus would take their innocent children from them. Many regarded the rapture as a type of death and refused to believe that a loving God would kill their children. It proved much easier to believe that aliens from another planet were responsible. People were especially indignant at being called sinners who were about to suffer the wrath of God. They considered this as hate speech deserving of death.

The worse persecution didn't come from the unbelievers but from pastors, ministers, and theologians of the institutionalized church who thought they were Christians. They interpreted Scripture allegorically and had long ago rejected the notion of a physical rapture of the church. Ignoring the teachings of 1 Thessalonians 4:13–18 and Revelation 3:10, they have insisted that nowhere in the Bible is the rapture taught. They didn't have an answer for what happened but they reasoned that if they were still here, this was not the rapture. They give the loudest ridicule to those who claimed the rapture occurred. They especially pounced on new believers saying that they had no proper understanding of Scripture. Those making dogmatic assertions about the rapture were considered heretics, and many were ostracized or put to death.

Few realized that, at the rapture, the "age of grace" or the "church age" came to an end, just as miraculously as it started. The rapture didn't mark the beginning of the tribulation, but it did mark the fulfillment of the age of the Gentiles that the apostle Paul spoke of in the book of Romans. At the rapture, the restraining influence of the Holy Spirit of God was removed from the earth and the spirit of Antichrist unleashed. With the spirit of Antichrist released, the world soon experienced evil such as it had never experienced since the days of Noah before the world flood. With the ending of the age of grace, the age of the law under Israel returned until the final week of years was fulfilled at the return of Jesus Christ.

Chapter 9
The Second Coming of Jesus Christ

As if the previous dream hadn't been disturbing enough, the eighth dream kept me awake for days. It took up where the previous one left off. It isn't possible to know the details of how Bible prophecy will unfold, apart from what has been revealed. In my dream, however, this is how it unfolded.

Upon receiving the messages to the seven churches, John looked and beheld a door that opened to heaven. He heard a voice like a trumpet saying, "Come up here, and I will show what must take place after these things." Just as the church will be taken up at this point in prophecy, so John too was taken up in the spirit. He immediately beheld a throne in heaven on which the Father was seated. No man in the flesh can behold the Father and live, but John was in the spirit. Thus he did not perish. Even so, he wasn't able to see the Father directly.

The Father sat on the throne, hidden by the radiance of a thousand suns. Around the throne was a rainbow that had the appearance of an emerald. Seated around the throne were twenty-four elders, clothed with white garments and wearing golden crowns on their heads. From the throne came flashes of lightning and peals of thunder. Before the throne stood seven lampstands of burning fire, which were the seven aspects of the Holy Spirit.

There was also a sea of glass like crystal with four living creatures in the center full of eyes. The first creature was like a lion and the second like a calf; the third had a face like a man, and the fourth was like a flying eagle. Each creature had six wings and was full of eyes around and within. They continuously said, day and night, "Holy, holy, holy is the Lord God Almighty, who is, and who was, and who is to come."

Each time they gave glory and honor and thanks to the One seated on the throne, the twenty-four elders fell in worship of Him, casting their crowns before Him. They stated, "Worthy art Thou, our Lord and our God, to receive glory and honor and power; for Thou didst create all things, and because of Thy will they existed and were created."

As you'll recall from the second dream, the earth had been yielded to Satan when Adam rebelled against God. The conditions for redeeming the earth from Satan were written on a scroll and sealed with seven seals. John noticed that same scroll was now in the right hand of the Father.

A strong angel proclaimed with a loud voice, "Who is worthy to open the scroll and break its seals?" No one was found in heaven, or on or under the earth, who was worthy to break the seals, for all have sinned and fallen short of the glory of God. Even the angels who had not sinned could not open the scroll for only a kinsman redeemer could open it. John wept, for no one was found worthy. Was there no hope for mankind? The twenty-four elders told him to stop weeping. The Lion of Judah, the Root of David, had overcome, so as to break the seals and open the scroll.

Between the throne and the four living creatures stood a

Lamb as if slain. It had seven horns and seven eyes, which were the seven Spirits of God sent out into the world. The seven Spirits—or seven aspects of the Holy Spirit as stated by Isaiah—were the Spirit of the Lord, the Spirit of wisdom, the Spirit of understanding, the Spirit of counsel, the Spirit of strength, the Spirit of knowledge and the Spirit of the fear of the Lord.

The Lamb who was slain took the scroll from the Father seated on the throne, and the four living creatures and twenty-four elders fell down before the Lamb, each having a harp and bowls of incense containing the prayers of the saints. They sang a new song of adoration, affirming that He was the Son of God who had been slain and had paid the price for the purchase of mankind from sin with His blood. To all those of every nation, tribe or tongue who agreed to partake of the new covenant He'd made with the church, He gave the right to be called children of God. Those who did not agree were called the children of Satan. Myriads and myriads of angels joined in the song of praise, as did every created being in heaven and on earth.

From this point, John was shown future events as seen from heaven. In my dream, I saw how they happened from an earthly viewpoint. The Lamb broke the first seal, and one of the four living creatures said to John, "Come." John beheld a white horse and he who sat on it was given a bow and a crown, and was sent out conquering and to conquer. He had a bow but no arrows indicating that he controlled the worlds weapons of war, but he didn't conquer by the use of these weapons. Rather it was by peace that he would destroy many. This rider was given a victor's garland as ruler of the world. He was none other than the false messiah who would become the beast Antichrist.

On earth, I saw him arise as a prominent player of the European Union prior to the start of WWIII. His nation appointed him an ambassador to the United Nations general assembly where he made a name for himself by providing an answer to the world's financial and economic crisis following the war.

Following the formation of the ten-nation confederacy, he was instrumental in reforming the United Nations to reflect this change. The ten super-nations replaced the nineteen nations of the Security Counsel and a parliament replaced the General Assembly. Eventually he was elected the United Nations Secretary General. Upon taking the oath of office, he insisted the world refer to him as Lord Maitreya (pronounced "My-tray-ah"). Maitreya, of course, wasn't his name. It was the occultic title for "messiah". By calling himself "Lord", he claimed to be God, and by taking the title of "Maitreya", he claimed to be the messiah that the world was looking for. Six months later an Israeli ambassador to the UN was elected as the Secretariat who presided over the parliament. The new Secretariat was a former rabbi and university professor in Jerusalem. He was destined to become the False Prophet. Shortly after taking the oath of office, Maitreya commissioned the rebuilding of Babylon in Iraq to be the new UN headquarters. His election as the UN Secretary General (SG), however, was not without opposition. Three of the ten leaders of the confederacy opposed him and rose up in rebellion against him.

The Lamb broke the second seal and the second living creature said to John, "Come." Another horse, a red one, went out. Its rider was granted the power to take peace from the earth and was given a great sword. In my dream, this rider was symbolic of the demonic prince of Russia, Gog. He went out leading a Muslim uprising in a surprise attack on Israel and making war that men would slay each other.

Immediately afterwards, the third seal was broken, and a black horse and rider came forth. This rider was carrying a pair of scales and was told to measure out a quart of wheat for a denarius, and three quarts of barley for a denarius; but not to harm the oil and wine.

Coming out after him when the fourth seal was broken was a sickly, pale green horse whose rider was called Death, and Hades followed after him. These three were given authority over a fourth of the world to kill with sword, famine, pestilence, and wild beasts. Children born after the rapture were especially susceptible to these things.

For several years following WWIII, Israel lived in peace and what they thought was safety. During these same years Israel became prosperous as she broke Russia's monopoly on natural gas sales to Europe. Through hydraulic fracturing technology called fracking, she was able to extract oil from her shale deposits and became the second largest exporter of oil, deeply cutting into OPEC's profits. Russia's desire for this wealth and the Muslims desire for Israel's destruction were hooks put in Gog's jaw to bring him against Israel.

Since Maitreya became the UN SG, the world experienced relative peace while Maitreya consolidated his power base. But the ten-nation confederacy was loosely united. Not all the nation's leaders, whom Maitreya referred to as kings, were completely supportive of Maitreya. Particularly those of the Russian Federation which included eastern Europe, the African Union, China, the Association of South East Asian Nations (ASEAN) which included India, and the Arab Confederacy which included Iran and Turkey. During the last three years, the kings of the Russian Federation, the African Union and the Arab Confederacy secretly built up their military strength and made plans to invade Israel.

At the Lord's timing, Russia and its allies invaded israel. This invasion was permitted that the Lord would reveal Himself to the world and that Israel would see that God had not abandoned her and is still her God. When the attack came neither Israel not the world expected an attack. The whole world was completely taken by surprise. It helped that they were distracted by certain signs in the heavens. The kings of the New European Union and the North American Union made diplomatic protests against the invasion. They demanded a reason for it and accused Russia of seeking riches.

The Russian led coalition invaded Israel by land, sea and air. The Israeli Defense Forces fought valiantly for several days but were pushed back on every side. Eventually Jerusalem was surrounded and Israel looked on the verge of defeat. During their desperate hour the Lord God intervened. With earthquakes, torrential rains, hail and fire from heaven, the Lord caused confusion among the invaders so that they turned on each other and defeated themselves. The Russian forces attempted to destroy Jerusalem with nuclear weapons but the missiles only detonated over their own people causing further confusion. At the Lord's intervention aircraft fell from the sky and the warships attacked each other and destroyed themselves. The surviving ships ended up beached and abandoned on the shores of Israel.

At the same time this war was being fought, the three kings of the invasion forces rose up against Maitreya and attempted to assassinate him. The UN Secretariat, who called himself Elijah, led the secret police to defend Maitreya and defeated the attempted coup. The ensuing fight left Elijah blind in his right eye and one arm hung uselessly by his side. This fulfilled the prophecy of Zechariah 11:17 that states, "Woe to the worthless shepherd who leaves his flock! A sword will be on his arm and on his right eye. His arm will be totally withered and his right eye will be blind."

With the three kings imprisoned, Maitreya led the NATO forces in defense of Israel. They arrived just as the invaders were starting to flee. The NATO forces ran down the fleeing invaders and destroyed them. While the Lord defeated Israel's enemies, Maitreya took credit and rode into Jerusalem triumphantly.

During the Gog invasion of Israel, the Muslims attempted to force sharia law on the European people as huge riots and violent clashes raged across the country. This uprising spread throughout the European nations and into North America. America had experienced a huge increase in Muslims in the last few years which now accounted for over a third of the population. The ensuing religious civil wars in Europe and America caused disruptions in crop production and food distribution, causing hyperinflation of food prices. It cost a man a day's wage to pay for a day's meal. Famine and disease spread throughout the land as food became scarce. The rich, however, were still able to afford and obtain their luxury and prepackage foods and wine.

True Christians had no part in the religious civil wars, but because of their intolerance for other religions, they were blamed for instigating the war. At the breaking of the fifth seal, they became the target of hate as the world church and government-sponsored persecution resulted in the deaths of millions of post-rapture Christians. They were rounded up and put into concentration camps around the world where they were systematically murdered by all manner of atrocious methods. The preferred method of the world government was beheading on a guillotine.

True Christianity, the Bible and proselytizing were subsequently outlawed. Millions of "pretend" Christians were forced to make a choice; to follow Christ wholeheartedly or to deny Him. Sadly, millions took the cowardly way out and denied the name of Jesus. The millions that refused to recant their faith in Jesus Christ faced persecution and death not seen since the first century. Not being properly discipled, these post-rapture Christians had never learned the love of Jesus. Like John before he learned what it meant to love, they sought justice and vengeance. In heaven, the martyred Christians were given white robes and were told to be patient until the number of their fellow servants to be killed was completed.

At Gog's defeat, the Israelites saw this was the hand of God who came to their defense. But Maitreya presented himself as the conquering messiah they've been waiting for whom the Lord sent to defeat their enemies. He brokered a seven year peace treaty between the Jews and the Muslims with him acting as Israel's protector. Control of the Temple Mount, however, remained in contention. The Muslims wanted to rebuild the Dome of the Rock while the Jews wanted to rebuild their temple so they could properly observe the Laws of Moses. As a compromise, Maitreya gave control of the Temple Mount to the world church. The Jews were permitted to build their temple in the center, the Muslims were permitted to rebuild the Al Aqsa mosque at the southern end, while the world church built a cathedral on the northern end. The Jewish temple was built with an inner sanctuary and an inner court, but without an outer court. The outer court was to be trampled by the gentiles for the next forty two months before the Abomination of Desolation was erected. Around the world millions of Jews became zealous of observing the Laws of Moses and in the coming years returned to Israel to properly worship God and make their sacrifices.

After brokering the seven year peace treaty, even though Maitreya wasn't of Arab descent or a Muslim, the Muslims recognized him as their long awaited Twelfth Imam, the Al Mahdi who was prophesied to return and deliver them from a catastrophic war. Maitreya, after all, was a man of all faiths (except Christianity). Elijah was recognized as their returned Jesus who served the Al Mahdi.

Just prior to the signing of the covenant, the three kings

that rebelled against Maitreya were publicly put to death and the remaining seven kings yielded their crowns to him, giving him complete control of the entire world. The kings of the east (China and Southeast Asia), however, did so reluctantly. Though they both shared animosity toward Maitreya, they were not friends by any means. In fact, there was a great deal of contention between them. The formal signing of the seven year covenant marked the beginning of the seven year tribulation, which corresponded to he Lamb's breaking of the sixth seal. The sixth seal announced that the "Day of the Lord" had arrived.

In the weeks prior to the Gog invasion of Israel, a previously undetected comet appeared. The comet was a spectacular sight, having three tails of different colors. The comet produced the signs in the heavens that distracted the people's attention from Israel and the impending invasion. The people were assured the comet would not collide with the earth but their attention was riveted to the sky.

On the day the covenant was signed, the comet made a near-miss pass of the earth, coming within a few thousand miles. As the earth passed through the tails, the ejecta burned up in the atmosphere looking like falling stars. Some of those ejecta reached the ground causing much destruction and wreaking havoc among the people. Suddenly, a great earthquake shook the entire planet. The comet didn't cause the quake, but its passing was timed by the Lord to coincide with the great earthquake and the signing of the covenant. So great was this quake that mountains and islands moved from their places. Entire continents moved as the mid-oceanic ridges experienced rapid spreading.

Of all the mid-oceanic ridges, the Mid-Atlantic Ridge experienced the greatest spreading, particularly in the North Atlantic. Between North America and Europe, the Atlantic ocean widened by a little over a hundred miles. The southeastern section of England from Portsmouth to Dover collapsed into the sea taking half of London with it. In the eastern Mediterranean, several islands in the Aegean Sea disappeared, and the Bosporus at Istanbul was closed when the land rose and cut off access to the Black Sea.

While the North American Plate and the Eurasian Plate were pushed away from each other in the Atlantic, they pushed against each other in Siberia. This put pressure on the Siberian Steps, the location of the worlds largest super-volcano that covered an area about the size of Alaska. The pressure caused hundreds of vents to open and release copious amounts of greenhouse gases into the atmosphere. Alaska and Siberia were pushed closer together and the Bering Sea landbridge emerged from the sea.

The movement of the North American plate caused the roof of the Yellowstone caldera to collapse. This triggered a massive eruption that destroyed everything within a five-hundred-mile radius and covered most of North America with as much as five inches of ash. Yellowstone wasn't the only super-volcano in North America to erupt. The Long Valley caldera at Mammoth Mountain, California, had been showing signs of building up to an eruption since the 1980s. The Long Valley caldera was North America's second-largest super-volcano. The movement of the North American Plate weakened the growing dome enough that the volcano violently erupted, adding its ash to Yellowstone's ash. The natural beauty of Yosemite National Park that bordered the caldera and nearby Kings Canyon and Sequoia National Parks was instantly obliterated. In addition to the eruption of the two largest super-volcanoes in North America, great rifts opened up and divided the land.

The nearby town of Fresno in the San Joaquin Valley was buried in ash but the people had little time to concern themselves with it. The movement of the North American plate caused the entire San Joaquin and Sacramento Valleys to drop below sea level allowing sea water to rush in from the San Francisco Bay. At the same time the El Centro Valley rift, which the Salton Sea east of San Diego was part of, opened southward to the Gulf of California and northward along the San Andreas fault past the south base of the San Bernardino Mountains and into the Los Angeles Basin. The rift continued north through the Cajon Pass along the northern base of the San Gabriel Mountains, cutting through the Tehachapi Mountains and connecting with the sunken San Joaquin Valley. Baja California northward to the Santa Rosa Mountains and the Coastal Ranges north of Los Angeles to San Francisco became two separate islands. San Diego, though leveled by the quake, was still intact, but Los Angeles was divided in half and was mostly under water.

The southeastern section of the former United States didn't move at the same rate as the rest of the continent. This caused the failed Midcontinent Rift to open from the western end of Lake Superior through central Minnesota, south through the center of Iowa, turning west into the southeastern corner of Nebraska, and into Kansas. The cities of St. Paul and Minneapolis, Minnesota, along with Des Moines, Iowa, and Omaha, Nebraska, collapsed into the rift along with numerous small towns in its path. The rift immediately began filling with water from Lake Superior and the numerous inflowing rivers. The Missouri River south of the rift partially reversed its flow until it dried up. The Mississippi River was cut off from it's headwaters, but other rivers flowing into it kept it flowing. It was rerouted in several places, however—particularly along the New Madrid Fault between St. Louis and Memphis. A small rift opened along the fault, which the Mississippi River promptly filled.

South of the equator, South America tried to move farther away from Africa but was impeded by the Nazca Plate, which was trying to push away from the Pacific Plate. This pushed up the Andes Mountains several hundred feet higher and devastated the western coastlines of South America. Because South America was impeded by the Nazca Plate, it didn't move as far as the North American Plate did. The Caribbean Plate was squeezed between the North American Plate and the South American Plate like a squashed meatball, resulting in a number of Caribbean Islands disappearing beneath the sea. Central America was also torn from South America at Panama, leaving an open seaway several miles wide where the canal was formerly located.

The Pacific Plate tried to move westward but the whole plate couldn't move at the same rate. Some parts of it moved slower than other parts. Slippage occurred along the transform faults, called *fracture zones*, causing the seafloor to sink in some areas and rise in others. This produced a number of tsunamis racing in all directions across the Pacific. Uneven slippage along the Tuamotu and Austral fracture zones caused several Polynesian coral atolls, which were only a few feet above sea level to begin with, to slip beneath the waves, taking thousands of people with them.

As the Pacific Plate tried to move westward, it was subducted beneath the eastward moving plates. The Philippines were about the only lands that didn't move, but more land was added to them. The Philippine Plate, caught between the Pacific Plate and the Eurasian Plate, was pushed upward as the Pacific Plate was subducted under it, merging the islands of Luzon, Leyte and Mindanao. But in the west, other islands disappeared, as the Philippine Plate was subducted under the Eurasian Plate.

Southward, as the Pacific Plate was subducted under the Australian Plate, two more super-volcanoes erupted. The Toba caldera in Sumatra, Indonesia, and New Zealand's Taupo caldera. As with the Yellowstone and Long Valley calderas, each one spewed enough ash and greenhouse gases to cause a mass die-off of plants and animals around the world.

Like the Philippines, the continent of Africa didn't move that much. The great Rift Valley in East Africa, however, did drop a couple thousand feet and partially filled with water doubling the size of Lake Victoria. The poles were by no means immune to the earth's contortions. Under the Arctic Ocean, undersea volcanoes erupted, which gradually warmed up the water and started the ice caps melting. In the Antarctic, Antarctica was literally torn about which direction to turn as Lesser Antarctica was ripped asunder from Greater Antarctica.

This was the first judgment the world recognized as coming from God. The people were so fearful that they hid in holes in the ground and called on the mountains and rocks to fall on them to hide them from the face of the Father who sits on the throne. Tens of millions perished in the great sixth-seal quake.

Following the breaking of the sixth seal, there was an interlude in heaven before the seventh seal was broken, to give mankind another opportunity to repent. But, even knowing that the sixth-seal judgment was of God, they still did not repent and give Him the glory.

During the interlude, four angels stood at the four corners of the earth and held back the four winds so that no wind blew on the earth. The four corners of the earth were the four compass points. One angel stood to the north and another to the east, one to the south and another to the west. The four winds they held back were the four major jet streams. Without any wind blowing, the ash thrown up by the volcanic eruptions fell back to the earth much quicker than normal. This buried surviving crops, causing further food shortages and famine. The angels holding back the four winds were granted the power to harm the earth, the sea and the trees, but they were instructed not to harm them until the bondservants of God were sealed in their foreheads.

John heard the number of them was 144,000; twelve thousand from each tribe of Israel except the tribe of Dan. The two half-tribes of Joseph made up the difference. There are many who say that all but three of the tribes of Israel have been lost. Perhaps to man they are, but not to God. He knows precisely where each and everyone of them is.

These 144,000 Israelites were sealed so no harm would come to them by the four angels empowered to harm the earth and the sea. These would be the witnesses of God during the years of Jacobs trouble, the final seven years of Israel's seventy weeks of years. These people would take the gospel of Jesus Christ to the world during the tribulation and complete the commission Jesus gave to the apostles as recorded in Matthew 10. The apostles had only been able to complete half the commission. The other half was reserved to be fulfilled during the tribulation. These witnesses were faithful witnesses of God who were separate from the church and followed Jesus wherever He went. Their ministry continued throughout the tribulation bringing millions to Jesus Christ. Most of those new Christians ended up losing their lives for believing in the Christ.

As John stood watching, a multitude of people from every tribe, tongue and nation on earth appeared before the throne, wearing white robes and holding palm branches. These sang praises to God as they waved the palm branches. It was explained to John that these were those who had come out of the tribulation. These were the fruits of the 144,000 witnesses.

The world earthquake of the sixth seal announced the coming day of the Lord. At the signing of the covenant, Israel continued to play the harlot to the world. Mankind was united under a single world religion that became increasingly intolerant towards true Christianity. The breaking of the seventh seal brought the judgments of God upon mankind who refused to repent and believe in the name of the Son of God.

At the breaking of the seventh seal, there was silence in heaven for half an hour, while seven trumpets were given to seven angels. How long this silence will last on earth is unknown. In my dream it lasted the first three years of the tribulation.

On earth during this time the civil war in Europe and America lasted a year and a half to two years before peace was restored. The sixth-seal quake added to the conflagration as the Muslims attempted to take advantage of the chaos the quake caused and tried to overthrow their respective governments. After the Muslims were defeated, a pseudo-peace followed as the world recovered from the wars and the sixth-seal quake. Though the world would never fully recover from the sixth-seal quake, it wasn't long before the quake passed into history and became a distant memory.

In Israel, seven months were spent cleaning up the wars aftermath and burying the dead. In a valley east of the Dead Sea in Jordan, the army of Gog was buried. The valley became known as the Valley of Hamon Gog. A town was built in the valley known as Hamonah. Professional contractors were hired to clean up the radioactive land and wreckage. Whenever a body part was found, a marker was placed by it to be retrieved and properly buried. Enough nuclear weapons and fuel was recovered to provide Israel with enough nuclear energy to last seven years. These things were done as prophesied in Ezekiel 38 and 39.

As time passed without any further judgments, the people forgot about God and concentrated on becoming gods themselves. The Jews became more zealous about observing the Laws of Moses and worshipping God. Elijah, however, insisted they observed the Kabbalah instead of the Torah and instigated Jew on

Jew persecution against those who would not comply. The world church became more intolerant of true Christians who would not submit to the church. It increased in power and wielded great influence in the world government. Maitreya grew to detest the Pope for the influence he wielded over him and longed to be rid of the world church. The rest of the world both loved and hated the world church. They wanted to partake of its riches but hated the control it had over their lives.

For the Christians, and other undesirables, who survived the fifth-seal judgment it was hell on earth. Persecution was severe—particularly from the world church—as many had to go into hiding and live like animals. They were hunted down like animals and put into concentration camps. Those that weren't murdered were made into slave labor or used for hideous medical experiments. The world during the first half of the tribulation remarkably resembled Nazi Germany prior to WWII.

During this period, the silence in heaven was like the silence of a courtroom just prior to the passing of judgment. Another angel took a censer containing the prayers of the saints, filled it with fire from the altar and cast it upon the earth. The prayers of the saints were about to be answered and judgment poured out on those who had persecuted and killed the saints of God. The saints were those whom God declared righteous when they put their faith in Jesus Christ, not those rewarded for righteous deeds by the Catholic church.

The casting of the censer on earth was followed by flashes of lightning, peals of thunder, and an earthquake. The inhabitants of the earth had no idea of the significance of the event, but it reminded the people that God was still there and many cowered in fear.

The seven angels with the trumpets stood prepared to sound them. When the first trumpet sounded, hail and fire mixed with blood were thrown to the earth, and a third of the trees and all the green grass was burned up. When the second trumpet sounded, a mountain burning with fire was cast into the sea. A third of the sea turned to blood, a third of the sea creatures died, and a third of the ships were destroyed. When the third trumpet sounded, a great star burning like a torch fell from heaven. The star was called "Wormwood." It fell on a third of the rivers and streams, and the water became bitter. When the fourth trumpet sounded, a third of the sun, moon, and stars was darkened. The day and night were both darkened by a third.

With six months remaining of the first half of the tribulation, the first four trumpets sounded in quick succession. These announced four effects of a single catastrophic event—the effects of a large comet impacting the earth. While John watched from heaven, there was pandemonium on the earth.

Three years after its first near miss of the earth during the sixth-seal quake, the comet was now on its return trip. This time it was on an intercept course with the earth. The comet, which scientists were now calling "Wormwood," became visible to the unaided eye. As the third year of the tribulation ended, the comet was now on its outbound course, moving away from the sun, tail first. Unlike other comets that circled the sun in a counterclockwise direction like the planets do, this one circled the sun in a clockwise direction.

Already the people were expressing concern about the comet's possible collision with the earth. The scientists assured the public the second visitation would not be as disastrous as the first. They lied through their teeth, saying the comet would not hit the earth.

In their official report, the scientists indicated that the comet was traveling at speeds of forty-five miles per second (144,000 miles per hour) and they estimated the size of the comet's nucleus of about thirty miles in diameter with a coma ten times that size. This comet was unusual in that it had three tails. Its primary tail was measured at about a million miles long, while the other two tails were half that length. The primary tail was the usual white, but the other tails were red and yellow. The head of the comet had a slightly reddish appearance. This comet was a true monster, leading the scientists to conclude that the impact would be an extinction level event.

As the comet drew closer to the earth, people began hoarding supplies, as it became evident that the scientists and government were wrong. Store shelves emptied within hours and rioting broke out. Stores and warehouses were looted and set on fire. Maitreya declared martial law and ordered the civil defense forces and militias to put down the rioting. They were given orders to shoot to kill those who would not comply with the law.

While all this was going on, the comet's primary tail reached the earth, as ejecta burned up in the atmosphere and produced a spectacular light show in the heavens. The comet, by this time, looked like a second sun visible in daylight. The closer the comet came, the larger the ejecta became. Some were beginning to reach the ground and produce huge explosions. They set cities on fire and produced wildfires that burned uncontrollably all around the earth. One of those ejecta, about the size of a football field, hit San Francisco and exploded with a force equivalent to twenty megatons of TNT. The explosion decimated an area about a hundred miles in diameter.

After bombarding the earth with ejecta for a month, the comet finally reached the earth's Roche limit, the point at which large heavenly bodies break up above the atmosphere from a difference of gravitational forces exerted upon it. The comet Wormwood almost passed through the Roche limit unaffected, but thermal stress and an increase in internal gas pressure caused the comet to break up into five large pieces and a few smaller ones. Most of the small pieces never reached the ground before burning up or exploding in the atmosphere, but the same could not be said of the five large pieces. The largest one led the group and entered the atmosphere above Siberia. It streaked across North America with a thunderous noise, looking like a burning mountain. In the night sky of the western hemisphere, it shone four times brighter than the sun.

It impacted almost dead center in the North Atlantic ocean. Upon impact with the water, it exploded, producing a wall of water over two thousand feet high racing outward in all directions at several hundred miles per hour. Every ship at sea in the Atlantic Ocean was destroyed. Some were caught broadside, capsized and broke apart. They sank in a matter of minutes. Others managed to turn into the wave thinking they could ride over it, but this was no tsunami. These ships were lifted up vertically bow-first as they were carried along and engulfed by the wave. If they weren't flipped over on their backs, they pitch poled and sank immediately, stern first. Even the largest ships couldn't avoid destruction.

Submerged submarines didn't fare any better. The pressure wave produced by the impact was so great that it crushed the hulls of any sub within a few miles of the impact. Those farther away were tossed about by the pressure wave so that equipment and machinery broke loose from their moorings and became missile hazards. The missiles injured or killed crewmen and damaged other equipment. Internal explosions or loss of control caused many of the disabled subs to sink below their crush depth and implode. Only a few of the lucky ones survived intact enough to blow their ballast tanks and return to the surface. Unfortunately for them, the water rushing back into the void caused by the explosion produced a secondary wave several hundred feet high.

Those vessels that miraculously survived the first wave, were in no condition to survive the second wave.

As the first wave reached the continental shelves, its momentum was slowed, but its height was increased. The slowed primary wave allowed the secondary wave to catch up with it adding its destructive force to it. When it reached land there was nowhere for the people to run. All the hoarding and looting was for naught. The wave swept hundreds of miles inland destroying everything in its path. Every island was wiped clean of all life and human habitation.

To the north, the wave swept around Greenland and Iceland, destroying the coastal cities and villages, into the Arctic ocean and breaking up part of the ice cap. In Europe, the wave washed inland as far as the Alps. In North America, it washed inland as far as the Appalachian Mountains and into the Ohio valley. It swept over the Bahamas and Florida into the Gulf of Mexico completely stripping the land of all life. In Mexico, only the Occidental Mountains prevented the wave from traveling any farther. The wave swept over the Caribbean Islands and Central America. In South America it washed inland as far as the Amazon Basin. In North Africa, it washed several hundred miles inland destroying every coastal city and carried most of the Sahara Desert sand into the sea when it receded. As the wave progressed through the South Atlantic it eventually reached Antarctica, where it broke up the ice shelves on the Atlantic side and carried the ice pieces a hundred miles inland.

Before the waves of the first comet fragment's impact reached Europe, the other four fragments streaked overhead resembling brightly burning torches, The second one hit in the center of the Algerian Basin of the Mediterranean Sea between Spain, and the Sardinia and Corsica islands, flooding the coastal regions a couple hundred miles inland. Sardinia and Corsica bore the brunt of the tidal impact, saving Italy from the worst of the wave's destructive flooding. The third fragment hit in the Aegean Sea between Greece and Turkey. The tidal wave it produced destroyed much of Greece, Bulgaria, western Turkey, Crete and the northern shores of Egypt and Libya. Much of the water that flooded Turkey spilled into the Sea of Marmara and flooded the coastal cities, overflowing the Bosporus into the Black Sea.

The fourth fragment hit in the Mesopotamian Valley in Iraq a mile south of Bagdad, completely destroying the city. The impact left a crater thirty miles wide and forced the Tigris River to change course. It ended up flowing into the Euphrates River north of Babylon instead of south of it. The impact put a temporary halt to the second phase of Babylon's reconstruction and caused minor damage to the first phase, which had been completed only a few months earlier.

The fifth comet fragment hit in Pakistan over the Indus River between the cities of Larkana, Shikarpur, Sukkur, and Khairpur. Between these cities was a host of small towns and farming communities, an area where about a million people lived. The comet exploded a hundred feet above ground, leaving no crater. The shock wave flattened everything for about forty miles in all direction. The cities of Sukkur and Khairpur were about fifteen miles from the detonation. Virtually nothing was left of them. Larkana, being the farthest away received the least damage. Of all the people living in the region, about two thirds of them were killed.

Each of the last two pieces exploded with the force of a one-hundred-megaton nuclear bomb. They each destroyed an area of about a thousand square miles. The impact plume carried dust and ash into the upper atmosphere. The dust and ash were carried around the world, darkening the sky by a third for several months. The glow in the sky that the comet fragments produced upon impact could be seen half way around the world for several days.

While tens of millions of people died from the impacts, hundreds of millions more died from the aftereffects. As the comet fragments entered the atmosphere, the heat shock caused the oxygen and nitrogen molecules to dissociate. Through a series of chemical reactions these molecules recombined to form nitrogen oxide (NO_2). The atmospheric moisture around the comet fragments was compressed by the shockwave to form large hailstones that fell to the earth among the burning ejecta. Some of the NO_2 molecules were broken down by the sun to produce tropospheric ozone, but most of them combined with atmospheric moisture and the dust thrown up by the comet's impact plume to produce acid rain (HNO_3). The acid rain had a pH level as low as 0–1.5 (the lower the number, the higher the acidity). It combined with toxic materials thrown into the atmosphere by the comet impacts, and was dispersed mostly throughout Asia. When the acid rain fell to the earth, it removed the insoluble elements from the soil and washed them into the water, streams, rivers and lakes. Many of the insoluble elements in the water were toxic to plants and animals. Untold numbers of animals that depended on these plants died. Millions of people and animals who drank the toxic water also died.

In the Atlantic Ocean, the elements making up the comet—ammonia, methane, aluminum nitrate and a lot of iron oxide—turned the sea red and lowered its pH level well below 7.8, killing off all the animals and plankton in the mixing zone (the top 250 feet). The toxic sea water that flooded the land poisoned the soil. For many months, nothing grew on the European coastal regions, or on the eastern coasts of North and South American.

When the seawater receded from the land, the devastation was beyond imagination. Hours later, officials at the Denver fusion center reviewed the live satellite feeds. They could scarcely believe what they were seeing. Within the big cities along the North American eastern seaboard they found the high-rise towers leaning against other towers or completely missing. They had all fallen over in a general southwesterly direction—the direction in which the massive tidal wave had washed over them. In various places they saw clumps of tangled wreckage containing vehicles of various types, twisted steel structures, uprooted trees and countless bodies of animals and humans. Ships of various sizes were found in the strangest places. Among the ruins of Greenville, South Carolina, an aircraft carrier lay on its starboard side, its hull nearly split in two. In many places they saw whale and shark carcasses where they shouldn't be.

Satellites overlooking Europe revealed the same degree of devastation. The Atlantic and Mediterranean coastlines had suffered from the same type of severe flooding as North America. The night terminus was passing over Italy at that time, making it difficult to determine the extent of the damage there. From there eastward, infrared images revealed fires still burning throughout the Middle East. The growing smoke and dust clouds, however, made it impossible to visually determine the extent of the damage. There seemed to be two large areas on fire in Iraq and Pakistan, with several other smaller impact areas burning around them.

It was a catastrophe the world would never recover from. The psychological impact shook people to their very cores. They hadn't yet fully recovered from the sixth-seal quake, and now this had been added to it. After all this, they still refused to repent of their evil deeds, and turn to Christ for salvation. Instead, they grew angry with God and vowed to avenge themselves for this unconscionable act. They didn't realize that this was just the first of a number of judgments against them. Compared to what was coming, this was a minor judgment.

An angel flew through the heavens, saying, "Woe, woe, woe, to those who dwell on the earth, because of the remaining blasts of the trumpet of the three angels who are about to sound." The earth was not given time to recover before the fifth trumpet sounded.

An angel, having the key to the bottomless pit, opened it and out came something like smoke of a great furnace. The bottomless pit exists in the second heaven and thus has no physical boundaries, but its corresponding location was near the comet fragment impact site near Babylon. From Babylon, the world's false religions had emerged, and Babylon was the location of Satan's seat before he relocated it to Pergamum. Out of the smoke of the pit came locusts; demons having the power of scorpions. These were told not to hurt anything on the earth except men who did not have the seal of God on their foreheads. They were commanded not to kill anyone but to torment men for five months. The 144,000 witnesses weren't the only ones bearing the seal of God. All those who had put their faith in Jesus Christ and received the Holy Spirit also bore the seal of God that no physical eye could see.

These locusts were demonic beings who had no choice but to obey the commands of God. They had as their king a demon with the name of Abaddon, which in the Hebrew means "destroyer", and Apollyon in the Greek. John described these locust-demons as appearing like horses prepared for battle. They had gold crowns on their heads and had the faces of men with hair like women and teeth like lions. They wore breast plates of iron, and their wings sounded like a herd of horses rushing into battle. They had tails with stingers like scorpions, with which to torment mankind. For five months, those who didn't have the seal of God on their foreheads were stung with a type of poison that gave them a foretaste of what hell feels like, a type of poison that felt like liquid fire coursing through their veins. They sought death, but death fled from them. This was the ultimate tough love, by which God showed mankind what they would be enduring for eternity if they didn't repent. The first woe was past. There were two more woes remaining.

The sixth trumpet sounded, and four angels—bound at the Euphrates River for this moment in time—were released that they might kill a third of mankind. These angels led an army consisting of two hundred million men. Presently, China and India and a few other far-east Asian nations has the densest populations on earth. They were the only nations capable of putting together a two-hundred-million-man army. Never before in the history of man had this been possible. The soldiers wore breastplates (body armor and/or biological suits) the color of fire (red), hyacinth (dark blue or black) and brimstone (yellow). This army operated vehicles including main battle tanks that sported dragon figureheads resembling lion heads on the gun barrels. On the back of these tanks was another fearsome weapon that resembled serpents' heads possibly rocket launchers. With these vehicles, this army used nuclear, biological and chemical (NBC) weapons to destroy a third of the world population.

The feud over the disputed Kashmir region became a full-out war. China and her allies, which included Pakistan, attacked India. The rest of Southeast Asia came to India's aid. When this war was over, the population of far-east Asia had been decimated but they still had enough surplus population between them to put together the largest army the world had ever seen. Following a devastating nuclear exchange, the two bitter enemies reached a peace accord. These enemies became allies and directed their attention toward Israel, with the goal of wrestling world control from Maitreya. Despite the NBC plagues, mankind still would not repent of their fornications, sorceries (drug use), thefts and murders.

An army from the Far East would have to cross the Himalayas to get to the Middle East. The Karakoram Highway, designated N-35, was the only highway running from China through the Kashmir region into Pakistan. It took the army several months just to get through the Karakoram pass. The two-hundred-million-man army took three years to reach Israel. Airlifting an army that size with all its equipment was not economically or logistically feasible.

Between the blowing of the sixth and seventh trumpets, there was another interlude in heaven. During this time, the kings of the east began waging their nuclear war—a war that would last through the second half of the tribulation and end at the Valley of Decision in Israel.

A mighty angel, shining bright as the sun, came down from heaven. He placed his right foot on the sea and the other on land. In his hand he held a small, open book. This angel made seven pronouncements in a loud voice like a roaring lion. He then raised his right hand and swore by the living Father who had created heaven and earth and everything in them that there would be no further delay in the restoration of the kingdom of God. In the days before the seventh angel sounding his horn, the mystery of God had been completed as preached by His servants and prophets. The plan for the restoration of God's kingdom under Jesus Christ had become known to all and were now completed as planned. Satan's plans to the contrary had utterly failed.

John was told not to write the seven pronouncements. They were meant only for the people on earth at that time, not for the church or anyone else. Anyone claiming to know what these pronouncements will be, are self-deceived, false prophets. After these pronouncements, John was told to take the little book from the angel's hand and eat it. It tasted sweet in his mouth, but turned bitter in his stomach, as the angel had said it would. He was told to prophesy again the contents of the book, which contained additional information about events that were to occur in the first half of the tribulation. John was given a measuring rod and was told to measure the temple of God and the alter—but not the outer court, which would be trampled under foot for forty-two months.

At the signing of the seven-year covenant, two more witnesses to Israel appeared. They wore sackcloth and prophesied to Israel for three and a half years. Sackcloth was worn by those in distress and mourning. The two witnesses were distressed that God's chosen people had rejected the true Messiah and had instead, embraced a false messiah. For three and a half years, the two witnesses testified of Jesus Christ and warned Israel about Maitreya and his sidekick, the false prophet. Those who refused to repent by the end of the three and a half years were sent a strong delusion so that they believed the lies of the Antichrist and his false prophet. Because they did not love the truth that they might be saved but chose instead to believe a lie, they were doomed to perish.

The two witnesses were given authority to hold back the rain and torment the earth as often as they wished. If anyone attempted to harm them, fire came out of their mouths to consume their enemies. The four angels formerly holding back the four winds carried out their judgments. These two witnesses' mission was to warn Israel of the works of the Antichrist and to remind Israel of her obligation to finish the transgression—to make an end of sin, to make atonement for iniquity, to bring in everlasting righteousness, to seal up vision and prophecy, and to anoint the most holy place.

About halfway through of the tribulation, the seventh angel sounded his trumpet. The whole world heard the voices from heaven that proclaimed, "The kingdom of the world has become the kingdom of our Lord, and of His Christ; and He will reign forever and ever." This announcement proclaimed that the conditions of the seven seals to purchase the earth and return it to its rightful owner had been completed. The people of the earth who didn't want to be ruled by Jesus Christ raged with great anger. The twenty-four elders gave praise to God and the temple in heaven opened. Within the temple there appeared the ark of the covenant. This was a sign to Israel testifying that the rule of the earth had been returned to the God of Heaven. There were lightning flashes and thunder, and the earth suffered another earthquake and a great hailstorm.

John beheld the ark with awe, and there appeared to him great signs in heaven. While John was shown the signs in heaven and the symbolic beasts of Satan's empire, I saw in my dream what was happening on earth.

These were the visions of the events that occurred at the halfway point of the tribulation. The earth was reeling from the effects of the comet impacts, the locust demons and the war in the Far East when Maitreya paid the Pope of the World Church a visit at the Vatican. One of the world church's elite Roman honor guards exchanged his ceremonial sword for an ancient Roman Hispanic sword—a double edged sword a little under three feet long, used for slashing and stabbing. This honor guard was a Jew who fully understood what Maitreya was. Thinking that he was going to save the world from the Antichrist, he wounded three people and killed two defenders before he succeeded in killing Maitreya. He practically split Maitreya's head in two with his sword before being killed himself.

Maitreya laid dead for three days. During that time, Satan waged war in heaven, attempting to take God's place on His throne. Michael the archangel, defender of Israel, defeated Satan and cast him and his fallen angels out of heaven. Never again would Satan be permitted access to the throne of God, where he had constantly accused the brethren.

The world witnessed an unexpected meteor falling from the sky, but no one knew where it came from or where it hit the earth. Many speculated that it just burned up in the atmosphere. That same day, the meteor news was overshadowed when Maitreya inexplicably rose from the dead. His mortal head wound was completely healed, but he was not at all the same person. The world never realized that the meteor and Maitreya's resurrection were related.

Seeing that he was cast out of heaven, Satan turned his wrath on Israel. But first he gave Elijah the power to resurrect Maitreya from the dead and appointed Apollyon, the king of the locust demons, to take possession of him. He gave Apollyon/Maitreya authority to rule over the people of the earth and to overcome the children of God. Elijah, who was now recognized as the False Prophet, was appointed Maitreya's aid and given all authority to enforce his decrees by performing miracles or by death.

At the place of the skull called Golgotha, where Jesus Christ had been crucified, God's two witnesses waited for Maitreya. He just threw his hands toward them, muttered something unintelligible and they fell dead. The world gasped in amazement. "Who was this man?" they wondered. "If he can do this, who could stand against him?" The bodies of the two witnesses were left where they fell for all the world to see. Cameras were constantly trained on them to remind the world that they were indeed dead.

When the world realized that the two witnesses were dead, they rejoiced that their torment had ended. For three days the world celebrated and even exchanged gifts. As Maitreya and the False Prophet worked on their next big event, the partying came to a sudden end. Fear once again gripped the world as they watched the two witnesses rise from where they had fallen. A loud voice was heard in the sky saying, "Come up here." They rose into the air and disappeared from sight. As the witnesses ascended into heaven, a great earthquake shook the city of Jerusalem. A tenth of the city collapsed and seven thousand people died.

When the great dragon, Satan, who had resurrected Maitreya, heard the proclamation that dominion of the earth had been returned to Jesus Christ, he raged with anger and vowed revenge. Maitreya immediately took possession of the Jewish temple, put an end to the sacrifices, and set up a statue of himself. The Abomination of Desolation that the Prophet Daniel foretold about.

Over the past few months, a robotic statue of Maitreya had been made in preparation for this day. Animatronic and robotic technology had progressed considerably in the last couple of decades. The statue appeared completely natural-looking and its movements were fluid and natural. Even its facial expressions were lifelike, not mechanical looking. It could mimic any movement a man could make. It even walked around.

The statue stood about thirty-three feet tall and was clothed with six plates of golden armor. Its skin appeared golden bronze and sported a full beard giving it the appearance of the Greek god Zeus. On its head sat a golden crown adorned with six different jewels. In its right hand, it held a scepter resembling lightning bolts. It was truly an awesome spectacle to behold.

The statue was erected between the golden alter and the Holy of Holies, seated on a great golden throne. Several cameras were mounted around it that tracked its every movement. The cameras were arranged in such a manner that a 3D image of the statue was broadcast, giving it a lifelike appearance on every 3D monitor and holographic projector around the world. Built within the statue were scalar transmitters that could broadcast the image of Maitreya and its message into every home and business around the earth without the aid of satellites. The transmissions were broadcast on every channel regardless of its source and overrode anything presently being broadcast. It even took over the internet's cloud network when it made its broadcasts. Each day at six AM and six PM, six trumpets announced the time to stop all activity and worship the image of the beast.

The False Prophet, wearing religious robes with a patch over his right eye and one arm hanging limply, made a show of bringing the statue to life by uttering a few mysterious words that sounded like incantations. The computer within the statue recognized the coded commands, and activated the statue. When the lifelike statue came to life, it stood up, took a couple steps and spoke with a booming, hypnotic voice. Through the statue, Maitreya proclaimed himself as God and commanded the whole world to bow down and worship him.

The Jews immediately revolted against him, and war broke out in the city of Jerusalem. Even the world church revolted against him. They were willing to recognize him as their messiah, but they weren't willing to submit to him or recognize him as God. As pandemonium broke out throughout Israel, an airlift was arranged to fly the faithful of God to the place of safety. Maitreya tried to halt the exodus to Edom by all manner of supernatural means at his disposal, but to no effect.

While Michael the archangel spread his protective wings over the faithful remnant of Israel, a million-man army was sent in pursuit of these Jews who fled to the hills in southern occupied Jordan, a place formerly known as Edom. A sea of humanity and machines of war raced towards Edom to destroy the faithful remnant of God. In the great rift valley between Israel and Jordan, the army gathered in pursuit of the sons of Israel.

Suddenly the rift valley opened up beneath them, forming a

great chasm as deep as the earth's mantle. A monstrous wall of fire shot skyward from the chasm. Nearly the entire army fell into it with all their equipment and were consumed by the fire. Those that didn't fall into the chasm were consumed by the fire just a surely as if they had fallen into it. Hundreds of aircraft flying over the chasm lost power and plunged into the consuming fire. When every last man had perished, the chasm closed over them leaving a canyon about three miles wide, a mile deep and 130 miles long. The Dead Sea drained into it, but the chasm did not yet open to the Gulf of Aqaba. When Maitreya heard the fate of his army, he flew off in a rage and turned to Israel's offspring. He ordered the False Prophet to find every last Christian and destroy them all. He was to use every means at his disposal and mercilessly hunt them down, even if it meant scorching the entire planet to rid Maitreya of all those who dared to oppose him.

It wasn't just the true Christians who were targeted but every so-called Christian of the world church that had rebelled against Maitreya. The Pope fled the Vatican and was never seen again. The False Prophet then called down fire from the heavens upon the city of Rome. The Vatican in particular was the focus of the firestorm. From Anzio, the False Prophet watched Rome burn, just as Caesar Nero had done two thousand years earlier. It was necessary to destroy the Vatican, both as punishment to the world church and to move the world religion headquarters to the newly rebuilt city of Babylon in Iraq, Maitreya's new world capital. Babylon was built near the location of the original Tower of Babel, the place where the world's false religions originated.

The city of Rome burned with such intensity that nothing on earth could put it out. The fire burned unchecked for several days before burning itself out. The world mourned the loss of Rome and the world church with which it had committed spiritual fornication.

Maitreya rejoiced to finally be rid of the harlot that had ridden his back the last few years. For too long the Vatican had stood apart from the ten-nation confederacy and defied his rule. The kings of the earth committed acts of immorality with the world church to win her favor. The entire world fornicated with this church for they were pleased with what she offered. The Vatican was drunk with the blood of the saints, and having great wealth, she thought of herself as a queen. She played the harlot with Satan and had become the great whore known as Mystery, Babylon; the mother of harlots and abominations of the earth.

Pleased with this, Maitreya made the False Prophet his high priest. This completed the counterfeit, unholy trinity; Satan as the invisible counterfeit Father God (represented by a great dragon with seven heads having ten horns and seven crowns); the beast Maitreya, the visible counterfeit god/man or Antichrist as the Son of God (represented by a seven headed beast like a leopard with feet like a bear and a mouth like a lion coming from the sea which represented the gentile nations); and the False Prophet as the counterfeit Holy Spirit (represented be a beast that spoke like a dragon having two horns of a lamb coming from the land of Israel). As the Holy Spirit never promoted Himself, but promoted the Son of God and spoke the words of the Father; so too the False Prophet never promoted himself, but promoted Maitreya and spoke the words of Satan. These were the triune aspects of the Antichrist who opposed the true Christ.

The False Prophet was given control of the secret police. Like the SS of Nazi Germany, the secret police enforced Maitreya's decrees. The False Prophet decreed that everyone take a mark of loyalty to Maitreya regardless of their station in life. Both free and slave, and both rich and poor were required to take the mark of the beast. Without this mark, no one would be able to buy, sell or trade anything. Bartering was made illegal. Those who refused to take the mark or worship the image of the beast were put to death.

On the right hand or forehead each person was to bear the mark of the Beast or the number of his name, equalling six hundred and sixty six. The number seven was the number of God, indicating perfection, while the number six was the number of a man indicating he had fallen short of God's perfection. In the Hebrew and Greek alphabet, each letter had a numerical value. The occultic title of "Maitreya" in the Hebrew added up to six hundred and sixty six. As stated earlier, Maitreya was not the Antichrist's name, only his title. What his actual name will be, at the present only God knows.

When the decree to take the mark of the Beast was issued, the voices of three different angels were heard in the heavens. The first angel preached the gospel of Jesus Christ so that every person on the planet would be without excuse. With a loud voice he said, "Fear God, and give Him glory, because the hour of His judgment has come; and worship Him who made the heaven and the earth and the sea and springs of water."

This was followed immediately by a second angel saying, "Fallen, fallen is Babylon the Great, she who has made all the nations drink of her wine of the passion of her immorality."

A third angel was heard saying with a loud voice, "If anyone worships the Beast and his image, and receives a mark on his forehead or upon his hand, he also will drink of the wine of the wrath of God, which is mixed in full strength in the cup of His anger; and he will be tormented with fire and brimstone in the presence of the holy angels and in the presence of the Lamb. And the smoke of their torment goes up forever and ever; and they have no rest day and night, those who worship the Beast and his image, and whoever receives the mark of his name."

Not surprisingly, very few chose to believe the voices of the angels. Instead they chose to believe the words of Maitreya who stated that this was nothing more than the antichrist waging psychological warfare in preparation for his invasion of the earth. He once again reiterated the need to take the mark of his own name that he might know friend from foe, who was loyal to him or to the antichrist. For in taking this mark, they would become more than a mere human. They would acquire godlike power, and nothing would be impossible for them. For only with godlike powers would they be able to defeat the antichrist's invasion of the earth.

The mark of the Beast was no mere tattoo. It was formed by two short incisions that crossed each other in an 'X' pattern. The skin was folded back at each corner and a one-millimeter square chip was inserted. It was called a Multiple Micro Electrode Array (MMEA), containing ten thousand microscopic electrodes on one side. It was the advanced form of the rice-sized RFID chip that led to its development. The chip was placed so the electrodes made contact with the nerve cells in the center of the forehead or the right hand. When the skin flaps were closed, they were sutured so that the incisions would scar and make the mark visible. When healed, the scar had the shape of an 'X', the Greek chi, which stands for "Christ."

The MMEA gave the recipient unlimited access to the wireless Internet cloud network. Anything a person wanted to know— what was *permitted* for them to know—was transmitted directly into their brain. The signal was sent to the optical processing center of the brain to give the data or images the appearance of floating directly in front of them. In order for the MMEA to access the cloud network, it was necessary to program the chip with the individual's eighteen-digit international ID number which served as the individual's personal IP address. The number consisted of three sets of six-digit numbers. This embedded the 666 number of the Beast in each ID number and IP address.

The MMEA chip required no power cell of its own to function. The human body was a natural scalar wave receiver with a 7.2 megahertz resonant frequency. This was the natural resonant frequency of the entire planet and everything that lived on it. The chip was tuned to this frequency and pulled power from the body's reception of the naturally occurring scalar waves.

Scalar waves are longitudinal waves like sound waves able to pass through everything unhindered. Unlike electromagnetic (EM) waves (RF signals and microwaves), scalar waves had unlimited range regardless of wavelength and power. Also, their longitudinal orientation made them immune to EM interference and EMP emissions.

Scalar waves were the secret power behind the MMEAs and made it impossible for those who took the mark to hide from the Antichrist and his image. The voices and images that seemed to come from nowhere where sent from the image of the Beast that used these same scalar waves to control the people.

There was an even darker side to the chip that only the elite with the need to know were aware of. The Illuminati satanists had cast a spell on each chip that attached a demon to it. Whenever someone received one of these implants, the demon attached to it inhabited that person. What few people knew was that the chip also contained a tiny dose of a designer virus that was injected into the bloodstream when the chip was activated. Even the doctors who implanted the chip didn't know about this virus, which contained the genes of the fallen angels. Where the satanists had acquired the DNA was anybody's guess. When the virus penetrated the membranes of the body's stem cells, it spliced its genes into the stem cells' genes and forced the cell to reproduce the altered genes. New stem cells reproduced with the altered genes, eventually replaced the old cells. Gradually, the body was transformed into something they called a *transhuman*.

Because of this change, the evolution-infused scientific establishment, who were likewise ignorant of the virus, declared that these people had evolved into a higher order of existence. They were no longer classified as *Homo sapiens* but as *Homo noeticus* or the "god-man," a term invented by the new-age so-called "enlightened ones". It applied to those who had supposedly achieved a higher state of consciousness characterized by elevated extra sensory perceptions (ESP) and a change in psychological and physical chemistry. These "enlightened ones" had deceived themselves into thinking they had achieved spiritual perfection and had become like God. They believed that the Bible was metaphorical and symbolic. They condemned those who held to the literal interpretation of the Bible for holding back mankind and considered eternal separation from God an illusion.

Because the supposedly multidimensional *homo noeticus* was no longer fully human, they were no longer eligible for salvation. Jesus Christ died on the cross to save true human beings only, descendants of Adam, not human hybrids, the fallen angels, or even extraterrestrials. Like the Nephilim in Noah's day before the world flood, those who took the mark of the Beast were no longer considered fully human. They faced the wrath of God that was about to be poured out on the earth in full strength.

After seeing the beasts and hearing the declaration of the three angels, John was shown a couple events that would occur at the coming of Jesus Christ. First, he saw Jesus standing on Mount Zion with the 144,000 Israelite witnesses. He then saw Jesus being given a sharp sickle to harvest the earth. Because the faithful, represented by the wheat, and the pretenders, represented by the tares, tended to grow in the same field, they had to be reaped together. The tares were then separated from the wheat, gathered in bundles and burned. This happened during Satan's war against all those who stood in opposition to him or claimed to be Christian. The pretenders were taken to concentration camps around the world. Either they were burned with fire or they denounced their supposed faith in Christ and took the mark of the Beast. The faithful were also gathered up and beheaded.

This sounds like the faithful lost the battle, but they gained victory over Satan by not bowing to his image or taking his mark. Because they maintained their testimony in Christ, they overcame Satan and emerged from the tribulation victorious. These were the ones John saw appearing in heaven, standing on a sea of glass mixed with fire, holding harps of God, and singing the song of Moses. The sea of glass mixed with fire represented the believers of every nation who were purified by the fire of the tribulation.

At the end of the tribulation, the wicked of the world were gathered in the Valley of Decision in Israel like clusters of grapes cast into the great wine press of God's wrath. Out of the wine press came blood that reached to the horses' bridles for a distance of two hundred miles.

During the final year of the tribulation, seven angels with seven plagues came out of the tabernacle of the temple. These wore linen, bright and clean, girded with golden girdles. The four living creatures gave each of the seven angels a golden bowl filled with the wrath of God. The temple was filled with the smoke of God's glory and power. No one was able to enter the temple until the seven plagues were completed. God's wrath was fixed and could not be mediated or delayed. Since those on earth had willingly rejected God's mercy and His Son, all that was left for them was to receive the wrath of God in full measure. A loud voice came from the temple, commanding the angels to pour out the seven bowls of God's wrath on the earth.

The first bowl was poured out, and there appeared sores like boils on those who had the mark of the Beast and worshipped his image. These sores caused a debilitating, burning itch that could not be relieved. All the doctors' attempts to relieve or cure the sores were ineffective. God's judgments could not be reversed. Certainly not by drugs. Those who had taken the mark of the Beast were no longer eligible for salvation, however, for those who had not yet taken the mark, this served as a warning for them to not to take the mark or worship the Beast.

The second bowl was poured on the sea, and the world's ocean waters turned to blood. This was not a red tide or some kind of dye, but a toxic substance that killed every creature in the sea. This toxic substance was in fact human red blood cells and hemoglobin.

The blood in the oceans went down to about 250 feet, the top mixing layer in which 90 percent of ocean life resided. But it was only a matter of time before the entire ocean would become completely devoid of life, for even life at the bottom depended on detritus drifting down from the surface. Those who made their living by the sea suffered economic ruin and starvation. Every ship at sea had to pull into port. Without fresh water the crews could not survive.

The third bowl was poured out, and all the streams, rivers and lakes turned to blood. The angel of the waters said, "Righteous art Thou who art and who wast, O Holy One because Thou didst judge these things; for they poured out the blood of saints and prophets, and Thou hast given them blood to drink. They deserve it." Millions died from lack of fresh water to drink. Plants and animals died, leaving nothing to eat. Many went mad, for the blood was soon everywhere and could not be washed off.

The fourth bowl was poured out on the sun, and men were scorched with heat. The sun flared and scorched the earth with great heat, but it stopped short of going nova. This heat gave a new meaning to global warming. The heat was so intense that brown outs occurred around the planet. Temperatures in the shade were over 120 degrees Fahrenheit. There was no escaping the heat. The ice caps (what was left of them) soon melted, raising the sea level and flooding the coastal regions. Many men died from the heat and they cursed God for these judgments. They refused to repent and give glory to God. Instead they rallied around the Antichrist and sought vengeance.

The fifth bowl was poured out, and the kingdom of the beast was plunged into darkness. The darkness was so intense that it caused great pain. Men gnawed their tongues for the pain from the sores, the heat, and the darkness. Instead of repenting of their deeds, they blasphemed the God of Heaven.

The sixth bowl was poured out, and the Euphrates river was dried up to prepare the way for the kings of the east. The Oriental two-hundred-million-man army reached the Euphrates by this time and was ready to invade the kingdom of the Beast. Those armies of the Far East that had formerly fought each other now marched together toward Israel. They were in full rebellion against Maitreya and never took the mark of the beast or worshipped his image.

During the first two years after Maitreya's resurrection, the armies of the east had made their way through the Himalayas and across Pakistan. At the Indus River valley they destroyed every city and town that had escaped destruction from the comet impact and they plundered the land. The army paused long enough to build a large airstrip to fly in supplies and reinforcements. The airstrip was then used as a forward airbase for their bombers and fighter aircraft. While the bowl judgments were being poured out, they marched across the deserts of Iran in the searing heat until they reached the southern slopes of the Zagros Mountains at the northern end of the Persian Gulf. There they waited for the darkness to lift. When the marshes and the Euphrates River dried up, they marched toward Babylon.

As with the seals and trumpet judgments, there was an interlude between the sixth and seventh bowl. This wasn't to give the people time to repent but to give the armies of the world time to gather in the Valley of Decision for the final war that truly would end all wars. Out of the mouths of the unholy trinity—the Dragon, the Beast, and the False Prophet—there came three unclean spirits resembling frogs. These demons went into the world performing signs and wonders to gather the armies of the world for the war of the great day of God Almighty. And they gathered at a place called Har-Magedon.

Jesus said, "Behold, I am coming like a thief. Blessed is the one who stays awake and keeps his garments, lest he walk about naked and men see his shame."

Prior to pouring out the seventh bowl, the angels went out to gather the remaining faithful to a place of safety. This was the gathering Jesus spoke of, as written in the gospels of Matthew and Luke. Into Edom all the surviving Christians were gathered. This was where the faithful of Israel had fled three years earlier, protected by Michael the Archangel. At the ruins of Bozrah, the former capital of Edom, they were gathered to await the second coming of Jesus Christ.

In the Valley of Decision, the armies of the west met the armies of the east. There the Armageddon Campaign began. Prior to the armies of the east arriving in the Valley of Decision, they were joined by the armies of the north as they crossed the dried up Euphrates River. The armies of the east and north laid siege to Maitreya's capital city of Babylon. They laid waste to the land around the city so as to render it uninhabitable, but they were unable to destroy the city. Bomb after bomb was dropped in the city, but none fell on the inner city. This was the new location of Satan's seat, which he had relocated from Pergamum. He wasn't about to let his crowning jewel be destroyed by a horde of mongrels.

The city of Babylon was the most modern and magnificent city ever built. It consisted of an inner city surrounded by an outer city, separated by a great wall. The outer city was a garden city with glass and marble towers adorned with beautiful intricate Arabic architecture. Scattered throughout the city were numerous souks alive with the sounds of haggling. Buyers were everywhere trying to get sellers to lower their asking prices. Everything imaginable was on sale; gold and silver jewelry, wood carvings, finely woven tapestries, silk and fabrics of every type, exotic animal hides and even slaves.

The inner city complex was even more spectacular. It was surrounded by a great wall one hundred and twenty feet high and eighteen feet thick. It had twelve gates, thirty-three feet wide, three on each side. Inside the wall was another garden city that glittered with gold. Even the streets were lined with gold. No wheeled vehicles or beasts of burden were permitted within the inner city, only foot traffic. Supplies were brought in through underground tunnels. The buildings matched the buildings of the outer city in architectural style, but were much grander. The UN Capital building sported the largest dome structure in the world and was plated with pure gold. So large was this dome that, inside it produced its own weather. There was a coliseum large enough to hold half a million people with a facade of polished red granite. The city center was dominated by a 2,500 foot tall stepped pyramid tower. It was made of iron and stone with thirty-three steps and a long stairway leading to the top on the east side. Each step was covered with overflowing gardens and waterfalls. The lower step had three entrance gates on each side except for the side with the stairway. That side had only two gates, for a total of eleven gates. A continuous column of smoke rose from the top of the tower, while inside were numerous rooms containing temples for committing every imaginable act of immorality.

When the pyramid tower was completed, Maitreya decreed that everyone was to sacrifice their oldest child to Lucifer. This required people to make a pilgrimage to Babylon and climb the tower stairs to make their sacrifice. Those who could afford to were allowed to buy a slave child to sacrifice as a substitute for their own child. Most of those slave children had been taken from their Christian parents. Because their parents were Christians condemned to die on the gallows, these children weren't considered worthy of freedom nor of the New World Order.

At the top of the pyramid was an iron sculpture of a magnificent winged dragon that had seven heads with seven crowns. The leftmost head had ten horns representing the ten-nation confederacy of the New World Order. The beast stood on its hind legs with its forepaws extended in front of it. A fire burned continuously within the dragon, making it glow red hot. This was a representation of Satan, the god of the Beast's kingdom.

Those climbing to the top to make their sacrifices could strongly feel the presence of Satan. The child sacrifice was placed on the extended paws that glowed red-hot. The screaming of the child didn't last long as it was quickly consumed by the fire. Child sacrifice was one of the most heinous abominations in the eyes of God. This tower, the rebuilt Tower of Babel, was destined to be the focus of God's wrath.

Unable to destroy the city, the armies of the east and the north marched toward Israel, destroying everything in their path. They crossed the Jordan River and staged themselves at the eastern end of the Jezreel Valley. They watched with amusement as the armies of Maitreya gathered at the western end of the valley. The armies were arranged in battle array, but Maitreya never attacked. Instead he marched on Jerusalem.

While the armies were being staged in the Jezreel Valley, the remnant of Israel taking refuge in Edom attacked Jerusalem and destroyed the image of the Beast. This enraged Maitreya who then determined to destroy the sons of Israel, no matter what it took. His army managed to recapture Jerusalem and he chased the sons of Israel back across the Dead Sea into Edom. The sons of Israel thought they were safe once back in Edom, but Maitreya continued to pursue them. The armies of the east, in the mean time, marched down the coast of the Dead Sea and turned west toward Jerusalem. The two-hundred-million-man army occupied the entire West Bank area. Maitreya left a few divisions to encircle the remnant of Israel and the Christians encamped at the ruins of Bozrah. East of Jerusalem, Maitreya engaged the armies of the east.

To the remnant at Bozrah, it seemed that the end was upon them. The army of Maitreya had them encircled and were poised to destroy them. They fought the good fight and were prepared to meet Jesus in heaven. In their desperate hour, the ground shook mightily.

The seventh bowl was poured out on the air and a voice was heard from the temple saying, "It is done." And there came lightning and thunder and a great earthquake. This earthquake was greater than any earthquake since man had first been created, even greater than the earthquake of the world flood and the sixth seal. Jerusalem was split into three parts, and every city of the earth was destroyed. God remembered Babylon the Great and gave her the wine of His fierce wrath. With this mighty earthquake came hailstones weighing a hundred pounds. For one hour, the earth shook, and hail and lightning assaulted the earth. Every mountain was leveled and every island sank beneath the sea. Even the mighty Himalayas were reduced to mere foot hills. Millions died in the giant tsunamis racing across the oceans, and virtually every ship at sea was either sunk or cast upon the land. The continents heaved and shifted so that some parts were lifted up while other parts sank and flooded. Hundreds of millions of people died as the earth staggered mightily like a drunkard in its orbit around the sun. So severe was this judgment, that men blasphemed God. This final judgment destroyed everything that remained of the kingdom of the Beast including Satan's beloved city of Babylon. On the city of Babylon, the judgment was so intense that nothing remained that could be recognized as manmade.

The kings of the earth looked upon the smoking ruin of Babylon from a great distance. They lamented Babylon saying, "Woe, woe, the great city, Babylon, the strong city! For in one hour your judgment has come." The merchants mourned for there was no one to buy their cargo. They stood at a distance and wept in mourning, saying, "Woe, woe, the great city, she who was clothed in fine linen and purple and scarlet, and adorned with gold and precious stones and pearls; for in one hour such great wealth has been laid waste!" The sailors and passengers and all those who made their living on the sea stood at a distance, weeping at the sight of the smoke of her burning. They cried out in mourning, saying, "Woe, woe, the great city, in which all who had ships at sea became rich by her wealth, for in one hour she has been laid waste!"

In heaven there was the sound of music and great rejoicing at the destruction of Babylon. For in her was found the blood of the saints and prophets and all who had been slain on the earth. This was followed by the marriage of the Lamb prior to His return to the earth. All those who had been raptured before the tribulation, those standing under the altar, those waving palm branches, and all those standing on the sea of glass mixed with fire were invited. These constituted the whole of the Gentile church. Though the early church had been primarily Jews, the later church was primarily made up of Gentiles. This Gentile church was the body of Christ that was wedded to Him as His bride. Though it may wound the pride of some men, the church has always been symbolized by a woman who is under the authority of Jesus Christ, just as a woman is under the authority of her husband. The bride of Christ, the Gentile church, was given garments of linen, bright and clean. These were the righteous acts of the saints who kept themselves pure and holy. "Blessed are those who are invited to the marriage supper of the Lamb. These are true words of God." This bride then followed her husband on His return to the earth.

For a whole hour the earth shook, and every city was laid waste, but the remnant at Bozrah were unaffected. The hills of Jordan were all flattened, but the encampment at Bozrah found themselves on a large, circular plateau overlooking the rift valley. The quake had torn asunder the rift, and water from the Gulf of Aqaba rushed in to fill the rift valley and the Dead Sea, moving up the Jordan River and into the Sea of Galilee as far as the mountains of Lebanon. The inrush of water carried with it any surviving ships from the Gulf of Aqaba. Half of Maitreya's army that had encircled the remnant was destroyed. The rest were in disarray, but still deadly. Suddenly the darkened sky to the east was pierced by a shaft of light that peeled back the clouds like a scroll.

Then a bright orb of light appeared, followed by innumerable orbs of light. The orbs following the first descended onto Bozrah, where the Jews and Gentile Christians were besieged. The orbs became white horses with riders wearing white, clean, fine linen. The lead orb became a white horse whose rider was wearing a white garment dipped and sprinkled in blood. On His rode and on His thigh, a name was written; King of Kings, and Lord of Lords. From his mouth came the Word of God like a double-edged sword and He Himself was the Word. Jesus Christ descended on Bozrah but hovered above it while the army of heaven circled around Him. The army numbered in the tens of billions. They circled around Him with such speed, that they looked like a glowing disc-shaped cloud. With incredible speed, they cut down Maitreya's army that was arrayed against Christ and His people. All those who resisted were cut down. Not one person was left standing.

Jesus Christ then proceeded toward Jerusalem with His army of the saints and hundreds of legions of angels following behind Him. A small group, however, detached from the main group and stayed behind with the remnant of Israel. As Jesus rode toward Jerusalem, He spoke words of condemnation on the nations and words of truth about Himself. With these words, like a double-edge sword, He smote the nations.

When Maitreya and the kings of the east saw Jesus Christ descending from the heavens, they rallied their forces to oppose the coming of the true Messiah. Vainly they fought and learned the hard way that material weapons had no effect on the immortals or the angels. In the Valley of Jehoshaphat, the satanic army tried to destroy the heavenly army with their weapons of mass destruction. They only succeeded in destroying their own.

As the army of heaven swept over the satanic army, the mortals fell like wheat stalks put to the sickle. The one-sided battle really wasn't a battle at all but a slaughter of wicked men intent on freeing themselves from the law of God. In the valley, hundreds of millions of men attempted to stop the return of Jesus Christ, and hundreds of millions of men were slain in a single night. So much blood was shed that it flowed five feet deep. The carrions of heaven gorged themselves on the flesh of men for days.

While Satan's army was slaughtered, Jesus Christ set His feet upon the Mount of Olives east of Jerusalem. Immediately, a great earthquake split the mountain in two. Half the mountain moved north, while the other half moved south. The 144,000 Israelite witness stood on the mountain with Him. Jesus called to the faithful remnant of Israel in Jerusalem who were hiding from Maitreya's thugs to come out and take refuge within the newly created rift. Once they were safe, He entered the Temple Mount through the east gate while the army of heaven swept through the city. Maitreya and the False Prophet were both taken captive on the Temple Mount and the remainder of Satan's army surrendered.

Once the army of Satan was defeated, the legions of angels went throughout the world and lay hold of all the demons that had deceived and possessed the souls of men. These were brought to the bottomless pit where the locust demons and Apollyon emerged. All were cast into the pit, including Apollyon and the demon that inhabited the False Prophet.

The angel holding the key to the pit then went to Satan's lair in Babylon. Lucifer sat in his lair beneath the ruins of his tower, laughing at the stupidity of man and gorging on their blood. He knew his time had come to an end and was determined to leave nothing for Jesus Christ to inherit. When the angel holding the key to the bottomless pit arrived carrying a great chain, Lucifer fought with every ounce of his strength. But despite his great power, he was no match for the angel. The angel subdued the Dragon, that Serpent of old who was called Satan, originally called Lucifer, and bound him in a great chain. Bound and powerless, he was brought to the bottomless pit where the other demons had already been cast. Satan was cast in there with them and the pit was locked and sealed. There he would remain for the next thousand years, until he would be released to deceive mankind once again for the final rebellion.

Chapter 10
The Vision of the Consummation of Mankind

*T*he ninth dream was very troubling, indeed, but the second coming of Jesus Christ was not the end of the story. Rather it marked the beginning of the final chapter of mankind. The final judgment and consummation of believers in Christ Jesus. In this last dream, I was shown the millennial reign of Jesus Christ and John's vision of the new heaven and earth.

The return of Jesus Christ and the defeat of Satan marked the end of the great tribulation and Israel's seventieth week of years. Once Satan was bound, Maitreya and the False Prophet imprisoned, and their armies defeated, Jesus resurrected the martyred tribulation saints. During Maitreya's reign, over a billion Christians were beheaded or killed by some other manner for holding to the testimony of Jesus Christ. Like the raptured saints, the bodies of the resurrected tribulation saints were glorified and made immortal.

At the Temple Mount, the Beast and the False Prophet sat subdued in their cages. Without their demons, they looked like withered old men. Stripped of their power, they were made a laughing stock.

The surviving men and women of the world who had taken the mark of the Beast were brought to Jerusalem for their judgment. Without their demons and their implants disabled, they were now in their right minds. They looked at the wretchedness of their former masters and wondered how they could have been deceived by them. And to think that this pathetic creature who called himself Maitreya thought he was God. They shook their heads in wonder.

At their judgment, the Beast and False Prophet were given the opportunity to defend themselves, but they had no defense. Saying the Devil made them do it, simply didn't cut it, for they still had a choice no matter the circumstances. Instead of being cast into the pit of hell along with the rest of Satan's children, these two were cast alive into the Lake of Fire.

The survivors who had taken the mark of the beast were not permitted to enter the millennium. These were slain and cast into the fiery pits of hell to await the final judgment.

Then it was time for the judgment of the survivors of the tribulation who had not taken the mark of the Beast. Rather than being judged according to their faith or their works, they were judged according to how they had treated the 144,000 Israelite witnesses.

They were divided into two groups. To the right of Christ went those who had provided shelter, food, clothing, medicine and whatever else the witnesses needed. These were referred to as "sheep." Jesus told them what they had done for even the least of these, they had done so also unto Him. These were permitted to enter into the millennial reign of Jesus Christ.

The other group was sent to His left and were referred to as goats. These were the ones who had mistreated the 144,000

Israelite witnesses, refused to give them food or medicine, and ran them out of town or put them to death. Jesus told them the same thing He told the sheep. In the same way they had done these things to the least of these witnesses, they had done so also unto Him. They were then cast into the pit of hell along with those who had taken the mark of the beast. Many of them pleaded for one more chance, but at the judgment that time was long past. They had the chance to repent countless times in the past. Now it was too late.

Then came the cleanup, which took several months to complete. Outside Jerusalem to the east, a giant pit was dug to bury the bodies of the slain children of Satan. So great was this pit that it resembled a strip mine. All the skeletal remains of Satan's army were cast into the pit. With them went their machines of war that couldn't be recycled and the radioactive dirt and debris from their nuclear weapons. When the pit was covered over, it resembled a great mountain. It came to be called Har-Mishcheth (Hill of Corruption). On that hill, no memorial markers were placed. Only lots of trees were planted on it and around it. In a few short years, the hill was covered with a small forest.

As the millennial reign of Jesus Christ began, it was discovered that the judgments poured out on Satan's children had done more than destroy his kingdom. They had put the earth back into its preflood condition with the exception of rejoining the continents into one. They remained where they were, though their geography was greatly altered. The earths axial tilt had been restored to eleven degrees as opposed to twenty-four. This lessened the effects of seasonal change and made the weather milder. The earth's axial precession was also reset. No longer did the sun rise in Aquarius during the spring equinox. It now rose in the constellation of Leo. The Lion of Judah was here now, and the earth entered its Sabbath rest.

The seventh bowl judgment also ionized and recharged the ozone layer to its original level, and since Christ's arrival, the magnetic field had doubled in strength. It set the earth on the path of healing, as did many of the previous judgments. The blood poured out on the oceans and streams, for instance, cleansed the waters of pollutants and toxic chemicals, restoring sea life to its proper ecological balance. All life in the sea had been killed, but not all sea life was in the sea. Some were kept in sanctuaries set aside to restore life in the sea.

A new government was established that was quite different from the previous governments. It was a theocracy run by judges, the way Israel had done before Saul was appointed it's first king. Those judges were chosen by Jesus from the resurrected who had been beheaded for keeping His testimony. But not all of them were made judges. The rest served as priests who taught the Word of God and ministered to His people. Those who had not been beheaded served in other capacities.

The public school and college education systems were no longer used. In their place an apprenticeship program was established. No longer would students be brainwashed with various deceptions and be allowed to run amok the way they had been in the previous century. No longer would they be the useful idiots of wicked men intent on implementing change designed to control people. The public schools were replaced with a home school program where the parents were the teachers. No longer would the children be left in the hands of school administrators and neglected by the parents. School administrations were still needed, however, to establish curriculum, to oversee testing and to provide the parents with tutor services and the resources they needed.

Once the children completed their basic education, they were enrolled in apprenticeships of their chosen craft. Craft halls were established as part of the industry. Journeymen within the industry taught the apprentices their craft. With enough time and experience, the journeymen were eventually recognized as master craftsmen and given management positions.

The economy was established on a barter system with currency based on the weight of gold. Banks were no longer permitted to print or issue money or lend that money at interest. Jesus alone authorized the printing and distribution of money. No longer was the debt-credit system used to control governments and lead them into debt that could never be repaid.

No longer would the people be enslaved to the banks because of debt. No longer would there be free handouts to those who didn't want to work. No longer would the government be driven to bankruptcy by entitlement programs or pensions. The people alone were responsible for their retirement, welfare and healthcare—not the government. It was not the governments job to take care of people. The government's job was to protect the people's rights, enforce the laws and ensure that basic services were kept functioning. The rest was up to the family and community.

Following the return of Jesus Christ, the earth rapidly recovered from the devastation of the tribulation. It started to resemble conditions prior to the fall of man. Animal predation was virtually nonexistent. Just as the animals had been before sin corrupted the world, they were now once again. Unlike the days before sin, animals still died. While the predators were now mainly vegetarian, they were still scavengers that ate dead animals to keep disease under control.

In zoos, people were permitted to mingle with the free-roaming animals. There was no longer any danger of the predators harming anyone or the other animals. All the animals were fairly docile and ate vegetable matter. The people were allowed to handle the animals and to ride those that permitted them to. The kids particularly liked to ride the lions. They practically mauled the lions. The lions just rolled over, purring and enjoying the attention. The bears liked it when the men wrestled with them. They were gentle, though, for they sensed the strength of men was not as great as theirs. A little boy played with a passing viper and wasn't bitten. A lamb sometimes scampered by with a young wolf chasing it. The wolf caught up with it, gave it a little nip, then turned and ran away. The lamb likewise turned around and started chasing the wolf. When the lamb caught up with the wolf, it jumped on it. Then the lamb ran off with the wolf chasing it. When the lamb grew tired, it lay down with the wolf lying down beside it.

Throughout the millennium, Jesus preached from the Temple Mount. People came from all over by the thousands just to hear Him preach. "Come," they said. "Let us go to the hill of God and listen to His wisdom." Sadly, the later generations began losing enthusiasm for hearing Jesus preach. The believers found it incredible that Jesus Christ stood before these people, who knowing full well who He was and were unable to deny Him, yet they still refused to let Him into their hearts. The believers lived to be several hundred years old, but the unbelievers only lived to about a hundred if they were lucky. They grew increasingly frustrated with the life-span inequality. They resented the rod of iron by which Jesus ruled and desired to live free of God's law. They desired their own country to live according to their own laws, but it was denied them. They grumbled at what they perceived as unequal treatment and took their grievances to court, but the judges would not hear their case. They even brought their case to Jesus.

He said to them, "Do you not understand that the rebellion of mankind against God is what corrupted the earth? Do you not realize that it is this rebellion that brought suffering and death into the world? If you do what is right, you will live. For sin crouches at the door, and its desire is for you. But you must master it."

There was also a growing vegetarian movement among the unbelievers, who tried to force everyone to become vegetarian like the animals. They found it disgusting that the animals had turned away from predation, but people hadn't. Again they took their case to the judges but were turned away.

Jesus told them, "At no time has permission to eat meat been rescinded. Do not even the animals eat the carcasses of the dead? What God has declared clean, let no man declare unclean." The people were given free choice of whether or not to eat meat, and no one had the right to force them to do otherwise. The people had a right to choose for themselves what to eat and how much to eat, not some government agency or special interest group.

Throughout the millennium, technological development reached undreamed-of heights. In the second century, computer controlled flying cars finally became a reality. In the subsequent years, cruise ships lost their long rectangular shape and became more like floating islands. The tubular fuselages and engines of transport aircraft blended with their wings. Shielded X-ray units provided the heat source for the turbine engines instead of burning fuel. Eventually the flying wings were replaced by disk-shaped aircraft using antigravity propulsion systems. *Mag-lev* bullet trains crisscrossed the land as freight moved in a complex system of underground tunnels.

Communications and information sharing were instantaneous worldwide without the use of implants. Flat-screen 3D displays gave way to true, 3D, holographic interactive displays that could be rolled like a sheet of paper. Quantum-computers replaced the world's conventional computers and eventually were small enough for use as portable tablet computers and smart phones.

City skyscrapers reached almost a half mile high. Square or rectangular architecture was considered old-fashioned and didn't fit in. Towers built with odd geometric shapes and exotic material were in vogue. Many of the city towers were agricultural towers that replaced traditional old-fashioned inefficient farms. They were built in odd shapes and surrounded by gardens. They were a work of art in and of themselves.

A permanently manned space station orbited the earth and was serviced by space planes that took off and landed like normal aircraft. They no longer needed booster rockets, carrier planes, or maglev slingshots to get them into orbit. These space planes also served the mining colony that had been established on the moon, Mars, and a few asteroids in the asteroid belt.

Not all lofty dreams of the future, however, were realized. The moon was never a popular tourist destination. The Apollo moon mission artifacts left on the moon were not worth the price of transport to see them. Warp drive or hyperdrive engines powering starships to distant solar systems were never developed. Spacecraft never reached even a tenth of the speed of light. The laws of physics described by Einstein's theory of relativity would not permit it. The closer a spacecraft approached the speed of light, the more energy it required to propel it. Eventually they reached the point where they required more energy than they could generate. Even matter-antimatter reactors were not capable of providing the energy they needed.

Those same laws of physics also would not permit the teleportation of an object through space. Teleportation of electrons permitted instantaneous communication, but teleporting solid objects proved impossible. This would have required converting a material object into a beam of energy and back into matter again. The formula $E=mc^2$ was only an equivalence statement. It might hint at the possibility of converting matter into energy, but actually doing it was something else entirely. Reassembling an object also proved to be an impossible hurtle. To disassemble and digitize even the simplest object and reassemble it at its destination would have required an enormously powerful computer. Even the most powerful quantum-computers were not up to the job. Teleporting something as complex as a living cell would have required an impossibly powerful computer. And that was assuming the cell's life force wasn't interrupted in the process. It served no purpose to teleport a living person, only to have him arrive as a dead unrecognizable lump of flesh.

For these reasons, mankind never departed the solar system and had to transport objects and people the old-fashioned way. Restrictions aside, technology made great strides forward in leaps and bounds, but the one thing that never changed was mankind's sinful nature.

There was true peace on earth for a thousand years, but the rebellious heart of mankind continued to grow. In the heart of the land of Megog, rebellious men were allowed to gather. In the city of Moscow, like-minded men gathered to plot against the rule of Jesus. Their activities didn't go unnoticed, but they were permitted to gather for the final purge of wicked men from the righteous. All they lacked was a charismatic leader to unite them, for there was much division among them over who should lead. That leader came when Satan was released from the bottomless pit.

Satan appeared to them like an angel of light. He promised them fame and glory and a kingdom of their own if they would help him remove God from His throne. He promised them eternal life and freedom from the law. He promised he would make them gods if they would bow down and worship him. This they were eager to do. The original sin of pride once again welled up in the hearts of mankind. The original sin of pride rose up to make its last stand against God's righteous justice.

With the release of Satan, the unbelievers realized that the reign of Christ had come to an end. It was now time to rise up against the great oppressor and free themselves once and for all from His laws. The once beautiful garden-like cities quickly plunged into chaos and destruction. The judges and priests were withdrawn back to heaven and the believers in Christ were called back to Israel.

The rebel army of Satan gathered in the land of Magog and fashioned weapons for themselves. An army several billion strong marched on Israel and surrounded the beautiful land. With an army several billion strong behind him, Satan felt invincible. Now he would ascend the mountain of God and dethrone Him. Now he would take his rightful place on the throne of God and rule the heavens and the earth.

As the army encircled Israel, the sky suddenly darkened and a rain of fire consumed the army. Not one person was left standing. An angel descended from heaven and laid hold of Satan. Satan fought the angel with all the power he could muster, but he couldn't defeat the angel. When at last the angel prevailed, Satan was cast into the Lake of Fire where the Antichrist and the False Prophet had been for the last thousand years.

The dead were resurrected and those still living were raptured off the earth to be judged. Every man, woman and child that had lived throughout the earth's entire seven thousand year history—with the exception of those already made immortal—were raised from the dead.

With Hades now empty, it was cast into the Lake of Fire. Death was the last enemy defeated as it was likewise cast into the Lake of Fire.

Those awaiting judgment found themselves standing in a

room of light. Though the walls and ceiling couldn't be seen, they all knew they were standing in one large room with all the other billions of people from all of history.

One by one they were called and found themselves standing before a great white throne. He who sat upon it had no discernible form and shone with great glory. The light of Him shone with the brilliance of thousands of stars combined. So great was His glory that heaven and earth fled from Him, and no place was found for them.

Everyone who stood before the great white throne stood with great fear, afraid to gaze upon Him. Each one of them was permitted to give an account of themselves. When asked why God should let them into His kingdom, they gave all sorts of strange and irrational answers. These reasons covered a broad range; living a good and decent life, to going to church every Sunday and serving Him, praying every day, and even preaching His Word. Some claimed ignorance of Him, citing several reasons for not knowing of Him. Those who had worshipped false gods claimed to lived lives of purity that they thought was pleasing to Him. Others cited scientific reasons saying there had been no proof of His existence.

The real test came when He asked, "Have you put your faith in My Son for salvation from sin?"

Some claimed they had done so. Others cited the same excuses proclaimed for the first question. Then books were opened. The first book was the Book of Life in which all the names of those who had ever lived were written at the moment of their conception. But there were a whole lot of names missing. The names of those who had died without putting their faith in Jesus Christ as the Father had commanded, had been removed from the Book of Life. The other book was the Lamb's Book of Life, in which were written all the names of those who had put their faith in Jesus Christ. These two books were a check to ensure that no mistakes were made and that all were without excuse. Even those who had never heard of the Son of God, were convicted by their conscience. It only took one small sin to be found guilty, for imperfection could not be permitted in God's presence.

Those who claimed to have put their faith in Jesus Christ were checked against the books. Those found written in the Lambs Book of life were permitted to enter into the kingdom of God. Children too young to make a decision for Christ were also permitted to enter. Many claimed to be Christians but their names were found missing from both books. These followed a false Jesus and were deceived by a false gospel taught by false teachers and prophets. These were not permitted to enter the new heaven.

Those who gave excuses for not believing or who claimed to have no knowledge of Him but had been convicted by their conscience, found their names missing from both books. No mistakes had been made in their accounting, they were without excuse, for God had made Himself known to all generations through His works and by His creation. For all creation spoke of His glory and gave Him praise. All those who had ears to hear and eyes to see understood this and responded in faith. Those who refused to hear or see now found themselves condemned. They were sentenced to eternal separation from their Creator, Whom they had been created to be with. The angel that brought them before the throne bound them and tossed them through an unseen void leading to the Lake of Fire. This judgment was pronounced upon them according to their own will, according to their choosing. By choosing to reject Jesus Christ, they had chosen death. Many of them pleaded for another chance, but after physical death and at the judgment, it was too late to repent. They had plenty of opportunities to repent while they were still living, but they chose not to. Sadly, of the whole of the world's population throughout its entire history, about 97 percent were not permitted to enter into His kingdom.

The demons and the angels were likewise judged. The bride of Christ sat as their judge. Those that had rebelled were likewise cast into the Lake of Fire with the condemned, while those who remained faithful were permitted to enter the new heaven. When the last demon was cast through the void, it was permanently closed off and the Lake of Fire with all those within it were forgotten.

With billions of people to judge, the process would seem to take millions of years to complete. In heaven, however, time does not exist. While time is considered a fourth dimension by some, it is purely a material by-product of gravity and velocity. The rate of the flow of time was relative to the object in motion and the pull of gravity and it flowed in only one direction. In the spiritual realm, the laws of physics of the material universe had no effect. There, different rules applied. In the spiritual realm there was no gravity or motion of a heavenly body; therefore no time existed. This was why a thousand years to God was as a day, and a day was as a thousand years. Since time did not exist, the judgments were finished in literally no time at all. With the completion of the judgments, it was now time for the final consummation of mankind.

At the spoken word of God, the laws of physics were instantly altered. Both heaven and the material universe began a rapid contraction back toward the center of the universe. Only the city of God, where the inhabitants of heaven resided, remained, while the rest of heaven disappeared in a wall of fire. The wall of fire closed in on the universe and swept up all the stars. As they were swept up, the stars exploded and added to the intensity of the fire. Not one micro-speck of matter remained. For seven days the wall of fire contracted, consuming everything in its path.

On earth, the atmosphere gradually heated up until it reached a temperature where everything spontaneously ignited. On the sixth day the entire planet was aflame. When the wall of fire reached it, all the molten matter of the universe merged with it and swept it along. Yet the earth itself was not blown apart.

When the wall of fire reached the center of the universe, all that remained was a ball of fire about two light-years in diameter. The molten ball of fire called "earth" was at the center. The ball of fire was allowed to burn for an entire day, ensuring that everything manmade or corrupted by mankind had been destroyed. All of man's grand architecture, works of art and marvels of technology were all eliminated. Not one molecule was left attached to another that was of manmade origin. All trace of the glories and corruptions of mankind were completely destroyed and forgotten.

At the end of the seventh day, three more days followed, during which the earth was recreated. Out of the molten matter of the old heaven and universe, a new earth emerged, perfect and unblemished. First the landscape was created, but there were no oceans. There were a great many lakes, a few large enough to be called seas, but there were no great bodies of ocean. The plants appeared next to purify the air and to provide food to the animals that would be created the next day. Mankind didn't need to be recreated; the inhabitants of the city of God would inhabit the new earth.

There was no sun or moon above the new earth. No light came from the heavens, for God Himself was the light. On the new earth, there was no darkness—not even in the deepest hole. Everything glowed with the light of God. The earth was two lightyears in diameter, but it was also a four-dimensional object.

The laws of physics governing the three dimensional material universe no longer applied. The crushing gravitational forces that such a massive object would normally produce simply didn't exist. The new four-dimensional earth was governed by a whole new set of laws.

When the earth was complete, the Lord declared it perfect. Then the city of God came down and rested on the earth. As it descended, it shone with the brilliance of God's glory like crystal-clear jasper, as a bride adorned for her husband. It was a city of magnificent splendor that defied the imagination. It was a city of pure gold that was like crystal glass. It was roughly pyramidal in shape and measured twelve thousand stadia in length and width and height according to human measurements (about 1,377 miles). It had as it's foundation twelve massive stones of different colors representing the twelve tribes of Israel. The first stone was of jasper, the second of sapphire, the third of chalcedony, the fourth of emerald, the fifth of sardonyx, the sixth of sardius, the seventh of chrysolite, the eighth of beryl, the ninth of topaz, the tenth of chrysoprase, the eleventh of jacinth, and the twelfth of amethyst. The city was surrounded by a high wall of jasper with twelve gates, three on each side. Each gate was 144 cubits wide (about 216 feet), and made of a single pearl. Upon each gate was the name of one of the twelve apostles.

The streets were paved with crystal gold and lined with crystal that shone with such brilliance that they appeared as white fire. Throughout the city, crystalline mansions of unimaginable and intricate beauty soared skyward. Trees and flowering plants that glowed from within adorned numerous parks inhabited with animals of every kind. The flowering plants permeated the air with sweet perfume that mingled with the heavenly music of the entwined voices of the angels continually singing their praises to God. Within the city, the bride of Christ resided.

Round about the city, a river flowed. This was the River of Life that emerged from the throne of God at the top of the mountain. In the center of the river grew a magnificent tree that spread it's branches across to both sides of the river and bore twelve kinds of fruit every month. The leaves of the tree provided healing for the people of various ethnic groups (nations), and the fruit provided enrichment for their bodies. The river flowed down and around the mountain of God. At the bottom of the mountain, the river then flowed back to the top and out from under the throne.

The mountain of God was adorned with precious gems and jewels, trees and flowering plants that glowed from within. Atop the mountain sat the throne of God. On each side of the throne were six seats. These were the seats the apostles sat in. The throne was encompassed by a sea of glowing crystal, which in turn was encompassed by four crystals of different colors that turned together as wheels within wheels. Each one turned as the four heavenly beings before God turned. On the sea of crystal were millions of other seats promised to those who had overcome the world. And from the throne the glory of God radiated to all parts of the city and beyond, in which no shadow of turning could be found. In the city, there was no temple of God, for the Lamb of God, Jesus Christ, was His temple and those who were raptured prior to the tribulation were the pillars of His temple. On each pillar was written a new name.

The people of the nations and the kings of the earth walked in the light of His glory. There was no night, and the gates were never closed. Nothing unclean and those who had practiced abominations and lying were not permitted past the gates. Only those whose names were found written in the Lamb's book of life were permitted through the gates. On the foreheads of those whose name were written in the Lamb's

Book of Life was written the name of God. The bride of Christ came and went as she pleased. The people not only lived in mansions of crystal in the city of God, but they also took up residences and conducted businesses in various places on the new earth. Those born and saved during the millennium, had been born after the marriage supper of the Lamb, thus were not considered part of the bride of Christ. Nor had they been part of the first resurrection. These didn't reside in the city of God but throughout the new earth. They were given dominion over the new earth and they tended to it, conducted various businesses, married and had offspring. They did, like the bride of Christ, have the name of God on their foreheads, and went to and fro as they pleased.

God Himself resided in the city and on the earth, for heaven and earth were one and the same place. God resided among the people, and the people were united with Him, their fellowship with Him restored, never again to be separated from Him. Thus the consummation of mankind was complete.

Jesus Christ declared, "It is done. I am the Alpha and the Omega, the beginning and the end. I will give to the one who thirsts from the spring of the water of life without cost. He who overcomes shall inherit these things, and I will be his God, and he will be My son. But for the cowardly and unbelieving, and the abominable and murderers and immoral persons, and the sorcerers and idolaters and all liars; their part will be in the lake that burns with fire and brimstone, which is the second death."

After seeing all these things, John was instructed not to seal up the book of this prophecy, for the time was near. It was important that all believers of every age understood what was written. It was given both as a warning of things to come and as an encouragement that they would be reunited with their Creator, nevermore to be separated from Him. The wickedness of the world would not go on forever. Jesus Christ would come just as He said He would, and put an end to the madness.

John found himself standing near the entrance to his abode feeling like a new man. He wished what he'd just witnessed had already come to pass, for he desired to remain with Christ on the new earth in the city of God. At the same time, he was troubled at the things to come and feared for his brethren. Now he had the job of writing it all down before his memory dimmed. It just so happened at that very moment that his scribe, Prochoros, came climbing up the hill carrying a scroll of papyrus. Prochoros sat at his writing table, writing everything John related to him. The Holy Spirit ensured that John didn't forget anything. It was well after sunset when they finished. At the end of the book, John instructed Prochoros to write, "I testify to everyone who hears the words of the prophecy of this book; if anyone adds to them, God shall add to him the plagues which are written in this book; and if anyone takes away from the words of the book of this prophecy, God shall take away his part from the tree of life and from the holy city, which are written in this book." Jesus Himself testified to these things saying, "Yes, I come quickly."

These last words were a warning to those who insist on allegorizing or spiritualizing the words of the prophecy. God takes them seriously. Those who insist on making them say what they were not intended to say will find themselves eternally separated from the Father.

Prochoros took the book first to the seven churches it was originally addressed to. Copies of the book were made and sent to all the churches. Many repented of their wicked deeds and found salvation in Jesus Christ, while others found the book troubling and sought to keep it hidden.

Shortly after the book of the Revelation of Jesus Christ was written, Caesar Domitian was assaulted by his servant and four others. He struggled madly with his attackers, but death overtook him. The senators, upon hearing news of his death, ordered all his statues, images and inscriptions throughout Rome destroyed. He was the last of the Roman emperors commonly referred to as the Twelve Caesars.

Since John had survived martyrdom, Domitian's successor released him from his exile. He had spent a total of eighteen months on Patmos. Upon his release, he returned to Ephesus, where he encountered Gnosticism within the church. Ever zealous for the truth of Christ, he wrote his three epistles to counter the compromised teachings. At the urging of his disciples, he wrote his gospel. Tradition has it that Mary Magdelene served as John's scribe. Since she was there with John throughout Jesus' ministry on earth, she was able to bare witness of these things, as stated in the last two sentences, and testifying that John's witness was true.

During the reign of Emperor Trajan, John died of old age. It was said of him that he founded and built churches throughout Asia and died sixty-eight years after the Lord's passion. He was buried near the city of Ephesus leaving behind the most beloved legacy of all the apostles.

Chapter 11

The Triune God

Several days passed before the troubling dreams of the tribulation wore off. If not for the hope of the consummation, I would have been in a deep state of despair.

When I was able to review what had been written, I noticed numerous references to the Trinity of God. Just what is the Trinity? In short it is the Father, the Son, and the Holy Spirit; three persons in one God. Each one has a distinct identity and a different purpose, but all three are one and the same God. They are different aspects of the same God.

Many who don't understand the Trinity have accused Christians of actually worshipping three Gods. They don't understand that the trinity is not the addition of God's power, where $1+1+1=3$. Rather, it is the multiplication of God's power where $1 \times 1 \times 1 = 1$. No one fully understands the Trinity, but to get a good idea of what it is, I was shown the following illustration.

I found myself standing on the seashore of the ocean and noticed its vastness. It was everywhere present and all-powerful. Sometimes it was calm and serene, while other times it was angry and wrathful. Nothing could resist the power of the ocean. It builds up, and it tears down. It was the supporter and giver of life, and the taker of life.

God the Father is very similar to the ocean. He is all-powerful and everywhere present. He is all-wise and all-knowing. He is the creator of the heavens and the earth. He is the source and giver of all life. For life can only come from life; it cannot come from non-life. As the Father is the Creator of all things, He is also the destroyer and rebuilder of all things. Nothing in heaven or on earth can resist His power.

People ask, "How can a loving God send people to hell?" The question is really, "How can a loving God *not* send people to hell?" God is slow to anger and quick to forgive, but once His wrath is stirred there is no resisting it. He is both loving and just, two inseparable attributes that are two sides of the same coin. Without love, there is no justice. Without justice there is no love. He is perfect in every sense of the word and cannot tolerate any imperfection (sin) in His presence no matter how slight. He is the judge of both the righteous and the wicked. His judgments are righteous and He gives to each in full measure according to what they have chosen. In reality, it isn't God who sends people to hell but they themselves. God just passes judgment.

As I stood on the seashore, looking out over the ocean, I noticed the waves. They were another aspect of the ocean and inseparable from it. The waves had their own identity and purpose, but they were one with the ocean. The waves carried out the will of the ocean and could not be held back. It was also impossible to get into the ocean without first going through the waves.

The Son of God, Jesus Christ, is similar to the waves. He is one with the Father, and inseparable. He has His own identity and purpose, but at all times He seeks to do the will of the Father. He is the Word of God. Since the beginning He was with God, and He is God. As the Father is the Creator of all things, so is the

Son. The Father gave the commands and the Son carried them out. When Adam and Eve lived in the garden of Eden, Jesus was the One who walked and talked with them in the cool of the morning. When they sinned, it was He who slaughtered an innocent animal to make a temporary covering for their sin. It was He who gave Noah the instructions to build the ark to deliver him from the world flood. It was He whom Abraham spoke to on His way to Sodom and Gomorrah. It was He whom Moses spoke to in the burning bush.

It was He who Isaiah prophesied would came to redeem mankind from his sins. He came to earth in the form of a man according to the will of the Father. He came to seek and to save those who are lost. He came to fulfill mankind's obligation to the law, which we were not able to keep. In accordance with the Father's will, He was crucified on a cross to pay the price of mankind's sin. On the third day, He rose from the dead as proof that fellowship with the Father had been restored in accordance with our faith in His Son, Jesus Christ. At His resurrection, His body was restored to its former glory. Forgiveness of sin was made available to mankind, as only God can forgive sins. Jesus is the way, the truth, and the life. No one can come to the Father but through Him. Salvation has been made available as a free gift to all who are willing to accept it. By faith in Jesus Christ we receive this gift of forgiveness and eternal life. It is by faith that we are saved, not by works of any kind, lest anyone should boast. Without faith in Him, it is impossible to please the Father. Those who have faith in Jesus Christ have been given the right to be called Children of God.

As I stood by the sea, I noticed a third aspect of the sea that was invisible to the eye. The salt air is produced by the sea and is one and the same with the sea. It can be sensed long before reaching the sea. It invigorates, motivates and draws people to the sea.

The Holy Spirit is similar to the salt air. He has His own identity and purpose but comes from the Father. He is one and the same with the Father. As the Father and the Son are God, so the Holy Spirit is also God. He is invisible yet everywhere present. He cannot be seen by the eye of man, but His work can be felt. He works among men to convict them of their sins and draws them to the Father. Those who put their faith in Jesus Christ receive the Holy Spirit. The Holy Spirit gives life to the spirit of men who put their faith in Christ. As life only comes from life, only the Holy Spirit gives life to the spirit of mankind. Mankind was created in the image of God, having a spirit like God. Being born in sin and separated from God, however, his spirit has no life. When he puts his faith in the Son of God, the Spirit of God resides in his heart, giving his spirit new life and a second birth.

This is what it means to be "born again." Unless a man be born again, he cannot enter into the kingdom of God. Those who claim to be Christian yet say they are not born again either don't know what they're talking about or are not true Christians. Once the spirit of man has been born again, the Holy Spirit continues to work in him completing the work that the Son has begun. He comforts and assures man, and leads him in understanding of the Scriptures. When the believer in Christ prays, it is the Holy Spirit who makes intercession on his behalf with groans and moanings too deep for the spirit of man to comprehend. The Holy Spirit defends him from Satan and works to keep him from sin, but He does not violate man's free will.

Living within the sea are a host of creatures—fish, mammals, reptiles and cephalopods. Each one fills a specific niche in the ecology of the ocean. So too are those who have come to the Father by faith in the Son. The believers reside in the Father, who bestows upon each one gifts to perform a specific function to build up the body of Christ. As the fish cannot leave the sea and live, so too the believers will perish (spiritually) apart from the Father. Unlike the fish that can be drawn out of the sea, there is no power in heaven or on earth that can remove believers from the hand of God. This, however, doesn't stop Satan from trying to make the believers ineffective.

There is a great spiritual war raging around us that few are aware of. The battleground is the souls of mankind. The stakes are eternal life. Satan seeks to deceive everyone and tries to take as many as he can with him into hell. Jesus stands at the gates of hell and seeks to save as many as will believe in him to save them from the second death.

This material world we live in is only the temporal reality. One we must eventually leave behind. The spiritual realm is the true reality into which we will eventually pass. There are two parts to this spiritual reality; heaven and hell. Each of these two spiritual realms has a single path leading to it.

The path to hell is broad, easy-to-follow, and paved with good intentions. A great many people are walking this path blissfully following the crowd like lemmings to plunge into the dark fiery chasm of hell. They try to earn their salvation by doing various works, but in the end they find that they have fallen short. The second death eagerly awaits them.

The path to the kingdom of God is narrow and hard to follow. Few are they that find it and even fewer are they that chose to follow it. Many are called, but few are chosen. Those who answer the call are chosen by God as was predestined. This does not mean that our destiny is written in stone and is out of our control. Destiny is determined by an act of our will, not by what is foreknown. Faith in Jesus Christ for forgiveness of sins and eternal life is the only way to the Father Whom we were created to be with. Jesus said, "I am the way, the truth and the life. No one comes to the Father but through Me." (John 14:6).

The postmodernist and unbelievers can deny the truth all they want claiming that everything is relative. Their sins still remain, however, and in their hearts they know this to be true despite their denials. They claim that there is no scientific evidence for God's existence and they say, "Prove it."

Romans 1:18-22 states:

> For the wrath of God is revealed from heaven against all ungodliness and unrighteousness of men, who suppress the truth in unrighteousness, because that which is known about God is evident within them; for God made it evident to them. For since the creation of the world His invisible attributes, His eternal power and divine nature, have been clearly seen, being understood through what has been made so they are without excuse. For even though they knew God, they did not honor Him as God, or give thanks; but they became futile in their speculations, and their foolish heart was darkened. Professing to be wise, they became fools.

Every time people look up at the stars or look at themselves in their bathroom mirror, they see the evidence of God's existence. In their foolishness, not wanting to believe the truth, they attribute His work to the work of evolution, but in their hearts they know differently. For God has written His law in the hearts of mankind. Though they deny it to their dying breath, they instinctively know the truth of God. These unbelievers are truly without excuse and will perish.

I don't mean to sound like I'm passing a railing judgment against anyone. However, truth is truth and no matter how much it hurts or offends, people still need to be warned. Therefore, I implore you to change your mind about your sinful condition and turn away from it, that is repent. Jesus said,

> For God so loved the world, that He gave His only begotten Son, that whoever believes in Him should not perish, but have eternal life. For God did not send the Son into the world to judge the world, but that the world should be saved through Him. He who believes in Him is not judged; he who does not believe has been judged already, because he has not believed in the name of the only begotten Son of God. And this is the judgment, that the light is come into the world, and men love the darkness rather than the light; for their deeds are evil. For everyone who does evil hates the light, and does not come to the light, lest his deeds should be exposed. But he who practices the truth comes to the light, that his deeds may be manifested as having been wrought in God. (John 3:16-21).

The choice between two destinies have been placed before you; eternal life with God in heaven or eternal separation from God in hell, also known as the "second death." Nothing can impose upon your freewill. No matter how strong the influence, you always have a choice. The catch is that you have to make that choice before the first death. For it is appointed for men to die once, and after that comes judgment. Judgment is determined by the choice you make. I invite you, therefore, to choose life and put your faith in Jesus Christ for salvation while you still have the opportunity to do so. A word of warning; it is not enough to believe in Jesus Christ in your head. Satan and his demons also believe, but their place is in the Lake of Fire. It is our heart that

God looks at. It is your heart that you must open to Him in faith. Then you can be assured that your salvation is secured and you will be with Him for all eternity. Those who reject the free gift of eternal life have, by default, chosen death.

Those who claim to be Christian, pay heed to the four-point message given to the servants of God:

1. Understand that you are living in the Laodicean age of the luke warm church. The vast majority of self-proclaimed Christians are living deceived lives. They love the Christ, claim to be Christians, and play church, but they live like the Devil. Satan is a personal Devil, just as God is a personal God. Satan influences the personal affairs of mankind just as God is involved in the lives of men. These "Christians" have bought the lie of Satan that it is all right to go to church on Sunday and attend midweek services—and then spend the rest of the week getting all they can out of life. They have bought the lie of the seeker-friendly purpose-driven, and Word of Faith emergent church with their ten steps to self-improvement and watered-down gospel of Jesus Christ. They have deceived themselves with their feel-good spiritual mysticism they call Spiritual Formation. The Catholic church is no different in teaching heresy and insisting only a priest can understand the Scriptures. The same is true of the false Christian churches, like the Church of Jesus Christ of Latter Day Saints and the Watchtower Society, otherwise known as Jehovah's Witnesses. These false Christian churches and pseudo-Christian churches have led their members into compromising the Scriptures to the point where there is no discernible difference between them and the heathen. When the members of the pseudo-Christian churches aren't playing church, they're getting drunk, carousing, gambling, fornicating with the neighbors and watching pornography. They see nothing wrong with abortion and homosexuality with their same-sex marriage that is proving

so destructive to society. Foul language, hate speech and gossip drip from their lips. With their tongue they slay your neighbors and give praise to God. This ought not to be. They believe they are comfortable and have need of nothing, but they are poor, blind and naked. Unless these lukewarm Christians repent, if they are Christians at all, Jesus will spew them out of His mouth. The true Christians who have overcome the world, Jesus has promised to keep from the time of testing.

2. To those who claim to be Christians, understand that you are supposed to be ambassadors of Christ on earth. You cannot be a true witness for Christ if you do not live the Christian life twenty-four hours a day, seven days a week. The true measure of a man's character is what he does in the privacy of his home when no one is watching. You must walk the Christian life at all times, not merely talk about it. Honoring God with your lips but not your heart is unacceptable. You husbands, do you love your wives? You wives, do you honor you husbands? How can you say you love and honor God, when you don't love and honor your spouse? You, Christian, do you love your neighbor down the street who hates you? How can you say you love God when you hate your neighbor?

3. As the world was in the days of Noah, so it is now. In Noah's day humanity gave no thought to Noah's words and refused to believe that anything would change. They saw the signs the earth was giving them, but they would not repent. Today is no different. The earth is in its last days. Humanity sees the signs of the last days, but they don't believe that anything will change. They refuse to believe in Christ's impending return and do nothing to prepare to meet God. Instead,

"Professing to be wise, they have become fools, and exchanged the glory of the incorruptible God for an image in the form of corruptible man and

249

of birds and four-footed creatures and crawling creatures. Therefore God gave them over to the lust of their hearts, that their bodies might be dishonored among them. For they exchanged the truth of God for a lie, and worshiped and served the creature rather then the Creator who is blessed forever. Amen. For this reason God gave them over to degrading passions; for their women exchanged the natural function for that which is unnatural, and in the same way also the men abandoned the natural function of the woman and burned in their desire toward one another, men with men committing indecent acts and receiving in their own persons the due penalty of their error. And just as they did not see fit to acknowledge God any longer, God gave them over to a depraved mind, to do those things which are not proper, being filled with all unrighteousness, wickedness, greed, evil; full of envy, murder, strife, deceit, malice; they are gossips, slanderers, haters of God, insolent, arrogant, boastful, inventors of evil, disobedient to parents, without understanding, untrustworthy, unloving, unmerciful; and although they know the ordinances of God, that those who practice such things are worthy of death, they not only do the same, but also give hearty approval to those who practice them. (Romans 1:22–32)

Behold, the Father, the creator of heaven and earth, is hurting when the lowest earth-child is hurting. So great is God's love towards the least of these children, no mere man can possibly comprehend. As we do unto the least of these, good or bad, we also do unto Him.

4. The Father is in the process of raising an army that will put to shame the hierarchy of the so-called "establishment" religion. Through them, God will perform miracles and demonstrate His power to a greater extent than the disciples did in the Pentecostal age. Through this army, God is about to perform the miracles He has promised us. God has given each of us gifts to be used in service to that army. Will you use your gifts and be part of that army? Satan has an army that acts like an army. We are the army of God. We need to start acting like an army.

I implore all lukewarm and backsliding Christians to repent, as Jesus Christ requires. Eschew evil and avoid those who teach things contrary to the literal teaching of God's written Word as dictated by the context in which it is written. Get off the couch, pour out the bug juice you're drinking, put the smart phone down and turn off the video games. Cease your partying and carousing. The sun is setting, and the daylight for working is growing short. The crops are ripe for harvesting, and the workers are few. So pick up your sickle or rake and join those already in the field. Do the work the Lord has given you with all earnestness as unto God, for the darkness is quickly overcoming the world, and the work will not continue. Work fervently to win souls for Jesus and to disciple them while we still can. As Jesus has promised, your reward will be great.

To those who are already in the field and feeling overwhelmed; do not be discouraged, for soon you will enter into God's rest. Take heart, for God is well-pleased with your work and has promised you the crown of life (James 1:12). Feeling tired and weary? "Do you not know? Have you not heard? The Everlasting God, the Lord, the Creator of the ends of the earth does not become weary or tired. His understanding is inscrutable. He gives strength to the weary, and to him who lacks might, He increases power. Though youths grow weary and tired, and vigorous young men stumble badly, yet those who wait for the Lord will gain new strength; they will mount up with wings like eagles, they will run and not get tired, they will walk and not become weary." (Isaiah 40:28–31).

To those who are fearful; take courage, for God is with us. If God is with us, who could possible stand against us? Satan's children may hate and revile you, persecute you and kill your body, but after that, what more can they do? No matter what they do, they can't touch your soul. Our salvation is guaranteed and cannot be taken away from us. We are free, and there is nothing Satan can do to bind us. There is no power in heaven or earth strong enough to remove us from the hand of God. Don't worry if you don't feel qualified. God doesn't normally call the qualified, but he qualifies those He has called. Do not lose heart. "Ask, and it shall be given to you; seek, and you shall find; knock, and it will be opened to you. For whoever asks receives, and he who seeks finds, and he who knocks it shall be opened." (Matthew 7:8&9). Behold, He comes quickly. To God be the glory, amen.

Appendix A: Time Lines

Biblical Time Line of Earth's History

AC = After Creation
BC = Before Christ
AD = Anno Domini
Note: Dates are approximate.

Patriarch	Age	Born	Died	Date of Event(s)	Event(s)
				1 AC (4108 BC)	The earth and universe is created in six literal, twenty-four-hour days. Mankind is created on day six. The creation is declared perfect. Man, dinosaurs, and other animals live in perfect harmony. There is no death or suffering.
Adam	930	1 AC (4108 BC)	930 AC (3178 BC)		Disobeys God and is tossed out of the garden of Eden shortly after creation. Earth and universe are corrupted by sin. Death and suffering begins.
				129 AC (3979 BC)	The first murder occurs when Adam's firstborn son, Cain, slews Adam's second born son, Abel. Cain's descendants build cities and develop technology.

Patriarch	Age	Born	Died	Date of Event(s)	Event(s)
Seth	912	130 AC (3978 BC)	1042 AC (3066 BC)		
Enosh	935	235 AC (3873 BC)	1170 AC (2938 BC)		
Kenan	910	325 AC (3783 BC)	1292 AC (2873 BC)		
Mahalalel	897	395 AC (3713 BC)	1292 AC (2822 BC)		
Jared	962	460 AC (3648 BC)	1422 AC (2686 BC)		
Enoch	365	622 AC (3486 BC)			Finds favor with God and is raptured, 987 AC (3121 BC). Does not taste death.

Patriarch	Age	Born	Died	Date of Event(s)	Event(s)
Methuselah	969	687 AC (3421 BC)	1656 AC (2452 BC)		Dies in the year of the world flood, either in the flood or months before—most likely a few months before the flood.
Lamech	777	874 AC (3234 BC)	1651 AC (2457 BC)		Dies five years before the flood.
Noah	950	1056 AC (3052 BC)	2006 AC (2102 BC)	1556 AC (2552 BC)	Begins construction of the ark as directed by God. Takes one hundred years to build it.
				1656 AC (2452 BC)	World Flood occurs. Noah, his three sons and all their wives are saved on the ark. Forty days of rain occur after the fountains of the deep and floodgates of heaven are opened. Breakup of continents result. The flood lasts one year.
Shem	600	1558 AC (2550 BC)	2158 AC (1950 BC)		

Patriarch	Age	Born	Died	Date of Event(s)	Event(s)
Arpachshad	438	1658 AC (2450 BC)	2096 AC (2012 BC)		
Shelah	433	1693 AC (2415 BC)	2126 AC (1982 BC)		
Eber	464	1723 AC (2385 BC)	2187 AC (1922 BC)		During Eber's day, the people are led by Nimrod to the land of Shinar. Building on the Tower of Babel begins.
Peleg	239	1757 AC (2351 BC)	1996 AC (2112 BC)	1757 AC (2351 BC)	Languages are confused at the Tower of Babel, approximately one hundred years after the world flood. People separate and spread out over the earth. Various nations are established. Ethnic diversity begins.
Reu	239	1787 AC (2321 BC)	2026 AC (2082 BC)		

Patriarch	Age	Born	Died	Date of Event(s)	Event(s)
Serug	230	1819 AC (2289 BC)	2049 AC (2059 BC)		
Nahor	148	1849 AC (2259 BC)	1997 AC (2111 BC)		
Terah	205	1878 AC (2230 BC)	2083 AC (2025 BC)		
Abram	175	1948 AC (2160 BC)	2123 AC (1985 BC)		Noah dies in Abram's fifty-eighth year. Abram leaves Haran at age seventy-five in 2023 AC (2085 BC) God changes his name to Abraham. Pharaoh Khufu builds the great Pyramid of Giza after Abraham imparts knowledge of mathematics and astronomy to Egyptians.
Isaac	180	2048 AC (2060 BC)	2228 AC (1880 BC)		Tricked into giving Jacob his blessings instead of Esau.

Patriarch	Age	Born	Died	Date of Event(s)	Event(s)
Jacob	147	2108 AC (2000 BC)	2255 AC (1853 BC)	2236 AC (1870 BC)	Takes family to Egypt, beginning Israel's 430-year sojourn in a foreign land. Twin brother, Esau, becomes father of the Edomites.
Joseph	110	2198 AC (1910 BC)	2308 AC (1800 BC)	2228 AC (1880 BC)	Becomes prime minister (vizier) of Egypt.
				2558 AC (1550 BC)	Hebrews bondage begins at end of Semite Kings rule of Egypt. (1650 – 1550 BC)
Moses	120	2588 AC (1520 BC)	2708 AC (1400 BC)	2668 AC (1440 BC)	Sons of Israel depart from Egypt 430 years after Jacob entered Egypt.
Joshua	110	2648 AC (1460 BC)	2758 AC (1350 BC)		He is twenty years old at the exodus from Egypt.
				2708 AC (1400 BC)	Joshua leads Israel across the Jordan River into the Promised Land.

The Holy Land

Patriarch	Age	Born	Died	Date of Event(s)	Event(s)
				2728 AC (1380 BC)	Period of judges to rule over Israel begins. (1380 BC to 1072 BC)
				3036 AC (1072 BC)	Saul is appointed as Israel's first king. He dies approximately 1019 BC
David	70	3074 AC (1034 BC)	3144 AC (964 BC)	3089 AC (1019 BC)	Kills Goliath and is anointed king at age fifteen to twenty years old.
Solomon	70	3114 AC (994 BC)	3184 AC (924 BC)	3144 AC (964 BC)	Becomes king at age thirty.
				3148 AC (960 BC)	In the fourth year of Solomon's reign, 480 years after the exodus from Egypt, construction of the temple begins.
				3184 AC (924 BC)	Israel divides into two kingdoms following Solomon's death.

Patriarch	Age	Born	Died	Date of Event(s)	Event(s)
				3387 AC (721 BC)	The northern kingdom of Israel is taken into captivity by Assyria.
				3511AC (597 BC)	The southern kingdom of Judah is defeated by Nebuchadnezzar. This is the first deportation to Babylon.
				3522 AC (586 BC)	This is the southern kingdom's (Judah's) second deportation to Babylon.
				3665 AC (539 BC)	Babylon is defeated by Persia. King Cyrus decrees that the temple of God in Jerusalem be rebuilt. Israel's bondage to Babylon ends.
				3761 AC (443 BC)	King Artaxerxes issues a decree to rebuild the walls of Jerusalem. Israel's prophesied seventy weeks of years (490 years) begins.

Patriarch	Age	Born	Died	Date of Event(s)	Event(s)
				3870 AC (334 BC)	Alexander the Great begins his conquest of the Persian Empire and overthrows King Darius III. He establishes the Hellenistic Empire. Upon his death, the empire is divided among his four generals.
				3941 AC (167 BC)	Antiochus Epiphanes defiles the Jewish temple by erecting a statue of Zeus and killing a pig on the altar. Puts an end to sacrifices and the observing of Jewish religious laws. He becomes a type of antichrist, but is not the true Antichrist prophesied in Scripture.
				4059 AC (49 BC)	Julius Caesar becomes dictator of the Roman Republic.

Patriarch	Age	Born	Died	Date of Event(s)	Event(s)
				4064 AC (44 BC)	On the Ides of March, Julius Caesar is assassinated. Octavius (Augustus), Mark Antony, and Lepidus form the second triumvirate.
				4066 AC (42 BC)	Herod the Great is appointed as king of Judaea by Mark Antony.
				4068 AC (40 BC)	Herod the Great is elected king of the Jews, by the Roman Senate.
				4077 AC (31 BC)	Lepidus is forced into exile, and Mark Antony is defeated at the Battle of Actium. The Roman Empire is established when Octavian becomes the sole ruler of the Roman republic and takes the name of Augustus Caesar.

Patriarch	Age	Born	Died	Date of Event(s)	Event(s)
				4100 AC (8 BC)	Augustus Caesar issues a decree for a census to be taken of all Roman lands. The Census in Judaea is conducted by Quirinius, a military procurator in Syria. It takes two years to complete.
Jesus	40	4100 AC (8 BC)	4141 AC (33 AD)		Jesus is born in Bethlehem in late September or early October, before the sheep are brought in from the fields to protect them from the winter cold.
				4102 AC (6 BC)	Jesus is visited by several magi from the east. Joseph takes his family to Egypt to escape the wrath of Herod, who has every child two years old and under killed in Bethlehem.

Patriarch	Age	Born	Died	Date of Event(s)	Event(s)
				4104 AC (4 BC)	Israel divided at Herod the Great's death. Herod Archelaus is made Ethnarch (not king) of Judaea. Herod Antipas was appointed tetrarch of Galilee. Joseph takes his family back to Nazareth in Galilee.
				4114 AC (6 AD)	Herod Archelaus is deposed. Judaea province is formed under direct Roman rule at the time Quirinius is Governor of Syria. A second census conducted by Quirinius results in revolt.
				4134 AC (26 AD)	Pontius Pilot is appointed as fifth prefect of Judaea.

Patriarch	Age	Born	Died	Date of Event(s)	Event(s)
				4137 AC (29 AD)	Jesus is baptized by John the Baptist in the autumn of AD 29 and proceeds to the wilderness for forty days. Fifty days after Jesus is baptized, John the Baptist is imprisoned. Jesus begins His ministry and calls the twelve apostles.
				4141 AC (33 AD)	At the age of about forty years old, Jesus was crucified on Passover, April 3rd, which occurs on Friday that year. Israel's seventy weeks of years stopped at exactly sixty-nine weeks of years. Jesus is resurrected from the dead, Sunday, April 5th. He ascends into heaven on a cloud after the Great Commission had been given to all those in attendance —about five hundred men. The church age begins on Pentecost with the outpouring of the Holy Spirit upon the apostles. Three thousand new converts added that day.

Appendix B: Glossary

*T*he following provides definitions and/or explanations of terminology used in this book. The items are listed according to three categories: Scientific Terminology and Concepts; Dinosaurs and Other So-Called Prehistoric Animals; and Political and Religious Organizations and Programs. Some of the definitions include criticisms, which some readers may find objectionable.

Scientific Terminology and Concepts

Assumptions: By definition, an assumption is something taken for granted or believed to be true without proof. People make assumptions everyday of their lives. They assume their car will start when they head off to work. They assume nothing bad will happen to them throughout the day. They assume life will continue as it has without radical change. In the case of science it is a necessary starting point for researching the unknown. For instance scientists assume that the unknown is knowable. They assume that the laws of physics as observed on earth are equally valid everywhere in the universe. They assume that naturalistic processes are responsible for the origins of the world we know and that God does not exist. They assume that the present is the key to the past.

The problem with scientific assumptions, especially where origins are concerned, is that they often obscure the facts; and when they are accepted by consensus of the majority of scientists, they are treated as facts that are not to be questioned or challenged. Anything that contradicts accepted assumptions is automatically rejected or reinterpreted and forced to fit the assumptions. When something is accepted without question it ceases to be science and becomes philosophical or religious dogma.

Axial precession of the earth: Also known as *Precession of the Equinoxes*. This was first discovered in classical times by the Greek mathematician Hipparchus around 147 to 127 BC. It may have been known by the Babylonians, Egyptians, and Mayans. Axial precession refers to the slow and gradual change of the earth's axis of rotation. It describes the westward motion of the equinoxes along the ecliptic, relative to the fixed position of the stars, opposite the motion of the sun along the ecliptic. Clear as mud, right? One precession cycle is about twenty-six thousand years. Because of this precession, during the spring equinox (March 21st), the sun rises in a different constellation of the zodiac every 2,166 years. Today, the sun is in transition between the constellations of Pisces and Aquarius. The earth is entering what some call the Age of Aquarius.

The precession is a gravity-induced wobble of the earth's axis of rotation—like a wobbling top. All rotating bodies have this gyroscopic wobble. The rotation of the wobble runs in the opposite direction of axial rotation. On the earth, the axial precession causes the poles to continuously point toward a different location in space. Today the north pole points closest to the star Polaris, known as the North Star. Polaris is forty-eight minutes of arch away from true north. When the axial precession was reset during the world flood, the spring equinox occurred in the constellation of Taurus, and the north pole pointed almost directly at Thuban in the Alpha Draconis constellation. True north was a mere ten minutes of arch away from it.

Big bang theory: A cosmological model invented to explain the origin of the universe from the uniformitarian world view. It postulates that hot, dense matter exploded from a singularity the size of a dime and expanded outward to form the stars and galaxies, like glitter on the surface of an expanding balloon. It is based on the Copernican principle that assumes the universe is the same everywhere and has no boundaries or center. Relies on gravitational forces to coalesce the first primordial elements to form stars. The source of the gravitational forces is not explained. However, gravity requires mass and density, which implies an edge and a center. Without a sufficiently large enough mass to produce gravity, matter cannot coalesce and produce stars and other heavenly bodies.

There are ninety-two naturally occurring elements in the universe, arranged on the periodic table according to their atomic weight numbers. Between elements five and eight there is a gap where there are no stable atoms. Because of this gap, the lighter elements cannot transmute into the heavier elements. The lighter gases produced by the big bang could never have produced the stars with iron in them, or the planets. The only thing the big bang would produce is an expanding ring of hydrogen and helium gas with nothing in the middle—no galaxies, stars, planets and no you and me. The big bang theory claims to predict certain observed data like the cosmic microwave background (CMB) radiation, but the verified presence of the CMB and other predicted phenomena is not proof of the big bang. The observed data is interpreted according to uniformitarian assumptions as proof of the big bang. The theory is claimed to rely on general relativity, but it actually violates general relativity and other laws of physics. It does not have a first cause and cannot explain where the matter making up the singularity originated from.

Black holes and white holes: A black hole is a hole in the space-time continuum from which nothing can escape, not even light. It is formed by a star with sufficient mass to collapse upon itself, once its nuclear fuel is exhausted. At this point a super nova occurs in which the outer portion of the star is blown off while the inner portion collapses upon itself to form a compact mass with a strong gravitational field that pulls in everything coming near it. Around the black hole is a mathematically defined region called the *event horizon,* which marks the point of no return. The more matter that gets pulled into a black hole the larger its event horizon becomes. An object approaching the black hole with enough velocity can still escape the black hole, but once it passes beyond the event horizon, there is no escape. The farther an object falls into a black hole, the stronger the gravitational pull. The side of the object facing the black hole is subject to a stronger gravitational pull than the side facing away from it. This results in the stretching of the object. The stronger gravity also has the effect of slowing down the flow of time within the black hole. Inside the event horizon, time appears to slow down to a point where it appears to stop relative to an observer outside the event horizon.

Matter in the form of gas, due to conservation of angular momentum forms a disk-shaped structure around the black hole called an *accretion disk.* This permits matter to fall farther inward, releasing energy and increasing the temperature. The temperature becomes so hot that it releases vast amounts of radiation, typically X-rays, called *extragalactic jets.* Once the object reaches the bottom or center of the black hole there are competing theories of what happens to it. The most popular theory states that the object is crushed into a singularity having zero volume, along with everything else that is pulled into the black hole. Another theory suggests that the object passes a point where it is expelled out the other end into another region of the universe or into another dimension. Quasars are thought by some to be formed from matter expelled out the back side of black holes in another dimension.

Another theory suggests that once sufficient enough matter reaches the center of the black hole, instead of being crushed into a singularity, it rebounds out of the black hole like an object bouncing off a trampoline. This rebounding would reverse the effects of the black hole, turning it into a white hole. A white hole is merely the reverse of a black hole. The pull of gravity decreases until it becomes antigravity and expels matter. The flow of time increases, but does not reverse. Matter passing out of a white hole will reduce the size of the event horizon until the white hole ceases to exist. A white hole would only be seen when matter is expelled from it. Observed anomalous flashes of light seen in space could possibly be matter expelled from white holes. Quasars are the brightest objects in the universe and aren't fully understood. They are thought to be the oldest objects in the universe due to their location at the outer extremes of the universe, as postulated by the speed theory of redshifted light. They could possibly be white holes, though it is highly doubtful.

Chemical reactions: The interactions of two or more atoms of certain fixed proportions to produce a new chemical compound, e.g., the interaction of sodium (a metal) and chlorine (a noxious gas) becomes sodium chloride (common table salt).

Consensus science or scientific consensus: A general agreement and solidarity between scientists about a certain belief that has no scientific data or evidence to support it. Scientists are by no means immune to the irrational peer pressure of the herd. When a consensus is claimed, it is often treated as a fact that should not be questioned. It has shaped the thinking of most scientists so strongly that they are no longer able to accurately summarize or evaluate radical ideas. Anything that goes against the consensus paradigm is automatically rejected. Those bucking the consensus are persecuted, labeled as "deniers" among a few other damnable things, and prevented from researching their theories or publishing their findings. They often find themselves out of a job. Science has devolved to the point where it has become necessary to establish a consensus before any new ideas can be postulated. This is not how true science works.

The result is that scientific progress has been severely hampered and tightly controlled by the so-called elite. "Peer-reviewed" literature is actually *consensus*-reviewed and is misrepresented. It has resulted in the rise of atheism among the scientific elite and the shutting out of creationists. If creation scientist like Newton, Pasteur, Faraday and others had conformed to scientific consensus, we'd still be living in the dark ages. Scientific consensus, like everything else, has its place, but more often than not it has been wrong. Some examples include evolution, the big bang, global cooling in the seventies, abortion, eugenics (which is currently experiencing a resurgence), the benefits of adding fluoride to the water supply, the value of embryonic stem cell research, and more recently global warming—among a host of others.

Scientific consensus has been used to justify fraudulent manipulation of data to force-fit them into supporting desired political agendas like cap-and-trade and Agenda 21. It has been used to browbeat scientists into toeing the party line and used to deceive the public into thinking that anything backed by scientific consensus should not be questioned. After all, its just too complicated for us poor stupid folks to understand. There's an old legal proverb that states, "If you have the facts on your side, argue the facts. If you have the law on your side, argue the law. If you have neither, attack the witness." When supporters of a particular consensus start attacking the "deniers", be very suspicious. Question the consensus, research the facts and demand the truth.

Conservation of angular momentum: The total angular momentum of a system does not change unless acted upon by an outside force. In other words; if a planet orbiting a star moves to a lower orbit within its gravity well, it must increase its speed to keep from falling deeper into the star's gravity well. If it increases its speed, it must move to a higher orbit to keep from being flung out of the gravity well. An object in a vacuum has a natural tendency to travel in a straight line at a fixed velocity. It will not change direction or speed unless something acts upon it. Gravity acts like a string attached to a planet. Instead of the planet going off in a straight line, gravity keeps the planet in its respective orbit around its star at the appropriate velocity. Thus angular momentum is conserved.

Cosmic microwave background (CMB) radiation: Predicted by the bing bang theory and confirmed by the COBE mission in 1965, this radiation is said to be the "dying breath of the big bang" and touted is evidence of the big bang. However, it does not match the predictions of the big bang. The radiation should be coming from one direction—outward. Instead it comes from all directions. It should be ten to a thousand times stronger than it is and it does not have the total light absorption capacity. It should be about five degrees Kelvin, but it is only 2.73 degrees Kelvin. (Kelvin = absolute zero or minus 273.15 degrees Celsius.) It does not cluster enough to produce stars. Gas always pushes outward, not inward. In fact, the hotter the gas, the faster it spreads out. Studies have shown that it is not the left over remains of the big bang. Both microwave and infrared radiation appear to be nothing more than the outflow of radiation from the stars and galaxies all around us.

Empirical science: A method of scientific research in which a theory must be able to predict the outcome of a test applied to it. The results must be observable, able to be proven wrong (falsifiable), and repeatable by other researchers. This is the essence of *empirical* or *operational science*. Evolution and creation fall into the category of *origins* science. Origins science can't be repeated, observed or tested. Evolutionists claim to use the principle of empirical science to prove evolution, but in reality, evolution violates this principle.

At this point, it must be made clear what science is *not*. Evolutionists have hijacked science and incorporated it into evolution, making evolution and science one and the same. By incorporating the two together, they've turned science into a science *religion* that no longer resembles science. This science religion has impeded true science for over 150 years. Any scientist who even hints at the possibility that evolution and the big bang are in error, will find their research funds rescinded, lab and/or telescope time denied, and publications turned away. They are made to look like pseudo-scientist quacks and their careers are lost. This is the establishment's idea of science these days. If not for the creation scientists, society would have returned to the dark ages. This so-called scientific age of "enlightenment" has darkened the minds of countless unsuspecting souls. These poor souls have been deceived into thinking that rejecting evolution is the same as rejecting science.

Evolutionists want us to believe that evolution is a proven scientific fact. They want us to believe that nothing in biology makes sense except in the light of evolution. They deride those of us who reject evolution and accuse us of also rejecting science. The fact is, despite what evolutionists would have us believe, science and evolution are not interchangeable concepts. Science does not depend on evolutionary interpretation to be understood, and nothing in biology makes sense in the light of evolution. Science is not capable of proving anything and it depends on God's existence for it to make sense. Nothing in the universe makes sense without God, for He is the first cause and designer of everything we see. Without God, there is no universe to be observed, no you and me, and no science—plain and simple.

Hemoglobin ($C_{3032}H_{4812}N_{780}Fe_4O_{872}S_{12}$): The most complex and largest molecule ever created. It is carried by the red blood cells to transport oxygen from the lungs to the trillions of cells throughout the body and to carry carbon dioxide back to the lungs for exhalation. Remove one atom from this molecule and it ceases to function properly. The odds of something this complex coming about by pure chance as evolution demands is simply staggering. A molecule consisting of over ten thousand atoms arranged in precise order demands an all-wise omnipotent creator.

Hypothesis: An educated guess. A tentative explanation of data obtained from experiments. The National Academy of Sciences defines *hypothesis* as "a testable statement about the natural world." Generally it is a limited statement about cause and effect, but to be useful it must offer the opportunity for further testing.

Irreducible complexity: This concept states that all the parts of a system are required to be in place for that system to function properly. The removal of any part would disable the whole system. In the case of organisms, the removal or absence of any part results in the death of the organism. Dead organisms cannot evolve or pass on their genes to the next generation. Even the simplest of organisms have been found to be extremely complex. The complexity is such that every part of the organism needs to be present and fully developed to be functional. If each component evolved slowly over time by chance, that part would be useless and discarded. Thus the organism would never evolve. It is easy to see when examining these complex organisms that the probability of evolving by chance is exactly zero. Thus an intelligent designer is necessary for the organism to exist.

Kind versus species: Creationism has always taught the fixity of kinds, whereby no kind of animal or plant becomes another kind. It has also always recognized that speciation within a kind does and has been observed to occur. In the late nineteenth century, evolutionists started claiming that creationists denied speciation and started using the terms *kinds* and *species* interchangeably as if the two were the same thing. This has caused a great deal of confusion within the church and has lead many to compromise the Scriptures by reinterpreting the Word of God according to scientific teaching. In so doing, they gave science—or rather the fallible opinions of mankind—a higher authority than God and His written Word. The lie that *species* and *kind* are the same thing is still taught in evolutionist's text books.

The truth is, *species* and *kind* have always been two different things. The Bible describes two types of *kinds*. In the first chapter of Genesis, animals are grouped into very broad classifications: beast, cattle, things that creep on the ground, birds, and fish. No distinction is made between reptile, mammal, insect, etc. Birds are anything that flies, whether it has feathers or not. Bats and pterosaurs are not birds by any means, but because they fly, they are included in the same broad classification as the birds. A fish is anything that lives in the water regardless of whether it breathes through lungs or gills, or if it has scales or not. A dolphin is not a fish, but because it lives in the sea, it is included in the same broad classification as a scaled fish.

A more narrow classification of a kind is by *genus,* according to modern classifications, such as the cat kind, the horse kind, the eagle kind, the shark kind, etc. Through adaptation to the environment and available food, the kinds have been observed to branch off into sub-kinds or species. This is adaptation, not evolution. Within the cat kind, we have lions, tigers, bobcats, and domestic house cats. Each one is its own distinct species, but they are all members of the cat kind. No matter how much the species has changed within the kind, they have never become another kind. The original cat, whatever it was, contained all the genetic information for all the various cat species. As different cats specialized and became their own species, genetic information was lost, not gained. They have always been cats from the very beginning and will always be cats.

For a species to change into a different kind, new genetic information is required. This has never been observed to occur. Rather, it has been observed that there is a limit to how much the genes can change. It is this fixity of the genes, that prevent one kind of animal or plant from becoming another kind of animal or plant. It is this fixity of the genes that conserves each kind and it is one reason among a long list of reasons why evolution never happened.

Light year: The distance light travels in a vacuum in one Julian year. It is a constant unit of length equal to just under ten trillion kilometers or six trillion miles and is used to measure the distance of stars and other distances on a galactic scale. The preferred unit of measure is the *parsec* which is equal to about 3.26 light-years. A light-year is calculated by the speed of light which is a universal constant important in many areas of physics. It is denoted as c in physics' mathematical formulas. An example is the famous $E=mc^2$, where E is energy, m is the mass of an object and c is the constant speed of light. The speed of light is equal to 186,282 miles per second or 299,792,458 meters per second.

According to Einstein's *special relativity*, it is the maximum speed that energy, matter and information can travel in the universe.

Quantum mechanics (also known as quantum physics): A branch of physics dealing with the actions and behavior of photons, electrons and other atomic/subatomic objects. It provides a mathematical description of the wave-like/particle-like duality behavior and interactions of energy and matter. Photons, for instance, are particles of light that behave like a wave. The word *quantum* comes from the Latin meaning "how great" or "how much." It refers to a discrete unit assigned to certain physical qualities, like the energy of an atom at rest. Quantum mechanics is essentially a means for understanding the behavior of systems on the atomic or smaller scales. Since its inception near the turn of the twentieth century, it has branched into every aspect of physics, such as *quantum chemistry*, *quantum optics*, *quantum information science* and *quantum electronics*—which has led to the development of *quantum computers*. A reevaluation of nineteenth-century physics has led to more advanced developments in *quantum field theory*, *string theory* and the speculative *quantum gravity theory*.

Radiometric dating: A dating scheme employed by evolutionary scientists. It takes advantage of the natural decay of radioisotopes. An isotope is an atom among similar atoms that have the same number of protons but a different number of neutrons. A radioisotope is an unstable isotope that decays into a stable element while passing through a number of transitional stages, emitting radiation in the process. Uranium, for instance, will decay into lead while passing through intermediate elements of thorium, plutonium and a few other elements. Uranium, in this example, is called the parent element while lead is the daughter element. By measuring how long it takes for the unstable parent element to decay into the stable daughter element, the age of the specimen can be determined. Radiometric dating is based on four assumptions: (1) the present is the key to the past, (2) the rate of decay remains constant, (3) there has been no contamination (no intermediate or daughter elements) leeched or introduced into the specimen, and (4) age can be determined by the ratio of parent to daughter elements, giving the specimen the superficial appearance of age. Uranium takes 4.6 billion years to decay into lead according to the afore mentioned assumptions.

This was how the age of the earth was determined by evolutionary scientists. None of these assumptions has been verified by empirical testing. Observations show that the conditions of the past were radically different from the present. Laboratory testing, for example, shows that the decay rate *changes* under certain conditions. One of the by-products of uranium decaying into lead is helium, which being a much smaller atom, escapes fairly quickly. Zircon crystals found in granite have been found to contain uranium that has partially decayed into lead. Measuring the uranium–to–lead ratio gives an age of the granite at 1.5 billion years old. However, significant amounts of helium have also been found inside the zircons. If the age of the rock was 1.5 billion years old, there should be no helium present. A measurement of the rate the helium leaks out indicates an age between four thousand and fourteen thousand years old.

Another example is diamonds. Diamonds are thought to be millions of years old, but they've been found to contain carbon14 (^{14}C). Carbon14 only has a half-life of a few thousand years, as it decays into carbon12 (^{12}C). If diamonds are millions of years old, they shouldn't have any ^{14}C in them.

A third example is this: a fresh lava flow in a canyon thought to be millions of years old tests to be millions of years older than the canyon. A fourth example was demonstrated when Mount St. Helens erupted in 1980. Shortly afterward it produced a canyon having several layers of sedimentary layers that would normally be assumed to take millions of years to form (approximately one to five centimeters every million years). This canyon was formed in a single day and was observed by qualified eyewitnesses. Its exact date of formation is known, but radiometric testing shows it is millions of years old. These are just a few examples that shows that decay rates are not consistent and the radiometric dating assumptions are all wrong. When one starts out with the wrong assumptions, naturally the conclusions are going to be wrong and should not be treated as facts.

Redshift: The stretching of light toward the red side of the color spectrum. It is said to be caused by the speed of the stars moving away from us and is used as a measure of distance to the star. The *speed theory*, also known as the *doppler theory of redshift* is doggedly adhered to by evolutionists as proof of the big bang because it gives evolution more time to occur. The *speed theory* interpretation gives the stars and galaxies the appearance of moving away from us, indicating an expanding universe and an age in the billions of years.

It is known that the distance of a star has something to do with redshift, but the *speed theory* has numerous flaws. Galaxies connected by a bar of matter are the same distance and travel at the same speed. Yet they have been observed to have different redshifts. Quasars have also been observed being connected to galaxies by a bar of matter, yet these also have a different redshift, showing that quasars are not the most distant objects in the universe. These observations effectively disprove the *speed theory*.

Einstein's general theory of relativity show that light bends as it passes through a gravitational field. As it bends, it redshifts. Light traveling great distances must pass through a great number of gravitational fields. It is a known fact that the light traveling a right angles to an observer is redshifted. This gives the universe the appearance of rotating around a center instead of spreading out. Also, light traveling at great distances looses energy. (This is not to be confused with speed. The speed of light is constant regardless of the distance traveled.) This "tired light" has been shown to be the primary cause of redshift.

These observed causes of redshift show that the age of the universe is only in the millions of years at best, not billions of years. These known facts are ignored by evolutionists since anything that contradicts the evolution and big bang theories is automatically rejected, covered up and the opposition is eliminated.

Scientific law: According to the National Academy of Sciences, a *scientific law* is defined as "a generalization that describes how some aspect of the world behaves under stated circumstances." Generally speaking, a law *describes* a phenomena while a theory *explains* it—or at least attempts to explain it.

Scientific model: A construct of an object or system to help explain a phenomena that a theory cannot. It is particularly useful for explaining processes that can't be observed or repeated like evolution and creation. A model can be a physical construct such as model of the solar system or a purely mathematical construct. It can help explain the working of anything from the atom to the big bang, evolution to creation. They can include as much detail as necessary without becoming too complicated to be useful. They often incorporate assumptions, hypotheses and observed data.

Sedimentary layers: Layers of loose particles—like sand, silt, and calcium carbonate (shells)—that have become lithified (hardened into rock). The fossilized remains of various animals and plants found within the sedimentary layers indicate the order in which they died and were buried in the world flood, not when they lived. Evolutionist like to date the fossils by the sedimentary layers they're found in. They also like to date the sedimentary layers by the fossils found in them. The dates assigned (note they are assigned) by this circular reasoning are nothing more than assumptions, without any verifiable facts supporting them. Radiometric dating, which itself is based on unverifiable assumptions, doesn't support their dating claims. Without an unimpeachable standard, how is it possible to know the truth? The evolutionists have no such standard, only unverifiable assumptions and consensus based on illogical faulty human reasoning.

Theory: According to the National Academy of Sciences, a *theory* is defined as "a well substantiated explanation of some aspect of the natural world that can incorporate facts, laws, inferences, and tested hypotheses." It is a commonly mistaken notion that a theory becomes a law when enough confidence in it is acquired. A theory merely attempts to *explain* a phenomena while a law *describes* it. If the theory is wrong, the law is not invalidated.

Theory of creation: The first chapter of Genesis in the Bible presents a detailed description of the theory of creation. According to the Bible, God is the first cause and designer of the universe and all it contains. He is the giver of life, for life can only come from life. According to the Bible, everything seen and unseen was created from a ball of water that was created out of nothing, not from an explosion of matter. According to the Bible, all life was created according to their own kind, not from other kinds. According to the Bible, mankind was created in the image of God, not from an apelike creature. According to biblical genealogy, the earth is less than ten thousand years old, most likely about six thousand years old—though old-earth creationists, gap theorists and progressive creationists would disagree. They give science the final authority and judge the Scriptures by it. Young-earth creationists acknowledge God and His written Word as the final authority and judge over science.

Critics like to point out that creationists have never presented a "Theory of Creation." Apparently they have never read the first chapter of Genesis. Just because it's found in the Bible doesn't make it any less a scientific theory than other theories presented in science journals. The theory of creation was the first scientific theory ever presented to the world. However, the Bible presents creation as more than a theory, but as an unequivocal historical fact.

Theory of evolution: By definition, evolution is merely a process of change over time. This type of evolution has been observed to occur and is referred to as microevolution. Where origins is concerned, evolution is derived from the theory of natural selection in which modern organisms are the product of a series of changes from a single-celled organism over a period of three billion years. Presently it is defined as a change in the frequency of an allele (a number of alternative forms of the same gene occupying a given position within a chromosome) within a gene pool caused by natural selection, genetic mutation and changes in population structure. Evolution does not have a first cause; it changes over time and is a random process without purpose or direction.

The laws of physics, chemistry, and biology have proven that matter cannot create itself, order cannot come from chaos, life cannot come from non-life, and living organisms cannot increase in complexity or add information to its genome. These, among a host of other scientific facts, prove that evolution is impossible, yet evolutionists keep insisting that given enough time, by pure chance, the impossible becomes probable. Why? According to the following quote from Ernest Kahane, a French molecular biologist, "It is absurd and absolutely preposterous to believe that a living cell could come into existence by itself; but, notwithstanding, I do believe it, because I cannot imagine anything else." Sir Arthur Keith confirmed, "Evolution is unproven and unprovable. We believe it, however, because the only alternative is an act of creation by a God, and that is unthinkable."

So why is it considered unthinkable to believe in an act of creation by God? Why is it so hard to imagine? Why do people insist on clinging to something they know is a lie and deceive others into thinking it's a proven fact? Because to believe in God, they would have to abide by a set of rules not of their own choosing and be held accountable for not doing so. This would interfere with their perceived freedom to do whatever they want to do without having to pay the consequences for their actions. Anything that impedes on their perceived sexual freedom is considered anathema.

In justifying his atheism, Aldous Huxley, grandson of Thomas Huxley, stated, "I had motives for not wanting the world to have meaning; consequently assumed it had none, and was able without difficulty to find satisfying reasons for this assumption... For myself, as no doubt for most of my contemporaries, the philosophy of meaninglessness was essentially an instrument of liberation. The liberation we desired was simultaneously liberation from a certain political and economic system, and liberation from a certain system of morality. We objected to the morality because it interfered with our sexual freedom."

Because it interferes with their sexual freedom? How low can one get? Is sex the sole purpose for our existence? Is that the highest they can set their sights on? The truth of the matter is, this is the heart and soul of atheism and one of the main reasons, if not the sole reason, for evolution's existence. It has nothing to do with science. Science is used to deceive others into believing it.

Theory of intelligent design (ID): A theory that holds

that certain features of the universe can best be explained by an intelligent cause, not by undirected random processes. It acknowledges organisms having irreducible complexity as being intelligently designed. Those not having irreducible complexity came about by other processes. This theory claims to be a purely scientific research program. It does not acknowledge who or what the intelligent designer was and it claims no affiliation with creationism.

Theory of relativity: This has nothing to do with the philosophical concept that everything is relative. The theory of relativity was developed by Albert Einstein and superseded the theory of mechanics stated by Isaac Newton. It has two interlinked aspects. The *special theory of relativity* introduced in 1905 and the *general theory of relativity* introduced in 1915.

The *special theory of relativity* postulates that the laws of physics are the same for all observers in uniform motion relative to one another and that the speed of light in a vacuum is the same for all observers regardless of their relative motion or the motion of the source of the light. The consequences of special relativity include:

1. *Relativity of simultaneity:* If one observer in motion at a particular velocity sees two events occur at the exact same time, another observer in motion at a different velocity will see the same events occur one after the other.
2. *Time dilation*: An observer's clock in motion will run slower than an observer's clock at rest. The faster an observer's clock travels, the slower it runs relative to a clock at rest.
3. *Length contraction*: The faster an object travels, the shorter it gets relative to the direction of motion. At the speed of light, its length is zero.

4. *Mass expansion*: An object is measured to increase its mass the closer it gets to the speed of light. At the speed of light, its mass is infinite. Infinite mass requires infinite energy to maintain its velocity. The universe does not have infinite energy, nor is it infinite in size.

5. *Mass-energy equivalence*: $E=mc^2$, energy and mass are equivalent and transmutable. It is an equivalence formula, not a conversion formula.

6. *Maximum speed limit is finite*: No physical object, radio signal or electrons traveling in a wire can travel faster than the speed of light in a vacuum. Electrons and radio signals travel at the speed of light, but they can never exceed the speed of light.

General relativity postulates that accelerated motion and being at rest in a gravitational field (like standing on the earth) are physically identical. This overrides Newton's theory of gravity by saying that an object of sufficient mass and density will produce a curvature of the space-time continuum. This curvature of the space-time continuum produces a gravity well. The greater the mass and density of an object, the deeper the gravity well. It is this gravity well that attracts other objects to it, not the force of gravity. The consequences of *general relativity* include:

1. *Gravitational time dilation*: Clocks run much slower in deeper gravitational wells than in shallow gravity wells. The deeper the gravity well, the slower a clock runs the deeper it gets within the gravity well. An observers clock outside the gravity well will appear to run much faster than an observers clock within the gravity well. A gravity well can be compared to a depression a bowling ball makes on a trampoline, except that the gravity well

curvature completely surrounds the bowling ball in three-dimensional space.

2. *Orbits precess: Orbits precess* in unexpected ways other than those predicted by Newton's theory of Gravity. It is observed in the orbits of Mercury and in binary pulsars (a star that emits pulses of X-rays at a regular rate).

3. *Gravitational lensing*: Rays of light will bend and go around an object producing a gravity well.

4. *Rotating masses: Rotating masses* "drag along" the space-time around them; a phenomenon known as *frame-dragging.*

5. *The universe is expanding*: The outer parts of the universe are moving away from the center at a faster rate than the inner parts. The weaker the gravitation field, the more an object accelerates. The Voyager probes were observed to accelerate as they departed the solar system.

According to the big bang theory, the universe has no boundary or center. Everything is moving away from everything else on the surface of an expanding universe. It states that objects far from us are moving away from us faster than the speed of light. A clear contradiction to *special relativity* that the curvature of space-time continuum (gravity well of the universe) cannot account for.

White hole cosmology: A cosmology model developed by Dr. Russell Humphreys that explains the origin of the universe from a biblical creation point of view. It postulates that matter was created as a ball of water at the bottom of a black hole that, by gravitational forces, transmuted the basic elements of water into other elements. The black hole converted into a white hole that expelled the heavenly bodies already formed inside the white hole in successive layers. From earth's perspective, the entire universe was created in six literal twenty-four-hour days.

This concept, supported by general and special relativity, states that the universe does have a center and a boundary. The observed data interpreted by uniformitarian assumptions to validate the big bang is reinterpreted according to creationism to validate the *white hole cosmology*. Critics point to mathematical issues as reasons to reject it, but they ignore the far greater mathematical issues of the big bang theory. In a typical, emotional reaction to anything that contradicts uniformitarian assumptions, these critics consider *white hole cosmology* and *creationism* to be pseudoscience. *White hole cosmology* is a best-fit interpretation of the observed data and answers problems plaguing other creation cosmology theories, like the distant starlight travel time.

Dinosaurs and Other So-Called Prehistoric Animals

Allosaur: (AL-oh-SAWR) A meat eating dinosaur about thirty-five feet in length. Its fossils are found mostly in North America. It is assumed to live in the late Jurassic period. The skull is characterized by a ridge along the top that runs between the eyes to the tip of the snout, and bumps above the eyes.

Ankylosaurus: (an-KY-low-SAWR-us) A plant eating dinosaur over thirty-two feet long and built like a military tank. It had thick, bony plates covering its back, horns on the skull, spikes along the side and a heavy, knobby tail club.

Compsognathus: (KOMP-sow-NAY-thus) A small, meat-eating, bi-pedal dinosaur about two feet long. Its fossils are found mainly in Europe. The tail, used for counter balancing, took up half its length.

Dinosaur: (DIE-no-SAWR) A particular group of land dwelling reptiles. The term was invented in the nineteenth century that means "terrible lizard." Dinosaurs are not lizards but a group of upright standing reptiles. There are two types of dinosaurs: the Saurischia (sawr-ISK-ee-a, meaning "lizard hip") and the Ornithischia (orn-ith-ISK-ee-a, meaning "bird hip"). Lizard-hip dinosaurs had hip bones with three bones pointing in different directions while the bird-hip dinosaurs had hip bones with two lower bones pointing backwards. The dinosaurs' closest living relatives, the crocodile and alligator, don't have either of these types of hip bones, thus are not classified as dinosaurs. Dinosaurs are not lizards; did not live in the sea, nor did they fly or glide. They're assumed to have been cold-blooded like most reptiles today, but they may have been warm-blooded.

It seems curious that the bird-hipped dinosaurs were the huge, lumbering, long-necked dinosaurs like the apatosaurus (ah-PAT-oh SAWR-us) and brachiosaurus (BRAK-ee-o-SAWR-us). Clearly, birds didn't evolve from these dinosaurs. However, the evolutionists insist that birds evolved from the small lizard-hipped dinosaurs like the compsognathus. It seems that God designed the dinosaurs this way to confound the evolutionists. It's even more curious that many bird fossils have been found that predate the dinosaurs they supposedly evolved from. Clearly there's something wrong with the evolutionists assumptions.

Prior to the nineteenth century, dinosaurs, along with their airborne and seaborne cousins, were known as *dragons*. It is highly speculative that any of them breathed fire, but there is no reason why they couldn't have. The Bible describes one seaborne or amphibious dragon, called Leviathan, as breathing fire. The fiery serpents described in Isaiah may have been the rhamphorhynchus, a flying reptile that may have breathed fire. The idea that dragons are purely mythological and the work of an overactive imagination is based solely on the evolutionary dogma that dinosaurs and humans are separated by at least sixty-five million years. Thus dinosaurs could not possibly have coexisted with mankind. Yet artwork around the world in various isolated cultures all depicts these dragons consistently, though stylistically, in the same manner. Did these isolated cultures all have the same overactive imaginations? What are the odds?

And then there's the T-rex that was found with soft tissue and unfossilized bone still present. Only a complete moron would think that soft tissue could survive sixty-five million years. Clearly dinosaurs coexisted with mankind, and did not die out sixty-five million years ago.

The Bible says that dinosaurs and mankind were created on the same day. But the evolutionist ignore the facts and insists on clinging to the dogma of evolution no matter how much evidence proves that evolution is wrong. To an evolutionist, scientific facts mean absolutely nothing when they contradict evolution or can't be forced to fit the evolutionary dogma. This attitude, in effect, disqualifies them from being scientists. They are pseudo-scientists at best. I can't help but think that God is laughing at them.

Glossopteris: An extinct order of seed fern tree with tongue-shaped leaves. Fossils have been found throughout the southern hemisphere including Antarctica. According to evolutionary assumptions, it grew during the Permian period, 250 to 300 million years ago. According to young-earth creationist it became extinct in the world flood about 4,500 years ago or shortly thereafter.

Gopher wood: A type of hardwood produced from an unknown species of tree, which Noah was commanded to use to build the ark. Possibly it was a very large tree like the sequoia or redwood trees of California. Or perhaps an even larger extinct tree. It is speculated that it may have been several trees grafted together to produce a special kind of wood. Whatever it was, it was a very big tree.

Pachycephalosaurus: (PAK-ee-CEF-al-oh-SAW-rus) A bone-headed, bi-pedal dinosaur about fifteen feet long. It had a thick dome topped skull above and behind the eyes. The dome skull is thought to have been used to butt heads the way big horned sheep do during mating season.

Parasaurolophus: (par-a-SAWR-oh-LOAF-us) A bizarre, duck-billed, plant eating dinosaur with a six-foot long, tubular crest curving back from its snout. The crest is believed to have been used to make honking noises.

Protoceratops: (pro-toe-SER-a-tops) a six-foot long neck-frilled dinosaur of the Ceratopsia infraorder. It had no horns on its face, but it did have a horny beak and a small neck-frill. Found mostly in Mongolia, it is thought to be a primitive form of Ceratopsia even though it appeared much later than the supposedly more advanced forms, according to the evolutionary-assumed time scale. Shouldn't it be the other way around? To you evolutionists, God is still laughing at you.

Pterosaur: (TAIR-oh SAWR) An order of flying reptiles of the pterosauria (TAIR-oh-SAW-ree-a) order that ranged in size from the Rhamphorhynchus (RAM-fo-RING-kus) to the pteronodon (ter-ON-oh-DON). Though often associated with dinosaurs, pterosaurs were not dinosaurs (see definition of dinosaurs above). The rhamphorhynchus had a wingspan of about six feet and had a long narrow jaw with long teeth that pointed outward and forward. It had leathery wings with claws mid-span and a long thin tail with a flat oval bladelike tip.

The pteronodon was the largest known flying reptile, with a wingspan of about twenty feet. A large crest on their head angled upward and back and it had a long, toothless beak. It had no tail and its legs were attached to the wings by skin membranes like those of bats. It probably walked like bats. Their wings had claws mid-span and were covered with leathery skin that was suitable for high-altitude soaring.

Sauropod: (SAWR-oh-POD) A suborder of long-necked plant-eating dinosaurs belonging to the Saurischia order. They traveled primarily in herds.

Tiktaalik: (TICK-taw-LICK) A four legged freshwater fish with a flat head shaped like a spade shovel and eyes on top of the skull. It walked on the sea floor and among submerged roots with its limbs, each having eight digits. Its front limbs were akin to a crocodile, but they weren't able to support the creature on dry land.

Tyrannosaurus rex: (tie-RAN-oh-SAW-rus REX) Probably the best-known dinosaur and one of the largest meat-eating dinosaurs that ever lived. Rex is the species name of the Tyrannosaurus genus. It is a member of the Saurischia order. Characterized by a huge head and powerful jaws with seven-inch long teeth. It had very short arms with two claws each. It stood upright on its hind legs (as indicated by cave drawings), but it walked with its back parallel to the ground and tail raised.

Velociraptor: (vel-OS-i-RAP-tor) A lightly built, six-foot long meat-eater of the Deinonychosauria (DIE-no-NIKE-oh-SAWR-ee-a) infraorder. It had a long skull with a flat snout. It also had long arms and long, slender legs with scythe-like claws on each foot. Its fossils have mostly been found in Mongolia. A giant velociraptor was found in Utah that was called a Utah-raptor. A raptor is a bird of prey but these raptor dinosaurs are by no means relate to them.

Conspiratorial Political and Religious Organizations, and Programs:

Agenda 21: A United Nations master program for "sustainable development" agreed to by former President George H. W. Bush in 1992 along with 177 other world leaders. "Sustainable development" sounds nice on the surface, but it cloaks plans to impose social justice and socialism on the world. At risk are private property ownership, single-family homes, private car ownership, individual travel choices, and privately owned farms. Agenda 21 essentially eliminates the "sin" of private property ownership and individualism and makes social justice the rule of the land. It controls land use, energy production, transportation, industry and development, food production and water availability, and regulates population size and growth. In reality, sustainable development can only be obtained by an eighty-five-percent reduction in population, which many globalists are calling for. In fact, the plan is to reduce the world population to about five hundred million. Agenda 21 overrides national sovereignty and will be the tool used to bring about a strong global governance.

Agenda 21 has been well known for two decades, but Americans are surprisingly ignorant of it. Americans need to educate themselves and get their heads out of the sand. Our country is being stolen from us. Don't be fooled by the *newspeak* to make it sound like a good thing. In newspeak, the words have the opposite meaning from the dictionary definitions. For instance, the sustainable development logo consists if three interconnecting rings labeled, *social equity, economic prosperity*, and *ecological integrity*.

Social equity is essentially "social justice," which is newspeak for 'redistribution of wealth' where the wealth of those who worked hard to earn it, is given to those who refuse to work and who think they're entitled to other peoples wealth. Of course, this principle doesn't apply to the *elite* wealthy.

Economic prosperity means prosperity for the global elites but economic ruin for ordinary people.

Ecological integrity means that animals, like the lowly slug, have more rights and value than people do. The International Council of Local Environmental Initiatives (ICLEI) USA is an organization that pushes Agenda 21 policies. It has a network of over 1,200 cities, towns and counties. The Tea Party and even some liberal Democrats are standing against Agenda 21 and ICLEI, but their voices are being ignored. That needs to change or the United States will become no different from communist Russia.

Apostasy: The compromise of Scripture by self-proclaimed Christians who incorporate the teachings of other religions as doctrines of faith. Very few people these days care to do their own studying. Even fewer are willing to do their own thinking. This makes these people very susceptible to the lies and deceptions of false prophets. How many of them have thrown away their life savings by allowing themselves to be deceived by false prophets? If they had read the Scriptures they way they were meant to be understood, they would not have been deceived. That's assuming they read the Scriptures at all. Jesus specifically warned about false prophets and setting dates, yet people continue to ignore His warnings and refuse do their own thinking.

A great many people have allowed themselves to be deceived by the apostate teachings of the emergent church; the Saddleback cult with their seeker-friendly, purpose-driven life heresy; the Kingdom Now dominionist; the god makers in the Mormon temple; and the Watch Tower cult—among a host of others. Their mixing of Christian doctrine with new-age eastern mysticism, Buddhism, Hinduism, Satanism and Islam is leading the church into judgment and is nothing short of blasphemy against the Father, the Son, and the Holy Spirit.

The mixing of Christianity and Islam, called *Chrislam*, is the greatest blasphemy of them all. A study of the nature and characters of Jehovah and Allah shows that they are complete opposites. To say they are the same and join them together is blasphemy of the Holy Spirit, an unforgivable sin no true Christian would dare commit.

Anyone involved in a church that has adopted the "purpose-driven" doctrine of the Saddleback Church or the emergent church doctrines, which are very similar to each other, needs to flee from it. Flee from it; don't look back; and warn others of it. Find a group of true believers who are not afraid to preach the gospel of Jesus Christ and teach the truth of God's Word without fear of offending someone.

As a result of these deceptions, the last few generations have become like the Greeks in Jesus' day, having no understanding of sin or where it originated. Nor do they know anything about God. They have a distorted view of God and no longer know right from wrong, willfully rejecting the biblical definition of right and wrong. For these people, nothing is right or wrong unless they decide it to be. Everything is relevant except the Bible.

Many in these later generations refuse to work and become productive, prosperous members of society. They become jealous of the prosperity of those who do work. They think they're entitled to another's property and will steal and kill to get it. They think they have a right to government entitlements and they riot when these benefits are withheld from them. They do what is right in their own eyes and no longer understand their need for a savior. They cry out in pain and fear for a messiah to deliver them, yet they refuse to consider the one true Messiah.

There are many who say that the Bible is irrelevant and out-of-date. That it is no longer applicable or authoritative for this so-called age of "scientific enlightenment." The truth is; the Bible is never irrelevant or out-of-date. If anything, it is more relevant today, than at any time in the past. The entire Word of God, not just the convenient parts, is relevant for today. There are no contradictions in the Scriptures. Contradictions appear as a result of misunderstanding what was written—or just plain stupidity and deliberate distortion of the Scriptures. The Word of God is the final authority by which all things are judged. Atheists and postmodernist false prophets of the apostate church can think what they wish, but truth does not depend on what they think. It is God who determines truth, and He is Himself truth. It is God who has the last word, not the atheists, postmodernists, or even science. As for that so-called "scientific enlightenment," if it wasn't so dark, people might be able to see what's keeping them from finding the true light.

Atheism: Atheism is an irreligious belief that denies the existence of God. Atheists are not to be confused with agnostics, who think it can't be known whether God exist's or, if He does, whether He's even knowable. Atheism in some form has existed throughout the history of mankind, but the modern version has its roots back in the seventeenth and eighteenth centuries when people sought to be free of religious abuse. In the mid-nineteenth century, evolution was popularized to justify the atheistic belief that God doesn't exist.

The sole reason for evolution and atheism to exist is to escape the moral boundaries of society. Adherents believe it is their right to do whatever they want without having to pay the consequences. Any attempt by society to impose moral values on them is considered a restriction on their rights, especially where it concerns sexual freedom. That is why they're opposed to abstinence. They support teaching sex education to our children, encouraging them to have sex, and hand out condoms in schools. That is why homosexuals are militant about passing hate-crimes bills that grant them special rights, force society to accept their abominable lifestyle as normal behavior, and brainwash society's children accordingly.

Atheists justify their belief by claiming that science can't prove the existence of God. They say there is no scientific precedence for God's existence. Science, of course isn't capable of proving anything even in the material universe. How anyone can expect science to prove anything outside the material universe is a mystery. They say, "prove it," while the proof is all around them, for all of creation speaks of God's glory. In His creation, God has given us all the proof we need. The burden now falls on Atheists to prove that He *doesn't* exist. They point to the same creation and say it came about by naturalistic processes, basing their statements on uniformitarian assumptions. The assumptions themselves can't be proven, but they have no trouble blindly believing them to be a fact and have confused them with science.

Atheists also like to point to the atrocious suffering that religious people have wrought on mankind as justification for their beliefs. They ask how could religion be good for society when so many people have suffered at the hands of religion? Yet, in the last century, people like Stalin and Mao Tse Tung have murdered millions in the name of atheism. These weren't men who just happened to be atheists. They were communists where atheism is the core belief. In a single generation, more people have been killed in the name of communist atheism then in all the history of religion combined.

However, to an atheist, life has no value. Evolution has taught them that people are just animals of a higher order. What does it matter that a few million unborn babies are aborted, or a few million elderly and handicapped are euthanized? What does it matter if a few million undesirables are executed? According to evolution death is an ally that makes evolution possible. Since it's supposedly an integral part of nature, why blame it on a God they don't believe exists?

There are two groups of atheists. The majority of atheists are among the group known as "weak atheist". They are the "live-and-let-live" type who have no trouble with other people believing what they want. It's okay if they share their faith, as long they don't try to force it on others. A small minority of atheists are among the other group known as "strong atheists." They are the antireligion type who want to force religion, especially Christianity, out of society. They consider religion outdated, irrelevant, abusive and brainwashing of children. Some even consider the teaching of Christianity to children as psychological child abuse. They are of the sort that believe their own rights trump the rights of others. They also believe that society is better off without any kind of religion at all. What they don't realize is that, in the absence of religion, chaos breaks out and the horrors of communism take over. Who will they blame then?

Atheists say there are no absolutes, yet they claim they know that God does not exist. This is an absolute statement, claiming knowledge that only God would know. Only God has absolute knowledge. By claiming to have absolute knowledge of something, one is claiming to be a god. Atheists deny the existence of any god, therefore, since they are not gods, they can't possibly have absolute knowledge of anything. If absolutes don't exist, how can they claim absolutely that God doesn't exist? They claim that there is no established, scientific precedent for God's existence. As stated in the *Humanist Manifesto*, they reject the existence of God due to lack of scientific evidence. Atheists not only have a distorted view of God, but they also have a distorted view of science.

Because of the concept of evolution, atheists see mankind as just a higher form of animal having no value. They don't understand why Christians object to killing the unborn, euthanizing the elderly, and using cadavers and aborted fetuses to produce beauty and medical products. This is a trillion-dollar industry driven by greed. The love of money is indeed the root of all sorts of evil. These people accuse God of being evil for not stopping the suffering and death, and yet they murder millions each year and see nothing evil about it. Where's the logic of this hypocrisy?

Chrislam: An attempt to merge the mega religions of Christianity and Islam by blurring the distinctions and differences between the two. It has its roots in Nigeria, Africa where some think that by concentrating on the similarities there will be peace between the two religions. Nigeria has always been a hotbed of conflict between Christians and Muslims, where the smallest thing can spark violence.

Both Christians and Muslims claim to be spiritual children of Abraham. (Only the Jews are true children of Abraham. Contrary to popular belief, Ishmael is not the father of the Arabs.) Both believe in the virgin birth of Jesus Christ, both honor Mary His mother, and both recognize Jesus as a prophet of God and as the Messiah. But that's where the similarities end.

Christianity teaches that salvation can only be obtained by placing ones faith in Jesus Christ, who died on the cross to pay the price for our sins—something we are not capable of doing ourselves. Christianity teaches that Jesus is the Son of God, is Himself God and is equal with the Father.

Islam teaches that people must earn their salvation by keeping the requirements of the Qur'an. They do not believe that Allah had a son, or that it was his place to have one. They consider it offensive to claim that Jesus is the Son of God. They do not believe that Jesus died on the cross but that He was taken up by Allah. The Qur'an also condemns Christians and Jews as objects of Allah's wrath. These differences are irreconcilable.

Muslims believe they are under a mandate to kill all Christians and Jews, as well as those who will not convert to Islam. The Bible, on the other hand, teaches that we are to love our neighbors, even if they hate us, which is why we are not given to violence. The Bible also teaches that we are not to compromise our faith; we are to worship God only. Christians don't recognize Allah as God.

There are some who think that Allah and God are one and the same, but a careful study of their characters show that they are complete opposites. We know that God cannot lie and cannot contradict Himself. For Allah, lying is his "modus operandi." God and Allah are not one and the same. To worship both is apostasy of the highest order. It waters down the gospel and leads to compromise, in which Islam always comes out on top. Jesus said, "No one can serve two masters; for either he will hate the one and love the other, or he will hold to one and despise the other. You cannot serve God and mammon." (Matthew 6:24) To the modern day compromisers who push Chrislam, He might as well have said, "You cannot serve both God and Allah." Mixing the two does not lead to peace.

Doctrines of Lucifer: The teachings of Satan/Lucifer. These teachings are cleverly disguised to appeal to mankind's pride and desire to be a god. It was this clever deception that led to the fall of mankind in the garden of Eden. Satan is first and foremost a liar and the father of lies. One of the means he uses to get people to believe his lies is to mix just enough truth in them, that those who are not familiar with the truth are not able to discern his lies. Another deception is to get people to believe that he doesn't exist. That he is just a myth conjured up in the minds of men to scare people into submission or control their actions. In doing so, Satan is free to do things that he would not otherwise be able to get away with. He also tries to separate the names Lucifer from Satan to get people to believe they are two different entities where Satan is a myth and Lucifer is the brother of Jesus. Satan often disguises himself as an angel of light and tries to say he is the Christ himself. By calling himself Lucifer, the light-bearer, he conceals his true identity, getting people to believe he is a benevolent agent working for man's benefit and helping him to reach his potential to be a god. In essence, everything that is the opposite of what the Bible teaches is a doctrine of Lucifer. And that includes evolution, reincarnation, and the idea that salvation must be earned.

Dominionism: Also known as *dominion theology*, *Christian reconstructionism* and *Theonomy*. It teaches that the church is still bound by the old covenant given to Israel through Moses. It holds that Christians are duty-bound to build a world kingdom of believers who follow the Mosaic law. Adherents believe that the church has replaced Israel as God's chosen people and is responsible to hold dominion over the whole world in obedience to God's laws. They believe that Jesus Christ will not return until the church holds dominion over the whole world.

This is a distorted view of Scripture, which clearly teaches the church is distinct and separate from Israel. Prophecy revolves around Israel, not the church. The church is instructed to preach the gospel of Jesus Christ to the world, but nowhere does it say that the church is to convert the whole world and hold dominion over it. Prophecy indicates that the opposite will happen. Mankind, in his rebellion against God, hates the name of Jesus Christ and will not submit to Him. Very few will chose to follow Jesus Christ into salvation. When Jesus Christ returns, faith will be in extremely short supply.

Sadly, this dominionism deception has seeped into many Protestant churches and deceived many. Christians need to be like the Bereans, who were more noble-minded than the Thessalonians. They searched the Scriptures daily to see if what the apostles were teaching was true. Very few these days care to do their own research. They have fallen into a state of lethargy and apostasy; thinking that everything is going okay, following their ten steps to self improvement, going to church on Sunday and teaching Sunday school—while living like the Devil the rest of the week. They pay lip service to God and think He is pleased with them. A word of warning to people who believe such things; repent while you still can. God is not pleased with this lukewarm lifestyle.

Emergent church: An apostate church that has exchanged the absolute truth of the Bible and cold, hard facts for warm fuzzy feelings and subjective, illogical reasoning. It claims to be Christian, and its adherents say they love the Lord, but they have rejected the literal interpretation of the Scriptures and have embraced the so-called postmodernist way of thinking. No consensus can be reached on what postmodernism actually is, but there is general agreement that postmodernism rejects the core tenets of the Bible, such as that faith in Jesus is the only way to salvation. It rejects the notion of right and wrong, believing that everything is relative to the moment or to what the community decides is truth. What's true for one community may not be true for another community. In rejecting the presupposed truth and referential language of the Bible, they have deconstructed the language of the Scriptures to redefine the meaning of the words according to what they *feel* is right for the moment. What they *feel* is right today, could be different tomorrow, and the meanings can differ from one group to another. Talk about making one's head spin.

Emergent church adherents believe that for Christianity to reach the postmodern world, it must change its beliefs and practices. In so doing, they have exchanged sound doctrine for false doctrine and are tossed to and fro by every wind of change that comes along. They have watered down Scripture, never mention sin or speak of hell except as a curse—all for fear of offending someone. They scoff at those who adhere to the literal truth of the Bible, who are called "modernists," and consider them intolerant (heaven forbid!) and insensitive to the world around them. Modernists are considered throwbacks stuck on traditional church doctrines and methods of evangelism, people who are out of touch with the world and are the worst kind of person anyone can be. The emergent church employs mystical spiritual practices of other religions (something they call "Spiritual Formation") in worshipping God and seeks to merge the religions together into one ecumenical faith. Some have even embraced the Chrislam movement that has migrated from Nigeria to America.

They have turned their churches into corporate worship centers and social clubs. They live the same way the rest of the world lives, including hanging out at bars, cursing, gambling, getting drunk and watching pornography. Judging from the way they talk and live, there is no discernible difference between them and the atheist. Since there is no discernible difference, why should anybody listen to what they say and put their faith in Jesus Christ for salvation? Critics see the emerging church as not emerging from society, but as immersing itself in society and getting lost in it. Jesus said not to be conformed to the world but to be separate from it, for a friend of the world is an enemy of God.

Freemasons: The principles, institutions and practices of the fraternal order of the Free and Accepted Masons. Belief in a Supreme Being and in the immortality of the soul are two requirements to become a Mason. Masonry adheres to the ideals that all people are the children of God and are all related to each other and that serving people is the best way to worship God. Freemasonry is more than just a fraternal social and civil service organization. It is also a religion. It sees itself as superseding and unifying all religions. The first step in this process was to infiltrate the Catholic church. Not to make its members Freemasons, but to bring the church under Satanic control. Over two hundred years ago following the French revolution, the Freemasons issued the Permanent Instruction of the Alta Vendita. The Popes successfully fought this off until the arrival of Pope Paul II and liberal minded Cardinals and Bishops. Through his policies and those of his successors, the Alta Vendita was successfully implemented. Now its a matter of reunifying the Catholic church and the Protestant church along with the apostate emergent church.

Masons consider the Bible as the "Volume of the Sacred Law", but they don't adjust their beliefs to fit the Bible; rather they adjust the Bible to fit their beliefs. One of those beliefs contrary to Biblical teaching is that there are many paths to God. The Bible teaches there is only path to God and that is by faith in the Son of God, not by works or by any other means. Masonry is not based on the Bible, however, but on the Kabbalah, a medieval book of mysticism and magic that teach the Doctrines of Lucifer.

Members are required to believe in a supreme god, but they never say which god. Any god will do, whatever its name might be. The Supreme Being is commonly referred to as the "Great Architect of the Universe", but he is also referred to as Grand Artificer, Grand Master of the Grand Lodge Above, Jehovah, Allah, Buddha, Brahma, Vishnu, Shiva or Great Geometer. The name of Jesus Christ is not mentioned for fear of offending non-Christian members (Heaven forbid.) Masons don't recognize the deity of Jesus Christ and are not allowed to offer prayer in His name. What they do in private, however, is perfectly acceptable. They don't believe that Jesus is the Christ, but that He obtained "Christ-consciousness," which the Masons believe is available to all mankind. By rejecting the deity of Jesus Christ, they have embraced the Spirit of antichrist.

Masons teach salvation by works or character development, not by faith in Jesus Christ. The heart of Masonry is the *doctrines of Lucifer,* which only high-level Masons come to understand. The Scottish Rite Masons have thirty-three degrees or steps to spiritual enlightenment while the York Rite has thirteen. However, even a thirty-third degree Mason will never find the "light" he is looking for. Freemasonry keeps a great number of secrets from the public, and even from its own members. The lower initiates are deliberately lied to and are conditioned to believe whatever they're told.

But the greatest secret of all, which every thirty-third degree Mason knows, is the unknown god they worship is not the creator of the universe that the Christians and Jews worship. The supposed "lost" name of their "secret" god is Jahbuhlum. Like all false gods, Jahbuhlum is none other than Satan who calls himself Lucifer, the light bearer, and doesn't want the world to know he exists. Lucifer is just his front name to hide his true identity. Another great secret is that the Freemasons are actually a fraternity within a fraternity. The other fraternity that has infiltrated and controls it is known as the Illuminati.

Gnosticism: The roots of Gnosticism can be traced back to the end of the first century. It is derived from the Greek word *gnosis* meaning "knowledge". It teaches that salvation can be achieved through special knowledge dealing with the individual's personal relationship with a transcendent being. It claims that Jesus Christ descended from the spiritual realm to reveal the knowledge necessary for this redemption. Gnosticism is dualistic in nature, regarding the material universe as evil and God as too pure and perfect to have anything to do with it. Therefore, God is believed to have sent lessor divinities to deal with the universe.

One of those divinities was called Sophia ("wisdom"). During her journeys, she emanated a being with a flawed consciousness. This flawed being created the material universe in his own flawed image. Not knowing his own origin, he imagined himself to be the true God. He took preexisting, divine essence and fashioned various forms called Archons ("rulers"). This evil divinity, along with his Archon minions, kept mortal beings in bondage to the material universe and tried to keep pure spiritual souls from ascending back to God.

Human beings are regarded as having perishable physical bodies as well as souls containing the light of the true God, which is referred to as the "divine spark." Gnosticism teaches that the body and soul are separate, and what the body does has no effect on the soul. Humans are believed to be mostly ignorant of the divine spark. This ignorance is mired in human nature, which is influenced by the false creator and his Archons as they seek to keep humans attached and enslaved to earthly things. Death releases the divine spark from its earthly prison. It ascends to God, but if it didn't acquire the right knowledge (gnosis) before death, it is hurled back and imprisoned once again in human form to try again. According the Gnostic scholar G. Quispel, "The world-spirit in exile must go through the Inferno of matter and the Purgatory of morals to arrive at the spiritual Paradise." Whatever that means, apparently death alone isn't enough to bring spiritual freedom.

According to Gnosticism, humans are ignorant of their true origins, essential nature and ultimate destiny. They must find the right knowledge to overcome their ignorance. Gnostics don't seek salvation from sin but from *ignorance* that brings sin. Humans can find this knowledge within themselves, but it requires the aid of a "messenger of light" to find it. Gnostics consider Seth (the third son of Adam), Jesus, and Prophet Mani (whoever he is or was) to be three of the salvific figures, but they hold Jesus as the principal savior figure. Gnostics do not regard rules as relevant to salvation. Rather inner integrity originating from the divine spark is ideal. Thus the sins of the body have no effect on the divine spark. However, Gnosticism encourages nonattachment and nonconformity to the world, a lack of ego, and a respect for the freedom and dignity of others.

The recent resurgence of Gnosticism in Western culture resembles the Alexandrian movement of the second and third century. Gnostic allegory is found in the resurgent interest in magic wrapped in medieval themes. It has been popularized in film, books and video games, including *Harry Potter* and *Dungeon and Dragons*. It has found its way into some of the apostate churches, just as it did at the end of the first century. Gnostic allegoristic interpretations of God's Word have twisted its true meaning and intent. People have been mislead and confused by these altered interpretations. The epistles of John are thought to have been written in response to this heresy. Those in the apostate churches would do well to read them in the straight forward manner in which they were meant to be understood and to heed John's message.

Illuminati: The Illuminati (a.k.a. "Brotherhood of the Snake") is a secretive fraternity of Satanists who consider themselves "enlightened." (They are not to be confused with the Bavarian Illuminati or with a benevolent group that calls itself "The Illuminati".) This particular "brotherhood" is driven by power, greed, and the desire for control over other people's lives. It has been around for thousands of years in various forms and names. It uses the Kabbalah as one of its guides for oppressing the world's population. The Illuminati consist of thirteen families that make up the "royal bloodlines" of the group. The thirteen royal families are named Astor, Bundy, Collins, DuPont, Freeman, Kennedy, Li (Chinese), Onassis, Rockefeller, Rothschild, Russell, van Duyn, and Merovingian. The families of Reynolds, Disney, Krupp, and McDonald are also interconnected with them, along with a few lesser known families of less pure "royal blood".

These thirteen families own or control all the international banks, oil businesses, most of the powerful businesses of industry and trade, Hollywood, and the music industry. They control the media and most governments, including the US Government. The children of these families are initiated into the "outer court" at three years old and for the next thirteen years they learn "six disciplines of training"—military, government, spiritual, scholarship, leadership and science. Upon graduating they sign a lambskin "book of death" with their own blood. Only those born of one of these thirteen families or the less pure families is considered a true Illuminist. Those who worship Satan who are not born of these families cannot be Illuminists but are considered Satanists. To the rest of us, they're all Satanists.

The Illuminati's ultimate goal is the establishment of a one-world government that has been centuries in the making. This so-called "New World Order" is actually the same as the Old World Order except that it is run by one world government and a world dictator. To accomplish this they need to lower the standard of living in developed nations and increase the standard of living in third world nations to about the same level to make them easier to control.

Crisis' are also engineered in order pass laws that give them more power, erode the Constitution, and restrict the rights of the people. Crisis' like the terrorist attack on the World Trade Center and the Pentagon, the war on drugs, the housing bubble, the

BP oil spill in the Gulf of Mexico and more recently the public shootings of innocent by-standers in schools, theaters, and other public places by drug induced madmen.

Their plans are made in secret and are carried out by secret societies like the Freemasons. Ninety-eight percent of Masons are mere foot soldiers who have been deceived into thinking they are doing benevolent work. These members have been deliberately lied to, to keep certain kinds of knowledge from them and to condition them to accept what they're told as truth. The Illuminati didn't create the Freemasons, but over time they infiltrated it and took control of it.

Their god is called Lucifer. They don't recognize Satan and Lucifer as being the same person. They consider Satan to be a mythical creature invented by the Christian church to control its members.

Islam: A monotheistic religion established by Mohammad in the early seventh century AD. Arabs once worshipped hundreds of gods, but Mohammad united them in the worship of a single god. Islam literally means "submission to God." A Muslim, therefore, is someone who strives to submit to God. The name of the Muslim's god is *Allah*, which means "God". Muslims believe that he is the creator of all that exists, that he is just, omnipotent and merciful.

Allah is not to be confused with the God of the Christians and Jews. They are not the same God. Muslims believe that Allah is one god who has no son. He has a holy spirit, but that holy spirit is not a separate person. The Christian's God is a triune God, three persons in one God; God the Father, God the Son, and God the Holy Spirit. Muslims (like most other people of the world) misunderstand the triune God and think that Christians worship three gods. Muslims believe that Christians worship the Father,

Son (Jesus) and Mother (Mary). A misunderstanding acquired from the Catholic church.

Many of Mohammad's misunderstandings of Christianity came from the Catholic church. The Catholic church is not a Christian church; they are pseudo-Christian at best. It does not represent the true Christian church as the world mistakenly believes. Much of what the Muslims believe about Christianity is derived from movies, books and music produced by nations that claim to be Christian nations. These so-called Christian nations, including the United States, are not Christian nations and do not represent Christian values. Only those of their father Satan. Muslims, however, don't understand this, and with the prevalence of the apostate church, they are unable to discern the difference.

There are seven fundamental beliefs that every Muslim must accept.

1. *Tawheed* : "Belief in the unity of God (Allah)" There is no god but Allah, and Mohammad is his prophet.

2. *Mala'ikah*: "Belief in the angels." There are angels who are slaves to Allah, and there are "jinn" (demons), who do evil.

3. *Kutubullah*: "Belief in the revealed books of God." Muslims accept the Torah, Psalms, and the gospel of Jesus, but they believe they have been corrupted and are unreliable. Mohammad was supposedly given the Qur'an to correct these corruptions. Thus they regard the Qur'an is the only reliable book of god.

4. *Risallah*: "Belief in god's many prophets, specifically Mohammad." Other prophets include Adam, Abraham, Moses, David, Jesus and many others found in the Bible. Muslims claim that Abraham through Ishmael, is the father of the Arabs. History reveals this to be a fabrication. Abraham and Ishmael never traveled to Medina. The

only time Abraham left the land of Canaan was when he went to Egypt a couple times. Ishmael became a great nation in the land of Canaan while the Hebrews were in Egypt, but they were later conquered by the Hebrews, and the survivors assimilated into the neighboring lands. There is no traceable connection between the Arabs and Ishmael. Muslims believe that Jesus was a prophet born of a virgin, but they do not believe He was God or that He was crucified. He was merely "taken up" into heaven.

5. *Yawmuddin*: "Accepting that there will be a last day." A day of judgment all religions have in common.

6. *al-Qadr*: "Belief in the divine measurement of human affairs," or predestination.

7. *Akhriah*: "Belief in life after death," or resurrection of the dead.

Islam is a religion of salvation by works. Muslims earn their salvation by keeping the requirements of the Qur'an. These requirements form five pillars of faith the Muslims must perform.

1. *Shahadah*: "Say the confession of faith." They must publicly profess, "There is no God but Allah and Mohammad is the prophet of God," and submit themselves to Allah.

2. *Salat*: "Pray." They must pray five times a day: *Fajr* (after dawn but before sunrise), *Duhr* (early afternoon till late afternoon), *Asr* (late afternoon till sunset), *Maghrib* (just after sunset), and *Isha* (late evening till late at night).

3. *Zakat*: "Give alms." Muslims, on average, give about 2.5 percent of their wealth.

4. *Sawm*: "Fast during Ramadan." Ramadan is a month-long holiday based on the lunar cycle. It usually occurs during late summer or early autumn. From sunrise to

sunset, Muslim are not allowed to let anything pass down their throats. A good Muslim will even spit out his or her saliva. From sunset to sunrise, they can eat however much they desire. This fasting helps them develop discipline and relate to the poor. Travelers, young children, pregnant and nursing mothers are exempt from observing this fast.

5. *Hajj*: "Make a pilgrimage to Mecca." Muslims are supposed to travel to Mecca, the birthplace of Islam, at least once in their lifetime.

By observing these five pillars of faith, Muslims earn their salvation. Unlike Christians who are guaranteed salvation by faith in Jesus Christ, Muslims do not have any assurance they are saved. They believe they have two angels accompanying them at all times; one to record their good deeds, and the other to record their bad deeds. At the judgment day, if their good deeds outweigh their bad deeds, they will probably get into heaven, providing Allah is feeling charitable that day. Otherwise they go to hell for a while to burn their sins off and maybe afterward they'll be allowed in heaven. One way to be guaranteed they'll get into heaven, is to observe what some call the sixth pillar of faith. That is by *Jihad*. Jihad is often translated as "holy war," but it literally means "exerting force for God." Muslims can participate in jihad by writing a book about Islam, sharing their faith with others, or by physically fighting for the cause. Those who die in Jihad are guaranteed to get to heaven.

There are two major groups of Muslims who are divided over who the leader of Islam should be. The Sunni's, which are the ninety percent majority, believe the leader should be selected by a committee. While the Shi'ites believe the leader should be a direct descendant of Mohammad. There were twelve descendants of Mohammad, called Imams, who ruled the Muslim nations until the twelfth Imam disappeared in a well while still a child.

The Shi'ites believe he is in hiding in another dimension and will return as the prophesied messiah. The Sunnis don't believe in the twelfth Imam and since his disappearance, they have gained control of the Muslim nations and appointed rulers by committee. There is a third lesser-known group within both the Sunnis and Shi'ites called the Sufis. They seek a mystical experience with God rather than a mere intellectual knowledge. They are given to a host of superstitious activities.

Two trends have arisen within Islam concerning attitudes toward contact with the Western world. One is to accommodate and adjust to the Western way of life to some degree. This trend has manifested itself in countries like Turkey, which has instituted secular forms of government while maintaining Islamic practices. The opposite extreme—as in Saudi Arabia, Iran, Pakistan and Sudan—is to return Islam to a more traditional approach and implement Muslim law (Sharia law) in every area of life. These adherents are active in virtually every Muslim country and oftentimes resort to violence and terrorism to implement Sharia law.

Western news commentators and politicians have stated that Islam is a religion of peace, yet Muslims are actively engaged in jihad in an attempt to force the world into Islam. It claims to treat those of other beliefs with respect, yet it is the most intolerant religion on the planet. It cares nothing about political correctness (except to use it against you) and deliberately lies to those it calls infidels to get what it wants. It terrorizes nations and murders those—especially Christians—who refuse to convert to Islam. Christians and Jews aren't even given the opportunity to convert—not that they would. The goal of Islam is to bring the entire world under Muslim control by any means possible. It matters not how many lives are destroyed in the process.

Christians are murdered throughout the Muslim world, while

the rest of the world turns a blind eye. Will they continue to do so when the Muslim sword is on their own neck? Or will they take the cowardly way out and submit to Allah? Atheists like to use irrational arguments to refute Islam just as they do with Christianity. They cite lack of scientific evidence of God or the soul as proof. How lack of evidence proves anything is a mystery.

Muslims, however, are not concerned about scientific evidence or a lack thereof. They will put a sword to your neck and force you to chose. Submit to Allah or die. Which will you chose? Will you take the cowardly way out or are you willing to die for what you believe? True Christians throughout the last two thousand years have proved willing to die for the truth of Jesus Christ. However, under Islam, Christians and Jews will not be given a choice. Islam has always been at war with the world. When they don't have a common enemy, they fight amongst themselves. Is this what a peaceful religion looks like?

Kabbalah: An aspect of Jewish mysticism consisting of speculation on the nature of divinity, the creation, the origin and fate of the soul, and the role of human beings. Derived from the Hebrew root word *kbl* meaning "to receive, to accept." It is an esoteric teaching based on the belief that the Torah is encoded with hidden meanings. It resembles Eastern spirituality and Gnosticism by teaching reincarnation and mystical concepts. It teaches something called *Ein Sof*, meaning "endless, created God," which permeates everything so that even rocks have divinity.

One of the core teachings of the Kabbalah concerns the Tree of Life which represents the ten emanations and aspects of Ein Sof. This strange concept illustrates an upside-down tree where the branches grow downward into three branches with three points. The right one is masculine or positive energy, the left one is feminine or negative energy, and the middle one is neutral, which balances them. The divine light supposedly travels down these points toward man. The goal is to enable mankind to work his way up the Tree of Life and return to the divine source to restore the garden of Eden. This is another one of Satan's long list of deceptions that says we can be gods, working out our salvation by working up this tree, effectively bypassing the redemptive work of Jesus Christ on the cross.

Notice the tree is upside-down. One of the tactics of Satan is to turn everything backwards and upside-down. This is, in fact, how Satanists see the world. The book contains a host of other strange teachings that are foreign to the Torah and the Bible. It has been gaining popularity in Western cultures among people desiring to experience secret realities. There are some who desire to replace the Torah and the Bible with the Kabbalah in the churches and synagogues. It is another means of introducing people to the doctrines of Lucifer and turning the world away from God and keeping them from finding salvation through Jesus Christ.

New World Order (NWO): A term that refers to a bureaucratic, collectivist, one world government consisting of ten super-nations ruled by a single world dictator. Satanists see it as completing the work of the Tower of Babel, which God interrupted. The dream of the NWO is to unite mankind into a collective, global nation with a single world religion that observes the Kabbalah to establish world peace and a new garden-of-Eden type utopia.

Political correctness (PC): A form of communal tyranny that erupted in the 1980's, declaring that particular ideas, expressions and behavior, that were then legal, should be outlawed and the transgressors punished. This absurdity is aimed at preventing homosexuals, Muslims, women, non-whites, and the crippled, stupid, fat and ugly from feeling offended by something someone says or does—though it seems perfectly acceptable to offend white males and Christians. PC has effectively become a secular religion based on emotion.

The PC absurdity has resulted in restricting freedom of speech, freedom of expression, and freedom to stand up for righteousness and what you believe. It is the result of selfish, resentful and spoiled children rebelling against their parents values. It has degraded to the point that anyone disagreeing with the accepted liberal perception of truth is considered a bigoted racist or sexist hypocrite. Being labeled as such often results in a loss of one's job and reputation. Those who are so labeled are terrorized, harassed, and subject to judicial penalties and death threats.

In some places, political correctness has degenerated to the point where it is acceptable for the afore mentioned groups to attack white males and Christians, but it is not acceptable for those white males and Christians to defend themselves—especially if their actions to defend themselves results in the death of their attacker. This has led to a movement by a group of city and town mayors led by the mayor of New York City to outlaw self-defense, particularly with a firearm, essentially turning the victims into criminals and the criminals into victims. Law enforcement is pressured into prosecuting the victims who dare to defend themselves, especially if the victim is a white man, while ignoring the crimes of the other groups.

With each generation, selfishness and unrestrained immorality spreads the PC social cancer further. It has turned society on its head resulting in a complete disconnect from reality where the insane are considered normal and the sane are considered mutant deviants. Good has become bad, and bad is good. Up is down, and down is up. Many a great nation has passed into history and into a dictatorship because of political correctness. Those afflicted with this PC social dementia think that this insanity is the way the world is supposed to be. It is an outmoded method of social control that must be eliminated. If the PC madness isn't reversed, it can only result in chaos and death.

Purpose driven church: The brainchild of Rick Warren, the founder of the Saddleback Church in California, which repackages and waters down the Christian message to appeal to the postmodern society. He based his church growth model on the successful techniques of the founder of the Crystal Cathedral, a universalist who doesn't believe that Jesus is the only way to heaven, and who thinks telling people of their lost and sinful condition is the worst thing a pastor can do. He also thinks that being born again means changing from a negative to a positive self-image.

Rick Warren partnered with the business world to develop his cloned version of their business growth models. To reach the unchurched, he decided to meet their "felt needs" saying that they can have whatever they're looking for in Jesus Christ. Righteousness, self-control and judgment are never addressed. In preaching his needs-oriented sermons he has watered down the gospel message and turned Jesus into a magic genie in a lamp. Just rub the lamp, and your every wish is his command. He preaches that if you silently pray, "Jesus, I believe in You and receive You," and sincerely mean it, salvation is yours. No conviction of sin, no repentance, and no counting the cost. Just name it and claim it, and Bam!, it's yours.

The gospel isn't about making people feel better about themselves, but about making them realize they're lost and in need of a savior. It doesn't meet their *felt needs*, but their *real spiritual need* to repent and put their faith in Jesus Christ alone for salvation. The Saddleback church has essentially become an entertainment venue that makes people feel good about themselves by using spiritual mysticism disguised with Christian terminology. The false gospel and false doctrine taught has produced a multitude of false converts and shallow members who have no clue what it means to live for Christ.

The Saddleback church boasts of having over ten thousand members, but numbers don't mean squat. They are only making the founder rich. The only way the church will have true success is if it returns to biblical truth, biblical living, biblical preaching, and biblical church practices. If only one person repents and believes in Jesus Christ unto salvation and eternal life, the mission is a success. Those preachers who only care about numbers need to remember that preaching is a calling, not a profession.

Rosicrucians: A secret society of so-called Christian mystics founded in Germany during the medieval period by Christian Rosenkreuz. This is one of those secret organizations whose beliefs have been hard to pin down. They claim to espouse Christianity, but not the Christianity taught in the Bible. It holds to a doctrine it claims is built on esoteric truths of the ancient past. They claim to appeal to logic and reason rather than blind adherence to religion—something not likely to appeal to the postmodernists who are more into *feelings* than *reason and logic*. It claims to cherish the tenets of religious zeal but does not pretend to dictate how one worships God.

It calls itself a "cosmology" that traces the origin of the cosmos from chaos to its completion when it will achieve a state of incomprehensible perfection. This is contrary to the first chapter of Genesis, which states the universe and the earth were created in six days that God declared perfect. They were then corrupted when mankind sinned against God. This indicates that the teachings of the Rosicrucians are extra-Biblical and did not come from God.

Rosicrucians have a whole host of teachings that are contrary to the teachings of the Bible and should be avoided—things like using a form of spiritual alchemy to transform the soul into spiritual gold. Many of the teachings of the Rosicrucians have been adapted by the Freemasons, in which the eighteenth degree is called "Knight of the Rose Croix." The fact that the Freemasons have incorporated its teachings is an indication of the satanic origin of the Rosicrucians, intended to deceive the disciples of Jesus Christ. The Esoteric Christian Rosicrucian school, for instance, "provide esoteric knowledge related to the inner teachings of Christianity." According to the article, as stated in the "Rosicrucian Mysteries" by Max Heindel (accessed March 29, 2006 under "Rosicrucianism" by Wikipedia), the order was founded in 1313 and was composed of twelve exalted "beings" gathered around a thirteenth: Christian Rosenkreuz. Their mission was to "prepare the whole world for a new phase in religion—to provide safe guidance in the gradual awakening of man's latent spiritual faculties during the next six centuries toward the coming Age of Aquarius." This new-age nonsense sounds like something one would find in the doctrines of Lucifer. Beware.

Social Justice: A code phrase for the socialist left that believes capitalism and the economic inequality it produces must be replaced by a classless society. In such a society all differences in wealth and property will be eliminated—at the price of individual liberty. It is news babble for "redistribution of wealth" in which the elite get richer and the common folk loose everything, forcing everybody into government dependence. It has nothing to do with real justice nor is there any real equality.

Spiritual Formation: A form of Contemplative Spirituality Mysticism that has flooded today's apostate Emergent (so-called evangelical) churches. It is a form of eastern mysticism disguised as "western Christian" mysticism. Mysticism is the belief that knowledge of God, spiritual truth and ultimate reality can be acquired by subjective experience, which erodes the authority of Scripture. The Bible makes no distinction between bad (eastern) and good (western) mysticism. Both forms are occultic and of the same source. (Hint: it didn't come from God.) Both forms use the same technique for corralling and emptying the mind. The western version just applies Christian terms to them. The purpose is to enter an altered state of consciousness where the mind is no longer active or critically engaged. With their mind passive and their God-given barriers down, they think they are experiencing God and hearing His voice. They come away thinking they have come closer to God and often feel ecstatic. This is nothing more than a counterfeit Holy Spirit experience that is not of God. This plays into the post-modernist "feelings" they use to determine truth instead of using critical thinking.

In its broadest term, spiritual formation is a means of spiritual shaping and growth. All schools and religions apply it. In Christianity it applies to time-tested Christian disciplines like personal and corporate Bible study, worship, prayer, discipleship and service. However, the apostate Emergent church incorporates extra-biblical spiritual practices like contemplative prayer, meditation and yoga. They lifted them from Catholicism, eastern mysticism, and other religions and renamed them with biblical-sounding terminology. Wherever this form of spiritual formation is found, there is also contemplative spirituality (a method of meditation described above in pursuit of a mystical experience with God). This contemplative spirituality is the heartbeat of the spiritual formation movement. Our focus is supposed to be on the word of God. Contemplative spirituality focuses on literally nothing. By emptying their mind and letting their guard down, they leave themselves open to all sorts of demonic persuasions.

Many Christian colleges and seminaries now offer spiritual

formation as a required class. The graduates then teach the "spiritual disciplines" they learned in these classes to their church members that they may "feel" closer to God and more "Christ-like". These "spiritual disciplines" (fasting, meditating, chastity, repetitive prayer, simple living, submitting to a spiritual overseer whom they're not supposed to question, confession, etc.) have replaced traditional Christian doctrine, which they consider a failure. The form of spiritual formation now pervasive in the apostate churches teaches we can get closer to God by our own efforts rather than by the grace of God. It appeals to pride by teaching we can get into heaven our own way rather than by God's way. That is by faith in His Son, Jesus Christ. Proponents of the spiritual formation movement include; Dallas Willard, Rick Warren, Ruth Haley Barton, Youth Specialties and San Francisco Theological Seminary, Richard Foster, Larry Crabb, and the Willow Creek Association among a host of others.

For those caught in a church that promotes the spiritual formation movement, beware; subjective spirituality does not bring you closer to God, but draws your attention away from God and His truth. This can result in derailing your spiritual growth and cut you off from God's plan of sanctification. The heart is deceitful above all else. Never make an emotional decision and never trust feelings to determine truth.

God has given us a brain to employ critical thinking in examining what we are told to determine truth. Follow the example of the Bereans who were more noble minded than the Thessalonians and searched out the Scriptures daily to see if what Apostles taught was true. If they needed to examine the Apostles teachings, how much more so do we need to do today? Finally, leave that apostate church immediately, warn others about it and find a church that handles the word of God accurately. Pay heed to the words of Paul the Apostle; "I am amazed that you are so quickly deserting Him who called you by the grace of Christ, for a different gospel; which is really not another; only there are some who are disturbing you, and want to distort the gospel of Christ. But even though we, or an angel from heaven, should preach to you a gospel contrary to that which we have preached to you, let him be accursed. As we have said before, so I say again now, if any man is preaching to you a gospel contrary to that which you have received, let him be accursed." (Galatians 1:6–10).

The Church of Jesus Christ of Latter Day Saints (LDS or Mormon religion): Founded in the early 1820's by Joseph Smith in New York. Upon his death, Brigham Young led the Mormons to the territory of Utah which became the Mormon cultural center. Joseph Smith believed Christianity became corrupted after the death of the apostles and that God gave him the teachings to restore the lost and corrupted elements of Christianity. He taught that only those who practice the Mormon religion are true Christians. Mormons follow some of the teachings of the Bible, but give the Book of Mormon, Doctrine and Covenants, Pearl of Great Price, and the teachings of their apostles, prophets and presidents a higher authority than the Bible whenever the Bible disagrees with Mormon doctrine. Some parts of the Book of Mormon were plagiarized word for word from the King James Bible.

Mormons take offense when non-members say they are not Christian. After all, belief in Jesus Christ is central to their faith as the official name of the church suggests, the Mormon Tabernacle Choir sings Christian hymns and they are committed to high moral standards and strong families. Surely that makes them Christian. However, they deny most of the doctrinal tenets of Biblical Christianity. And while faith in Jesus Christ is necessary to be a Christian, the Jesus Christ the Mormons believe in is not the same Jesus presented in the Bible. The following are fourteen articles of faith (now there are thirteen) that form the foundation of the doctrinal teachings of the Mormon church that are completely contrary to the teachings of the Bible (these are official teachings of the Mormon church that not all Mormons believe):

God was once a man who lived on another planet. This is the most important of Mormon teaching. They believe he was once a mortal man who progressed to godhood living in obedience to the laws and ordinances of the gospel on his world. He died, was somehow resurrected and evolved into a god. He married, created this world and became the God of the children of this world. He wasn't the only god. There were hundreds of gods who inhabited other worlds. Jesus Christ even became a god who inhabits his own world. Mormons who say they don't believe this don't know their own doctrine.

We are co-eternal with God. Mormons believe we have always existed for all eternity as undefined "intelligences" who were given a spiritual body in heaven by our eternal parents (God and his wife). We have always been around God in one form or another, he just progressed ahead of us.

The origin of Jesus Christ. Mormons believe we were all "intelligences" floating around in the universe needing to be organized into spirits. Because the "intelligence" of Jesus was superior to the rest of us, he was the first born spirit created by God and his wife. For this reason he was the most important spirit creation. He was given a physical body when God had a physical union with Mary. He was thus part man and part God. Jesus was special because his father was God, while the rest of us only had a human father when our spirits were put into our bodies. Mormons believe death and sin came through the fall of Adam and Eve, but their deed was not actually a sin. Rather it was a blessing that enabled man to continue progressing towards eternal life. The death of Jesus on the cross canceled the death penalty imposed on all men, ensuring that all men would be redeemed, resurrected and given eternal life as a gift. Thus enabling men to become gods themselves.

Truth is determined by feelings. Mormons disregard any facts that contradict what they feel is true. For example; reading the Book of Mormon gives them a good feeling, therefore it must be true. When someone tells them Joseph Smith was a false prophet and a fraud, it makes them feel bad about being duped, therefore it must be a lie. Good feelings apply to all aspects of their lives. They determine if they should do something and know the truth of something by praying about it and feeling good about it.

What a prophet said can be revised depending on the circumstances. To the Mormons, a prophet is the head of the church. When he says something that is definitely wrong, he was not inspired at the time. He was just talking as a man. Newer prophets can override the older prophets. Mormons believe they have a prophet on earth today, even though he never prophecies anything.

Saving our dead ancestors shows we are the only Christian church. Mormons have temples where they get the handshakes and passwords that allow them to become gods. They also baptize dead people by proxy so they can become Mormons.

Ex-Mormons or apostates had sin in their life or never had a testimony. Mormons believe apostates will be cast into the outer darkness. Those who leave the church never had a testimony. If a Mormon becomes a true Christian, they believe he losses his salvation and will never become a god.

We will only read church approved materials. Any literature that is critical of the church is considered either Satanic, written by disgruntled apostates or by idiots who don't know the truth. Any reasonable arguments that oppose the gospel of Mormonism is considered unimportant and can be ignored.

We need to convert the whole world to Mormonism. They believe they should send all they young men ages 19 to 22 and most of their unmarried daughters on missions throughout the world. They think they should save their money so that when they are older, they can go on missions as a married couple.

By being Mormons we are assured of salvation - even if we are wrong. Mormons believe even if they're wrong about Mormonism, God will forgive them because they believe in Jesus Christ. If they're right then they will live forever with their families as gods. They reason they wouldn't want to be anything other than Mormons because they have all their bases covered.

Since we have the name of Christ in our church - our church is the only true one. For some reason the Mormons think if the church does not have the name of Christ in its name, it must not be a true church.

We believe in the book of Mormon. They believe in a book that has absolutely no archeological support. That it contains a record of peoples who inhabited the Americas between 2200 BC and 420 AD. They believe a second group of people populated the Americas who were Jewish, spoke Hebrew and kept records in reformed Egyptian. These people supposedly numbered in the millions, yet left no tangible proof of their existence. Some Mormons believe the church leaders will someday admit the people described in this book are fictional, yet maintain it still contains religious truths.

The fruits of Mormonism prove it is the true church. The Mormon church believes in manipulating the statistics to show they have a superior belief system. They disregard any statistics that are embarrassing to their position. If I recall right, lying and deception are the fruits of evil.

Since there are people who oppose our beliefs - our beliefs must be true. Someone must have spiked the coffee they supposedly don't drink.

They believe that because someone writes something against them or assails their beliefs, than their beliefs must be true as only the true church has anything bad said about it. Every religion on the planet is opposed by someone. Using this logic, they all also must be true religions, since only truth has anything bad said about it.

Watchtower Society (a.k.a. Jehovah's Witnesses or JWs): The JWs, like the Mormons, are another false Christian church that thinks it is the only true Christian church and is God's sole earthly representative. The JWs are controlled by a "Governing Body" of 10 to 15 mature men. The JWs are told they have direct guidance from God who use this guidance to instruct followers through the pages of the Watchtower and other publications. The JWs are told they cannot understand the things of God by the Scriptures alone. The Bible can only be properly understood by the Watchtower Society and the literature it produces. They are told they are the instruments of God to teach the world the deeper things of Scripture and to not think of themselves, but submit to the Watchtower Society teachings.

The JWs believe they are the only ones serving God and the only ones who will be saved. They dare not question the Watchtower Society teachings. In doing so, they are considered weak in faith and could be disfellowshipped. Disfellowshipping is used by the Watchtower Society to control its members with guilt and fear. A lot of rules are made by the Watchtower Society based on their interpretation of Scripture. Anyone found in violation or does not turn in someone in violation of these rules, are brought before three elders who serve as judge and jury deciding who is repentant and who is not. Those found unrepentant are disfellowshipped. Those found associating with a worldly person (a non-JW) could be marked. JWs can only speak with a marked person in the Kingdom Hall. They cannot associate with a marked person in a social setting.

JWs are not permitted to accept blood transfusions for themselves or their children. Many JWs have died because of the restrictions the Watchtower Society has placed on them. They are not allowed to salute the flag, recite the pledge of allegiance, sing the national anthem, run for public office or serve in the military. They are not allowed to celebrate Christmas, birthdays, Easter, Thanksgiving or any other holiday because of their alleged pagan origins. They aren't even allowed to associate with non-JWs even if they are family.

Some doctrinal beliefs include:

Trinity: They don't believe in the trinity of God. Jehovah (their name for God which is not supported by Scripture) is the only supreme being. Jesus Christ is the Son of God, but he is not equal with Jehovah. He was a created being who existed in a pre-human state as Michael the Archangel. The Holy Spirit is not a separate entity, but a force God uses to interact with the world.

Man's Soul: They believe a person is the soul the Bible speaks of. When he dies, nothing lives on. He is dead and conscience of nothing. When God resurrects him from the dead, He will create a new body from His memory.

Hell: They believe hell is the "common grave of mankind" where people go upon their death, not the traditional Christian view of hell. People are not conscience after death, they simply cease to exist. Believers remain in death until God resurrects them.

144,000 witnesses: They believe the Heavenly Kingdom took effect in 1914AD with the alleged invisible enthronement of Christ as King. (Only God knows where they came up with this nonsense.) An Anointed Class of about 135,300 people currently occupies the Kingdom. They were selected after Christ's ascension into heaven and in the following centuries. Supposedly the full compliment of 144,000 was competed in 1935 AD. They believe some 8,700 are still living on earth. They will spent eternity as spirit creatures with God and Christ, and will rule over the JWs who remain on earth. Those JWs who remain on earth are called the Great Crowd or Other Sheep.

Salvation (Grace vs. Works): For a Jehovah's Witness to be saved, they must accept the Bible doctrines as interpreted by the Governing Body, be baptized as a Jehovah's Witness and follow the program of works determined by the Governing Body. They say they believe in God's grace and cannot earn salvation by their works, but their actions say differently. A JW cannot survive the end times unless he remains "in good standing". That is, they must observe the rules and do the works set out by the Watchtower Society. Those who violate the rules are disfellowshipped and cannot survive the end times.

The Watchtower Society is essentially deciding who deserves God's grace and who does not. In the JWs Bible, grace is translated as undeserved kindness. The Watchtower organization claims they want to give deserving ones the opportunity to learn of Jehovah's undeserved kindness. If God's kindness is undeserved, how can anyone deserve it? By what standards are these mortal men using to discern who deserves God's kindness and who doesn't? Doesn't God have anything to say on the matter? Aren't His thoughts above man's thoughts? The Watchtower Society's attitude is that not all men are deserving of God's kindness and it's their job to decide who deserves God's undeserved kindness and who doesn't.

Jesus was crucified on a stake, not a cross: JWs believe the Christian cross as being of pagan origin. They view the cross as an idol and the wearing or displacing of one is considered idol worship. They translate the Greek word "stauros" as "torture stake", instead of "cross". They believe Jesus was crucified on an upright wooden stake with no crossbeam. This is contrary to known historical facts that the Romans used crosses to crucify people on, not upright wooden stakes.

No true Christian worships the cross. If that were the case it would be an idol. Rather they worship Jesus Christ alone who is God and equal with the Father. Whether displaying or wearing a cross is appropriate, is up to the individual to prayerfully decide.

A Final Note: The Watchtower Society, the Mormon church, and the Catholic church, among a few others, all claim that the Scriptures can only be understood by the teachings of their prophets, priests and elders. This should raise all sorts of red flags as a warning to flee from these false prophets and teachers. The Scriptures are meant to be understood by everyone, not just a select few. For those caught in these false Christian cults and pseudo-Christian churches, pay heed to the words of Jesus Christ:

> "Enter by the narrow gate; for the gate is wide, and the way is broad that leads to destruction, and many are those who enter by it. For the gate is small, and the way is narrow that leads to life, and few are those who find it. Beware of the false prophets, who come to you in sheep's clothing, but inwardly are ravenous wolves. You will know them by their fruits. Grapes are not gathered from thorn bushes, nor figs from thistles, are they? Even so, every good tree bears good fruit; but the bad tree bears bad fruit. A good tree cannot produce bad fruit, nor can a bad tree produce good fruit. Every tree that does not bear good fruit is cut down and

thrown into the fire. So then, you will know them by their fruits. Not everyone who says to Me. 'Lord, Lord,' will enter the kingdom of heaven; but he who does the will of my Father who is in heaven. Many will say to Me on that day, 'Lord, Lord, did we not prophesy in Your name, and in Your name perform many miracles?' And then I will declare to them, I never knew you; depart from Me you who practice lawlessness." (Matthew 7:13-23).

Shun the false Christian and pseudo-Christian cults with their false prophets and false teachers. Turn to Jesus Christ in faith who is the only way to salvation for there is no other name under heaven given unto men by which we must be saved. And don't worry about getting your act together first. Just come as you are. God will take care of the rest. He who has begun a good work in you will complete it to the glory of God. Praise be to God.

Appendix C:
Recommended Reading
and Other Resources

Books

De Young, Donald B. *Thousands... Not Billions Challenging an Icon of Evolution Questioning the Age of the Earth.* Published by Master Books, Green Forest, AR, copyright ©2005

Ham, Ken. *The New Answers Book.* Published by Master Books, Green Forest, AR, copyright ©2006

Humphreys, D. Russell. *Starlight and Time: Solving the Puzzle of Distant Starlight in a Young Universe* Published by Master Books, Colorado Springs, CO, copyright ©1994

Koenig, Don A. *The Revelation of Jesus Christ Through the Ages: a Complete Literal Common Sense Interpretation of the Prophecies.* Self published 2004. Available only as an e-book or PDF file. (This source contains expanded commentary on Babylon and other mysteries. See the website: thepropheticyears.com)

McDowell, Josh. *Evidence that Demands a Verdict, Volume 1 & 2 Historical Evidences for the Christian Faith.* Published by Here's Life Publishers, Inc., San Bernardino, CA, copyright ©1972, 1979.

Morris, Henry M. *Scientific Creationism.* Published by Master Books, El Cajon, CA, copyright ©1974

Muncaster, Ralph O. *Examine the Evidence: Exploring the Case for Christianity.* Published by Harvest House Publishers, Eugene, OR, copyright ©2004

Sunderland, Luther D. *Darwin's Enigma: Fossils and Other Problems.* Published by Master Books, El Cajon, CA, copyright ©1988

Whitcomb, John C. And Henry M. Morris. *The Genesis Flood, the Biblical Record and its Scientific Implications.* Published by P&R Publishing, Phillipsburg, IL, copyright ©1961

Websites

answersingenesis.org Was founded by Ken Ham, President and CEO of Answers in Genesis. It is an apologetics ministry dedicated to enabling Christians to defend their faith and to proclaim the gospel of Jesus Christ effectively. The organization and website provides numerous articles and study materials related to creation science.

gracethrufaith.com According to the author of this website it is, "a non-denominational, non-church, Christian ministry dedicated to providing believers with a deeper understanding of the whole counsel of God through His revealed word." It is authored by Jack Kelley who has written several books.

hallindsey.com Is a website of Hal Lindsey Media Ministries. Bible prophecy expert Hal Lindsey gives a weekly video report of world events and Bible prophecy teachings. His ministry provides a number of Bible prophecy study resources.

icr.org Is a website for Institute for Creation Research founded by Henry M. Morris Ph.D in 1970. The institute conducts scientific research and operates a graduate school near San Diego, Ca. The website contains numerous articles and study materials for various subjects relating to origins science and creation studies.

raptureready.com Is a website containing end-times related articles and news stories to help prepare and encourage Christians concerning the imminent return of Jesus Christ. It was founded by Todd Strandberg, and the general editor is Terry James.

s8int.com (pronounced saint.com), Home of Ooparts, is a website of out-of-place artifacts and ancient high technology that was perhaps evidenced at the time of Noah's flood. The website contains numerous articles of archeological evidence that doesn't fit the uniformitarian consensus.

About the Author

William Waldo served over ten years in the US Navy as an Avionics Technician. He became a born-again Christian in 1983 while living in San Diego after reading Hal Lindsey's writings on Bible prophecy. Presently works as an aircraft mechanic quality control inspector for a regional airline in Shreveport, Louisiana. He has done extensive self-study on creation science and biblical end-times prophecy. Currently he lives alone in Waskom, Texas with his cat, Licorice.

CPSIA information can be obtained at www.ICGtesting.com
Printed in the USA
LVOW08s0744270713

344872LV00001B/6/P